Aband...

Betrothed to an ea... ...lotte Haversham arrived at Balfurin, hoping to find love at the legendary Scottish castle. Instead she found decaying towers and no husband among the ruins. So Charlotte worked a miracle, transforming the rotting fortress into a prestigious girls' school. And now, five years later, her life is filled with purpose—until . . .

Seduced by a stranger

A man storms Charlotte's castle—and he is *not* the reprehensible Earl of Marne, the one who stole her dowry and dignity, but rather the absent lord's handsome, worldly cousin Dixon MacKinnon. Mesmerized by the fiery Charlotte, Dixon is reluctant to correct her mistake. And though she's determined not to play the fool again, Charlotte finds herself strangely thrilled by the scoundrel's amorous attentions. But a dangerous intrigue has drawn Dixon to Balfurin. And if his ruse is prematurely revealed, a passionate, blossoming love affair could crumble into ruin.

⌒~∞~⌒

"A writer of rare intelligence and sensitivity."
Mary Jo Putney

By Karen Ranney

If You've Enjoyed This Book,
Be Sure to Read These Other
AVON ROMANTIC TREASURES

Coming Soon

KAREN RANNEY

Autumn in Scotland

An Avon Romantic Treasure

AVON BOOKS
An Imprint of HarperCollinsPublishers

This is a work of fiction. Names, characters, places, and incidents are products of the author's imagination or are used fictitiously and are not to be construed as real. Any resemblance to actual events, locales, organizations, or persons, living or dead, is entirely coincidental.

AVON BOOKS
An Imprint of HarperCollins*Publishers*
10 East 53rd Street
New York, New York 10022-5299

Copyright © 2006 by Karen Ranney
ISBN-13: 978-0-06-075745-8
ISBN-10: 0-06-075745-0
www.avonromance.com

First Avon Books paperback printing: December 2006

Avon Trademark Reg. U.S. Pat. Off. and in Other Countries, Marca Registrada, Hecho en U.S.A.
HarperCollins® is a registered trademark of HarperCollins Publishers Inc.

Printed in the U.S.A.

10 9 8 7 6 5 4 3 2 1

TO LOVEY

It may seem silly to dedicate a book to a dog, but frankly, my Sheltie, Lovey, is one of my best friends. She listens to me expound about things I can never mention to anyone else. She's seen me naked and will never divulge her opinion on the experience. When I feel weepy, she puts her chin on my knee and sighs. She's learned to make a sound like a purr when I rub her ears, and her dark brown eyes mostly express love. Occasionally, they reveal annoyance, but that's when I'm not fast enough in giving her a cookie.

So, to Lovey: *Thank you for all the days of companionship when you listened—without comment— to my reading a manuscript aloud. Thank you for sitting on my feet in winter so my toes stayed warm while I was writing. Thank you for tolerating your teeth being brushed, "Beauty Shop Nights," and a dozen other indignities so beneath you. Thank you, mostly, for only barking at the computer when it went off, and not at leaves, birds, or cats. Thank you for never being a watchdog, which meant that I had to be brave enough to protect you. Thank you, finally, for being a perfect lady-dog in all ways.*

Friends, even four-legged ones, should be appreciated in life, and this is my way of appreciating Lovey.

I think she'd much rather have a cookie.

Prologue

March 1833

Scotland was a soggy, cold disappointment.

Charlotte Haversham MacKinnon had spent the last three days huddled in the corner of the carriage praying that the sun would emerge from behind watery clouds. The sun, however, was as stubborn as any Scot and refused to make an appearance.

Just like her husband.

However cold she was, however miserable and damp, however exhausted, she dared not utter a complaint. After all, it was her fault they were there.

The farther north they traveled, the more she understood her husband's professed love of England. In Sussex, flowers bloomed in shades of orange, red, purple, and white. Branches boasted a new growth of leaves in the spring. There was a look of beauty to the land as

1

if it gloried in life. Even London was a cheery place.

Scotland looked as if it had recently been burned to the ground, as if God Himself had decreed this place a dead and desolate spot. When it wasn't drizzling, it looked as if it might imminently storm. How anything grew in this place, Charlotte had no idea. If it did sprout from the barren earth, surely it must be the color of slate.

She kept her thoughts to herself. Her parents were not in the mood for conversation. Her father had spent the last two hours frowning, and when her mother did address her, it was formally: Countess Marne. As if by doing so, she was reminding her father that some good had come of all this—their eldest daughter had a title.

When she was first introduced to George MacKinnon, Earl of Marne, it hadn't mattered all that much to Charlotte. A woman must be married, and as her mother said, it was as easy to wed an Earl as it was a Mister. In this case, however, the Earl was as poor as any squirrel nesting in one of the oak trees near the garden. Perhaps more so, because at least the squirrel owned a few acorns.

George MacKinnon had a title but precious few coins to rub together. There was, supposedly, a castle he claimed as his ancestral right, and it was to Balfurin in the Scottish Highlands that they'd been traveling for the past week.

Charlotte leaned back against the cushions and closed her eyes. She hadn't done anything. Not anything that would make George leave her. Not even when she found him with the chambermaid. She'd simply gone back to her room and vowed never to say a word.

"Charlotte, are you feeling unwell? We do not need that inconvenience."

She opened her eyes and turned her head to look at her mother.

"I'm feeling fine, Mother."

Her father frowned at her again.

Everyone pretended, during this entire journey, that she was on her way to join George at his ancestral home. But she wasn't even certain he'd returned to Scotland. One morning he'd simply disappeared without a note of explanation. Only days later was it determined that her entire dowry, a not inconsiderable sum, had also vanished.

Charlotte leaned her head back against the cushions again. She had acted the part of besotted bride as well as she could. She'd been amenable, tolerable, and charming. She spoke only when she was addressed, and discussed a variety of subjects when conversation faltered.

She was even to be found in her bed, gowned and perfumed for her husband, her hands resting outside the bed, the lace at her wrists so fulsome that it almost covered her fingers. Her hair was always brushed and left loose, spread over the pillow because George had remarked once that he'd liked it that way.

But he'd never returned to her bed, not after that first night. Perhaps she should consider herself fortunate for that fact.

"I'm sure George has a perfectly good explanation for his actions," her mother said abruptly.

Since it was her mother's first effort at conciliation, weak that it was, Charlotte smiled. "Perhaps he will."

That was the extent of their conversation for several

hours. The coachman had said this morning that they'd reach Balfurin today, but the afternoon was advancing and the scenery looked less promising as they traveled. If they didn't pass a town or even a hamlet soon, they'd be doomed again to spend the night on the side of the road, the horses grazing on whatever vegetation they might find.

Charlotte dismissed George MacKinnon, Earl of Marne, and Balfurin from her mind. For a few moments, she amused herself by envisioning the gardens of her childhood home, lush with a hundred varieties of vibrant flowers. That vision done, she concentrated on the library, her favorite room in the palatial estate. She was always to be found there, even as a child. The reading nook was a sanctuary from her pestering sisters, and the governess who giggled incessantly and postured endlessly.

If she concentrated, she could list all the books in one section of the shelves from top shelf to bottom. Over the years, she'd read them all. Some were interesting, some boring, and some she could still recite, as if her mind had captured each page.

Such a memory should be used for some purpose, but it had not, other than to serve her up to ridicule from her sisters as some sort of freak, an aberration of nature.

"You'd better spend your time finding some way to bleach that complexion of yours, Charlotte. You look as dark as a blackamoor." That comment was from Adelaide, a formidable flirt, and the next girl to be wed—a state of affairs no doubt hastening Charlotte's own nuptials, the speed of which had been blinding. Either her parents had been beside themselves with the prospect of wedding Charlotte off, or George had been destitute and desperate.

Both circumstances could well be true.

"Damnation," her father said, leaning forward.

"Nigel!" Her mother frowned.

"Pardon, my dear. I didn't think. But look." He extended his finger toward the window.

"Is that Balfurin?" her mother asked faintly.

Her father knocked on the window separating them from the driver.

"Is that our destination?" he asked, and the man answered in the affirmative.

Charlotte had a feeling of impending doom as she turned her head. Her father's uncharacteristic lapse of gentility had warned her, but nothing could truly have prepared her for what she saw next.

Balfurin Castle was a disreputable ruin of a place, perched high on a rounded hill, surrounded by a copse of trees, like a bald man's shiny pate ringed by a fringe of hair. Three crenellated towers spoke of a warlike past, when such defenses were necessary. The fourth tower, in a crumbled heap, revealed that too many years had passed since anyone had stewarded Balfurin with pride.

The overall color of the castle was gray, with red brick showing vividly where it had been spared the elements. A yawning archway led to a courtyard. Charlotte somehow knew that a drawbridge had once been installed there, just as she suspected that the dry gully had once been a moat.

She loved Balfurin at first sight.

This was the place of dreams, of childhood fantasies, of stories she'd sighed over as a young girl. Without much difficulty she could envision a dragon, scaled and deeply green, creeping down the hill, and the banners of a worthy knight flying in the wind as he left the castle walls to engage in battle.

Within those sheltering walls a clan could live, kept safe by their number and their leader. Voices would be raised in celebration within the Great Hall, and the courtyard would be a hive of daily activity.

Such a place needed a chatelaine, a woman destined for the role, strong, resolute, and surrounded by the love and respect of her people. Charlotte could almost see herself wearing a long linen dress of pale yellow with a belt of hammered gold disks. Around her waist would be a knotted cord with keys to the granary and storerooms.

Her husband, the lord of Balfurin, would come to her as she stood on the battlements surveying the far crops and nearby garden.

A touch of silliness, then, to imagine herself loved by such a man, such a person. An illusion, when she was wed to an absent earl who was not much more attentive when he was standing beside her.

"Dearest Lord and all the saints preserve us," her mother said. "It's a horror."

"Damnation," her father said again, in evident agreement.

Her mother didn't correct him this time, wide-eyed as she was at the scene before her.

The carriage slowed, the driver expertly entering the arched entranceway as if he'd done so many times before. Only inches remained between the carriage's shiny black lacquered exterior and the darkened bricks.

The courtyard continued the impression of desertion. Hay was strewn over one side of the space, while a few broken crates were set against one wall along with a wagon wheel with most of its spokes missing and a ladder with three shattered rungs. A well in the center of the courtyard held a rusted pulley, but the bucket looked newly hewn. A mangy dog eyed them suspiciously from beside the wall. He and three scrawny chickens plucking at the dirt were the only signs of life.

"No wonder George wanted my dowry," Charlotte said. Both her parents glanced at her, but neither reprimanded her.

What, after all, could they say?

Charlotte had the impression that Balfurin was simply waiting, patient and eternal, and that it might have looked like this for hundreds of years.

"This whole journey has been nothing but a waste of time, Charlotte," her mother said.

Charlotte sighed inwardly, and turned to face her mother. *What would you have me do?* A question she did not dare ask. She didn't have a rebellious nature. If she had, she wouldn't be sitting here wondering about the whereabouts of her husband. For that matter, she wouldn't have found herself married at all, leastwise to a stranger, and a Scot.

A desperately poor Scot.

All her life she'd been proper and restrained. Every single moment, she'd done exactly as her parents had asked. She'd been a model daughter, a perfect paragon of decorum. She'd been an example for her sisters, a Haversham worthy of the name.

But it was getting harder and harder to remember

her role, especially after the humiliation of being abandoned so soon after being wed. She'd begun to entertain shocking thoughts of mutiny.

"Your mother is right, girl," her father said. "This has been a wasted trip. Your mother and I have suffered during this whole damnable journey. Nor does it look as if we're going to get much of a welcome here. But I'll be damned if my horses are going to be ruined for your selfishness."

My selfishness? How could he say that? All she'd wanted to do was find her husband. What about George? What about him, leaving his wife after a week of marriage? Thoughts that weren't verbalized. There were words for what George had done, but she'd never before spoken them aloud. Very well, in the silence of her mind perhaps—cad, bounder.

Bastard.

She clasped her hands together and watched as her father exited the carriage. He turned and stretched out a hand to help her mother descend. Charlotte was next, and when she stepped onto the ground she smoothed her dress down, wishing she had a mirror. Was her hair acceptable? She sent a questioning look to her mother, who nodded at her absentmindedly.

Not one single servant had appeared at the arrival of the carriage. Her father strode forward, calling out, "Is anyone here?"

The coachman leaned down and addressed him. "Shall I send one of the footmen searching for someone, sir?"

"That's a good idea, John. Do so."

The coachman nodded, and with a touch of his whip, pointed to one of the footmen. Immediately, he clambered from the carriage and strode toward the rear of the castle. Some ten minutes later he returned, walking slowly beside a stooped and aged man.

"His name is Jeffrey, and he says he's one of the few servants remaining at Balfurin, sir," the footman announced when they approached the coach.

"I'm old but I've not lost the ability to speak for myself," Jeffrey said, eyeing the footman with some disfavor. He turned and looked at her father, making no effort to welcome a stranger to Balfurin.

"And who would you be?" Jeffrey asked.

Her father drew himself up and frowned at the elderly man. "We are looking for George MacKinnon, Earl of Marne, my good man. Please be so good as to tell him that his wife and in laws are here."

"What makes you think he's come back?" Jeffrey asked. "He left us to starve without a backward glance. Married, you say?" He narrowed his eyes and looked at Charlotte, who took a step back. His expression left no doubt of his feelings either for George or her.

"What now?" her mother asked. "We've come all this way for nothing."

"A fool's errand, Jennifer," her father said, frowning at Charlotte. "We'll rest the night, and then return to England. That is, if this ungodly place offers us shelter."

He turned and strode up the broad stone steps to the door, lifted the iron knocker, and waited.

Suddenly, the door moved, groaning on its hinges as it opened slowly inward. A yawning chasm of black appeared, and then a face, lined, weathered, and topped with a shock of white hair.

"Who you be?" the elderly woman asked.

"Nigel Haversham, my wife, Jennifer, and our daughter, the Countess of Marne."

The old woman kept her gnarled hand on the edge of the door. Was she Balfurin's only protector?

"If you will move aside, madam," her father said. "We require lodging for the night."

"So, he married? And an Englishwoman at that?" The elderly woman shook her head. "That I've lived so long to see such a horror." She squinted into the bleary sun, her eyes sunken and faded. "Even so, how do I know you're who you say you are? I've not seen the earl since the spring when he came to have the chapel window removed and taken to Edinburgh." Her hand tightened on the door.

"I realize George is not in residence," her father began, but she interrupted him.

"He told me it would fetch a good price from those who were building their fine houses. I wouldn't let them take it. His grandfather would have curled up in his grave. That window has been at Balfurin Castle since before I was born."

"My dear woman, I do not care about one of your windows," her father said, becoming exasperated. "Move aside!"

The old woman looked offended by his command. She drew herself up, and frowned back at him.

"I'm Nan McPherson, sir. Eighty-seven years have I been on this earth. Too long to be cowed, even by a rude Englishman like yourself. I've not been given word you were coming. Go away."

She tried to shut the door, but Charlotte's father was having none of it.

Her mother stepped up and placed her hand on her father's arm. "Nigel, dear, shall I handle this? It is, after all, a domestic arrangement." She smiled at the woman at the door as if they were conspirators.

Charlotte knew the tactic well, since she'd been privy to it all her life. Nan did not stand a chance against her mother's determination.

"We know George didn't send word, Nan. But we are tired, and it looks to rain again. Surely, you don't begrudge us a night under a roof in a real bed?"

Nan stepped back, the door opening an inch wider. "The roof leaks, and I've not had the strength to air the beds myself."

"We've two footmen who could assist in whatever arrangements need to be made." Her mother smiled, and the door opened even farther.

"Well, I'll not stand here like a beggar," her father said.

He appeared genial, but her father had God's own temper when he was riled, and this journey had done nothing to soothe him. He pushed past Nan and gestured to his wife. "I'll be damned if I'm going to be treated like a supplicant at my son-in-law's door."

Charlotte turned and surveyed the courtyard again. It didn't improve with a second glance.

"Come, Charlotte!"

What choice did she have?

By nightfall, they'd managed a meal of something purporting to be a stew, and bread so hard that it felt like one of Balfurin's bricks. Her parents occupied the laird's suite of rooms, while Charlotte was installed in a smaller chamber across the hall.

She stood at the open window, shutters carefully folded back against the wall, and stared out at the night.

The hills were shapeless now, shrouded by darkness. Above them winked a thousand stars, glittering brightly in an ebony sky. A peaceful night, with the soft breath of a cool wind touching her cheek.

In winter the castle would be a cold place. A fire in every room would not be so much a luxury as a necessity for living in Scotland. But there could be warmth in this place, just as there could beauty. A few plants in the courtyard, a garden of sorts, now that the need for defense was not so pressing. The whole place could do with a bit of sorting through and order, not to mention a good cleaning. Once the windows sparkled, and the dust was gone, and a few repairs made, Balfurin might be as it had been once before: a proud laird's holding, a grand and stately castle guarding the Highlands.

The door abruptly opened.

"I've been told to turn the mattress, miss," one of the footmen said. He was followed by his partner, a man so young he still had an air of boyhood about him. "Himself gave me the order. But how that's going to make this place smell better, I don't know."

She wanted to warn him that her father didn't believe in servant's airing their opinions and he should use some caution. For that matter, he didn't believe in his daughters speaking their minds, either. Her mother was the only person she'd ever heard give Nigel Haversham the honest truth.

Was that the meaning of love, then? The ability to speak freely and without fear?

She turned and stared out at the night again, hearing

them work behind her. At the least the mattress would be fluffed for the night. Were clean sheets possible?

"Is it true, miss, that your husband comes from here?"

"True," she said, not turning to face them. She could only imagine their looks.

What do you think of him? Now, that was a question she dared herself to ask, but of course, she didn't. Her father would criticize her for even thinking of asking for a servant's opinion. But they knew most of what transpired, even in a grand house like the one in which she'd been raised.

She heard the door close, and knew they'd left her. A moment later, it opened again.

"Did you forget something? Have the good manners to knock, at least," she said.

"Must I beg permission of you, daughter?" her father asked. "I think not."

She sighed, and stared straight ahead, knowing the confrontation had finally come. She hadn't wanted it, had dreaded it, but knew her father would demand a reckoning of sorts. A bludgeoning not by fist or instrument, but the sheer power of his will. He would demand and she would accede. Perhaps.

She straightened her shoulders, fixed a smile on her lips, and forced herself to turn and face him.

"We'll leave in the morning, Charlotte. Back in England you'll comport yourself like a proper wife until George returns."

"From where?" she asked.

"Does it matter? He's evidently had business to transact, something he didn't feel necessary to impart to you."

"Or to you, Father?"

He didn't look pleased by that question, did he?

As he was deciding whether to chastise her for her words or offer sympathy to diffuse an emotional outburst, she delivered him another blow—the truth, hard won and very painful.

"George might not return, Father. He has my money, after all. Perhaps he sailed away with one of the maids."

Her father's nose was reddening, a sure sign that he was becoming annoyed. His next words verified that prediction.

"If that's so, it will not matter to your deportment, Charlotte. You will be a proper countess."

"A countess in waiting. Waiting for my husband to return. I don't think so, Father."

He looked startled. What an odd expression. She hadn't often seen her father surprised. Then he wasn't going to like what she had to say next.

"I'm going to remain here," she said softly. "Here at Balfurin."

"You can't be serious. I forbid it."

"You cannot," she said calmly. "I'm a married woman. A countess, Father, and capable of the command of my own self, if not my funds."

"You've no funds, Charlotte, and I'll not give you money for this misadventure."

"I've my grandfather's money," she said, having given this decision a great deal of thought. "Enough to live here in some comfort. George did not get that."

"That man was a fool to leave his money to you. I'll not have it."

"Fortunately, Father, there's nothing you can do."

She smiled sweetly at him, confident in her words. She'd visited her solicitor before leaving London. Her father was not the only Haversham who believed in planning and organization.

"What do you mean to do, Charlotte? Remain here like a lovesick wife, pining for George's return?"

"No," she said. She reinforced her smile. "Did you know that in Scotland it's possible for a wife to divorce her husband? I'm going to divorce George for desertion."

Her father, strangely enough, had no comment for *that*.

Chapter 1

October 1838

As homecomings went, this one would rank among the strangest.

Dixon Robert MacKinnon felt as if ghosts welcomed him, trailing their cold and lifeless fingers over his skin, greeting him with soft, almost soundless moans as if to warn him away from his destination. Yet the whole of Scotland was a place of ghosts, each hill and glen carrying memories of bittersweet victory or poignant loss. He'd forgotten how damp the air felt, as if the earth had wept and was now resting between tears.

How strange that he'd come halfway around the world for this moment and now he dreaded arriving at Balfurin.

He sat back among the cushions and surveyed his companion. Matthew was wedged into the corner of the carriage, arms crossed over his embroidered silk jacket, his gaze fixed at the tops of his pointed shoes. He'd been silent ever since yesterday when Dixon had announced it would be weeks before they left for Penang. In fact, it was very likely they would remain the winter in Scotland.

Dixon tapped on the ceiling, a signal for the coachman to slow. Another tap, and he felt the horses being walked to the side of the road.

"Come and have a look at Balfurin, Matthew," he said.

"I will remain here, if you do not mind, master," Matthew said, refusing to look in his direction. "The storm will be upon us shortly."

"A good Scottish storm takes the fire out of the blood."

"I have no more fire in my blood, as you say, master. I have spent too much time being cold and wet for any fire to survive."

Dixon stifled his smile, exited the carriage and closed the door, not remarking to Matthew that a carriage would be no protection in a Scottish thunderstorm. He might as well stand in the lee of the wind and delight in its fury with no shelter at all.

Dixon walked some distance from the carriage, feeling as if the years fell away with each step.

His parents had died in a boating accident on the River Tam, and he'd been brought to Balfurin for his uncle to raise. His mother's home had soon become his. How many times had he raced around the ruined tower? Or run up the steps to the battlements themselves? He'd played Robert the Bruce or Hannibal, Caesar, or a host of other warriors, and all during those pretend battles, he'd been the Earl of Marne, not George. Even as a child, he'd been envious of George's position in the world. Not just that his cousin had inherited the title, but that he would forever be known as the Laird of Balfurin.

The red streaks of sunset were a perfect backdrop to his first view of Balfurin. In the distance, the sky was already black, but not from nightfall as much as an approaching storm. An omen, perhaps, that Balfurin didn't welcome him back home with much enthusiasm.

He should have heeded the warning.

Balfurin was nothing like it had been. Dixon stared down at the glen, barely recognizing the castle.

The ruined tower wasn't there. Somehow, it had simply disappeared from the landscape. Had it finally crumbled and been carted away in a hundred barrows? Or better yet, had it been used to build the new addition to the east? A three-story building, rectangular and plain, seemed to have no relationship at all to the existing castle except for the fact it shared the same courtyard.

The curtain wall had been shored up, and the gate holding the portcullis had been repaired. The battlements looked as if their crenellated tops had been sharpened and there was a flag flying there, one that he couldn't make out from this distance.

The courtyard was filled with a hundred lit torches along the curtain wall. Candles outlined the path from the portcullis to the broad stone steps. Hundreds of flickering flames sat in every window of Balfurin, giving the impression that the castle itself was on fire.

A long line of carriages took turns before the steps,

each set of passengers being escorted up the stairs by a girl dressed in a long flowing white gown.

Females of all ages, each identically dressed in the same type of gown, were milling about the court-yard. A few were lining up in a queue. One, her hand holding the end of her hair, was racing to the three-story building to the east, as if distraught over a ruined coiffure.

"Is it a church?" Matthew asked. Dixon turned to find the other man at his side.

"I've never known George to be religious," he said. "But a decade can change a man."

"A man wills his own change," Matthew said. "Time does not matter."

Dixon stifled both his smile and his comment.

"Is this what you need, master?"

He glanced at Matthew.

"To ease your heart. Will it help?"

"We've agreed, Matthew. You will not speak of it."

Dixon looked down at Balfurin again. Would George welcome him home? Or would their rift, of a decade's standing, continue? Only the next few min-utes would tell.

They returned to the carriage and Dixon gave the signal for the driver to begin the long descent to the glen.

"Well, what do you think, Maisie? Will I do?"

Charlotte MacKinnon, Countess of Marne, stared at herself in the mirror.

"I think you look absolutely stunning, your lady-ship," Maisie said.

What had she expected? Maisie had been Charlotte's

fiercest supporter since the day she had hired her as maid four years earlier.

Maisie was always smiling, the small space between her front teeth and the dimple in her right cheek giving her an impish expression. The young maid found the world to be a pleasant place, all in all. However, being around Maisie was sometimes a trying experience, especially on those days when Charlotte wasn't in the mood to be excessively bright and cheery. But right at the moment she was appreciative of the girl's effusive disposition.

Tonight Charlotte was prepared for a little festivity. The ball she was hosting was the culmination of five years of work and worry.

The very first class of seniors were graduating from the Caledonia School for the Advancement of Females and embarking upon their lives. Families from all over northern Scotland had descended on Balfurin in order to see the graduation program. A column of seniors would march down the center of the Great Hall, each carrying a lit white pillar candle, held slightly forward as if each girl was following the light of knowledge itself. After the ceremony, the rest of the evening would be devoted to merriment, including the first ball to be held at Balfurin in decades.

When word of tonight's festivities spread through Edinburgh and Inverness, she expected to have even more applicants. Soon, she'd have to limit enrollment, the true measure of success for a school for girls.

She leaned forward to see her reflection more clearly in the mirror. Her forehead was shiny and she blotted the spot with a French powder puff and then picked an ostrich feather from her cheek. Excitement was making her warm, coloring her complexion pink, while worry was causing her to feel cold inside.

What if something went wrong?

Nonsense. Nothing could possibly go wrong.

She stood, smoothing out the folds of her white pleated dress. Exactly the same type of dress the graduating girls were wearing. After the ceremony in the Great Hall, she'd return to her room to dress for the ball in a frothy creation of feathers and lace that she worried about even now.

She turned and surveyed the dress hanging on the screen.

"You don't think it's too bold, Maisie?" She'd commissioned it from a dressmaker in Edinburgh, the first time she'd spent so much money on a gown in five years.

"Not at all, your ladyship. It's a bit different for your taste, that's true. But it's the most glorious thing, what with the feathers and all."

"But the décolletage, you don't think it's too risqué?"

"Oh no, your ladyship. You'd see worse than that on the streets of Edinburgh."

She didn't exactly want to be equated with the women on the streets of Edinburgh, but Charlotte didn't say so.

The feathers on the shoulders seemed an awfully daring touch, not to mention the plunging V of the neckline. Everyone had to be impressed by her demeanor, by her composure, by her appearance, else why would they send their daughters to her school?

"You'll be the most lovely woman at the ball, your ladyship," Maisie said, still trying to reassure her.

"Mr. McElwee will be over the moon to see you."

Spencer, dear Spencer. Whatever would she have done these past years without him? She'd been so lonely, and he'd been so attentive. Not to mention all the assistance he'd given her with her . . . problem.

"I'm not altogether sure he'll be in attendance," Charlotte said, feeling a spurt of disappointment. "Perhaps it's better if he isn't. I can't have it bandied about that I've a loose reputation."

"Still and all, it'd be nice to see you dance with him, your ladyship."

Charlotte nodded, thinking the same.

In a moment, she'd head for the Great Hall, for the speech she'd give before the assembled parents and students.

She pressed both hands against her midriff in order to calm her stomach. It didn't help. Her pulse was racing, her mouth dry. Tonight was the culmination of everything she'd worked for in the last five years.

Tonight was the realization of a dream.

Dixon's carriage pulled into Balfurin's courtyard slowly, the pace necessitated by the dozen vehicles in front of him. Along the interior curve of the curtain wall at least that many carriages were parked, waiting.

Was the whole of Scotland visiting Balfurin tonight?

"Perhaps it would be better to call upon your cousin when he isn't entertaining, master."

"On the contrary, Matthew. Tonight might be the very best time to call upon George. He may not have fond memories of our last encounter."

"You quarreled, master?"

Dixon shrugged. "Don't all families?" he asked.

"I do not know, master, having had no family."

Dixon didn't comment. The subject of Matthew's foster parents was a delicate one. He found it wiser to remain silent.

"We are evidently to be greeted, master," Matthew said, pointing to the carriage ahead of them.

As each carriage pulled up to the steps, a young girl attired in a long white dress moved from the head of the line to greet the guests. She spoke to another, older girl similarly attired holding a leather-bound book before escorting the inhabitants of the carriage up the broad stone steps.

"They're much too young," Dixon said, as their carriage halted. He disembarked from the vehicle, followed by Matthew. "I'd have liked to be greeted by an older woman with a hint of a good time in her glance."

Matthew shot him a chastising look. Matthew had strict and odd views of celibacy that Dixon didn't share. The fact that he'd been forced into a monklike state in the last few months had been due more to circumstances than inclination.

Dixon turned and called up to his coachman. "Find the stables, Donald, and introduce yourself. We're going to be staying for a few days."

Donald nodded and tipped his hat with his whip hand.

"Whose guest are you?" the young woman asked when she greeted him.

"Guest?" Dixon asked.

She nodded. "I need to indicate it for our book," she said, gesturing toward the other girl holding the leather-bound volume. "We're listing all the guests. You have come for the graduation, have you not?"

"I'm afraid we haven't," Dixon said. "Graduation?"

She looked annoyed, a strange expression for such a young and vibrant face. "The Caledonia School for the Advancement of Females, sir. The very first graduating class."

"We're friends of the family," Dixon said, hoping the information would wipe the look of annoyance from her face and summon a smile.

It didn't, but he forgot about her the moment he entered Balfurin.

Once, the entrance to the castle had been a narrow corridor leading to the Great Hall, with other rooms branching off that cavernous chamber. Sometime in the last decade, however, since he was last at Balfurin, massive changes had been made to the interior of the castle. He followed a steady line of people into a commodious foyer tiled in black and white. When he was last here, the area had been a narrow little closet of an entranceway. To his left was the Great Hall, and above, where once there had been a narrow curving stair, was a set of steps sweeping up to the very top of the castle.

He wanted to stop the press of people, demand some time to absorb the changes, but he was soon born along with the crowd into the Great Hall. Here, at least, there were few changes. The claymores and broadswords had been removed from the walls, but the flags and banners belonging to the MacKinnons were still in evidence.

Thank God. For a moment, he'd thought George had found a way to circumvent the primogeniture laws and sold the castle outright.

He moved to the back of the hall, Matthew accompanying him. With some difficulty he found a place beside a pillar. In moments, a procession began, white gowned girls walking two by two through the middle of the Great Hall holding thick white pillar candles before them. They were chanting something he couldn't translate. He could speak French, German, and in the last ten years, Malay, but his Latin was rusty. He was reminded of his schoolboy lessons of ancient Rome, and wondered what the hell George had gotten himself into that a group not unlike the Vestal Virgins were parading through Balfurin.

An older woman stepped up to an elevated area at the end of the Hall. She waited until the crowd became aware of her and then began to speak. "It is my great pleasure and privilege to introduce Charlotte MacKinnon, the Countess of Marne."

Applause greeted the woman who replaced her at the podium.

She was dressed in a similar fashion to the girls who stood in front of her, their candles still flickering. Her auburn hair had more than a touch of red to it, as if there was fire in it. He was too far away to see the color of her eyes, but he somehow knew they'd be green. Her face was pale, but spots of color showed on her cheeks, as if she were embarrassed or excited to be standing in front of the crowd of people in Balfurin's Great Hall.

She began to speak and he found himself fascinated by the low timbre of her voice.

"Those women who are graduating from the Caledonia School for the Advancement of Females have completed a rigorous course of work in Latin, geography, mathematics, linguistics, French, history, and art appreciation. They have also been schooled in household management, millinery, and fashion, all subjects that will enable them to become good citizens, wives, and mothers. When our students leave Balfurin, they do so armed with a knowledge of the world, and hopefully a thirst for education that will continue throughout their lives."

She smiled, and her face was transformed from simple prettiness to beauty. He moved closer, his back to the pillar, eager to see her in a better light.

The crowd laughed at one of her comments and she blushed, looking down at the podium for a long moment before continuing to talk. One by one, the teachers were introduced, a fair number of young to middle-aged women being acknowledged to applause. She was artful at sharing praise and singling out those who appeared shy.

Finally, the girls advanced onto the stage, received their rolled diplomas, and stepped away, each one to a thunderous round of applause.

At the end, the redheaded woman hesitated, and then stretched out her arm, indicating the assembled column of girls in a sweeping gesture.

"Ladies and gentlemen, fathers and mothers, I give you the first graduating class of the Caledonia School for the Advancement of Females."

A very nice speech, but it didn't answer his question—what had happened to Balfurin, and where was George?

In the last four hundred years, the Great Hall had probably been as crowded. Instead of a graduation from the Caledonia School for the Advancement of Females, however, the talk had no doubt been of warfare, stealing a neighboring clan's cattle, or going to battle against the English. Dixon couldn't help but wonder if the first earl—ensconced in a heaven reserved for Scottish warriors—was wincing at Balfurin's new, less warlike demeanor.

When the ceremony was over, and the crowd invited to ascend to the ballroom for dancing and refreshments, Dixon gradually became aware of the looks sent in his direction.

He moved through a door he doubted many people knew about since it was set flush into the wall and looked like part of the decoration. He didn't worry that Matthew had followed him—Matthew was always five feet behind him, a constant, protective shadow.

People passed him, intent on the curving staircase. He ignored them and walked through the first floor of Balfurin.

The framed souvenirs of war that had been mounted on the wall were gone, replaced by watercolors of native plants. Bouquets of heather brightened the shadowy corners. Heather should be growing free in the glen, not looking oddly miserable and out of place confined to copper urns.

A footman, tall and straight, in blue livery, bowed to him.

"May I direct you to the ballroom, sir?"

"No," he said, as amenably as possible in the midst of the unpleasant experience of rediscovering Balfurin.

The castle had been softened, the interior furnishings almost feminine. Dixon wasn't certain he liked the change. It played hell with his memories.

Were there any servants left who might have known

him as a boy? Anyone at all, who could recall the shape of his boyhood face in the man who stood before them? Was that the reason he'd come home to Scotland after all this time? To find a trace of himself? To find his identity? He'd spent the last ten years of his life immersed in a culture where family was valued over wealth or prestige, where ancestors were more honored than the living. Perhaps he was simply trying to find his own roots.

The area where he walked had once been dreary from the absence of light. Now the corridor had been widened and windows added. He wondered what view they would reveal in the daylight. Candles illuminated a room he could call a parlor in another home, comfortable with overstuffed couches and chairs angled to catch the best of the light from the mullioned windows.

What the hell had happened to Balfurin?

"It is a very big place, master," Matthew said. Dixon glanced at him, surprised to realize that he'd forgotten the other man's presence for a moment.

"Balfurin's larger than I remember. Aren't places from your childhood supposed to look smaller?"

Balfurin both resonated in his memory and yet felt alien. Too many things had changed and yet the castle itself was timeless.

A couple passed him, intent on the stairs. He gestured to Matthew and followed them, annoyed that strangers seemed to know Balfurin better than he. At the head of the stairs, the crowd bunched together and then stalled. It wasn't until they moved forward that he discovered why—they were being announced by an elderly man in stiff brocaded blue livery and wearing a powdered wig.

Finally, someone he recognized.

"Hello, Jeffrey," he said as he came abreast of the old man.

Jeffrey turned and frowned at Dixon, his bushy white eyebrows meeting together over soft brown eyes that looked too young to belong to the old man. Abruptly, his annoyed expression changed, becoming almost frightened. His mouth hung open; he stepped back a pace, and stared at Dixon.

"I know I've been gone some time," he said, "but it's really me, Jeffrey."

Jeffrey's hand quivered as he stretched it toward Dixon, one finger extended, as if Jeffrey thought he was a ghost and had to touch him to assure himself Dixon was corporeal. His eyes softened, and for a moment Dixon thought the elderly servant was going to cry.

Instead, Jeffrey took a step forward. He cleared his throat, straightened his shoulders, and thumped the wooden floor with his gold-topped staff. In a voice louder than he'd announced the other guests, he intoned, "The Earl of Marne, and Laird of Balfurin."

Conversation abruptly stopped. People ceased mingling. A quiet as profound as midnight on the ocean stole over the room. As Dixon moved closer to correct Jeffrey, the woman from the Great Hall stepped forward. The crowd parted silently for her.

Her face was flushed and then seemed to grow paler the closer she came to him. She'd changed clothes, and the feathers on the shoulders of her gown bobbed as she walked. She looked not unlike a cygnet, a young swan of grace and dignity.

"A most exquisite female," Matthew said from

beside him. Since Matthew was rarely given to comments about women, he glanced at him curiously. There was an expression of intensity on his companion's face that he'd never before seen.

He didn't have time to comment, because suddenly she was standing not two feet from him. Unlike some women who do not improve on proximity, this woman was even more striking up close than she was from a distance. Her complexion was perfect, her skin clear and radiant, her teeth—her lips were parted in a determined, if grim smile—were perfectly formed and white. Her hair was truly more red than brown, and her features so perfect that he was tempted to ask her to remain still for a few moments so that he might be able to measure each against the other.

How odd that the music was still playing.

Nor was her figure to be missed. How could he? He was a man who'd been celibate for too long.

"George," she said, her voice low and intimate, "I might have expected this of you."

Instead of waiting for his reply, however, she walked past Jeffrey into the corridor. He had no recourse but to follow her, Matthew at his side.

"Madam, you are mistaken," he said, annoyed that she'd taken him for his cousin.

She smiled at two late arrivals, and waited until they were announced before turning to him.

"In what? The fact that you are here? Or the fact that you chose the worst night in five years to return? Where have you been? And why in the name of the archangels have you come back?"

"Madam, I must correct you," he began, only to be interrupted once more.

"Why now, after all this time? You're not welcome here, MacKinnon. I don't have any use for a husband, especially you." She fisted her hands and held them out in front of her as if they were playing a children's game. Perhaps she wanted to hit him and was only barely restraining herself.

He took a precautionary step backward.

"Did all my money run out, George? Is that why you're back? I've not got any spare to give you, and you'll not take from the school's coffers. It's barely paying its way as it is."

Now that was really too much.

"A MacKinnon has never been a thief, madam."

She answered with an unladylike snort of derision and a quelling look. "Pity I didn't know that five years ago when you absconded with my dowry after a week of marriage."

"The actions of a man betray his soul," Matthew said.

Dixon glanced at Matthew, wondering why he chose now to become inscrutably Oriental.

"Who are you?" she asked, then shook her head as if chastising herself for her rudeness. But she didn't alter the question or soften it.

Matthew tucked his hands into his sleeves and bowed from the waist. "I am Matthew Mark Luke and John."

She looked startled, but then so did everyone upon learning Matthew's full name.

"Matthew was raised by missionaries," Dixon said. "They couldn't decide which book of the Bible to name him after so they picked four."

"It's a good thing they weren't reading the Old

Testament at the time," she said. "Nahum, Habakkuk, and Zephaniah would have been much more difficult."

Matthew smiled, a rare enough expression that Dixon stared at him. The younger man wasn't easily charmed, and it was disconcerting that this red-haired virago had been the one to do it.

"Is it your hair?" he asked. "Does it give you your fiery nature? Or were you born a blond and your temper colored your hair?"

"You claimed, once, to have liked my hair," she said, her eyes narrowing.

"A lot of things that were real five years ago may not be real now." Including his identity.

"I haven't been able to divorce you, George. Perhaps I should just kill you instead. It's something I shall have to consider."

With that she turned and walked away, leaving him staring after her.

Chapter 2

The orchestra was playing, the sound of lush music traveling through the corridors of Balfurin, bringing the old castle to life. Moonlight streamed in through the archer's slits, recently fitted with glass. Everyone looked as if they were having a delightful time. The food on the sideboards was disappearing at a rapid rate, as were the wines. Even the overly sweet punch, set aside for the younger students, was being refilled in the large silver bowl.

Charlotte skirted the dance floor, nodding and smiling at her guests. The effort to appear cordial and welcoming was nearly killing her. She wanted to stand in the middle of the ballroom, spread her arms wide, and start screaming.

A cluster of girls stood in the anteroom, and she nodded to them, hoping they wouldn't engage her in conversation. She needed a few minutes to gain her composure, calm herself, before becoming the chatelaine of Balfurin once more.

Damn him.

Closing her eyes, she took a few deep breaths but it didn't work. She was still furious.

Damn him. Damn him for showing up tonight of all times. Damn him for not disappearing forever. Damn him for ruining the one evening in the world that mattered to me. Damn him for his interference. Damn him for being alive.

Gradually, she became aware of the whispers on the other side of the anteroom. If the three girls clustered there wanted a bit of privacy, they should have considered how high the ceilings and how well sound carried.

". . . it was in her family for ages, and she's heartsick."

"Marybell can't locate the ring her grandmother gave her either."

"My mother will never forgive me. She told me not to bring it to school and if I tell her it's missing, she'll just get all puffed up like she does when she's right."

Charlotte pushed aside all thoughts of George in view of this new crisis. She crossed the anteroom and addressed the three girls.

"What is missing?"

None of the girls looked eager to impart any information, but Charlotte merely waited. She'd found that silence was a remarkable persuader.

"My brooch," Anna finally said. "I had it yesterday, but when I went to put it in my case, it was gone. It's gold, with a lock of my parents' hair inside."

"And Marybell's ring, and Jessica's necklace," another one of the girls said.

"Why haven't you reported any of these items?" Charlotte asked, even though she knew the answer. They wouldn't be found, any more than the other jewelry gone missing this term.

The regrettable fact was that one of her students had a habit of thievery. She could only hope that it was one of the graduating seniors and they wouldn't return to school.

"Make sure Miss Thompson gets the list before you leave," she said. Each of the girls nodded, and Charlotte forced a pleasant expression on her face as the three girls left the anteroom.

What else? Surely, this night would soon be over. She'd been so elated earlier in the evening and now she only wanted her bed.

"Your ladyship?" She turned to find Maisie standing there. "Is there anything I can do?"

Turn back time itself to five years earlier. She'd have refused to marry George MacKinnon.

Charlotte shook her head and began to pace back and forth. What was she to do now? Every time she turned, one of the feathers brushed her lips. Finally, too annoyed to tolerate it any longer, she grabbed the offending feather and jerked it free, hearing the worrisome sound of stitches ripping as she did so.

Maisie came to her side. "Your ladyship, you'll ruin your dress."

"At this moment, I don't care."

The maid drew her hands away from the feather, and carefully removed it. "Is it true?" she asked. "Is he your husband?"

"I'm very much afraid he is."

"It's a wonderful thing for him to have returned after all this time, your ladyship."

She turned her head and looked at her maid. "No, Maisie, it isn't. The man should have greeted me on his knees, hands outstretched, with an apology on his lips. Instead, he arrogantly stood there smiling at me."

"He's very handsome," Maisie said. "Every woman in the ballroom noted it."

"Did everyone hear what I said?"

"I don't think so," Maisie said, and at this moment Charlotte didn't care if her maid was being tactful or not. She was going to choose to believe that no one else had heard the words she'd thrown at George.

"Damn him," she said, uncaring whether or not she shocked her maid.

What if he intended to claim his place at Balfurin? Become the long-lost laird? Dear God, he could even close the school.

Charlotte forced a smile to her lips and a bit of patience to her mind. Now was not the time to panic.

"Go find him, Maisie, and make sure he's settled in the Laird's Chamber."

"Your ladyship?"

"I can't have him leaving again. Not now. I couldn't divorce him because he'd disappeared. I want to know exactly where that man is at all times."

Maisie nodded.

"Send him a tray," Charlotte added as an afterthought. "As much as I want to, I can't starve my own husband. Damn him."

* * *

She had simply turned and walked away, leaving Dixon standing there, an object of intense scrutiny. People were staring at him, and although he was used to the sensation in Penang, he found it disconcerting in the middle of Scotland, in his ancestral home.

He turned and walked out of the ballroom, heading for the stairs.

"Shall you correct her, master?" Matthew said in a low voice. "She labors under the mistaken notion that you are who you are not. You are not this George."

"No, I'm not George," Dixon said.

"How could a wife not know her husband?"

"We were close enough in appearance as boys," Dixon said. "People mistook us for brothers more than once. Sometimes, even twins. But I'm taller than George." A sore point with George. "And my eyes are darker as well."

"A wife should know such things." Matthew made a clucking sound, one of his habits when distressed.

Dixon halted halfway down the steps.

"We are to be leaving this place, correct, master? There is no cousin here, and no welcome from your family."

"Which is exactly why we're not going anywhere," Dixon said.

"Should we not return to Edinburgh, master? Our ship will be waiting for us." Matthew looked hopeful.

Dixon's answer was interrupted by a small voice. "Sir? Your lordship?" The sound of footsteps on the stairs behind him made him look up.

A girl stood there, attired in a dark blue dress with white collar and cuffs. Her black hair was arranged in a bun, but riotous curls escaped the back and the sides.

Her face was pale, but two dots of color appeared on her cheeks as if she were embarrassed.

"Your lordship." She did a credible job of curtseying on the steps, one hand carefully holding onto the banister as she did so. "Her ladyship has asked me to show you to the Laird's Chamber."

He would have bet that her ladyship couldn't wait to see the last of him. "Why?"

The young girl blinked at him. "Why, sir?"

He moved to the side of the stairs as another couple ascended, leaned against the banister and surveyed the girl. He'd learned patience in his years in the Orient, and it served him well now as he waited for her to answer him.

"I'm to show you to the Laird's Chamber, your lordship, and then fetch you a tray if you're hungry. Do you not wish me to?"

He didn't know what he wanted at this moment. Yes, he did. He wanted to be acknowledged for who he was. He wanted someone to recognize him, to welcome him home, to greet him the way he'd expected to be greeted. He wanted to be called by his name, and asked about the last decade of his life. Above all, he wanted this sense of discordance to fade, and he wanted Balfurin back the way he remembered it, ramshackle and worn, and familiar.

She turned to face Matthew, and then halted in the middle of her curtsey. The young girl looked dumbfounded as she stared.

The Scots were traditionally a welcoming people, less quick to judge than the English, less xenophobic than the French. But here at Balfurin, just like Edinburgh and Inverness, he doubted that many people had seen an Oriental man, let alone someone dressed like Matthew.

Matthew chose to wear floor-length robes of embroidered silk over a sarong or skirtlike garment. Asking Matthew to look differently—just like asking him to behave differently—would be taking away his identity. Years with a missionary family had almost done that, and Dixon would not add to the sins of his fellow countrymen. In Edinburgh, Matthew had been a source of amazement. In Inverness, people had actually stopped him on the street, asking him questions fueled by curiosity.

Dixon had witnessed prejudice, had experienced it himself as one of the first Europeans in Penang. But Maisie's reaction to Matthew was not so much aversion as it was amazement. Whereas her gaze had been fixed on the floor just a moment ago, now she studied Matthew's face intently as if fascinated by the almond shape of his eyes and the flat bridge of his nose.

"Matthew is a native of Penang," he said.

"Pulau Pinang," Matthew corrected, using the historical name for the island.

Finally, she smiled and turned to Dixon. "Will you come with me, sir? Your lordship?"

"Lead on," he said, ignoring Matthew's look.

She led them back up the stairs, glancing at Dixon periodically as if to make sure he followed.

"What's your name?" he asked, accompanying the young maid to the wing where the family quarters were located. At last, something that hadn't changed.

A gate-legged table sat at the end of the corridor. Atop it was a small brass lamp, its light barely enough to illuminate the walls with their raised dark mahogany panels and the crimson patterned carpet running down the center of the polished floorboards.

"Maisie, sir. Your lordship. I'm named after my mother's sister. Her name was Maisie Abigail Lawrence, but of course my mother didn't choose the whole name. She liked the Maisie part, though."

She glanced at him, looking as if she'd like to bob another curtsey.

"I'm sorry to take you away from the festivities, Maisie."

"Oh, it's no bother, sir. I was looking for an excuse to leave anyway. I can't dance, you see, even if someone was foolish enough to ask me."

Maisie hesitated beside a wide brass-handled door. She looked down at the floor and then back at him. "It's silly to pretend that I'll ever be able to. I'm lame, you see."

"Lame?"

She faced the door and stared steadily at it. "There was a problem when I was born. My foot is not right."

He glanced down at her feet and only then did he realize that one shoe was elevated more than the other. The sole of her left shoe was twice the depth of her right.

"I wouldn't consider you lame, Maisie. In fact, if you hadn't said something, I wouldn't have known."

She smiled, the expression so filled with joy that he was startled at how much it transformed her face from plain to pretty.

"Thank you, your lordship."

"It's only the truth, Maisie," he said, oddly embarrassed.

"Even a fallen flower can have beauty," Matthew said, the first time he'd spoken since they'd begun to follow Maisie.

She looked down at the floor again as she opened the door to the chamber and stepped aside. "You've been given the Laird's Chamber, your lordship, as you're the earl and all."

Dixon didn't comment, and pointedly ignored Matthew's sidelong glance as he stepped across the threshold.

He'd been in this room exactly twice in his life, as a young child on the night his grandfather had died and ten years ago when his uncle had succumbed to influenza. The heavily carved mahogany four-poster bed looked the same, positioned as it was between two floor-to-ceiling windows.

The ceiling was decorated with plaster saints, dating back to a time when the family was Catholic. As a child, he'd thought one of the statues was the likeness of his grandfather. Only later had he learned that they were effigies of the saints, and had been brought from the old castle before it was abandoned.

The armoire was in the same position, as were the crimson armchairs in front of the fire. Everything looked in readiness for another inhabitant.

"It's been vacant for five years, sir, but we've kept it up all the same. The maids dust and sweep in here every month or so. I don't think we have mice anymore, but it's always wise to be prepared."

"What about snakes?" he asked. But Maisie was

too intent upon her duties to realize he was jesting.

"Oh no, no snakes, sir. None that I've ever seen."

He took pity on her and refrained from teasing her further.

"If you're sure you need nothing else, sir, your lordship," she said, her gaze fixed firmly on the floor, "I'll show your manservant to his room."

"Matthew isn't my manservant," he said. "He's my secretary."

She looked at Matthew and then at Dixon. "Would you like another room, then, your lordship? The third floor's where most of the servants sleep."

"That room will be acceptable, miss," Matthew said, stepping forward, tucking his hands in the commodious bell sleeves of his jacket and bowing from the waist. "I would not like to trouble anyone."

"You're not, Matthew," Dixon said firmly. "Balfurin is my home, and you are its honored guest."

Maisie looked startled by his words. Matthew only looked at him cautiously, as if he knew the veneer of Dixon's politeness was whisper thin.

"The third floor will be fine, master. If that is acceptable to you."

After a moment, Dixon nodded, and watched as the two of them left the room.

They called her Old Nan, or Mother, as if she had given birth to every creature who lived at Balfurin. In fact, she'd never given birth at all. Her only claim to everyone's good fortune and well wishes was her advanced age.

She had been born in the year of our Lord 1746, which made her exactly ninety-two years old. While it was true that she'd never heard of anyone living to her great age, the maid assigned to bring her meals had told her once about a woman in Edinburgh who was ninety-six when she died.

If she could believe that silly girl.

Her knees hurt, but it had been the day for that—the sky had been overcast and the wind brought with it a touch of chill. It was autumn in Scotland, after all. Tomorrow, her hands would pain her as well as her back. Or even her hips, although she didn't walk as much as she once did. How many times had she strode across the moors, intent on meeting Robbie? All other men were forgotten the first day she'd seen him, with his bright blue eyes and his smile.

Sometimes, a good memory was a torment.

She grabbed one of the straight-back chairs sitting at the little table along the wall and scooted it across the wooden floor. She'd done the same thing so many times that there was a rut in the wood planking where the chair legs dragged. Strange, that no one had ever seen fit to comment on her habit of watching the inhabitants of Balfurin from her tower room. Perhaps they all knew, and they simply respected her age too much to say. Either that, or they thought her eccentric and wandering in her wits. She'd done that too much lately.

Or perhaps they never noticed her at all.

For years Nan felt as if she was the protector of Balfurin when its own laird could not be present. When she couldn't manage the stairs any longer, she sat at her window and guarded the castle with her will, protecting it from strangers.

Sometimes, her eyesight wasn't very good and her mind wandered, so that she could almost envision a male figure standing on the broad stone steps in front of the castle just like the long-ago laird she'd loved so fiercely. He lay in his grave now, dust and bones, his spirit no doubt out hunting instead of being in heaven where it should be. Or perhaps he was laughing, an arm extended, his hand gripping a tankard of ale, bidding all those companion ghosts with him to drink up in eternal merriment.

Her heart ached for the touch of him.

Earlier, before her nap, when the torches had been lit and those silly little girls in their flimsy dresses had all congregated on the steps, she'd thought she'd seen him again, standing there looking up at the tower room.

That was one thing that surprised her about age. The body might wither and eventually die, but the heart never lost its capacity for yearning, or its ability to feel pain.

She'd not seen him, of course; it had only been the darkness or a wish or a dream she'd had during one of her frequent naps. She slept often these days, and she thought it was God's way of leading her into forever sleep, a way of acquainting her with what was to come.

She wouldn't mind death if it meant being with Robbie for all time. What a way to spend eternity: with laughter on her lips and a taste of his kisses there. She'd be young again, as would he.

Nan clenched her hands tight and then released them when the pain in her joints made her realize what she was doing. A tear fell down a lined cheek, but she didn't bother to brush it away. There was no one to see her weep. No one but ghosts.

She sat ramrod straight in her chair, years of practice causing her to ignore the discomfort of her posture. Instead, she concentrated on the torches still lit at the front steps. Perhaps if she wished him there she would see the coach arrive, and him emerge again, along with his strange and unusual companion.

Had he come for her?

A knock on the door followed that thought so perfectly that she jumped, startled. She didn't bother to call out. If it were a ghost, it would not need her summons; and if it was the maid assigned to her, the silly girl ignored all of her wishes anyway.

Once, she'd been the housekeeper for Balfurin. If the girl had been under her thumb, she'd have dismissed her, but not without whipping her first.

"I've brought you some refreshments, Mother," the girl said, entering the room. "Her ladyship thought you would like some punch and maybe some of the food that's being offered tonight. There's meat and cheese and apple and peach tarts."

The girl held out the full tray like an offering. Nan could have lived on its contents for a week. During the lean times, she would have wept with joy to see such bounty. But she didn't bother to lecture the girl on frugality. The silly thing wouldn't care. She'd not a thought in her head, spending all her time dreaming of the young footman with the yellow hair. An English lad. In her day, such a pairing would never have been allowed. But then, the English had not been welcomed at Balfurin.

And now an Englishwoman was the laird's wife.

Nan reached up for one of the pastries with a trembling hand. Using her other hand to steady her wrist, she brought it to her mouth. Age brought about several changes that she could no longer fight. Better to simply ignore them. She took an appreciative bite, grateful that she still had most of her teeth. More than she could say for some of the English she'd seen.

The pastry was flaky and sweet. A delicious confection, but she wouldn't tell the girl. Instead, she only nodded when she was done.

"Would you like some of the punch? It has a bit of a spike to it. I took the punch from the man's bowl, knowing how you like good whisky."

Oh, so now the silly girl was remembering she was Scot, was she?

She said nothing as the girl put the tray on the small table beside the window and then handed her a cup.

The girl would spend another few minutes readying her bed, as if Nan didn't know where to sleep. She'd fluff her pillow and smooth the blanket and generally make herself as annoying as possible.

Nan ignored her, sipping at the punch as she stared out at the dark night, far beyond her reflection. The window was fogging, a sign that the air was growing colder.

The wind was bringing more than winter. Changes were coming to Balfurin. What was the poem? For a second she couldn't remember it, and that frightened her more than death. She'd promised, after all. Then, it came to her, and she relaxed, sinking back against the chair.

She didn't want to think of the rest of the poem. Wasn't it a bad omen that it came to her mind so quickly and easily these days?

Who needed treasure? As long as the body was warm, had food, shelter, and a measure of love, however fleeting that might be—that was all a body needed to make a life, a good life.

Asking for more was foolishness, but then the world was populated with fools.

Chapter 3

Dixon sat on the end of the bed watching as Matthew unpacked his trunk.

"I can help, you know," he said.

Matthew looked offended by the suggestion.

"Do you not think I can do the job correctly, master?"

"You are not my manservant, Matthew."

Matthew only smiled and shook his head. A moment later, he spoke. "A man is born to what he must be. Trouble follows when he tries to be more than he is."

"Or less," Dixon said. "I know only too well about the layers of society, thank you. I'm an earl's cousin, and not privy to the accompaniments of his rank or position."

"I would think, master, that there are not that many accompaniments to being an earl," Matthew said, glancing around at the dimensions of the room.

"This castle is smaller than your home in Penang."

Dixon nodded. He'd spent three years building a house in the hills, a magnificent structure overlooking the lowlands and surrounded by lush gardens. At the time people thought it was a gift to his bride. In reality, the house was a way of demonstrating—without a word spoken—just how powerful and rich he'd become.

"You are much wealthier than the earl, I think. You have fifty servants, and numerous concubines."

"No concubines," Dixon said, his smile fading. "Surely the women of my household do not think they're employed for that purpose?"

"Every day there are one or two more who ask to labor for you, master. The whole island would be at your feet if you wished. They know of your loneliness."

"It's been a year, Matthew."

"Master, the heart does not know the meaning of time."

One day, he would have to tell Matthew the truth. Then, perhaps, he'd stop making Dixon into a figure of sorrow, a grieving husband who dreaded the coming of every day.

Guilt kept him silent.

"Nevertheless," Matthew said, waving his hand at him as if to dismiss everything Dixon had said, "there are women waiting for you to return. They would give you massages with warm oils, and drink tea with you and converse on any subject you wish. When night falls, they will give you comfort of another sort. There is no need for you to hunger after a European woman."

Dixon raised one eyebrow. "Just what European woman am I hungering after, Matthew?"

Matthew shook his head and reached into the trunk.

"Why is it that you're silent when I wish you to speak and when I wish a little peace, you insist on chattering?"

"I am sorry that I displease you, master," Matthew said, but his tone was light and unconcerned.

"Is there a particular woman you wish me to bed, Matthew? Are you acting as her agent?"

Matthew turned and faced him fully, folding his hands within his sleeves. His face was devoid of expression.

"No, master, there is no one I would represent to you. But the women of Penang are attuned to you in a way a European woman is not. She would not know of the last ten years. She has no idea of your loss."

Dixon ignored that last comment. "You seem to think I lust after my cousin's wife. Why is that?"

"I saw the way you looked at her, master. As if she were a meal and you a starving man."

"You're imagining things, Matthew. I appreciated her appearance, nothing more."

Matthew looked doubtful, but he didn't speak.

"European or Oriental, I'll choose my own woman," Dixon said.

When Dixon glanced at him it was to find that the other man had turned back to the trunk, intent upon his chore.

That's how it was with Matthew. A confrontation never lasted more than a moment, rarely longer than a sentence. Matthew simply stopped, as if knowing how dangerously close to insubordination he tread. As if sensing that he was allowed so much leeway and no farther.

There were times when Dixon wanted a brawl, an argument, a spirited debate, but Matthew wouldn't give it to him. He would voice his opinion and then retreat, not unlike a badly abused dog that barked and then cowered.

"You don't like Balfurin, do you?"

Matthew straightened and, for a moment, Dixon wondered if he would speak at all. Or had his capacity for honesty been reached?

"If you will forgive me, master, may I speak freely?"

"You've always had the ability to do so, Matthew. You need not ask my permission." A speech he made repeatedly.

"There is something dark about this place, master." He hesitated as if searching for the correct word. "Not evil, exactly, but close to it. Something that dwells in darkness and feeds on pain lives here. It has waited for you to come and it is happy now."

"The Countess of Marne? She doesn't seem a creature of the darkness to me."

Matthew looked offended at his jest, turning back and bending over the trunk again.

"If not her, then who?"

"You are angry," Matthew said.

"Not angry, impatient. I'll grant you that something is wrong here, and I don't know what it is, but I'm going to withhold judgment about it being evil at the moment."

"What kind of woman does not know what her

husband looks like? Who accuses another man of being him?"

"What kind of man leaves a woman such as her?" Dixon countered. "I don't have any of the answers, Matthew, which is why we're not leaving here until I do."

"The darkness will be happy. And it will grow."

"I thought Buddhists were supposed to believe in attracting good?"

Matthew closed his eyes and held them closed for a full half minute. When he opened them, his gaze was calm, serene.

"You know I am not a Buddhist, master. I am a Baptist."

"I think you're Oriental when you wish to be and something else entirely when it suits your purpose."

He was annoyed, especially when Matthew smiled.

"You see, the darkness is working on your soul already. It is making you unpleasant."

Dixon strode toward the door, anxious to rid himself of Matthew's presence.

"Avoid the woman, master," Matthew said.

The command was so unlike him that Dixon turned and glanced at his secretary.

"She is a danger to you, master. I feel it very certainly. She will bring harm to you. I know you are grieving, but you must not seek comfort in her arms."

Dixon opened the door without looking back. "Do not speak of it, Matthew. I forbid you to do so."

"Has this visit eased your heart, master?"

Dixon didn't answer, leaving the room and closing the door behind him. For a moment he rested his back against it, eyes closed. He'd been a fool to think that coming home would relieve his conscience.

What the hell did he do now? He could attend the ball again, but he wasn't in the mood for levity or celebration or any more threats from George's wife. Despite what Matthew thought, he wasn't anxious to encounter the Countess of Marne again.

He could find his way to the kitchens since he'd done so often enough as a boy. Hunger was an impetus for seeing if his memory was correct as to its location. But he didn't want to see anyone, let alone a harried kitchen staff.

Instead, he headed toward the south wing, away from the ballroom and the bedchambers, to a room he remembered all too well, his uncle's library.

Dixon opened the door slowly, allowing memory to sweep over the threshold and overwhelm him. He half expected to hear Uncle Stan's booming voice, "Close the door, can't you feel the draft? How's a man supposed to work in this infernal cold?" His uncle, however, was no longer there, seated behind the massive desk that had served generations of MacKinnons.

He stepped inside. This was a well-used room, one not overly changed in all the years since he'd been to Balfurin. The only change was in himself. The desk did not look so commanding. Nor was the chair thronelike. How many times had he stood here while his uncle imparted another stern lecture?

He'd been ten the first time he'd been summoned to this room.

"You'll not shame this family, Dixon. I'll not have your shenanigans bandied about Scotland. You'll behave with some decorum as befits a MacKinnon."

"Yes, uncle."

For years, that had been the only acceptable answer to any question his uncle asked. Later, he'd been more courageous.

"Is it true you manhandled the maid?"

"Is that what she said, Uncle?"

"She won't say anything. She only giggles when anyone mentions your name. The cook, however, has stated that you two were seen kissing in the pantry. Is that true?"

He'd only shrugged. His uncle had not hesitated to beat him for it.

When he'd been sent home from school with a warning from the headmaster about his lack of application, he'd been summoned here.

"I'm paying for your schooling, young man."

"Thank you, Uncle."

"I don't want your gratitude as much as your excellence. You will remember who, exactly, you are."

He'd been expelled in his third year, sent home in disgrace with a letter outlining his exploits. His uncle had decreed him a disaster and a blight on the family name.

"Do you understand anything that I am saying, boy?"

"I'm not a boy, Uncle," he'd said. "I'm a man."

"No, you're a child. A boy does what you have done. A man owns up to his faults."

He'd had no response to that, so he'd kept silent.

Strangely enough, he'd never begrudged his uncle his strict discipline. But he'd never understood why

George was not treated in the same way. Once he'd had the courage to ask his uncle why he'd not disciplined George for the same infraction. His uncle's answer had been swift. "George does not have to aspire."

The two cousins may have resembled each other, but there the similarities ended. George was the heir, the future earl, educated and treated as if he'd already ascended to the title.

His uncle's funeral had been well attended. People had come from miles around simply to bid farewell to the man they'd known and loved so dearly. Dixon had stood in the rain and marveled at their genuine grief, and thought that perhaps that was the measure of a man after all. Not what he left behind but how many people attended his final ceremony.

He'd left Scotland several months after that day, after realizing there was nothing here for him. He no longer wanted to watch George gamble away the family fortune or spend it on mistresses and horses.

More than a decade had passed since Dixon had stood here. More than enough time to understand what his uncle had tried to teach him. This empty room seemed to echo with all those long-ago lectures. Dixon felt a deep and abiding pain—he couldn't reach past the veil of death and send a message to the man he'd come to respect and admire.

"Forgive me, Uncle," he said softly in the stillness. "For all my foolishness. For all my stupidity and childishness. For not listening, and for being such a trial to you."

He rounded the desk and sat in his uncle's chair.

The room didn't smell like tobacco anymore; it smelled of roses. A leather blotter tooled with flowers sat in the middle of the desk. On the blotter sat a silver quill holder and an inkwell in the shape of a swan.

The Countess of Marne evidently used this room as her own.

She didn't belong here, and yet her claim to this place was greater than his. He should find some other room to haunt, some other chamber in which to revisit the past. But no other place evoked Balfurin and his childhood as strongly as this library.

A stack of correspondence sat at his right hand. She liked heavy cream-colored stationery, and wrote in an elaborate script. Her signature was telling. She didn't use her title in her correspondence but simply signed Charlotte MacKinnon. Nor did she use George's crest.

Had George wed her for her money? If so, why had he deserted her after such a short time? A week, she'd said. She was either a liar, or George was a bounder. Since Dixon knew his cousin better than he knew his countess, he suspected where to put the blame.

He rearranged her quills, and moved the inkwell so that it was perfectly aligned next to the blotter's edge.

George was missing and Charlotte thought he was his cousin. Balfurin had been transformed to the Caledonia School for the Advancement of Females. Matthew was predicting doom and gloom, and Dixon hadn't yet rid himself of the suffocating guilt that had fueled this journey.

Why the hell had he ever come home?

Maisie knocked on the door softly, and when it wasn't answered, she balanced the tray in one hand while she pushed down on the handle with the other. The Laird's Chamber was empty, but to be sure, she called out his lordship's name, wondering if he was using the attached closet for his personal needs.

When no one answered, she left the tray on the small writing desk and returned to the kitchen.

The trip to the third floor was harder, and she allowed herself to limp a little, as long as no one was around to see. It was a matter of pride that she didn't give in to her affliction. Like her Mam said, everybody was born with something. Some faults were obvious, some were deeply hidden, but everybody had one or more.

Once on the third floor, she knocked softly on the third door from the end. The chamber Matthew had been given had once been occupied by one of the footmen, but he'd gone off to Edinburgh when the country silence had grated on his nerves.

She knew the room well, had cleaned it herself. The window looked out over the loch and the room got most of the morning sun. There was a pretty little blue coverlet on the narrow bed and the pillow was fluffier than hers. But it had been newly stuffed and she'd seen to it that there was a selection of herbs in the middle of all the feathers so that it smelled fresh no matter what time of year it was.

She knocked once more, wondering if she should leave the tray on the floor in front of the door. But if he wasn't inside, it would be an invitation to any rodents who might be making their home at Balfurin. And what a waste of food that would be. She'd made the same selection for both the earl and his secretary from the silver platters in the kitchen. The cook had fussed at her a bit, saying they were for the ballroom, but she'd stood her ground, told her they were for the earl. Cook had stepped back, wiped her hands on her apron and muttered something under her breath.

The door abruptly opened and she was left staring at the Oriental man.

For a moment she forgot about politeness, lost in wonder. He was the most different-looking person she'd ever seen, what with his tilted eyes and his nose all but flat in the center of his face. His mouth was perfectly formed, his eyes the color of peat, a deep dark brown. His hair, cut short all around his head, was black and she wondered if it was as soft as it appeared.

He looked straight at her, and she had the strangest thought that although he wasn't smiling, he was amused.

"I've brought you dinner," she said. "I'm sure you're hungry."

"I have learned to deal with hunger, but I thank you."

"But why should you have to? Balfurin always has food."

She stretched out her arms and for a moment she wondered if he would take the tray from her. Should she enter his room and put it on the small table beside his bed? But while she debated, he reached out and took the tray.

"There are small little bits of food called hors d'oeuvres, something French, I think, and roast beef, cheeses, and a pastry that looks like a cherry tart.

Cook and her helpers have been working for days on the refreshments. A buffet, it's called, something I've never seen. But today is a day for strange occurrences, I think. My Mam said that a day when you learn something is a day never wasted."

"It looks very good," he said.

"If you don't like it, I can try to find something more to your taste. Do you like Scottish food?" she asked.

"I find it very different from what I am used to."

"What are you used to? Or is that a very rude thing to ask? You see, I don't know where Penang is."

"It's on the other side of the world."

"Oh." She'd never met anyone who wasn't from Scotland. Well, the English, but they were considered countrymen now, weren't they?

"I like your fish," he offered. "Salmon. With rice. And I have a particular liking for vegetables."

"There's some salmon," she said, pointing to one of the hors d'oeuvres. "But there isn't any rice, I'm afraid."

"I will try the salmon, and I thank you."

He bowed to her, and so surprising was the gesture that she stood frozen in place.

"Thank you," he said. An obvious comment of dismissal, but she truly didn't want to leave. Instead, she would love to simply stand here and study him.

"May I ask why you are staring? Is it because my appearance is so very different from your countrymen?"

"Oh no," she said, embarrassed. She looked down at the floor, wishing that it might open up and swallow her. "It's that you're quite the most beautiful person I've ever seen, sir."

He looked surprised, and then he smiled. The loveliest smile she'd ever been given, one that she had no choice but to return.

Chapter 4

The ball and the revelry continued unabated until the wee hours of the morning. As Charlotte watched the dancers, she missed Spencer even more. If he'd been here, he would have taken her in his arms, out of sight of the others, and just held her for a moment. Before he released her, he would have pressed a chaste but warm kiss on her temple and given her a smile that imparted courage at the same time it did compassion.

He might also have passed on some solicitor's advice. Advised her what to do, how to handle George.

But Spencer wasn't here, and George was.

She hated him. The confession startled her. She remained where she was, back braced against a carved wood panel as she watched the dancers. She hated George, Earl of Marne. The emotion came rolling out of her as if a door had recently been open. She hated him for all of the humiliation she'd had to endure, all of the sleepless nights, and all of the fear.

In all this time, no word had ever come. No apology, no letter of explanation, no notice that he had simply tired of married life and her, and taken himself away. No inkling of what had ever happened to him.

Her heart beat so fast that she felt faint with it. She walked to the sideboard and nodded at some of the parents in passing, making polite conversation with another couple.

At the end of the buffet table, she encountered two of her students and endured their giggling with what restraint she had left. She reached for a glass of spirits, something mild, designed for the female guests and older students. At the moment, she would have gladly traded her locale for her father's wine cellar. Let her pick a bottle of carefully matured wine and sit in the silence until she was in her cups.

Not exactly a ladylike thought, was it? But then, she hadn't time to consider being a woman, not when she was trying to survive—first as an abandoned wife, and then as the headmistress of the Caledonia School for the Advancement of Females.

Until Spencer, that is. She'd consulted him as a solicitor a few years ago, when she'd had the money to consider divorcing George. Over these past months their relationship had deepened.

She took another sip of the oversweet punch and smiled politely at a couple on the dance floor. They looked to be in love. Was that what she felt for Spencer? Certainly, she always felt in a good mood in his presence, as if she were smiling deep inside when she was next to him.

But if it was love, it felt too light, too insubstantial, almost a fluttery feeling. Surely love should be more weighty.

Like rage?

Never before had she felt this fierce anger. She realized she was frowning, and smoothed out her expression, pressing a smile to her lips with some degree of difficulty.

The ballroom was a cacophony, an overwhelming sea of noise. She felt like a tiny island in the middle of it. Or perhaps a sea creature floating in an ocean. A headache bloomed between her eyes, pierced her temples as well. What she really wanted was to leave the ballroom and seek out her bed. She'd drink a tisane for her headache and place a cold compress on her forehead, take off these incredibly uncomfortable shoes, and wiggle her toes in freedom. She'd toss her stays to the other side of the room and might even lay naked beneath the sheets.

The headmistress was not nearly as restrained as she appeared.

But she was not done with polite chatter. Parents came up to her, cups in hand, questions on their lips. She responded to their worries with as much tact as she could.

"Mary is doing quite well in her studies," she told one mother. "She seems to have an aptitude for the poets." In other words, the girl spent endless hours staring out the window and uttering dreamy little sighs from time to time rather than paying any attention to her instructor.

"Janet is, perhaps, more suited to marriage than to books," was the advice she gave to another parent.

Janet, the sweet girl, could not find her way out of a darkened room with a lit candle. She desperately needed a husband to protect her from the world and herself.

At three in the morning, the ballroom began to thin. At half past, she moved to the door, a signal that the celebration was officially over.

She stood at the doorway and watched as one by one her guests descended the stairs. Those who were staying the night were directed to the guest rooms. Those who couldn't be accommodated at Balfurin would take comfort at a nearby inn.

By noon, Balfurin would be empty of chattering, laughing girls. By afternoon, the teachers would leave as well. Another school year would not begin until March. She and the staff of Balfurin would have four whole months of blessed quiet.

And George.

George, who picked the very worst time to reappear.

She smiled at one of the last couples to retire for the evening, suspecting that her expression was less than successful coming on top of the surge of anger at her husband.

Husband, the word didn't even sound correct. For five years she'd been little more than a widow. The subject of rumor and speculation. One courageous student had actually asked her, "Your ladyship, did your husband die on your wedding night?" Since the girl was a dear sweet innocent who was already engaged, she saw the question as it was, an almost tearful request for reassurance.

"No, he didn't, Annabelle, and it won't happen to

you, either. I'm sure your marriage will be a long and happy one."

What an utter hypocrite she was, lying about marital bliss. Thank God the subject didn't come up often.

Her last guest was the aunt of one of her students. A woman no longer in the prime of her life, but beautiful nonetheless. She was leaning on a cane. Charlotte couldn't remember Lady Eleanor being so afflicted.

"It's a bother, my dear," she said when Charlotte approached her offering assistance. "I've been kicked in the leg by a horse, can you believe it? Vicious brute, not fit to be ridden, but I would try."

"I am sorry, Lady Eleanor. Do you need some help with the stairs?"

"Lend me one of your footmen, will you? The one with the blond hair and the devilish smile. He can carry me all the way to my bed." She smiled wickedly at Charlotte. "Oh, my dear, are you shocked? Of course you are. How very odd. I find that disturbing, actually. My niece shouldn't be exposed to such puritanical thought." She looked thoughtful for a moment. "But then, my brother would probably be very happy about it. He's a bit of a puritan himself."

"Puritanical thought?" Charlotte said. She really didn't know what to say.

"We must discuss this narrow-mindedness of yours. But first you must lead me to a chair. I find confidences are easier when I am not thinking of my leg."

The very last thing Charlotte wanted to do at this moment was talk to Lady Eleanor. She was related to a duke, and having her niece attend the Caledonia School for the Advancement of Females had been one of the reasons enrollment had suddenly jumped in the last two years. Moira's father had interviewed Charlotte quite thoroughly, and he'd found no fault in her establishment or her thought patterns.

Narrow-minded? Of course not.

She loved learning for the sake of it. She enjoyed filling her mind with extraneous facts and each day acquiring some knowledge that she didn't have the day before.

They found a set of chairs outside the ballroom door.

"Is there anything I can get for you?" Charlotte asked.

"Other than a footman?" Lady Eleanor asked, laughing gently. "Nothing but information, my dear. Who was that delightfully handsome man you greeted earlier?"

A moment passed while Eleanor looked expectantly eager, and Charlotte searched her memory for the men who'd approached her.

"Black hair, my dear. Devilish eyes. Blue, I'm certain. And a dimple in his cheek."

"George," Charlotte said flatly. "My husband."

"Your husband?" Lady Eleanor sat back in her chair and surveyed her with interest. "Then why are you looking so stricken? If I had a husband as handsome as that, I should be smiling the whole time."

Charlotte didn't quite know what to say to that.

"The ceremony earlier was a bit long, I think, but the ball more than made up for it. And your selection of footmen certainly added to the charm of the evening." Lady Eleanor smiled, glancing at the procession of young men who were carefully descending the stairs while laboring under trays of cups and glasses. "A veritable selection of young gods. I could sit and watch them for hours."

What is the female word for satyr?

"Tell me," the other woman said glancing at her, "do you not feel the same? A handsome man must surely make your heart beat stronger."

"Not particularly."

"Truly?" Lady Eleanor looked surprised. "Not even that handsome husband of yours?"

"I have found that men on the whole are an encumbrance," Charlotte said.

"I am indeed sorry to hear that, my dear. Someone must give that husband of yours a little instruction. It's a sin to be so arresting in appearance and so deadly in the bedroom."

"I beg your pardon?"

"He's evidently a bad lover," Eleanor said, swinging her cane from side to side in an arc.

"I don't remember," Charlotte said, wondering if she should admit the truth. "He's been gone for some time. We've been estranged."

"Only arriving tonight? Oh, my dear, why didn't you say? I've been chatting on and on and you've got that delightful creature waiting for you." She stood.

"I sincerely hope not," Charlotte said, joining her. "I haven't seen him in five years, I'm not about to welcome him into my bed."

"Why on earth not?"

She glanced at Lady Eleanor. The woman wasn't even looking at her but was ogling one of the footmen. What was worse, he was grinning right back at her.

"It's late," Charlotte said. "Let me have someone escort you to your chamber."

"Him," Lady Eleanor said, pointing the end of her cane at the blond footman.

Charlotte clasped her hands in front of her, wiping any expression from her face. Evidently, she was not entirely successful, because Lady Eleanor only laughed.

"I am beginning to think that Providence led me to speak with you tonight, my dear. Such innocence is not an altogether good thing in a woman of your years."

"My years?"

"You're not a young girl, my dear. You're a mature woman, and if you don't take care, you'll be an old woman before your time."

With that, she stepped away, placing her hand on the footman's arm. As Charlotte watched them walk slowly down the stairs, she was suddenly grateful that Lady Eleanor's niece had graduated tonight. She wouldn't have to see the woman again.

Chapter 5

At seven o'clock, before the breakfast bell rang, in fact before the bell rang to wake up the dormitories, a knock on her door roused Charlotte.

Thinking it was Maisie, she rose up on one elbow and called out, then fell back on the pillow and closed her eyes. She hadn't slept well the night before. Her feet hurt from standing for hours in those hideously uncomfortable shoes. But the main reason she couldn't sleep was because of her thoughts.

George no doubt slept without nightmares in the room across the hall.

She wanted to slam her fist against the door more than once and wake him up. Discretion kept her in her bed, frowning at the tester above her, frustrated, angry, and plotting.

Unfortunately, she hadn't come up with any way to rid herself of her husband. Murder was both immoral and illegal. She couldn't stab him, although any woman in Scotland would side with her, she was certain.

She hadn't been able to divorce him, even though she'd tried. An action for divorce could not be started until four years after desertion, and the fact that no one knew exactly where George was living had complicated that process.

She'd gone through the process of adherence—attempting to legally acquire George's assets so that she'd have some way of supporting herself. Unfortunately, there were no assets except for her missing dowry. Balfurin was entailed and exempt from any adherence procedures. The adherence petition had ultimately been dismissed, since she couldn't prove that George was still living in Scotland.

Had she been successful, however, she would have had to go to civil court to have George declared a rebel, and "put to the horn." After that process was complete, she was expected to present a petition to the presbytery asking that George be excommunicated. This was only a formality and not truly expected to be granted. But only after these cumbersome steps were completed could she raise the action for divorce.

Maybe George would go back to where he'd come from, as long as she knew where that was. He hadn't been forthcoming with any details. But the fact that his companion was Oriental was a clue. He'd gone to the Far East, evidently, when he'd left London.

Far enough from a new bride not to be found.

But this time, perhaps her divorce petition would be granted. If he remained in Scotland, that would be even better. How did she convince him to leave Balfurin?

She doubted he would go, and she wasn't about to abandon the school.

What was she going to do?

The knock came again, and this time she sat up.

"Oh, come in, Maisie," she said crossly.

But it wasn't Maisie. It was Lady Eleanor.

Charlotte grabbed the sheet and held it up to her throat. "Lady Eleanor."

Eleanor smiled brightly at her and held the door open for two more women. Charlotte recognized them immediately—Gladys McPherson, the English widow of a Scottish industrialist. Following her was Mary Holmann, a Scot who'd married a German baron. On his death she'd returned from Germany to live in Scotland again.

Each one of the women were either parents or patrons of students.

"Ladies," Charlotte began, only to be silenced by Lady Eleanor.

"We haven't much time, my dear. The girls are in a hurry to leave. Each of them is in a rush to spend a fortune on dresses. Why ever do you insist upon uniforms?"

"They're more conducive to learning, I've found," Charlotte said. But Lady Eleanor was not listening. Instead, she was gathering up chairs from the adjacent sitting room, and placing them around the bed. Mary and Gladys joined her in sitting down and looking intently at Charlotte.

Gladys's gray hair was arranged in a coronet.

Surprisingly, even at this early morning hour, she had flowers arranged in her hair as if she were a sprite of spring. Her dress was a pale yellow, and flattering, bringing out the sparkle of her brown eyes.

Mary was dressed in a subdued reddish brown, the color of rust. But her hair was loose, with tresses that looked as if they might fall from a few well-placed hairpins.

But Lady Eleanor was the most surprising of the three of them. Her dress was a solid deep blue, with white cuffs and collar. As somber as any of Charlotte's dresses.

"As I said, my dear, we haven't much time. Mary and Gladys and I have agreed that you should be included in our little gatherings. We normally meet for tea at Mary's house, but these are special circumstances."

"I have the fewest relatives who might be scandalized should the purpose for our meetings be learned," Mary explained.

"You're a great deal younger than our normal members," Gladys said.

"But that's a good thing, I think," Mary said.

"Indeed, we've agreed," Lady Eleanor added.

"What group would that be?" Charlotte asked.

"Oh dear, didn't we say?" Mary asked.

"We call ourselves The Edification Society."

Mary giggled. "We've come up with other names, of course, but none that bore people so successfully."

Lady Eleanor smiled. "It's true, my dear. The curious want nothing to do with our meetings. They're afraid we're discussing Egyptology and women's suffrage."

"Not that we don't occasionally, of course. One can't talk about men all the time."

"Men?" Charlotte asked, subsiding back against the pillows.

Eleanor tapped her cane on the floor. "You have an emergency and we've decided that you should be included."

"Especially now."

"Why now?" Charlotte asked weakly.

"Because your husband has returned," Mary said.

"An errant husband is a problem," Eleanor said. "Especially one who's been gone so very long. Four years, hasn't it been?"

"Five," Charlotte said.

"All the more vital that we meet."

"I do wish we could have discussed the footmen." This surprising comment was not from Eleanor, but from Mary.

"Perhaps next week, dear. For now, we must address Charlotte's issue."

All three women looked at her expectantly, as if they were waiting for her to comment.

"Very well," Eleanor said after an interval of silence. "We shall begin."

She pointed her cane in Mary's direction.

"It is very important that your husband be considerate of you after such a very long time without conjugal relations," Mary said.

"I beg your pardon?" Charlotte said.

"There are a great many substances that can be used as lubricants," Gladys said. "We provide our members a list."

"We have an entire package of substances available

for new members. There is no need for discomfort during relations."

"I'm afraid you have the wrong idea," Charlotte said.

"Are you naturally orgasmic?" Mary asked. "What a delight! You must tell us how that feels."

"I have no intention of bedding George," Charlotte said. "In fact, I wish very much for him to go away. Just as he had for the last five years."

They stared at her as if she'd been the one saying shocking things.

"He deserted me." She faced them down and wondered if she was doing the wrong thing by being so honest.

"Yes, but he's back."

"He's a very good-looking man, Charlotte."

"He has very healthy-looking attributes," Gladys said.

Charlotte glanced at her, eyes widening. The older woman wasn't even blushing.

"Attributes?"

"John Thomas," Lady Eleanor explained. "His twig and berries. Or, if you insist upon the most medical of terms, his penis."

"And testicles," Mary said. "Although I've often found them to be superfluous at best."

"Oh dear no, Mary," Lady Eleanor said. "If you mouth them properly, it causes quite a sensation."

"As well as the anus," Gladys said. "Bung hole," she explained. "A most curious orifice capable of a great many sensations."

Charlotte looked from one to the other, certain she'd never before been quite so discomfited.

"Are you giving me instructions on my marriage bed?"

"In the absence of your mother, my dear, why should we not?" Lady Eleanor asked.

"Although I doubt she would have as much experience as all of us. You see, we're only a small contingent of our group." Mary leaned forward. "We even have a former kept woman among us. She's been most instrumental in teaching us all sorts of things."

"I really have no intention of replaying my wedding night," Charlotte said.

"Oh, then you haven't been instructed properly. Were you told to lay there and bear it all? What a very great pity. Men are like bulls, my dear. You must give them a whiff of the pasture before letting them loose. You must demand of them your full measure of satisfaction before allowing them to climax."

Charlotte didn't know quite what to say to that. Another protestation that she had no intention of bedding George MacKinnon would fall on deaf ears, she was certain.

What on earth *did* she say to them? None of her training, either received as a child, or as the Headmistress of the Caledonia School for the Advancement of Females, prepared her for this group of women.

"You must demand your conjugal rights of him as soon as possible, my dear," Lady Eleanor said, "for your health. Intercourse is very good for the digestion, not to mention the circulation."

"Oh bother, Eleanor, it's fun!" This comment was from Gladys, the oldest of the group, whose eyes shined with merriment at the moment.

All three women laughed in a convivial agreement that went completely over Charlotte's head.

Lady Eleanor was the first to sober. "You haven't had a good time of it, have you, my dear? George has had all the fun, then?"

When Charlotte remained silent, she sighed. "Well, we need to change that. You must demand your rights."

"My rights?" Charlotte nearly choked on the words.

"Her reaction means something," Gladys said.

"Of course, how foolish we are not to have noticed." Lady Eleanor leaned forward and patted Charlotte's hand. "You haven't had any pleasure, have you, my dear?"

"Is it too late for a lover?" Mary asked.

"I do believe so. Her husband is in residence. I doubt he would accept a lover with alacrity."

"Unless he enjoys voyeurism," Gladys said. "Is that the case, Charlotte?"

Charlotte shook her head, less in negation of the question as to banish the sight of them from her vision. This must be a dream. No, a nightmare. They were the products of a distorted mind.

She'd drunk too much punch at the ball.

Charlotte closed her eyes and pushed away the women's conversation. After a moment, she opened her eyes again, but they were still there.

"Well, we cannot solve this problem in one meeting," Lady Eleanor said crisply, standing and motioning to the other women. "It might be interesting to have a few meetings here, instead of in Edinburgh. You certainly have the staff to accommodate us." She smiled. "Especially that delicious young footman, Mark. Do make sure he's here the next time."

Charlotte felt ice travel down her spine.

"You can't have your meetings here. What if someone finds out?" She pushed herself to an upright position. What would dissuade the woman? "There is my reputation to consider, Lady Eleanor. And that of the school's."

"Nonsense, my dear. It shouldn't signify. The Edification Society has adopted you, Charlotte. Besides, our sponsorship will guarantee your school's success."

"I offer a good curriculum," Charlotte said weakly. "I teach the graces, of course, but I also offer mathematics, philosophy, Latin, and logic. I'd prefer to attract students in that fashion."

"Very well, but having twenty of the most influential ladies of Edinburgh behind you will not be amiss."

"Behind me?"

"I must communicate with the other members, but we cannot allow George to continue as he is."

"You can't?" Charlotte asked.

"It wasn't well done of him. He needs to be punished for his sins."

"A velvet whip," Gladys suggested.

"A little deprivation," Mary added. "But first, he needs a taste of what he's missing."

"I mean to divorce him." Charlotte could swear the inward gasps nearly sucked the air from the room.

"Oh, that will never do," Lady Eleanor said. "Divorce scares off potential suitors and even lovers, my dear. Besides, he is such a lovely specimen of manhood.

Why on earth would you banish him from your bed?"

"He did that on his own."

"The cur," Mary said. "You should most definitely punish him. Tongue him nearly to release, then refuse to let him climax. That should do it."

"Make him suffer," Lady Eleanor said. "Make him writhe in agony, my dear. Women have always had the upper hand. The problem is that they haven't known how to use it."

Could this day—the last two days—be any worse? First, George returns without a regretful bone in his body. And now this, adopted by a bizarre group of women whose sole intent seemed to be to interest her in the wifely arts.

Dear God, what had she ever done to deserve this?

She wanted to pull the blanket over her head, sink down under the covers and pretend they really were part of a nightmare. But Lady Eleanor was looking at her oddly, as if she knew exactly what she was thinking.

"We shall return," Lady Eleanor said again. "When we do, we'll bring our entire group and some of our supplies."

"Creams that smell delightful," Mary said, "for use in the most interesting ways."

"A few velvet whips," Gladys added.

"Really, it's not necessary." Charlotte held up her hands, but the women paid no attention to her.

"Nonsense. If you don't do it for yourself, you must do it for womenkind."

"Must I?"

"He has not acted in the best manner, Charlotte,"

Lady Eleanor said sternly. "He must be seen to have learned his lesson."

"But I don't want him as a husband."

"Then take him as a lover, but teach him a lesson first."

All three of them smiled.

Chapter 6

She dressed by herself, banishing Maisie with the excuse that she wasn't fit for company. Let her maid think it was George's appearance that had so discomfited her. His sudden restoration to Balfurin was only partly responsible for her mood—The Edification Society was responsible for the rest.

She'd worked long and tirelessly to accomplish something with the school. Charlotte had modernized Balfurin, transforming the crumbling castle into an institution of learning. It was she who poured over the lesson plans, who spent the last of her grandfather's legacy on new books, and who had restored the gardens so the girls would have a place to stroll.

When she'd first started the school, she'd only had five students, but she'd persevered. By the second year, after a great many luncheons, teas, and talks with groups of women, she'd increased the enrollment to nearly a hundred. Now, the school housed nearly two hundred students for the eight months of term.

She must dissuade Lady Eleanor and her friends from meeting here. She left her chamber, her mind on ways in which she could suggest that it wouldn't be convenient, in a way that wouldn't insult the relative of a duke.

"It's one thing to starve me, madam, but I would have thought your generosity extended to the servants. Matthew shouldn't be punished for his affiliation to me."

She jerked to a stop and stared at him.

"George."

She couldn't help but think of what Lady Eleanor had said—something about tonguing him almost to satisfaction and then leaving him frustrated. Heat traveled from deep inside her to her cheeks as she stared at him.

"Good morning, Charlotte." He smiled at her. What a very pleasant smile he had, and why hadn't she ever noticed it before? Perhaps because he'd never smiled at her.

"Are you always sunny in the morning, George?"

"Something you should remember, surely."

She blinked at him. "A week is hardly long enough to be accustomed to a husband's moods. Besides, I don't believe I ever saw you in the morning."

"Truly?" He smiled again, and she decided that it wasn't so much a pleasant expression as it was a goading one.

"How annoying you can be."

"I'm hungry," he said, "and I'm always annoying when I'm hungry."

"Something I shall endeavor to remember," she said, preceding him down the stairs.

"Aren't you going to ask if I slept well?"

No, she wasn't going to be amiable to him at all. It was better if she recalled that he'd deserted her after a week, stealing her money and leaving her to find her own way in the world. Besides, he looked rested and well dressed. Surely, if he'd slept poorly there would have been lines around his dark blue eyes, or dark circles beneath them.

Irritating man.

"Come with me," she said, deciding that the clamor of breakfast in the student dining room was exactly what he deserved.

They reached the bottom of the stairs, and she turned left. He followed her, silent and menacing, like a giant shadow she'd somehow acquired.

"Are you glad to be home?" she asked, more for something to say than truly wishing to know.

"It's been a melancholy visit," he said.

Surprised, she glanced at him.

"The people I loved are gone, and the others don't seem to recognize me."

She flushed again, wondering if he was referring to that moment last night when she'd stared at him as if he were a ghost.

How odd that she didn't remember George being quite so, well, handsome.

"Perhaps if you hadn't been gone so long you wouldn't find that to be true," she said. "Perhaps people's memories have faded."

"Perhaps there were reasons I was gone."

"What reasons could there have been? Are you

saying I forced you from London? From England?"
She waved her hand in the air. "Forgive me, now is
not the time to discuss your reasons for leaving. We
will have to make time to do so."

"Will we?"

"Yes," she said. "But don't think there is any chance
of a reconciliation for us, George. I have no intention
of letting you into my life. Once was quite enough,
thank you."

Besides, she'd already decided that she much preferred Spencer to George.

She halted at the entrance to the dining room and
faced her husband. "It would have been better if you'd
not returned, you know. People had grown accustomed to your absence."

"You mean yourself, of course."

"Among others."

"Do you find it easy to live alone, then, Charlotte?"

"Better alone than in tandem with a man I cannot
respect."

"You mean me, of course," he said.

"It's time for breakfast."

"I'd prefer an answer more than I would a meal."

"I have no intention of answering you, George. Perhaps later. Or perhaps I'll just disappear like you did."

"Ah, but then I'd welcome you home with open
arms, Charlotte. I might even keep a candle burning
in the window until you returned. There were so many
candles burning last night that surely some of them
must have been for me. Didn't you ever think I'd return?"

"No," she said.

"Never? Why shouldn't I return? Everything I left is still here. My home. My wife."

"You haven't shown any concern for either Balfurin or me in the last five years, George. Am I supposed to believe that you care now?" She forced a smile to her face more for the benefit of the watching students than him.

"Perhaps I've changed," he said.

"Perhaps you want money. I haven't any to spare."

"I do."

Startled, she just stared at him, uncertain what to say. He'd never been generous in the past. She didn't want him to change, be someone she had to know all over again. Annoyed, she frowned at him.

"I'm considered quite wealthy. Almost a pasha, if you believe Matthew."

"How fortunate for you," she said, the words bitten out one by one.

"Do you need anything, Charlotte? Tell me what you need, and I'll provide it."

"Your absence, George. Please."

"I'm afraid I can't leave," he said. "There's something I must do."

"What?" She folded her arms around her waist and forced her shoulders level. Her chin tilted up and she prayed that her smile was somewhat genuine, at least to him. Those who knew her well would know she was wearing her parents' face, that expression a headmistress wore when dealing with either exasperating parents or the too lenient parents of exasperating students.

George, however, was the most exasperating person she'd talked to in five years.

"Balfurin is mine."

She felt the blood leave her face. She bit her lip and then immediately released it. He mustn't know how upset she was by that comment.

"Balfurin was a disaster when I came here. There were chickens in the Great Hall, and there wasn't a room in the castle fit to sleep in. I spent every cent of my grandfather's legacy to modernize Balfurin, and now you claim it as yours?" She laughed, and the sound was curiously hollow. "I'll buy it from you," she said suddenly.

"What price would you put on a legacy?"

"A legacy? Why didn't you think that five years ago? The Orient evidently called to you more than your legacy."

"I'm sorry, but I cannot sell it. Surely you know that. It's entailed for the heir. Shall we have an heir?"

She had never been a violent person. She'd never wanted to strike anyone until this moment. Now she wanted to slap that half smile off his face, see her hand-print on his cheek. She wanted to shock him, startle him out of his charm, and to reveal the real person he was beneath his sudden affability.

He looked as if he knew it, too, with his half smile and the lines crinkling around his eyes. He must have smiled a great deal in the last five years. Strange that she didn't remember his eyes being quite so blue.

George was George, but he wasn't. It was as if he were more than himself, taller, broader, his eyes a more intense shade, his smile more charming. Five years had matured him, changed him from a man who could leave a young wife to . . . what? A man who'd offered her money.

"Why did you return?"

He shrugged, an effortless gesture that annoyed her. "Perhaps I missed you, wife. We hadn't time to become acquainted. A week, you said, wasn't it? I wonder what I was thinking?"

"That the downstairs maid looked ripe for the plucking, no doubt."

From the look on his face she'd finally managed to startle him.

"Surely I wasn't so foolish as to dally with the servants."

"I found you with one of the maids one night. You didn't even bother to go to her room. The corner was good enough. You flirted outrageously with my sisters, our guests, anything female. I'm surprised you didn't go after the bitches in the kennel."

He smiled, as if genuinely amused. "Charlotte, I was an idiot to look at anyone if you were nearby."

"Do you really think I'm foolish enough to listen to your blandishments? I wasn't jesting, George, I've tried divorcing you. It's not a rare feat in Scotland."

"On what grounds, Charlotte?"

She really wished he wouldn't smile at her in that way.

"Desertion."

"Ah, but I've returned. And I've no intention of leaving."

She stared at him for a moment. The impulse to strike him was so strong that she almost gave in to the temptation. But her hand was too soft. Perhaps if she had a brick. Or a boulder. Or a stick.

Two girls dashed out of the doorway to the dining room, both giggling. At seeing her they sobered momentarily, long enough to walk in a subdued fashion to the corner. Once there, however, they began to race down the corridor, the sound of their laughter an odd backdrop to the tension between the two of them.

"Go away, George," she said wearily. "There's nothing here for you. As far as a legacy, Balfurin survived without you. Perhaps even despite you."

He looked as if he'd like to say something, but he only smiled. His pleasant mood was becoming increasingly annoying. But why should he be agitated? He hadn't remained behind all these years. No, he'd traveled the world—on her money.

"Refund my dowry," she said abruptly.

Once again she'd managed to surprise him. Good, it was about time he looked as discomfited as she felt.

"The money you took when you left me." She named the amount, and one of his eyebrows arched in surprise.

He didn't say anything, and she was grateful to note that his smile had slipped. His face was carefully bland, but his eyes betrayed his emotions. George was annoyed, perhaps even angry.

"Is there someone waiting in the wings, Charlotte? Is that why you're so desperate to divorce your husband?"

She'd never met anyone who referred to himself so distantly. She frowned at him, but answered him anyway. "Whoever I feel affection for is none of your business, George."

"On the contrary, I find it's very much my business. If nothing else, I'm head of the family."

Before she could comment, he moved beside her,

and then inside the dining hall. She'd wanted him to feel awkward among so many young girls, but it was obvious he was comfortable with being the center of attention. All of the remaining students fell silent and one by one they began to stare.

He was too attractive to remain in residence. His black hair gleamed in the sun streaming in from the upper windows. His blue eyes were the color of the fair Scottish sky, and his smile could have charmed hearts from Edinburgh to London.

Damn him.

She thanked Providence that the term was ending today, and all of the suddenly awestruck females were going home.

Chapter 7

Breakfast was abysmal, and it was all George's fault.

She and the other teachers didn't normally share their meals with the students—it was one of the few times during the day that she was exempt from being the headmistress. The young maids who worked at Balfurin took turns being both chaperones and servants to the two hundred girls at the school.

She and the ten teachers ate in the smaller, more private dining room adjacent to the Great Hall. Here they discussed their morning or their afternoon classes, depending upon what meal was being served. They rarely paid any heed to the noise in the dining hall. For that matter, there was rarely any sound emanating from the dining room except for the low drone of young female voices.

Today, however, every time she leaned forward to

speak to her companion, a burst of laughter interrupted her. More than once, she sent an irritated look toward the connecting door.

"Whatever can he be doing?" she finally asked after a resounding bout of laughter.

"It sounds as if he's charmed them completely," the mathematics teacher said. Charlotte shook her head and returned to her breakfast.

Perhaps she should have insisted that he eat with her and the teachers. But then, he would no doubt have charmed the adult females as well. He had that sort of smile.

The door to the hall opened suddenly, and for a fleeting second she thought it might be him. She framed a scathing response as she turned. But it wasn't George; it was his servant, Matthew. Today the man was dressed in a brilliant red jacket embroidered with fanciful birds with multicolored feathers. The black garment beneath his jacket looked suspiciously like a skirt. His slippers were silk with the toes pointing skyward.

He was quite the most exotic thing she had ever seen, especially at Balfurin.

Irritated that she didn't know exactly how to treat him, Charlotte stood, pushing back her chair.

"Good morning, Matthew Mark Luke and John," she said, determined to be the consummate hostess. The man did not deserve the treatment she had set aside for George. It was, after all, not his fault his employer was a snake. Besides, by being friendly with his servant, she might find out some additional knowledge about her errant husband. It was much better to be armed with information than to be confounded by ignorance.

"If it is more comfortable for you, your ladyship, you may call me Matthew."

She gestured to the empty chair beside her, normally occupied by the French teacher who'd departed for France two days ago. She expected Mademoiselle Douvier back at Balfurin in March, like the majority of the teachers.

Instead of sitting, Matthew bowed from the waist and declined. "I could not, your ladyship. It would not be proper. I came to ask you only if you knew the whereabouts of my master."

"I insist," she said. She gently placed her hand on his elbow, pretending that she didn't feel him flinch from her touch. Her breakfast companions were looking at her strangely. Not one of them had commented upon George's abrupt appearance the night before, probably because they'd already discussed the matter before she arrived.

"You would do us a service. We'd very much like to know about your travels here from the Orient. How long did it take you? There's a great deal we would like to know about you as well, Matthew. You cannot deprive us of the opportunity for education. We're teachers, after all."

The poor man looked as if he would prefer to be anywhere but here, but she was relentless in her determination. He would sit with them, and she would obtain any bits of information she could about George. As if he'd heard her, another burst of laughter came from the dining room.

As Matthew settled in the chair beside her, she leaned over and smiled brightly at him, an expression that did not come at all naturally this morning.

"How long have you been with George?" she asked.

Matthew stared at his plate, and then at the young maid who was serving him porridge. For the longest time he didn't answer. The moments stretched out long enough for Charlotte to feel the knife edge of embarrassment. Normally, people were quick to obey her summons and answer her questions. Nothing, however, had been remotely normal since George had come back to Balfurin.

"I'm truly not hungry, your ladyship. I have already partaken of my morning meal. I have just come to find my master."

"Why do you call him master? You're not a slave, Matthew."

"I am, your ladyship," Matthew said, shocking her. He looked straight at her, and she found her gaze held by his. "I am indebted to my master for the extent of my life. He saved me, you see. My life belongs to him."

She sat back in her chair, wishing she'd never insisted upon Matthew joining them at the table.

Each of the teachers was staring at Matthew. Not only was he dressed more richly than any of them, but what he was saying was so alien that all they could do was stare at him.

"He saved you?" Charlotte finally said.

"I was being punished, your ladyship. My master intervened, and nursed me back to health. My fate is bound to his."

"And George won't release you?" Her hand was at her throat, her thumb rubbing up against the onyx intaglio she'd inherited from her grandmother.

"He has released me, your ladyship. Many times. It is I who refuse to go. My honor would suffer greatly if I had no gratitude toward the man who saved me."

"Where do you come from, sir?" the music teacher asked.

"From Penang," he said, staring at the cooling porridge in front of him with a look of revulsion.

"Is it very different from Scotland?"

"As different as the sunset is from a rock," he said. He raised his eyes to address the teacher. Whatever she saw in his gaze silenced her. She only nodded as if she understood completely. No one at the table was under any illusion that Scotland was the sunset in this case.

"My country is surrounded by a sea of greenish blue water. White sands lead to the ocean. The sky is blue, but when night comes it changes to pink and violet as if the sun cries in despair to leave. The ocean breezes cool the heat and make Penang a place where it is always temperate. When we have rain, it comes like a burst of tears from God himself, quickly over and forgiven."

"It sounds like a beautiful place," one of the teachers said.

"Yet you are Oriental," Charlotte said.

He glanced at Charlotte. "My father was Chinese, yes."

Matthew was obviously uncomfortable seated with a group of women. She wondered if it was because his society was a patriarchal one. But then, most societies were except for the small oasis of peace women managed to create within the broader world. Such as the school. Here, women ruled, and men were not in abundance. If they were present, they were not in a position of power.

Unlike George. A fox among the chickens. A burst of laughter punctuated that thought.

"Does your master," she asked, bowing to the inevitable when referring to George, "feel the same about Penang?"

"My master is content as long as he is able to ply his trade."

"What is his trade?" Exactly what does a Scottish earl do in Malay?

Matthew glanced at her and then looked away, evidently finding the bowl of porridge more to his liking than her gaze.

"I do not speak of my master without his approval."

"I can only commend your loyalty, Matthew," she said sweetly, more sweetly than she felt. "In fact, I'd wish the same loyalty of my servants."

Matthew didn't respond.

"Your master is probably finding the weather rather dismal," she said. "In fact, I believe we're due for a storm soon." That wasn't difficult to guess. The autumn had been filled with thunderstorms.

A corner of Matthew's mouth turned down, but otherwise he made no comment.

"In a few weeks it will be quite cold. Penang would be warmer."

Matthew glanced over at her. "My master can accommodate himself to the weather."

Yes, but she couldn't accommodate herself to George.

"I doubt he can," she said, as an ember of something devilish curled up in her stomach and fueled her words. "He'll probably take himself off to Edinburgh. Or London. Not that it's warmer there. But there are more braziers. And stoves. Here at Balfurin, we are forever shivering."

To her dismay, three of the teachers tittered behind their hands as the others nodded emphatically. The conditions were not quite so dismal as she'd announced. Evidently, however, the teachers did not agree.

"Once the students leave it's quiet here. Other than reading or studying or preparing for the next school year, there isn't anything at all to do. George will be quite bored, I'm certain."

"I doubt you will find that is true of my master, your ladyship," Matthew said. "My master occupies himself in great pursuit most of the day. When he is not managing his companies, he is planning on more adventures."

She felt a slight pinch of irritation at Matthew's loyalty. "Companies? Well, good for George, then. But he'll find Balfurin a very out of the way place. It's not convenient to send correspondence. You'll find that the world ignores us here, Matthew."

Another burst of laughter had her looking toward the door.

"Your master is a very entertaining man, it seems."

Should she go inside? Or send reinforcements—someone sedate and less amenable to George's charm? Who? She glanced over at Mrs. Brant, an older woman from England who taught decorum. If anyone had an effect on the girls it would be Mrs. Brant. Unfortunately, the woman was smiling at the moment, and glancing longingly at the door from time to time. Charlotte sighed heavily.

"Women find my master to be charming," Matthew said.

"Do they?" Charlotte forced a pleasant smile to her face, a singular feat since she wanted, at the moment, to snarl. "He has not changed, then. Has he scores of maids in Penang? He seems very partial to maids, as I recall."

"Many women work for my master. They find him very agreeable."

"No doubt," Charlotte said.

If Charlotte had ever imagined a moment as hellish as this, she'd have surrounded herself with flames at least twelve feet high. She'd be bathing in boiling oil. Demons would be assaulting her ears with high-pitched squeals while her flesh was being singed from her very bones.

"How odd that he's returned home to his wife," she said, knowing that her smile had an edge to it. It was a very good thing her students were leaving today. They would not serve as an audience for George's *charm* after this morning.

She stood, annoyed and near to tears. At this particular moment, she couldn't tell if she was more angry because she was close to crying, or wishing to cry because she was so angry. Either way, she mentally cursed George MacKinnon in all the languages she knew.

Matthew was wise enough not to speak. He only stood and bowed to her, the perfect servant.

"I pity you," she said in a low enough voice that the others could not overhear. "You're loyal to a man who does not deserve it."

"Your ladyship, you are mistaken about many things. I thank you for your pity, but I think you should keep it for yourself."

She whirled and left the room, intent on any place but here. She strode through Balfurin, her expression no doubt causing others to look away. Not one person summoned her in the entire time it took to walk from the dining room to the other side of the castle. Her name was not called once, no one solicited her advice, her opinion, or asked a question of her. That, alone, was monumental. The fact that she reached the door and actually exited Balfurin before anyone could stop her was a strange and unsettling event.

She walked out into the morning and kept walking, intent for a nearby hill. No one in Scotland would call it more than a roll of the glen. But from here she could see all of Balfurin's land. Here was where the carriage had stopped five years ago and where she'd first viewed the ramshackle castle.

Five years had passed since she'd stood and watched her parents' carriage drive away from Balfurin. She'd made a life for herself, and carved a future from an impetuous decision. True, there had been too many waking hours spent being afraid, but she'd soon learned that it was better to be occupied at some task than to simply sit and worry.

She'd come to love this wedge of Scotland as if it were a person—a recalcitrant, irascible, prideful character who challenged her at each step. The sunsets were magnificent, and the sweeping hills and gray blue skies were signs of home.

As she walked, the chilled wind brushed against her face, summoned forth the tears she'd been so careful to keep at bay. They came, flowing freely down her face to her chin where they dropped to the serviceable dark blue of her headmistress's dress, soaking into the wool and becoming part of the cloth itself.

She would not be an object of pity. She especially would not be an object of Matthew's pity. *How dare he!* She brushed at her tears with the back of her hand as she mounted the crest of the hill.

Ahead of her in the distance, between two rolling hills, were the ruins of the old castle, a place the Mac-Kinnons had abandoned years ago. It stood too close to the River Tam, and had been subjected to periodic flooding whereas Balfurin had been built on higher ground.

For a long moment she stood with her back to Balfurin, wondering at her curious reluctance to view it in the light of the morning sun. She might see *him,* and his very presence had spoiled it for her. He had left her and she had transformed his family home to a place that was almost magical in her mind, an institution where girls were encouraged to learn, a place for knowledge that was not thought of as unfeminine or ungainly but something to be treasured and cherished.

In one day, George had put it all in jeopardy, had pushed everything she'd worked so hard to accomplish to the edge of the cliff and dared her to watch it fall and shatter upon the stone.

She would not allow him to ruin her life. She would

not allow him to ruin the Caledonia School for the Advancement of Females.

Him and his women. How dare he!

She would go and see Spencer. As her solicitor, he would know what to do.

Chapter 8

The courtyard was a hive of activity. Matthew walked to the outer ring of girls, stopping in front of Rebecca McKnight, who looked wide-eyed as he reached up and plucked an egg from her ear. She clamped both hands over her mouth as her companions giggled. When he did it again to Moira Campbell, the entire group of girls squealed in delight.

"What is he doing?" Charlotte said to one of the teachers, a woman who looked as enamored of Matthew's behavior as any of the girls.

"Magic," she said, sighing. "His lordship mentioned at breakfast that Matthew is quite adept at it, and the girls insisted on a performance."

"Indeed," Charlotte said, jerking on her gloves.

George stood to the side, smiling fondly at the scene he'd arranged. Had everyone lost their minds this morning?

"The girls should be leaving soon," she said. "This demonstration will delay them." In fact, the carriages were all lined up, ready to take the rest of the students back to their homes.

"Oh, I don't think so, your ladyship," the teacher said, not turning. "Some of them have a long trip. Shouldn't they enjoy themselves now?"

Had she lost all authority?

Very well, she had a choice, to stay here and insist upon an orderly transition of the girls from the dormitory to the carriages, or continue with her mission to see Spencer. George turned and smiled at her, solidifying her resolve. The girls would just have to be chaperoned by the attending teachers. Charlotte needed a solution to the problem of her newly arrived husband.

Matthew suddenly began to spin, his wide sleeves bellowing out at his side. He abruptly stopped, and twin tongues of orange flame emerged from where his hands would be. A collective scream emerged from the girls, all of whom either looked at Matthew with amazement or George with too much admiration.

Thank God it was the end of term.

"I put you in charge, then," she said to the teacher. "I trust you will see them off safely, and not in flames."

"Of course, your ladyship," the woman answered, but her attention didn't veer from Matthew.

Charlotte sighed and descended the steps to her carriage.

Where was she going?

Dixon stood near the circle of girls surrounding

Matthew and watched as the carriage left Balfurin's courtyard, heading north toward Inverness. *Where is she going in such a hurry?*

He really shouldn't have teased her so unmercifully this morning. There was something about her that made him want to make her angry, force some emotion into her eyes. She was too controlled, too cool. He'd finally succeeded, and the flash of anger she'd showed had warned him that Charlotte MacKinnon might be the consummate headmistress, but she was also a woman.

A very interesting woman.

Matthew's words kept coming back to him. What kind of woman mistakes another man for her husband? The kind who didn't know George well. The kind who'd only been married a week.

His cousin had to answer for her charges—had George really absconded with Charlotte's dowry? As much as Dixon disliked to admit it, George could well be capable of that kind of behavior.

Their last conversation came to his mind as it had often lately.

"How the hell do you expect me to make it through life with Balfurin to support, not to mention my ancient servants? Thanks to my father's will, they've got a home for life, but even the old man couldn't have foreseen them living to such an advanced age."

"I don't care how you do it, George," Dixon had said. "But do it honestly. Don't shame our name by palming cards. Find yourself an heiress to marry."

"You really truly do want me miserable, don't you, cousin? Why, so you can laugh in your whiskey? I've got the title, but damn little else."

"Then, for God's sakes, be the best Earl of Marne you can. And I don't mean by cheating at cards."

Ten years had passed since that conversation. What had those years been like? What, for that matter, had George been doing? Gambling away the rest of his inheritance? Living off a succession of friends and women? Dixon didn't know, anymore than he knew what George had done since marrying Charlotte.

Intellectually, he knew he wasn't responsible for George. But Matthew was a walking testament to the belief that one man did owe another. Dixon couldn't rid himself of the thought that if he left Balfurin today, he'd always feel a measure of guilt. Matthew wasn't going to be happy, but he had to find out what had happened to George.

In the courtyard, a dozen large barouches were lined up in readiness. A group of women stood huddled on the top of the steps like blackbirds bidding farewell to the girls. A momentous day, the end of term. He remembered when he'd gone away to school. He couldn't wait to return home to Balfurin.

"If you please, your lordship, I've come from Old Nan."

He turned, pulled out of his reverie by the young maid's words. He hadn't seen her before, and as he nodded, she curtseyed, holding out her apron with both hands as if it were the full skirt of a ball gown.

"She'd like it if you'd call upon her."

"Dear God, is she still alive?" he asked.

The maid smiled and then smoothed the expression on her face as if afraid she'd be punished for her levity. "Aye, your lordship. She's ninety-two now. A great advanced age. But my granny was near as old as her when she died in her sleep last year."

"And she wants to see me?"

"Aye, your lordship. She saw you in the window, and there's nothing she'll have but for you to come and visit her."

The very last thing he wanted to do was to call upon Old Nan. The woman had terrorized him as a boy, always insisting on a standard of behavior that he and George mocked behind her back. He, especially, always seemed to be a target of her wrath.

"You're named after Dixon Robert MacKinnon," she'd told him more than once. "You'll be a proper namesake, you will."

No climbing in the forest for him. No tricks on cook, or his uncle. Nan always insisted upon inspecting him before gatherings or ceremonies, in case his breeches were stained or wrinkled, or his waistcoat was buttoned improperly. George was exempt from such supervision, which Dixon never thought especially fair.

"Tell her I will," he said reluctantly now. "Is she still in the tower room?"

She nodded.

"Ten minutes, no more."

She curtseyed again as he turned and strode up the broad steps of Balfurin, heading for his room. Once inside the Laird's Chamber, he moved to the dresser. He released his hair from its queue, took his military brushes, one in each hand, and brushed his hair until it shone before retying the queue at the back of his neck. A great many years had passed since he'd been subjected to Nan's appraisal, but he inspected himself critically with an eye for detail.

The dark blue of his jacket was immaculate. His waistcoat, embroidered with yellow and green butterflies, was colorful but not gaudy. His trousers were of the same material as his jacket, and thanks to Matthew's ministrations, perfectly pressed. His boots were highly polished, enough that he could almost see his reflection.

He looked exactly as he was—a man of some substance, a man of wealth, a man who'd traveled the world. If the expression in his eyes was a little wary, that was easily explained. He'd learned to trust himself more than any other person. If there was something missing from his life, no one could discern it from his appearance.

He turned to the window. Charlotte's carriage was almost out of sight.

Where was she going in such a hurry? Did she have a destination in mind, or was she simply escaping Balfurin? Because of him? Questions he couldn't answer.

Nor could he answer a more important question. Why didn't he simply go to Charlotte and tell her that he wasn't George? The elderly servant's error could easily be explained away—in the dim light, Jeffrey had simply been mistaken. Only a day had passed since he'd been announced as her husband. He could simply go to her and say: I'm not George. I'm Dixon, his cousin. Then all would be well. He could assist her in looking for George and do so without hiding his identity.

Then why didn't he? Why continue with the ruse?

When Balfurin was empty of its students and the school had disbanded for the term, he and Charlotte would be alone except for the servants. Balfurin was a large castle, but not large enough to silence the gossips.

He left the Laird's Chamber, heading for the tower room. In all these years, he'd not forgotten the way. At the moment he felt like he was twelve again and summoned to Nan's presence for another misdeed.

Nan had been a scullery maid, advancing over the years to a position of housekeeper at Balfurin. She was revered for what she knew about Balfurin, and the history of the MacKinnons, and possibly because she had been his grandfather's leman.

Her punishments were generally upheld by his uncle. Once, Dixon had to sweep the stables for a week because he'd ordered one of the stableboys to exercise his horse and Nan had heard of it.

"You'll learn to give orders once you've learned how to take them," Nan had told him. "And don't you go looking at another man as being less than you."

He passed through the corridor leading to the tower room. This was the oldest part of the castle, where the walls were four feet thick. Over the years the arrow slits in the outer walls had been filled with stained glass, and now a pattern of multicolored light followed his passage.

At the end of the corridor, he turned right to a small door. He opened it, remembering a time when he didn't have to stoop beneath the lintel. The stairs, cut into the masonry, had a depression in the middle worn by countless pairs of feet over the generations. At the top of the stairs was another door, and again he had to stoop to enter the tower. When he straightened, he glanced to his left, to the lone window. From here the vista of Balfurin was magnificent. In the distance, he could see Charlotte's carriage. On the horizon, another storm was coming, the dark clouds warning of high winds and lightning.

He knocked on the small door, and when a faint voice answered, took a deep breath and entered.

Old Nan sat in a chair beside the window, her hands resting on her lap. Time had wizened her, as if she were shriveling with each advancing year. Her face was a mass of wrinkles, giving her skin the appearance of the softest leather. Her eyes were sunken, lids almost disappearing in the sockets. Her hair, once thick and pure white, was now wispy and sparse, arranged in a coronet that barely covered her scalp. Blue tinged veins, like engorged worms, skittered over the skin of her hands, seeming to knit the joints together.

Her smile, however, was oddly lovely, as if age could not quite destroy the last remainder of her beauty.

"It's been more than ten minutes," she said, her voice barely more than a whisper. She studied him, her soft green eyes still capable of pinning him in place.

He felt strangely as if he should bow to her, if nothing more in honor of her age. She was a survivor, and the expression in her eyes seemed to indicate that she knew it only too well.

"Nan," he said, coming to stand in front of her. She leaned back in the chair, making a slow and leisurely inspection of him from the tip of his shiny boots to the top of his black hair.

"The girl tells me that George has come home. Finally."

"Is that what she said?" He wasn't foolish enough to lie to her.

"There was no celebration for your homecoming. No fatted calf."

"No," he said.

"There should have been," she said, looking out at the horizon. "You've been gone a very long time, Dixon Robert MacKinnon."

He pulled up a chair from the table and sat in front of her. "Yes, I have," he said, grateful that someone at Balfurin had finally recognized him. That it was Nan could be a complication, however. She had a very stringent sense of honor, for all that she'd been his grandfather's mistress. He should admit his identity to Charlotte before Nan told her.

They eyed each other for a moment.

"Why would you tell them you're George? You're more handsome than him."

"I didn't tell them," he said. "Jeffrey announced me as the earl. I merely allowed them to continue to think what they would."

Her face changed, became harder. Now she would lecture him on his behavior, he was certain. Instead, she clenched her hands together and leaned back in the chair.

"Are you unwell?" Asking that question of a woman of her years struck him as idiotic, but she fixed her gaze on him and gave him a little smile.

"I am healthier than most people here, and destined to outlive most of them, especially the English."

"My grandfather wouldn't be pleased at the English," he said with a smile.

"Do not say his name," she said sternly. "You've

lost the right. Gone for ten years, Dixon Robert MacKinnon. Gone for ten years. Did you think to turn your back on Balfurin?"

"I thought to create my own life," he said. "There was nothing here for me, after all. Balfurin belongs to George, not me. What would you have me do, Nan, be his whipping boy? Remain here grateful for the crumbs from his table?"

She didn't answer.

"Why are you here?" she finally asked. "Why have you come home?"

He stood, too uncomfortable to remain seated. The lone window offered little respite, since the view was of Balfurin and its hills and glen. What he needed, perhaps, was the oblivion offered by sleep or spirits. Unfortunately, all he had was Nan's uncompromising stare.

"I needed to feel anchored," he said, offering a confession to her. Would she absolve him? Or would she simply delve further, seeking more of an explanation.

"Has the world been too cruel to you, Dixon?"

"The world has been exceedingly kind," he said, turning and facing her. "By anyone's standards, I'm a wealthy man."

"Yet you're poor in your spirit. Why?"

"Greed," he said, giving her more of a truth than she'd recognize.

She nodded, as if she somehow understood. The gesture made him uncomfortable. Venerable and stern, she managed to get beneath his skin.

"Where's George?" he asked, certain that she'd know.

"Why do you care? Leave him where he is. He's

probably gambling and whoring, and shaming the name of MacKinnon. He's not welcome here at Balfurin. He would've torn apart the place brick by brick and sold it if he could. Besides, he brought an English woman here."

Her expression left no doubt that she was angrier about the last statement than the first.

"Who kept Balfurin alive. Or are you angry because of the school?"

"It's a fair enough destiny. An honorable one, better than allowing the place to fall into rack and ruin. Robbie would've been sad to see it the way it was before the woman came."

"But you can't quite forget she's English. It's been a long time, Nan. Things change, including hatreds."

She nodded. A sign of her age, that she allowed him to contest her comment.

"He didn't want to marry, you know. George. He once told me that he didn't want to be chained to a rich wife because of a building. I told him that Balfurin was more than a building. It was his heritage, his honor, his responsibility. He only laughed."

He sat in the chair again, leaning forward to take one of her hands in his. Her skin was papery thin and cold. Retrieving her shawl from the back of the chair, he wrapped it around her shoulders, draping the ends over her arms.

Her lips curved into the faintest of smiles. "You remind me so of Robbie," she said. "You both had the same temperament. Stubborn as goats, the two of you."

This, too, was new. She'd never before mentioned

his grandfather in less than glowing terms, and always with a sense of formality. As if Dixon didn't know that his grandfather's will had stipulated she was to live in the tower room until she died.

When he was a small boy, still grief stricken by the loss of his parents, he watched her make a daily pilgrimage to the chapel. She placed flowers on his grandfather's plaque, and then sat on the pew in front of the altar. Sometimes, she'd talk to the man he'd only known as old, as if sharing her day with him.

She'd found him there once, crying over his parents. Instead of scolding him, she'd simply hugged him close. Ever since that day, his life had been molded by two adults who'd given him both instruction and a grudging affection: his uncle and Old Nan.

"George didn't understand that he had to choose duty first, because he was earl. But he never remembered that. He always thought it was more important simply being George."

"Why do you talk about him as if he's dead?" Dixon asked.

She turned her head and regarded him. "He is, to Balfurin. He's gone away, and I doubt he'll ever be back."

"Why did he come here?" Dixon asked.

"To ask me about the treasure, of course."

"He hasn't given that up?"

"Perhaps he found it," she said, pulling her hand away and wrapping the end of the shawl around her fingers. "Perhaps that's why he's not here. He found the treasure and he went away. We'll not find him again until he's spent all the money."

"There isn't a treasure," he said. All his life Dixon had heard the tale of the missing MacKinnon treasure. Pots of gold hoarded for generations, insurance for the heirs of Balfurin when they needed it. As a boy, he'd been fascinated with the tale, but that's all it had been, just a story handed down from father to son to excite the imagination, and then to be put away as a child's fable.

He and George had badgered every single adult at Balfurin about the treasure. He'd even sought information from his aunt before she died, but she'd just shaken her head, smiling at him fondly.

"There's supposed to be a treasure map somewhere. Your uncle and your mother tore through the library when they were children, trying to find it. I think it's a nursery rhyme, something to keep the children of Balfurin occupied for years. There's nothing more to it, I'm afraid, my dear."

He and George had explored the caves along the bank of the river, finding assorted items that they excitedly carried back to Balfurin: a scrap of tartan, an old pipe, a rusted knife blade, and a long thin reed that looked as if it might have once belonged to a set of bagpipes. But they'd never found the Balfurin treasure.

"The treasure is real," Nan said, focusing her attention on his face once again. For a moment he forgot what she said, concerned as he was with the tears that pooled in her eyes. "You are so like your grandfather. How could anyone mistake you for George?"

He brushed aside her question for one of his own. "What do you mean, the treasure's real?"

"I only know the poem. Your grandfather made me

memorize it. Some days I think I've remembered it all. On others, I'm certain I've forgotten something."

She leaned back in the chair and closed her eyes.

> *"When changes come*
> *And the wind blows cold*
> *Ancestors will speak*
> *Of things foretold."*

She opened her eyes, fixed her gaze on the ceiling. "That's the first part of it. Anyone who asks is to receive the first part."

He sat back and studied her. "Did you tell George?"

"Weren't you listening? I had to. I was to tell anyone who asked me. Even George."

"But there's more?"

"I can't tell you that. You must follow the riddle."

She was old and frail, but she was still stubborn.

They sat in silence for a moment as she stared out the window.

"It's been a very long time since I've been able to leave the tower," she finally said. "But I don't mind that my world is only this little room. He used to visit me here." She sighed and closed her eyes.

"You didn't mind that it was wrong?"

She didn't speak for a moment, and when she did, her voice was laced with such sadness that he regretted the bluntness of his question.

"Adultery? Of course I minded. I hated him every time he came. And yet I couldn't wait for him to come to me. I'd vowed that I would never ask about his wife, and I never did. I told myself that my sin was less because I didn't know what excuse he gave for leaving her bed and coming to mine.

"The MacKinnons do not have happy marriages," she said, opening her eyes and glancing at him. "But they always have love."

"What else did you tell George?" he asked gently, turning her back to the subject.

"You want the whole of what I told him? Are you seeking the treasure as well, Dixon?"

"I have enough money. I am seeking my cousin."

"Should you not let him be, wherever he is? He'd do the same for you, less out of caring, I think, than because it's too much of a bother."

"I'm not George."

"Why do you feel such responsibility for your cousin?"

Because he'd not felt enough responsibility for someone else in his care. Perhaps looking for George would help to expiate his guilt, make amends for the fact that his greed and ambition had caused the death of another human being.

Instead of telling her the full truth, he gave her a partial answer. "Perhaps because I once envied everything he had. Perhaps to show him I'm the better man."

"You've become an honest man, Dixon, but one, I think, who's too hard on himself."

"Or not hard enough."

"Life will do to you what your own nature does not, have no fear of that. We do not know, any of us, how long we will have. Some of us will outlive our usefulness, and some of us will outlive our loves."

She leaned her head back and began to speak. For a moment he didn't understand, but then he realized she was reciting the poem again. This time, however, there was an additional stanza.

> *"Where once we came, so where we'll go.*
> *The fates have said what no mortal will know.*
> *Swords and shield and treasure foretold,*
> *A fortune for those brave and bold."*

When she finished, she looked at him. "Is that any clearer, Dixon?"

He shook his head. She laughed in response, a gentle tinkling laughter that sounded almost young.

"Did you think I gave you more, simply because you look like your grandfather sitting there? Do not be so foolish." She closed her eyes again and lifted her right hand, flicking her fingers at him in a dismissive gesture as regal as a queen.

Chapter 9

Had she been too rash?

Normally, it took a little more than an hour to reach Spencer's home, a pleasant manor house on the outskirts of Inverness. But this morning it seemed to be taking much longer, perhaps because Charlotte was so conscious of the passing of the moments.

There was a storm coming; the clouds were black on the horizon and the wind already rising, whipping the last of the leaves from the trees lining the road. The air was chilled, and she held her cloak tight around her neck, feeling a shiver travel the length of her body.

Autumn was evidently impatient for its death.

She ended the term in mid-October because of the weather. By spring, Balfurin would be hospitable again. For the first time, however, she dreaded the coming of winter, wishing there were hundreds of people left in the castle. There were days when even Spencer could not make it through, and she and the staff were cut off from the rest of the world by the snow and ice.

And now there was George.

She couldn't even think of him without feeling her temper rise. Perhaps she should do what Lady Eleanor suggested and give her errant husband a reason to think she wished him in her bed. Then, at exactly that moment when he expected her to welcome him, she'd draw back and smile at him in a very cool, calculated manner and banish him from her room.

The thought alone was almost worth touching George.

She'd have to kiss him first. She'd have to stand on her tiptoes and place her lips against his. Why had she not remembered that he was so tall?

She pushed any thought of kissing her husband out of her mind and concentrated instead on the journey. Her horses were very calm, unexcited by the approaching storm, but then they were not thoroughbreds but of sturdier stock. They'd never race for sport, but they could pull a plow.

George had liked horses, she recalled. He'd even wagered on a few races, if what her father had said was correct. More than a few, if he'd been so desperate to marry an heiress.

"It's no sin for him to marry for money, Charlotte," her mother had said five years ago. "He has a title, and we have a fortune."

"It doesn't seem like a fair trade," Charlotte had replied.

"For whom? A woman's destiny is fulfilled in a good, stable marriage arranged by her family. Your father's business will be strengthened by a relationship with an earl, not to mention you'll become a countess."

She'd believed her mother, as a good daughter should, and she'd had no difficulty marrying George. The problem had been in staying married to him.

They were almost in Inverness, the coachman needing no further directions before turning down the lane and making the final climb up a small hill. Spencer was also a gentleman farmer, he liked to tell her, but she never commented in return that he didn't seem very prosperous at that endeavor. Most of his fields were fallow and those that had been cultivated had not yet been harvested. At the moment, however, Charlotte didn't care about his success at farming.

She needed a friend.

When the carriage stopped in front of his house, she sent the driver to the door and waited. An unaccompanied woman did not attend a man in his own house, even a woman with her odd marital situation. But Spencer could join her in the carriage without causing any eyebrows to lift.

If she'd only brought Maisie, the two of them could have waited in Spencer's drawing room as they'd done many times before. But Maisie had been given instructions to give each of the teachers an envelope prior to their departure. Inside was a bonus that they would not expect: their final pay plus a little extra stipend, a reward for such a very good year.

The young girl at the door seemed to be arguing with her driver. For a moment, Charlotte was almost tempted to disembark from the carriage and mediate. Whatever he was saying was causing the girl to shake her head back and forth.

She knew before Franklin returned to the carriage, his hat in his hand.

"Your ladyship," he said, "he doesn't seem to be at home."

"Truly?"

"He's in Edinburgh, your ladyship, on court business."

How very odd. She shouldn't have been so surprised, but Spencer, from his own words, didn't travel often. "I have all that I need in Inverness, Charlotte. Why ever should I go anywhere else?"

He'd been looking at her at the time, in what she'd construed as a tender fashion, and she couldn't help but feel that he was stating something else entirely different. Something intimate and warm, and until she was divorced, utterly scandalous.

As she decided upon her course of action, the rain began, spotting the driver's cloak.

"Very well, Franklin," she said reluctantly. "We'll return to Balfurin."

"Is there a message you would like to leave, your ladyship?"

"Simply that we called, perhaps." She reached into her reticule and pulled out her card, handing it to him through the open door. "If you'll give the girl this."

He bowed slightly, and returned to the doorway while Charlotte leaned forward and closed the door against the rain. She sat back against the cushions, wondering what she should do now.

She had no other choice but to return to Balfurin, but she hated to do so since George was there. George, with his smug—and charming—smile, who had fascinated most of her students. George, with his strange and loyal companion. George, who kept looking at her as if there was something on the tip of her nose that fascinated him.

She rubbed the end of her nose now with one gloved finger.

He'd won again. A second later she chided herself. How foolish. He'd had no inkling of her errand. Nor was she desperate to talk to someone. Not at all. Most definitely not.

Ever since she'd come to Scotland on that fateful day five years earlier, she'd ceased being dependent upon anyone. Who could she talk to in those early days? Old Nan? The woman wouldn't have anything to do with her because Charlotte was English. Jeffrey? The old man was the same type of Scot but whereas Nan avoided her, Jeffrey made a point of being obnoxious and in her way all the time.

There had been one young boy at Balfurin in the beginning. Thomas, she recalled, had gone to sea, an undertaking she'd blessed with some misgiving. But he'd left Balfurin without a backward glance, making her wish, for an hour or so, that she was as courageous about her future.

"Why did he come back now?" She addressed the question to the roof, and a thunder of raindrops answered her. Why not two years ago when she had to ask cook to be especially economical in her meal planning because Charlotte was concerned about paying the greengrocer? Why not three years ago when she was so distraught about money that she wondered if she could afford to pay the teachers' salaries? What about four years ago, when she'd spent all her money on the most expensive of Balfurin's renovations and there were still few students? Or what about when she'd stood in the courtyard looking about her, determined not to go back to England and yet uncertain she'd made the right decision to stay.

No, he had to arrive now, just when things were looking their brightest.

She closed her eyes and listened to the wind. Leaves scratched against the windows as if nature were indulging in a bit of mischief and flinging them at the carriage.

A gust of wind swayed the vehicle, and she grabbed the strap above the window to keep her balance. The storm hadn't seemed so fierce when it had begun, but then, everything in Scotland was unexpected, from the sheer raw beauty of spring to the gentle tranquility of summer. But she hated winter—it seemed like the season of death, when living things became dormant and there was nothing to the landscape but ice and snow.

George probably loved the winter. How odd that she didn't know. But there were few things about him that she did know. He liked mustard, that she remembered from their few dinners together. And roast beef. He claimed that Scottish cows were tastier than English ones. As if she ever knew the nationality of what she was eating. He liked the feel of silk against his skin. He'd said that once; she couldn't remember the occasion but she did recall that it had been inappropriate at the time. What was his favorite color? His favorite song? His favorite book? Did he even choose to read?

She knew more about the footman who'd stayed in Lady Eleanor's room last night.

What on earth should she do about that situation? Should she even mention it? Did she need to reprimand the young man? Or congratulate him?

Yesterday, she'd been the headmistress of a soon to be profitable school for girls. Simply that and no more. Her life was manageable, if a little dull. Her days were orderly, her routine fixed. She knew what Monday would bring, and Tuesday, as well as every other day of the week.

Today, however, her missing husband was in residence, and she was the center of attention for a very determined and not easily dissuaded group of women who wanted to instruct her on the amatory arts.

The wind howled around the carriage as she heard Franklin shout to the horses. Slashes of lightning darted from the clouds to spear the hilltops. The frightened whinnies of the horses mixed with the drumming sound of the rain, and the crack of Franklin's whip.

Perhaps she should have considered the weather before setting off from Balfurin.

Charlotte braced herself against the seat as another gust of wind threatened to tip over the carriage. Was this how her life was going to end? Not as ancient as Old Nan, looking out over Balfurin with a feeling of accomplishment, but crushed by a carriage in a brutal storm?

Now was the time to pray, but she couldn't think of a word. Perhaps she'd given God too many reasons in the past five years to punish her, including a host of sins for which she'd ultimately have to provide an explanation. Pride, the greatest. She hadn't gone home as a good daughter would. Instead, she'd remained at

Balfurin, stubborn, determined, shamed. Vanity, that was a sin, wasn't it? She'd liked the way she looked last night in her new and only ball gown, and had regretted that Spencer hadn't seen her entrance into the ballroom.

The horses screamed, and she clenched her eyes shut and wished she could do the same for her ears.

Was she being punished for not welcoming her husband home? God did like unions, didn't He? He also approved of submissive wives, and she could easily recall a dozen or more passages from the Bible proving it.

She'd seen that look in George's eyes, a strange and vulnerable expression lasting only a moment, but it had pulled at something in her. But she'd ruthlessly pushed away the surge of tenderness she'd felt. She was doomed to die by storm, then, because she had absolutely no intention of being submissive to George MacKinnon.

If only Spencer had been home, she'd have waited out the storm in his company. Perhaps she might even have moved into the drawing room, certain that anyone would understand in the circumstances.

But it wasn't Spencer's fault. If blame had to be assigned, she was the one who should bear the brunt of it. She'd needed comfort, support. A moment of weakness that she was paying for now.

George was no doubt sitting warm and comfortable beside the fire in the Laird's Chamber. Or was he entertaining the last of the girls in the Great Hall?

The thunder boomed again. She pitied Franklin in his exposed perch. The farther they traveled, the more tempted Charlotte was to rap on the ceiling and tell

Franklin to slow down. Perhaps they could just simply stop in the middle of the road and wait for the worst of the storm to subside. As it was, the carriage was being buffeted from one side of the road to the other. As they began to travel up the largest hill, it felt as if a celestial hand was pushing them backward.

She was not a woman given to fainting spells, and she discouraged such histrionics in her students. But there were times when it might have been preferable to lose consciousness for a moment or two.

This was one of those times.

The thunder was booming directly above her, the noise so deafening that she lost her hearing for a moment. Unexpectedly, the carriage shook with the impact of lightning striking right outside.

The horses reared, and suddenly, the carriage lurched and they were off the road, careening downward, and then slipping sideways. Charlotte held onto the strap with both hands as she was thrown from one side of the carriage to the other. Her elbow hit the glass of the window and she heard it crack. She tried to grip the seat but her hands slid off the tufted cushions.

An eternity later, they stopped moving. Charlotte knelt on the seat, her breath matching her heartbeat in rapid cadence. She kept her eyes closed for a minute, forcing herself to have the courage finally to open them and take stock of the situation.

The carriage was wedged sideways as if the wheels on one side had snapped. The sound of the storm was still raging above them, but now she could also hear the screams of the horses.

Her body shook, and she was very much afraid she

was going to have a bout of hysterics, but she was still alive. Evidently, God didn't think she deserved to perish in such a fashion.

A few moments later, she heard Franklin's voice coming from the window near the roof. She looked up but she couldn't see his face through the grill.

"All you all right, my lady?"

"I think so," she said, hearing the quaver in her own voice. She must be in control of the situation. But at this particular moment, she was barely able to speak, and movement seemed impossible.

"We're on the side of a hill, my lady."

She nodded and then realized if she couldn't see him, he probably couldn't see her either. "I have deduced that, Franklin, from our angle."

"I could come around and get you, my lady, or we could wait until the storm passes. No sense in your getting soaked."

At the moment, she didn't want to move a muscle, let alone disembark from the carriage.

"I think it's better if we wait," she said. "You should come inside the carriage, Franklin."

"I'm already soaked, my lady, but I thank you." A moment later he spoke again. "One of the horses is badly injured, my lady."

Even if Franklin hadn't told her, the animal's screams would've alerted her to its condition. She closed her eyes again and wished herself far away from here. But wishes didn't transport her anywhere. She remained exactly where she was, witness to the dying screams of an injured animal.

"Do what you must, Franklin," she said, knowing without being told what would happen.

A few minutes later the screams stopped.

How long did the storm last? Probably no more than a quarter hour, although it felt much longer. She left her watch brooch at Balfurin and had no idea how fast or slow time was passing. Finally, however, the storm seemed to wane and move off, no longer pinning them in place. The roof was leaking, the silk on the ceiling now stained and water marked. She measured the path of one droplet from the edge of the window to the middle of the roof, and then watched as it fell to her skirt.

The door abruptly opened and Franklin stood there, drenched from the top of his bare head to his muddy boots.

"I could go back to Balfurin, my lady and get help. It's nothing but mud up to the ankles as far as the eye can see."

"I do not melt, Franklin," she said firmly. "I can certainly walk in a little mud."

"You'd be safe enough here, my lady."

"Nonsense," she said, wrapping her scarf around her neck and inserting her hands in the slits of her cloak. She wished she'd had the forethought to wear heavy gloves. But she'd wanted to be fashionable more than she'd wanted to be warm. Vanity—she'd already judged herself guilty of that sin.

"It is not all that far to Balfurin," she said, stretching the truth a bit. She had no idea how far they were from the castle, but if Franklin could make the walk back, so could she. "We'll make it in an hour or so." Or double that, she corrected mentally.

"If you're sure, my lady."

"I am," she said. She was the headmistress of the

Caledonia School for the Advancement of Females. She was no fainting flower.

Franklin helped her climb out of the carriage, and she slid into the mud. He was wrong; it wasn't ankle deep, it was nearly knee deep. They were at the bottom of an incline. On a sunny day, she wouldn't have considered it much of a hill, but now it seemed nearly impassable.

Franklin turned toward the horse at the front of the carriage, and she resolutely headed in the other direction. The earth had been transformed into wide muddy rivulets. Each step was an effort to pick up her feet and then allow them to sink down into the mire.

She'd worn her most fashionable shoes. Vanity again. It no longer mattered, because in the next step, she lost her left sole. She rooted around for it with her hand, and finally found it, holding it in front of her like a dark, dripping trophy. Halfway up the hill she lost the rest of the shoe. She unbuttoned the other shoe and continued climbing in her stocking feet.

She was wet, covered in mud, and sweating profusely beneath her wool cloak. One of the bones of her stays was digging into her side, and she was almost tempted to unlace it and free herself from the discomfort. Her bonnet had slid down until it covered one eye, and a very peculiar odor was emanating from the dark blue ribbon. But she was the headmistress of the Caledonia School for the Advancement of Females and, as such, was an example of decorum.

Even muddy, sweaty, dripping, and exhausted.

"Are you all right?"

She looked up. Of course *he* would be there, sitting atop a horse as if he were born to it. One of *her* horses. One of her best horses. Equine ability was one of the courses taught at the school, and she'd purchased two mares for her students to ride.

Of course, George would look none the worse for wear except for being a little wet from the rain. He wore a heavy greatcoat that was dotted with moisture but was otherwise perfectly attired.

She felt bedraggled, a female wreck, and the ugliest possible creature compared to him.

"What are you doing here?" she asked.

Instead of merely answering, he dismounted and came to her side.

"I wanted to know where you'd gone. Unfortunately, I was caught by the storm."

She held up a muddy hand holding part of her shoe as if to keep him at bay.

"I'm fine," she said. "I do not need your assistance."

"Of course you do, don't be foolish."

She stared at him, wondering if it was possible to dislike a man more intently than she did him at this moment. She walked around him and began to head for Balfurin.

"Where are you going?"

"Home," she said.

"Wouldn't you prefer to ride?" He turned his horse—her horse—and began following her.

She ignored him, intent on the sight of Franklin coming up the hill walking the remaining horse. George went to help him, and together they managed to get the struggling animal to the road. The two men conferred over the animal's leg. Twice, Franklin nodded, as if George had said something especially brilliant. She looked away and sighed, wondering when, exactly, the two men had become such fast friends.

George startled her by unwrapping his stock and winding the silk garment around the animal's knee.

When had he become so altruistic?

"It should be all right if you walk him slow," he said. "A little liniment tonight, and a compress, and he should be good as new."

Franklin nodded.

And when had George become such an expert on horses?

She continued walking, determined to put as much distance between them as possible.

A few minutes later she heard him behind her, but she determinedly ignored him. A little harder to do when the horse he was riding began mouthing her bonnet. Charlotte swatted at the mare, but evidently, the decorations on her hat were enticing. Or maybe it was simply the smell, something that reminded Charlotte of wet hay.

"It's some distance back to Balfurin," he said. "Are you certain you wouldn't like to ride?"

The rain had subsided to a drizzle as if he'd commanded it. She pretended he hadn't spoken, and walked faster so the horse couldn't nibble on her bonnet.

"Do you allow your pride to rule your life, Charlotte? I didn't think you that foolish."

She stopped and turned, wishing she didn't have to crane her head back to look up at him. She didn't like it, but what he said made sense; it would be foolish to walk all that way when he'd offered her some comfort. Besides, her feet hurt. The rocky road was painful in only her muddy stockings.

"Very well, I would like to ride back to Balfurin."

She had expected him to relinquish the horse to her, not bend down and effortlessly pull her up to sit sideways in front of him. She wasn't exceptionally good at riding anyway, but she could have managed. This was like riding sidesaddle without a pommel for her knee. Consequently, she was forced to allow him to extend his arms around her for some sort of support.

"Where did you get that back of yours?"

"I beg your pardon?" she asked.

"You're very stiff."

"I have excellent deportment," she said.

"You have an iron bar up your back, Charlotte."

She didn't know quite what to say to such an insult. Silence was always the best recourse. She looked toward the direction of Balfurin, hoping that she wouldn't have to endure George's company and comments any longer than was absolutely necessary.

"Did you really come in search of me?" she asked a few minutes later.

He hesitated for a moment. "I did."

"Why?"

He didn't answer her and she didn't press the issue. She didn't know what to think, whether to be insulted or pleased that he'd been concerned for her. Or perhaps he'd only been curious. George had never been curious about her before.

"I went to see my solicitor. *Not*," she said, emphasizing the word, "that it is any of your concern."

"While I visited Old Nan," he said.

She glanced at him, surprised. "Did you?" Honesty compelled her to add, "I haven't seen her lately. She prefers to pretend I'm not a resident of Balfurin."

"You're English," he said. "She comes from an era when the English weren't welcome in Scotland."

"We're not welcomed now."

"You haven't been to Edinburgh lately, have you? There are more English there than Scot. It's become fashionable to own land in Scotland."

"Regardless, Nan has never accepted me and she's too old to change."

"Probably not," he said, so easily that she glanced at him again. At her look, he smiled. "Did you expect me to lie to you? I won't, you know. However unpalatable, I'll always tell you the truth."

She searched her memory for times when he'd lied to her. She couldn't think of an occasion, but then they'd spent so little time together. Barely seven days of marriage after meeting him on exactly three occasions.

"You've done well with the school," he said, startling her. "It must have been difficult converting Balfurin into something profitable."

"It was."

She turned and looked at him. They were so close she could see the gold flecks in his blue eyes. Strange, how she'd never before noticed them.

"Is it necessary that we converse all the way back to Balfurin?" she asked.

She looked away, uncomfortable with his proximity, his curiosity, and, strangely enough, the expression on his face. As if he were feeling some kindness for her.

She didn't want his kindness or his regard. She wanted nothing from George MacKinnon.

"Do you know that I haven't been alone with you since I came to Balfurin? Your school is an achievement, Charlotte, but four hundred giggling girls is not conducive to conversation."

"We only have two hundred students currently enrolled."

"Really?" he asked. "It seemed a great deal more."

"You looked pleased to be seated among them. Practice for all your women, no doubt."

"All my women?"

"Matthew says you employ a great many women. I gather they all think you're some sort of pasha. Is one of them your concubine?"

He smiled slightly. "Matthew doesn't like Scotland, and he actively dislikes Balfurin. He would do or say anything to precipitate my departure."

"Pray, do not stay on my account." She was growing tired of straining her eyes for a sight of Balfurin in the distance.

"I've never known a wife so eager to rid herself of a husband."

"I'm only emulating you, George. Unlike you, however, I'm leaving no doubt of my intentions."

"Surely I left a note."

"You don't know?" She turned to look at him. "I will not countenance a story of a lost memory, George. You cannot simply arrive at Balfurin one day with a tale of not knowing who you were for five years."

He returned her look, his gaze more somber than she'd expected.

"I'm sorry, Charlotte. It shouldn't have happened."

She looked away, discomfited by his apology. She hadn't expected it of him.

He looked into the distance. "Shall we say that I was an ass? An unmitigated ass?"

"We could say that," she said, feeling slightly mollified. But only slightly.

"Again, I'm sorry, Charlotte. It should not have happened."

"I'm not entirely certain I like you in this mood, George. I certainly don't trust you in this mood. You've never attempted to curry favor with me before."

"Nor am I now," he said stiffly. "I'm simply apologizing for abysmal behavior."

"Your abysmal behavior."

He didn't say anything in response.

For a few moments they rode together in silence, the rising wind making the only sound. She wondered if the storm had abated only to gain more strength. She frowned up at the sky, and then heard George laugh behind her.

"You can't scold the storm into submission, Charlotte. It'll either rain or it won't. Nothing you do will have any effect on it."

"I don't want to be rained on again. This day has been disastrous enough without me getting ill on top of it."

"Do you get ill often?" he asked.

"Never."

"Then why do you worry about it?"

She glanced at him and then away. His smile was firmly fixed in place and too charming. "I'm not worried about it. I'm simply cautious."

"You've had ample reason to be, I think."

"You mustn't do that, you know," she said, frowning at him.

"Say nice things?" he asked.

"And don't do that, either," she said. "You really don't know what I'm about to say, and it's annoying that you would even try to figure it out."

"Very well, I shall attempt to be obtuse. Isn't that what you women think of men?"

"Another point you should learn," she said. "I'm not like most women."

"And you dislike being labeled by a group as well, or am I being too perceptive again?"

"You must have a great many women in your harem," Charlotte said. "I'm sure you've learned a few things from them."

He was smiling again, and this time she couldn't help but wonder how many of her students had departed Balfurin sighing dreamily and casting woebegone looks toward the Laird's Chamber.

"I haven't a harem, despite what Matthew says."

"I sincerely doubt that," Charlotte said. "I know what those countries are like. I'm sure you were given women as gifts."

He laughed, the sound startling her so much that she almost fell off the horse.

"Welcome to the country, here's my daughter? I can assure you, it wasn't the case."

"A great many cultures in that area of the world have no respect for women."

"Unfortunately, I must concur," he said. "But I wasn't given women as gifts, even by the men who were grateful to me."

"Why were they grateful?"

"I made them rich," he said. "They became investors

in my export company. I trade, simply put. What Penang doesn't want, Europe does."

"Something else you should learn about me, George, I'm very intelligent. I don't need to be addressed as a child. I understand economics."

"Then you understand supply and demand. I find what the demand is and I supply it. Wherever and whenever."

"Do you traffic in opium?" she asked cautiously.

"Never."

"Slaves?"

"What a fine character you must think me. But then, the Earl of Marne hasn't been an example of virtue, has he?"

"You're doing it again," she said.

"Doing what?"

"Distancing yourself from your actions. Talking about yourself as if you weren't there, as if everything you did was done by someone else."

"Maybe I'm a totally different man from the man you used to know, Charlotte. Maybe in the last five years I've changed, so drastically as to be a different person."

"Even physically?" she asked him.

He looked startled.

"You're taller than I remember, and broader in the shoulders. And your eyes were not quite so blue. But then, perhaps I tried to minimize you in the last five years and make you less attractive in my eyes."

"You think I'm attractive?"

She nodded, just once. It wouldn't do to give the man a swelled head. Just consenting to talk to him was complement enough. He should consider himself fortunate. Any other woman would have barricaded herself in her chamber and refused to have anything to do with him.

But she wasn't any other woman. She had a life separate from George, a very busy and fulfilling life, and he must be made aware of that. He could not—and would not—be allowed to alter her life by any measure.

As if he had heard her thoughts, he said, "I haven't come to Scotland to make you miserable, Charlotte."

He tightened his arms around her, and she responded by sitting up straighter.

"Balfurin isn't much farther."

She looked up to see that he was right. It would be only a matter of moments until they reached the outer courtyard. Then she would be free of him.

For how long?

"What are you going to do, George?"

He pretended to misunderstand. "I'm going to change into dry clothes," he said. "Then I have letters to write, and business to transact with my factor in Edinburgh."

"Factor?" she asked.

"An agent of sorts, who sells goods on my behalf."

"How long will you be staying? You used to tell me that you despised Scotland."

"While you seem to have taken to it like a native," he said.

"I hate the winters."

"Any thinking, rational person does. Although," he countered, "I have been anticipating the cold and snow. Perhaps I've been living in paradise too long."

"You could experience winter in England. It's cold and wet there."

"My tastes have changed in the last five years. I find that England is a good enough place, but it doesn't have the spice of Scotland. There's something about the country that speaks of freedom, of the very nature of man, both warlike and peaceful. I think we're closer to who we truly are in Scotland, whereas in England we've become too civilized."

She'd never thought George to be reflective, or introspective. This new person both annoyed her and interested her too much.

"So, you're staying through the winter at least."

"Charlotte, if I didn't know otherwise, I would think that you are anxious for me to leave. Have you given any thought to the idea that if I leave, you'll be in a predicament? Neither wife nor widow."

"It's the same if you remain," she said, remarkably calm despite the fierce beating of her heart. "I'm neither wife nor widow."

When she glanced back, she found him smiling that half smile of his. He wasn't, thankfully, looking in her direction, but toward Balfurin.

He placed his hand against the small of her back. When she stiffened, he looked at her.

"I'll not hurt you, Charlotte. Do you act the same around any man, or is it just me?"

When she didn't answer, he moved his hand upward, flat against her stays as if daring her to protest.

"I have something to do here. When I have accomplished that task, I'll leave. Not before."

She turned to look at him. They were closer than they'd been in years, linked by a bond even the Scottish courts were slow to sever. Yet he was a stranger to her, a maddening man who had control over her in a way she despised and loathed.

Make him suffer. Lady Eleanor's words. *Make him writhe in agony, my dear. Women have always had the upper hand. The problem is that they haven't known how to use it.*

She smiled, gratified to see that he narrowed his eyes in response. Evidently, he was as suspicious of her sudden amiability as she was of his cordial nature.

"Then you must tell me, George," she said pleasantly, "what I can do to make your stay here more comfortable. I wouldn't like you to want for anything."

"Your companionship? A smile from time to time?"

She didn't answer him, grateful to note that they'd passed the outer courtyard now. A great many of the carriages had departed. She would go and be a headmistress again for another hour or two. In that time, she could dismiss George from her mind almost totally. She had other events and other duties that would wipe him clean.

Only tonight, when she was alone in her chamber, would she give him any thought at all.

Until then, he was as nothing to her.

He moved his hand up further, and she deliberately forced herself to relax. When she could, she slid from the horse, stumbling as one of the grooms reached out to help her.

Without a backward look, she strode away from him.

"Charlotte."

She pretended she didn't hear him, but when one of the iron-banded oak doors shut behind her, she was tempted to turn and kick it.

Chapter 10

***

Dixon sat astride the horse he'd commandeered, watching as Charlotte stomped into Balfurin. She bristled so much when she was required to accept his help. For a moment there, he'd thought she might refuse a ride back to Balfurin, if only to prove to him that she could manage quite well on her own.

Damn George.

He felt caught between honesty and a righteous duplicity. Matthew would tell him there was no honor in lies, but Matthew's family had been killed when he was young. There was no one to whom he felt a familial loyalty, unless it was Dixon himself.

But it was getting difficult to continue pretending to be his ass of a cousin.

No man is entirely evil, but Dixon was hard pressed to find something good about George. The longer he knew Charlotte, the more asinine his cousin appeared.

Unfortunately, he had no problem envisioning George being insensitive and cruel to his new wife. George had always put himself first. If his wishes and wants were in violation of another human being's best interest, George simply didn't care.

But even if George could have overlooked her wit and her intelligence, there was the matter of her appearance. Or had George become so jaded by the whores he'd frequented that he didn't see the striking woman right in front of him?

Dixon wanted to see her hair down on her shoulders and wanted to comb his fingers through it. Was it really a shade of brown or did it shimmer with gold and red?

Her skin was creamy, yet at the same time it had a tint of gold, as if she didn't avoid the sun like so many women of his acquaintance. There was something about her soft green eyes that invited a man to simply sit and stare in wonder at them.

And that mouth. He stopped himself before he could think thoughts that were not the least bit cousinly.

She was tall for a woman and so beautifully shaped that he hadn't been able to keep his hands from her, all in the guise of making sure she didn't fall from the horse. He could still feel the shape of her back beneath the stiff wool of her cloak. His excuse? He'd been celibate for more than a year, and prior to that, he'd been a husband.

A thought occurred to him and it was so distasteful that he waved the groom away when he would have grabbed the reins of the horse. He dismounted and began to walk the horse to the stables himself.

Was that why he was adamant about remaining at Balfurin? Not for George. Not for any family loyalty or any noble reason, but because he was lonely? He was coveting his cousin's wife, which, even if George didn't want her, was a sin. He was surprised that Matthew hadn't continued to comment on his weakness, especially since the other man had set himself up as Dixon's conscience and spiritual protector.

God knows he needed one.

At the first sign of thunder and lightning, Matthew had no doubt retreated to his room, spending the duration of the storm in meditation and prayer. They'd encountered a summer storm on the Indian Ocean, and Matthew had remained tucked into his bunk for an entire day. When he'd emerged, he'd been pale as death, his appearance so changed that Dixon hadn't commented on his fear.

But instead of being in his room, Dixon found Matthew in the stable, talking to the coachman. Evidently, the two had conspired in the last few hours. Both men glanced at him and then looked away. Another deduction—he'd been the subject of conversation.

"Is there a mutiny happening?" he asked.

Matthew turned and bowed to him, a gesture of obeisance that didn't fool him one bit. Whenever Matthew wanted to accomplish something, he seemed even more submissive than usual.

No doubt they'd been trying to find reasons to urge him to leave Balfurin. Matthew may see the spirits of his ancestors, hear ghosts, and read prophecies in tea leaves, but Dixon didn't.

He was grounded in reality, not a mystical world. Even his belief in God was tempered by experience.

He'd witnessed events that could not ordinarily be explained, just as he'd seen the magnificence of nature. He was willing to concede that God might exist, because only a universal intelligence could have conceived of a world both so brutal and so beautiful.

He folded his arms and waited.

"Donald and I are not at peace in this place, master," Matthew said.

"Is it absolutely imperative that you be at peace, Matthew?"

Matthew bowed again, but not before Dixon saw the look of surprise flicker across his face. Up until now, Dixon had been very conscious of the wishes of his secretary since it had been a spur of the moment decision to return to Scotland and one in which Matthew had had no say.

"There are portents and warnings in abundance here, master. A stench that speaks of death," Matthew said.

"I think what you're smelling is peat, Matthew. The good earth of Scotland."

"Begging your pardon, sir," Donald said, stepping forward. "Would you see your way clear to telling me how long we'll be remaining?"

"Are you under a time constraint, Donald? If so, I'm surprised that you haven't given me any warning of that until now."

"Well, I didn't know you were no earl, did I? Nor did I know you were all fired up to see your ancestral home, either. I've no business waiting me at Edinburgh, but I'm with the Chinaman, I don't like this place and I don't feel bad telling you so."

He wished someone had a few constraints. First

Charlotte, with her blatant honesty. He was torn between wishing to pummel George and wanting to confess to her that he wasn't her husband. And then Matthew, who called him master, but was no more a docile creature than he had two heads. And now the coachman, who had up until now been polite and accommodating.

"Perhaps if you and Matthew occupy yourselves in worthwhile tasks," he said, "you will have less time colluding with the other about how dismal a place Balfurin is. It is, after all, my family home, infested with spirits or not."

The coachman touched his hand to his forehead, and took one step back. Matthew tucked his hands into his sleeves and bowed low once more.

"There's a coachman walking back to Balfurin with an injured horse. See if you can assist him in some manner." Annoyed, Dixon turned and left the two of them.

Where the hell was George? Perhaps if he concentrated on that task, he wouldn't have any thoughts about Charlotte or worry about his two rebellious servants.

Had Old Nan recounted the conversation with George correctly? Or had her mind simply been wandering? Had he really come back to Balfurin only to locate the treasure?

He walked into the foyer, nodding to one of the maids, and a few of the girls he'd breakfasted with, but then mounted the stairs two at a time, intent upon his room.

He entered the Laird's Chamber and closed the door behind him, locking it. At the moment he wasn't in the

mood for any of Matthew's incantations or pronounce-
ments. He changed his clothes and then grabbed his
writing desk where Matthew had placed it, putting it
on the bed. He read through the riddle he'd written
earlier.

> When changes come
> And the wind blows cold
> Ancestors will speak
> Of things foretold.
>
> Where once we came, so where we'll go.
> The fates have said what no mortal will know.
> Swords and shield and treasure foretold,
> A fortune for those brave and bold.

For a moment Dixon stared at the riddle, wondering what George might have thought.

Balfurin was only about four hundred years old,
but there was an older structure dating back to the
first earl, a powerful warrior granted his lands as a
reward for both his sword arm and his loyalty. He
was buried in the crypt in the ruins of the first castle
abandoned because of continual flooding.

Ancestors will speak of things foretold. Was there
a clue in the crypt? It looked as if he was going exploring.

The afternoon was well advanced, the skies a pewter gray, hinting of another storm. But he'd crossed
Cape Horn, nearly drowning in the process. A Scottish storm was no match for his determination.

A quarter hour later, he left the room. At the top of
the stairs he saw her. Charlotte had changed as well

since coming back to Balfurin. She was dressed in something filmy and yellow, more fashioned for spring than autumn. But at least at wasn't serviceable blue or black, like she'd worn this morning.

He'd seen two versions of Charlotte since coming here—the fashionable woman with bare shoulders in her ball gown with the fluttery feathers, and the stiff, stern headmistress intent on propriety. This yellow-gowned woman was another incarnation, one that struck him as closer to the truth.

She held a light cream shawl against her shoulders and her hair was curling against her shoulders as if she'd left it loose to dry. As he watched, she walked from the entrance to the Great Hall down the corridor and back again, almost as if she were counting the steps. He heard her sigh, stop, and then begin pacing again.

Was she trying to decide on a course of action? Or was she simply missing the cacophony that was the new Balfurin? The silence might be disorienting to her, but it was more familiar to him. He could almost hear the relieved sighs of his ancestors as peace settled over the castle.

Suddenly she looked up.

She didn't seem startled to see him, making him wonder if she'd known he was there. Instead, she nodded as if winning an argument with herself.

"You didn't have your lunch," she said. "Cook has set aside a meal for you in the family dining room."

"I thank you for your concern, but I'm not hungry. I don't know if Matthew has eaten, however."

She nodded again. "I'll make sure he has."

Most people with a veil of mystery around them

created the impression on purpose, the better to heighten others' interests or to make themselves seem more important. He preferred to deal with individuals who were genuine, regardless of whether or not they were of good character. Give him a thief who made no pretensions of being otherwise than a lord who hid his crimes behind a sincere smile.

And Charlotte? What was she?

An enigma. A puzzle. But he doubted she cultivated the impression on purpose. She was both uncomfortable around him and oddly cosseting, as if unable to come to a decision whether he should be shunned or welcomed.

"Why the sudden interest in my well-being?" he asked, slowly walking down the stairs. "I had the impression from our ride that you would just as soon I starve to death, and now your concern is that I might miss a meal."

"If nothing else, George, you are my husband. I will not have it said that I treated you badly in your own home. Or that I make you seek comfort from another."

"Why on earth would I be an ass for a second time, Charlotte?"

She flushed, her skin mottling to a bright pink hue that was not at all attractive. Most women blush in a flattering way, as if nature gives them that trick to attract the wandering eye of a male. Not Charlotte. Not only did she not blush well, but she looked angry about it.

He found her endearing in a way that was dangerous. The very last thing he should feel for Charlotte MacKinnon was fascination.

At the bottom of the staircase he held up both hands, palms toward her. A universal gesture of surrender.

"Very well, I concede. You were only exhibiting Highland hospitality."

"It has nothing to do with Scotland," she said in a clipped tone. "I was simply being polite."

"Then I was a bore. Forgive me."

She nodded again, and he couldn't help but smile.

"If you would ask Cook to hold back my meal, I'll eat when I return."

She looked startled. "Where are you going?"

"I have something to do. A visit, if you will."

Her face changed, stiffened and his smile disappeared.

"Not to a willing woman, Charlotte. Nor to one of the maids. And to the best of my knowledge, I have no female friends in residence."

She moved aside, clutching her shawl as if it was a garment of some protection. If she'd wanted to be that covered, she wouldn't have chosen a dress with a décolletage. He wanted to reach out and pull the shawl closed at her neck, shield her from prying eyes, including his.

His masquerade was blurring. Many more days of this, and he would come to believe that he really was George. He shouldn't feel anything for her—not concern, jealousy, or any kind of protectiveness. He had no right to touch her throat with his fingers, to soothe her fast beating pulse. Nor was it proper for him to want to slide his hand over the fabric of her sleeve, to feel the softness of the silk, to measure the shape of her arm, her elbow, her wrist. He was standing too close but he didn't step back, feeling instead as if he were engulfed in a cloud of the scent warmed by her body.

Abruptly, he left her, walking to the front door without another word. Perhaps it was better if he didn't converse with Charlotte at all. Every time she spoke, he was left with more questions and an insidious kind of interest and curiosity about her that wasn't healthy. Every time he was around her, he felt as if he were being drawn closer into the role circumstance had prepared for him, as if he were losing his identity.

He'd been here two days and already he was losing his objectivity. If he ever had any from the moment he saw her.

"You didn't say where you were going," she said from behind him.

"No, I didn't, did I?" he said, being deliberately rude. He closed the door behind him, hoping that she wouldn't follow. When he was far enough away, he turned around and looked back at Balfurin, ridiculing himself for the disappointment he felt.

She stared at the closed door, feeling as if he'd slapped her. Very well, he was being mysterious. He'd reverted to type, then, hadn't he? For a moment, on the ride home, she'd thought there might be some . . . what? Hope? He'd never given her hope. He'd never said that he'd come home to stay. He'd apologized for his behavior, but was that enough? Here I am, Charlotte, forgive me?

Did she?

The man who'd returned was substantially different from the man she remembered. That was both certain and disturbing.

Annoyed, she retreated to the library, deliberately focusing on something other than George.

The moment she entered the room, however, she knew he'd been there.

Someone had rearranged her quills and moved her inkwell. No one else but George would have dared. Had he looked inside her desk as well?

She'd always advised her students to be calm in the face of disaster. "It is by keeping a level head that you will survive almost any calamity," she'd said on more than one occasion.

However, she wasn't feeling calm right at the moment. She was incensed. He'd been here less than a day and he'd already made his presence known.

She closed her eyes, thinking that she could still smell his scent. Something exotic and foreign. He smelled of sandalwood as well, and she couldn't help but wonder if his soap was tinged with the scent.

His soap?

Why on earth was she thinking about his soap? Next, she'd care about his other habits—whether he bathed often and cleaned his teeth twice a day, although from that white-toothed smile he had to care for his teeth in some fashion—and what his underclothes were like. Then she'd be thinking more thoughts she had no business at all thinking, like how often he'd been unfaithful to her and with whom.

She'd be much safer concentrating on the most important question of all: why had he come home now?

Maisie opened the door slightly and peered inside.

"Your ladyship, he hasn't come to eat."

There was no doubt of who *he* was.

"Has the entire castle simply stopped because George

has not had a meal?" she asked. "He has an errand to perform. Some task, and before you ask, I have absolutely no knowledge of it." She frowned at her inkwell and very deliberately moved it back into place.

"The downstairs maid saw the earl walking in the direction of the old castle, your ladyship." Maisie delivered that information with an expectant look.

"Truly?" That was interesting. A strange trysting place for George. Or not, if she believed him.

Maisie didn't move from the doorway.

"I have absolutely no intention of following him there, Maisie."

"No, your ladyship. Matthew hasn't come to eat, either."

"Whether or not two men have decided to eat one meal does not mean we simply have to cease our routine and forfeit all of our other activities."

"What would those be, your ladyship?"

Maisie wasn't trying to be amusing; she was simply seeking information. The fact was there wasn't anything they actually needed to do. Not today. For the last four or five weeks they'd been focused on this one day, in bidding farewell to all of their students, in settling down into an almost empty castle, in relaxing from the term's grueling schedule.

She was free for the first time in months. Free, if she could call it that in light of George's return.

"He might not know we've prepared a meal for him, your ladyship. Matthew, I mean."

She glanced at the younger woman, hearing the forlorn note in Maisie's voice. "Aren't you supposed to be visiting your parents soon, Maisie?"

"Not until next month, your ladyship."

"I could spare you sooner if you'd like to go next week."

"That's all right, your ladyship," Maisie said. "They're not expecting me until then. Perhaps I could go in search of him. He'll be hungry."

"Matthew is a grown man, Maisie. If he's hungry, he can find his way to the kitchen well enough."

"Oh, no, your ladyship, Matthew would never be so forward. I think he'd starve in his room rather than cause any trouble."

Charlotte sighed. "I doubt very much that that will happen, Maisie."

A moment later, Maisie spoke again. "Cook says that she can heat up the soup, but she's worried that the lamb will suffer."

"Lamb? I don't recall having lamb. Exactly how many courses is this meal?" Charlotte asked.

Maisie flushed and stepped back. "I'll tell Cook to simply set everything back. Perhaps his lordship will want an early dinner."

Charlotte stood, and came around the desk, smoothing her hands down her skirt.

There is something special about every day. Who said that recently? The French teacher, Mademoiselle Douvier. The woman always looked on the bright side of things. What would she say to this situation? Since she was French, she would no doubt have some romantic advice, not unlike Lady Eleanor.

"George will simply have to fend for himself, as will Matthew. They did not starve before they came here, and no doubt they will not starve when they leave. They are not infants, after all, but grown men who should not be coddled. I will not have my household disrupted, Maisie."

"Yes, your ladyship."

If George was an ugly man, she doubted half the women at Balfurin would be willing to serve him.

She closed the door, and returned to her desk, thankful that her maid didn't wish to continue the conversation. Charlotte wasn't behaving rationally, and she knew it, and that made her feel even more irrational.

Damn George.

Fog often shrouded the old castle, especially on spring and autumn mornings. One end of the structure still bore a standing wall with a massive arch that was now covered with dark green lichen. Long, thin shadows were formed by the still standing columns, once needed to support the now missing roof.

He and George had played in the old castle as boys. He'd been fascinated by the stories of the first earl, and his grave in the crypt had been a place where six-year-old Dixon had first gone on a dare. Later, he'd visited the earl whenever he was troubled and even when he needed advice, finding a curious kind of comfort from speaking his problems aloud.

He'd never believed in ghosts, but they might exist here. Silence so heavy that it was almost a sound crept over the structure, greeting him and reminding him of when he was a boy.

Dixon descended the five steps at the edge of the foundation, turned right and unhesitatingly took the next ten steps down to the earthen floor. Long ago, parts of the foundation had crumbled, letting bars of light into the crypt. Puddles sparkled in the sunlight, the air still damp from the storm.

Pillars stretched up from the rock floor, widening at the top to support the vaulted ceiling, still in place. Carved vines traced across the expanse, ending in the corners where they entwined to form a wreath. The wreath shape was replicated several times throughout the crypt, and Dixon couldn't help but wonder if the form had some meaning like rebirth or renewal. If so, the crypt was the perfect place for it.

Although there had been plans over the years to move these ancient graves closer to Balfurin, the money had never been spared for the task. The living had more priority than the dead.

Not a bird sang. The wind didn't whistle through the trees in the nearby forest. There were no noises made by a small animal. A leaf didn't fall. There was nothing, except for the sound of his breath, dividing him from those who occupied this place.

He stood there in the silence for a few moments. There was nothing in the crypt that hadn't been here a decade ago, except perhaps the accumulation of a few more years of leaves. The crypt was, like death itself, unchanging.

The first earl lay alone in the middle of the space, his coffin surrounded by stone and topped with a life-sized effigy of the earl attired in full armor, holding the hilt of his sword that stretched from mid-chest to his knees. Beside him was a shield on which his crest was inscribed.

His ancestor had been a shorter man and slighter of build, but their features were remarkably similar.

Dixon's nose, perhaps, was not so prominent in his face.

Dixon had seen the world since he'd last stood here, had challenged himself and discovered his flaws as well as his attributes. Yet at this moment, he felt strangely adrift as he'd been as a fifteen-year-old about to be sent back to school. He'd come here then, standing in the crypt and desperately lonely for his parents, for a place to call his.

There had been nothing for him at Balfurin so he'd been forced to travel the world, only to find himself full circle a decade later.

For the first time Dixon wondered if this man had been as conflicted as Dixon felt at this moment. Had he ever questioned his actions? Had he debated about his path? Had he felt guilt over his deeds? Had he done things he wished he hadn't in an attempt to win his earldom and his lands?

Or had he felt no twinge of conscience at all? Had his every action been noble, his quest pure?

The first earl was the founder of a dynasty, one that ended with George. For all his faults, for all his self-ishness, despite his irritating qualities, George was the last of his family. It felt wrong that he wasn't here at Balfurin.

"It is a place of ghosts, master."

Dixon glanced over his shoulder to see Matthew carefully descending the shadowed steps.

"It's supposed to be. It's a crypt."

"Ah, but here the ghosts are not confined to their burial place. They wander like stray dogs."

Dixon smiled. "We're staying, Matthew, however much you dislike Balfurin."

Matthew shrugged. "I have little to do with your decision, master. I merely wished to inform you of what I know."

"You can't know about ghosts."

"I am of Penang, master. We are closer to the spirit world."

"Have you ever noticed that you take off your nationality like a coat? Some days you're of Penang, while others you're more than happy to learn of European ways."

"I adapt to my surroundings," Matthew said, glancing around him. "Is it a rudeness to ask why you are here?"

"A bit of foolishness on my part, I'm afraid. Revisiting favorite places. Perhaps trying to find a treasure. Evidently, my ancestors hid a fortune for their descendants, to use when needed."

"You think this treasure ties in with your cousin's disappearance?"

"At this moment, I don't know what to think," Dixon admitted.

"Maisie believes that you—he—abandoned the countess. Is this your belief as well?"

"It's possible. Evidently, George hasn't changed since I left Scotland."

"You will try to find your cousin, then?" Matthew asked.

"Have you any warnings to issue? Angry chickens, fierce storms, signs in the tea leaves?"

Matthew only shook his head.

"Come now," Dixon said. "You can tell me. Better a danger known than one suspected, correct?"

"I saw only that which confused me, master. I saw

joy and prosperity for you, but with it certain danger. I'm uncertain whether or not the danger overwhelms the joy, but it is there regardless. You should be on your guard."

"Then let's hope the joy compensates for it. We're both due for a little joy, don't you agree?"

Matthew didn't answer him for a moment.

"I have had great joy in my life, master," he finally said, "regardless of my outward circumstances. My inner self knows great serenity."

"You are a better man than I, Matthew," he said. "I crave serenity as well, but not as much as physical joy. Preferably with a willing woman."

He grinned at the look on the other man's face. In many ways Matthew was a prude. "Do you not wish the same?"

"I have nothing to offer a woman, master. My blood is cursed."

"So says the missionary."

Matthew glanced at him.

"I hope to God I'm not required to be as pure," Dixon said. "I'm sure there are a few Irish girls in my background, as well as an Englishwoman or two. Who knows, perhaps the first earl was a Norseman."

"You are ridiculing me, master."

"Indeed I am," Dixon said.

"You do not understand."

"I understand, Matthew. I don't accept. There's the difference."

He turned and began to walk out of the crypt. "You put up a wall between yourself and happiness."

"You have done the same as well, master."

He didn't want to talk about his life at the moment.

But Matthew, once on the subject, showed no sign of giving it up.

"You are the one who has not forgiven yourself, master. No one else holds you responsible for her death. Only you."

He stopped on the stairs, tempted to forbid Matthew from mentioning her name. Perhaps Matthew was right and this was a place of ghosts and spirits. He could almost see Annabelle standing there, her mouth pursed in a moue of discontent, her eyes swimming with tears.

Now was not the time to summon her memory.

"She was under my care. I should have protected her."

Matthew was blessedly silent.

As they walked back to Balfurin, Dixon wondered if Matthew's plan had been to silence him. If so, the ploy had worked. He would not mention Matthew's happiness again as long as Matthew didn't mention Dixon's dead wife.

Chapter 11

The smell woke her.

Charlotte turned over on her back and blinked until she could focus on the tester above her. Something wasn't right. Was Balfurin on fire? She abruptly sat up and looked around the moonlit room.

She slipped off the bed, thrust on her slippers and donned her wrapper. She jerked the garment closed, tightening the belt before opening her door and looking both to the left and right.

There was no smoke in the corridor, but something was definitely wrong. She had never before smelled anything quite so . . . strange. As if a marsh were burning.

She frowned at the door across the hall, wondering why George had not awakened. A reminder that she didn't know if her husband slept lightly or heavily. Her ignorance annoyed her. She jerked on her sash again and began walking toward the smell.

As she descended the staircase, it occurred to her that the odd odor might well be coming from the kitchen. Who would be cooking at this time of night? What could they be creating that smelled so loathsome?

When she pushed in the door to the kitchen, she half expected to find Matthew there, engaging in some sleight of hand like his magic. But it wasn't Matthew at all, but George, a towel wrapped around his dressing gown, and a cloud of noxious smoke wreathing his head.

"What are you doing?" she asked, forced to raise her voice over his muttering.

He didn't even glance in her direction. Instead, he was attempting to wrestle a large black bowl-like vessel, the source of all the smoke, off the surface of the stove. "Creating havoc for the moment. Would you care to assist me?"

"If it means that you'll cease trying to burn the place down, yes."

"I can assure you, it isn't meant to be quite this bad." He glanced at her. "I need some water, I think."

"I wouldn't think water would do all that much good."

"Are you a cook?"

"I never thought I would say this, but I think I have more skill in that area than you."

He set the large instrument to the cooler side of the stove. "I was in the mood for some *soon hock*."

She raised one eyebrow.

"Marbled goby—a fish," he said. "Although, I confess, I'd have settled for some shark's fin soup."

"I've never heard of marbled goby, and I can assure you we haven't any shark."

"I know," he said, sounding like a disappointed little boy as he stared down at the smoking remains of his food. "But I had some dried noodles and thought it would go with the salmon Cook served for dinner."

"Are you missing the Orient?"

"The food," he said. "Fried eggs with oysters, prawn fritters, *sotong bakar, nasi goreng ayam, burbur chacha,* or my favorite—*muah chee*."

She sent him another look. He smiled. "*Muah chee,* a dessert made from peanuts."

"It smells hideous," she said, and then mitigated her comments. "But perhaps I am simply not used to Oriental cooking."

"I'm afraid no one is, the way I've done it. Matthew's a better cook, but I didn't want to disturb him."

"You're very considerate of your servants," she said, moving to the table. She sat at the bench, propping her elbows on the scarred wooden surface. She clasped her hands together and rested her chin on them all the while regarding him solemnly.

"I wouldn't exactly call Matthew my servant."

"Yet he calls you master."

"Old habits die hard, sometimes. He was taught to call any European master as a form of respect."

She remained silent, wondering if he'd explain.

Finally, he spoke again. "As an infant he was orphaned and taken into the home of missionaries. He was raised more as their slave than their child.

Whenever he wasn't quick enough to do something, he was punished severely. I believe the minister called it 'beating the heathen' out of him."

"How vile." She lowered her hands and leaned toward him. "How could he get away with something so horrible? Isn't it strange, I've always considered missionaries the very best of us, those people touched by God."

"Perhaps some are," he said.

"But not the ones you've met."

He seemed to consider her question for a moment before finally answering. "The man who raised Matthew was more a barbarian than Matthew could ever have been. But he considered himself superior because he was European. Perhaps he was an oddity, however, one of a kind. No doubt the other missionaries are people touched by God."

"I'm sorry," she said gently.

He glanced at her in surprise. "You didn't do anything."

"I know," she said, "but I'm sorry for Matthew. I'm sorry for anyone who must endure cruelty simply for its sake. It's one thing, I think to suffer for a cause, quite another when there seems to be no virtue at the end of it. Pain for the sake of pain doesn't seem quite right, does it?"

"No," he said, smiling faintly.

"Did I say something amusing?"

"On the contrary," he said, joining her at the table. He folded his arms and regarded her with the same somberness with which she'd earlier studied him. "I don't believe I've ever had such a profound conversation with a woman before."

"What do you normally talk about with women?"

He stared off into the distance and she wondered if he was recalling all those hundreds of conversations he must have had. Even during their abortive marriage he'd been a favorite of her sisters, always flattering them, whispering things into their ears that made them giggle and blush. He was one of those men who knew what women wanted to hear.

What an idiot she'd been to ask that question.

But he seemed to take it seriously, and when he spoke, his answer surprised her. "I think, on the whole, men discuss ideas more than women. Women choose to talk about feelings."

"That's a rather broad assumption, don't you think? I know a great many women who discuss ideas. We're living in an age of enlightenment, after all. Women are encouraged to think, to do, to more than simply exist for the sake of a man."

"You are the headmistress of a school," he said. "I'd be very surprised if you espoused any other opinion."

She shook her head, annoyed at him. "What kind of feelings did these women want to discuss with you?" Now, that was a question she really should not have asked, and she almost called it back the minute it left her lips. But she was more curious than polite at the moment.

"Perhaps they were madly in love with me," he said, his eyes sparkling.

"Or perhaps you wished to believe so. They probably disliked you intensely," she offered. "And couldn't wait to tell you exactly how much. That's certainly a feeling."

"Perhaps they were afraid of the strength of their own emotions."

"Or they were made nauseous by the power of their antipathy."

His smile broadened, and she couldn't help but answer with one of her own. He really shouldn't be as charming as he was.

"If you're still hungry," she said, "I could make you something. I learned to cook in a middling fashion when I first came to Balfurin."

"No," he said, shaking his head. "My appetite has vanished for now."

"Now that you've perfumed the air with your efforts."

"I'm sorry for that, but not if it summoned you from your room. I didn't see you at dinner. Were you avoiding me?"

If she'd truly been avoiding him, she wouldn't now appear before him dressed only in her nightgown and wrapper. But she didn't want to call attention to her attire, so she only shrugged.

"Am I that frightening?"

"Frightening?" She shook her head.

He didn't argue the point, but left the table and began cleaning the bowl-like vessel.

"What is that you're cooking with?" she asked, genuinely curious.

"It's called a wok. It's Chinese." He began scraping it with a long handled spoon. "Are there any ill effects from your mishap this afternoon?" he asked. "The carriage accident," he added.

"I'm a little sore," she said. "But that's to be expected."

"Franklin arrived safely. I think the horse can be saved."

She nodded, having spoken to Franklin before retiring. "Did you find what you wanted in the old castle?" she asked.

He glanced over his shoulder and smiled at her, as if in praise of her curiosity. "I didn't. But it was nice to see the old place. It's been years since I was there." He didn't say anything for a moment, and the only sounds were the scraping of metal against metal. "It's odd to see all those relatives in the crypt. A reminder that I'm only one in a long line."

He glanced at her. "What about your family, Charlotte? Do you ever see them?"

The question so surprised her that she stared at him. "No," she said realizing it was the first time in all these years that anyone had inquired about her parents. Indeed, of any of her relatives. She might have sprouted, full grown, on the steps of Balfurin five years ago. That's as much interest as anyone had expressed in her previous life. Even Spencer.

"No," she said again. "I sent a few letters." Two years ago, her last letter had been returned, with no notification as to why. She'd simply been rejected, and she'd felt so affronted that she'd never written to her parents again. "They didn't seem to want to know me," she said, giving him the brutal truth. "They left me here, no doubt convinced I would come home in abject misery. I vowed never to do so, of course, and consoled myself with Mary Wollenstonecraft's words. Have you read her? She wrote a treatise on the rights of women nearly fifty years ago."

At his silence, she continued. "She said that: 'The

simple definition of the reciprocal duty, which naturally subsists between parent and child, may be given in a few words: The parent who pays proper attention to helpless infancy has a right to require the same attention when the feebleness of age comes upon him. But to subjugate a rational being to the mere will of another, after he is of age to answer to society for his own conduct, is a most cruel and undue stretch of power; and, perhaps, as injurious to morality as those religious systems which do not allow right and wrong to have any existence, but in the Divine will.' "

He turned and looked at her, his expression a little bemused.

"You've never seen them since they left you here?"

"It wasn't a case of leaving me here," she said. "You mustn't think so badly of them. I refused to go. I simply dug in my heels. My grandmother's trait, my mother said. I wish I'd known her. We'd probably have been fast friends."

"But you've never seen them since?" he asked, relentless.

"No. But why do you care? You never liked my father."

"I suspect the feeling was reciprocated," he said.

She reluctantly nodded.

Her father had taken every occasion to avoid George whenever possible. Even at dinner the two men did not converse. The women held up their share of the conversation. Otherwise, the table would have been occupied by stilted, silent people, the only sound the clinking of silverware against dishes.

"You liked my mother, though."

He didn't answer, but she expected it, coming to understand that there were a great many things that George didn't say. He left holes in the conversation, as if he didn't wish to reveal more of himself, or comment in a negative fashion. He was not as petty as he'd once been, perhaps, choosing silence rather than sarcasm. On the whole, she approved of the change.

"So you lived here all alone."

"All alone, without any money," she added.

He looked surprised. "I thought you were an heiress."

"My father announced that he'd disown me if I remained behind. My mother was shocked and appalled. I had a choice. To remain at Balfurin and be a rebel, or return to England a dutiful daughter.

"I knew that I had my grandfather's legacy. It was supposed to be saved for my children, but since it was evident that I was not going to have any since my husband had disappeared, there was no reason not to spend it on Balfurin."

"So you became the chatelaine of the castle."

She smiled. "Queen of the mice."

He turned and faced the stove again making a great deal of noise as he beat at the wok. Was he angry at it?

"There were more mice here than people at the beginning," she said. "I grew accustomed to the sound of them squeaking in the corners. Every other creature had decided that the castle was inhospitable. There was not one single part of the roof that was lacking a hole. In the rainy season, it was like living in a sieve."

"In Scotland, that's twelve months out of the year."

She smiled. "Yes, it is. There were five of us here, and every morning we congratulated ourselves for surviving another night without drowning or freezing to death. Nan and Jeffrey considered me beneath their contempt, so that left Thomas, who went off to sea, and Cook."

He turned and faced her, crossing his arms over his chest, and leaning back against the stove. His face was carefully bland, and she wondered if he practiced that expression so as to not reveal what he was thinking.

"It took nearly a year for the bank to release my grandfather's funds to me. I suspect my father had something to do with that. Until then, we subsisted on chickens, and what we could grow in the vegetable garden. There is a great deal of land at Balfurin, but not much of it will grow anything. It's better suited for cattle, or sheep, but unfortunately there was no money to buy them. But of course you know that," she said, feeling curiously embarrassed.

She glanced down at her left hand. "Even my wedding ring was gone."

"Did you sell it?"

She looked down at her hand again and then over at him. "Surely you remember that you took it with you when you left. I always assumed that you'd sold it."

He didn't speak, and for a moment she wished she'd not been quite so honest. She sounded as if she were soliciting his sympathy. Perhaps she was. She knew quite well that he'd considered her an oddity, a book-ish heiress with no discernable wit. Did she want him to view her differently now? As a courageous figure? A woman of tenacity and spirit?

"What made you stay? Especially that first year? It

would have been so much easier to simply leave, return to England."

She glanced at him and then away. Honesty could be a weapon, and she felt the sharp bite of its blade now. Did she tell him the truth—that too many times, she'd had that same thought? Life would have been much more pleasant in England. She wouldn't have had to worry about her next meal or the roof or a hundred other irritations. One thing had always stopped her, however, the thought that she would forever be known as the bride whose husband had left her. Poor Charlotte MacKinnon, deserted after a week of marriage.

She neither demanded anyone's pity nor wanted it.

"Once my grandfather's money came," she said, annoyed with herself for wanting anything from him, "life was a lot less difficult. We were able to shore up the roof and begin to make plans for the school."

"Why a school?" He turned back to the stove and began to use the curious implement to clean the wok again. This time, however, he was not quite so aggressive.

"It had become my dream, you see. At first, I had simply not wanted to go back to England a failure. A bride who had somehow lost her husband. Then, over the winter, it occurred to me that I was best suited to teach. I needed something to occupy the rest of my life when it was all too evident that I was not to be a wife and mother."

He didn't comment.

"I was comfortable around books," she confessed. "In fact, more comfortable in my library than I've ever been anywhere. I have an affinity for the written word.

I like the way it looks upon the page. I wonder what a writer was thinking about. I especially enjoy the way one thought travels from an author's mind to mine. I feel the same way when I teach. A Latin proverb states that by learning you will teach and by teaching you will learn."

She looked down at her hands. "I am doing it again, aren't I? You used to hate it when I'd quote something I'd read. Some people would consider it a blessing to have such a memory as mine. I read something one time and can remember it for a very long time."

"I think you misunderstood. Perhaps I was only envious of your recall."

She laughed, the sound too brittle to be amusement. "You used to say I was a walking library, that there was no need to waste money on buying another book, that you could simply set me inside a bookseller's stall and at the end of the day I could parrot anything on the shelf."

"I was a cruel bastard, wasn't I?"

She didn't reply.

"Perhaps I was so filled with my own consequence that I couldn't see the value of others," he said. "Time alone sometimes cures that malady of youth. I trust you will accept my apology for my words. And my actions. Evidently, the missionaries are not the only ones who have a great deal to answer for."

She didn't know what to say to that, so she asked another question. "Did Matthew ever forgive his foster father?"

"It's not a question I've ever asked," he said, abandoning the wok and coming to sit at the table again. "Matthew is one of the truly good people in the world.

He wouldn't inflict pain consciously on another human soul, and I don't doubt he'd forgive with the alacrity of the truly angelic. Sometimes I think he's too kind for the world."

"So you've set yourself up as his protector, determined to shield him from the world's cruelty. I wouldn't have thought it of you, George," she said gently, realizing it was true. The man she'd known five years earlier would not have had any compassion for another soul. He might have ridiculed Matthew's sweetness and lack of guile, but he wouldn't have sought to protect it.

"Do not make me out to be a saint, Charlotte. You, of all people, know that I'm as far from that as one of Satan's minions." But he smiled at her as if to soften the words.

Strangely, it was a moment of perfect accord. A truce, perhaps.

"Why have you come back?" she asked him, knowing that she might have broken the mood by asking the question. But it had been festering ever since she'd seen him in the ballroom.

"I was lonely," he said, tracing a path along the grain of wood with his finger. "As much as I enjoy the Orient, and as much as I enjoy traveling, I needed to come home."

"What did you miss the most?" she asked, and then inwardly flinched. It sounded as if she wanted him to say something complimentary about her. There was little chance of that. George had made no secret of his dislike for marriage and his dislike of her as well.

He halted in his actions but remained staring down at the table.

"I missed knowing people who'd known me." He glanced at her. "Perhaps that's why I returned, to feel a sense of homecoming." He smiled. "In the Orient, I'm an inch thick. People have only known me for a few years. There is no one there who knew me as a child, no one who knew my family. I crave a sense of history, a feeling of heritage. I think Matthew must feel the same way, being an orphan."

"There is no one at Balfurin who has known me longer than five years," she contributed, feeling a curious sense of kinship. "Sometimes I feel the same, as if I don't quite belong here."

"Perhaps it's up to us to find our home, wherever it is in the world. Or create it from nothing."

"*Nullus est instar domus*," she said.

"There is no place like home," he translated, smiling. She nodded.

"So, you are well versed in Latin as well?"

"On the contrary," she said. "We have a linguistics mistress who teaches Latin and Greek. I, myself, only have a smattering of the language."

"I remember my Latin teacher at school," he said, smiling reminiscently. "He was an old man who insisted on wearing a brown robe like a monk and smelling of sandalwood. He'd terrify all us boys by waving a stick around and snapping it against any object, threatening to use it on our backside or any available surface of our person if we failed to conjugate our verbs correctly. I recalled that I escaped that class with quite a few bruises, but at least I was more adept than my cousin. He was even a worse student than I."

"I didn't realize you had a cousin," she said. "You've never spoken of him before."

His face changed, and for a moment she wondered if she'd said something wrong.

"I am very sorry," she said, stretching her fingers out so that they almost touched his arm. "Is he dead?"

"Not dead," he said, placing his hand on hers. "Missing, perhaps. I've lost track of him."

"Were you very close?"

How very warm the palm of his hand was. She allowed her fingers to rest beneath his, feeling a strange comfort at his touch.

"Not as close as we should be. We quarreled the last time I saw him."

"Why hasn't anyone ever mentioned him?" she asked.

"He's been gone from Balfurin a great many years. He was filled with wanderlust, a yearning for something other than what was here."

She pulled back her hand. "In that, you and your cousin are alike. Why do you care so much for a man with whom you quarreled?"

He smiled. "Matthew asked the same question of me. Because he's family. The last of my family. For some reason, it's begun to matter that I belong somewhere, to someone."

A feeling like tenderness swept over her, made her want to lean forward and put her hand against his cheek, perhaps even press a kiss there in comfort.

The last person she should want to console was George MacKinnon.

She stood, pushing back the bench. "It's late, and if you're sure that you don't need my cooking skills, I'll leave you." She nudged the bench with her knee until it fit under the table.

"Must you go?"

She smiled and began to recite:

> *"The sun descending in the west,*
> *The evening star does shine;*
> *The birds are silent in their nest.*
> *And I must seek for mine."*

"William Blake," he said, surprising her.

She nodded.

"I've enjoyed this time with you, Charlotte. Is that something a husband would say?"

"You've never said it before," she admitted. "In fact, you seemed to go out of your way to avoid me." *And the one time you did come to me, it was in the darkness as if you were ashamed I was your wife.*

"I'm surprised that you even deign to speak to me now. Your husband was an ass."

She smiled, oddly warmed by the look of disgust on his face.

"I would never have thought that five years could make such a monumental change in a person, George. But I am willing to concede that it might be possible. You don't seem the same man or even the same type of person as you were."

He looked as if he wished to say something else but in the end he remained silent, watching her from where he sat at the table. As she left, she was acutely conscious of his gaze, more so than she'd ever been.

She wanted to ask him why he was regarding her in that solemn way of his. Why did he make her feel both happy and miserable at the same time? Why did his presence in a room make it seem smaller, more intimate?

Why had he ever come back? And what was she to do now? Why did she feel as if he was a danger to her?

She left the room quickly, knowing that there were no easy answers to her questions.

Chapter 12

Over the next two days, Dixon occupied himself with tasks, some of which weren't completely necessary but had the added benefit of taking up time. He approved the plans for a new ship being built in the Glasgow shipyards and another awaiting repair at the Falmouth docks. Some of his funds were transferred from an American institution to an English bank. Diversification was the key to his success even in the volatile trading market of Malay.

Matthew was happiest when he was at his most frenetic, and by the end of the second day, when a mound of correspondence sat in readiness for the mail coach, he was smiling from ear to ear.

Or perhaps Matthew's budding contentment was only due to the list Dixon had sent to his factor, detailing all the supplies he wanted to take with him to

Penang, proof that the two of them were eventually returning to the Orient.

Dixon stood and stretched, finding the chair in the parlor uncomfortable and too soft. But he'd not wanted to invade Charlotte's sanctum, and there were only so many places at Balfurin where he could demand privacy.

This masquerade was troubling him, perhaps because he was adjusting to it so adeptly. Whenever Jeffrey opened the door for him, addressing him as *my lord,* Dixon didn't have any reservations about accepting the title. When the maids curtseyed, he didn't once want to correct them.

The truth was that he'd always wanted to be the Earl of Marne. He'd always envied George, not only his title but the fact that he was Laird of Balfurin, one of a long line of distinguished men who'd protected the castle and the clan.

Until he'd come home, Dixon had contented himself with establishing himself as an importer of goods, a trader, a man with an uncanny ability to take chances, and thereby increase his fortune many times over. In the Orient, a title hadn't been necessary. A man's courage had counted, as well as his word.

Now, he was pretending to be the man he'd always wanted to be.

Shame should have assaulted him every morning, but it didn't. He woke and looked around him with the pride of ownership. Part of him wanted to find George, another more despicable part never wanted George to come home.

What did that make him?

"We should be leaving here," Matthew said.

He glanced over at the other man, wondering if Matthew had suddenly acquired the talent of reading minds.

"Yes, we should." His departure would solve all his difficulties, wouldn't it? His attraction for Charlotte would fade away as would his lust for George's life. He would become himself again, however difficult the role.

"You have not found the treasure."

"I haven't been looking," Dixon admitted. It seemed a foolish exercise, especially since he didn't truly believe in it, and found it difficult to accept that George might have. George was probably on the continent, enjoying himself in the company of a woman who agreed to support him while he, in turn, comforted her. An arrangement that George would have found entirely agreeable.

"Then why do we stay, master?"

A question Dixon didn't want to answer.

Matthew sent him an admonishing look but otherwise said nothing. Matthew's silences, however, were always filled with meaning.

"You're right, of course," Dixon said. "We should leave." But he left the room before the other man could say anything, or worse, ask him the date of their departure.

Until he reached the library, Dixon wasn't conscious that it was his destination. Until he saw Charlotte, her head bent over some paper in concentration, he wasn't entirely sure she'd been the one he needed to see.

Curiosity, that's all that brought him here to stand in the open doorway to the library. Curiosity, and perhaps something else, something he couldn't as easily identify. She intrigued him, because she sought the unknown, because she wasn't afraid of change, perhaps because she'd dared to do as other young women had not: defied their parents and their upbringing, and carved a life for herself in a strange land.

How odd they were so similar. He'd done the same in leaving Scotland.

He leaned against the door and watched her, lit as she was by the waning light of the sun. Although she was truly striking, Charlotte wasn't conventionally pretty. Her nose was a little too sharp and her lips too wide. Her cheekbones were high and her eyes seemed tilted at the edges. However, it was an arresting face, an almost exotic one.

She had beautiful shoulders, and a lovely form even hidden as it was now beneath her ubiquitous navy blue dress. Her hair, tucked up in a bun, revealed a long slim line of neck.

He wanted to kiss her there.

If he were truly her husband, he'd have financial control of Balfurin, even over the school she'd founded. Although women in Scotland had a great deal more freedom than in other parts of the empire, his word and wishes would be law.

But if he were truly her husband, he'd never have left her.

The perfect irony, wasn't it?

He'd had a wife he didn't want, and now he was tempted by a wife who wasn't his.

The honorable thing to do was to tell her who he was, and then leave. Two very simple tasks, but not so easy to execute.

He didn't want to leave her. Instead, he wanted to watch the curve of her lips as she fought against a smile. He wanted to tease her to laughter. But most of all, he wanted to ease the discomfort between them. A curious edginess existed whenever they spoke or met, as if they were each too aware of the other.

Hunger, that's what it was, at least on his part. He wanted her in a way he'd never before known.

At that thought, she looked up. Her face changed, stilled, as if she had given herself a command to not reveal her thoughts or her emotions. Her face simply became a mask behind which the real Charlotte hid.

"Am I interrupting you?" he asked.

She inclined her head. "Is there anything I can do to assist you?" she asked in that headmistress voice of hers.

He should warn her, perhaps, that it had an effect on him. He didn't think of schoolrooms, chalk, and dusty books when he heard her speak. Instead, he thought of warm flesh, soft whispers, and the scent, strangely enough, of persimmons.

"Nothing, thank you. Is there anything I can do for you?"

"Other than leaving Balfurin?" she asked pleasantly, smiling.

Now was the time to tell her that he was contemplating doing just that. He remained silent.

"How hospitable you are," he teased. "If you do not cease, I shall think you don't want me here."

Her face changed then, became even more severe. "Perhaps if I give the order to have soiled linens put on your bed and serve you only spoiled food and brackish water, you'd reconsider your stay."

"Oh, but the Scots are notorious for their hospitality, and haven't you embraced all the tenets of your new country?"

"If anything," she said, putting her quill down, "I've acquired the Scottish traits of tenacity and ferocity. Perhaps you should be on your guard."

"I have not ceased being on my guard since the moment I entered Balfurin," he told her honestly.

At least he'd succeeded in startling her out of her mask. Her cheeks flushed as she looked down at the letter she was writing.

"Do you wish to use my library? The library," she added a second later, as if to remove from their conversation any hint of possession. More likely, she didn't want to enter into an argument over who actually owned the room. The law would say that he was master of Balfurin, despite the fact that he'd been gone five years.

If he was George.

How odd that he was finding it difficult to remember his identity.

This pretense was dangerous and addictive. Without too much difficulty he could convince himself that they'd actually been married, down to remembering the ceremony and writing his name in the register. His mind wanted to recall holding her hand, slipping the ring on while her fingers trembled. At the altar he'd have bent his head solicitously to hear her whisper, and been rewarded with the subtle scent of her rose perfume. Warmed by her body, it almost dared him to find where she'd applied it—wrists, throat, between her breasts.

"Was I a brute on our wedding night?" he asked

abruptly, startling himself. The question had lurked in the back of his mind, but he'd no intention of asking it.

Her flush deepened, traveling to the end of her nose. He had the most absurd desire to kiss the tip of it, and then simply hold her until she calmed.

What an idiot he was becoming. She didn't want anything to do with him. For all she knew, he'd deserted her. He couldn't forget what she'd carefully left out of the conversation a few nights earlier. Balfurin, until her stewardship, hadn't been known for its comforts. At his father's death, George had simply stopped spending any money on the castle. Anything that fell into disuse was left to rot or crumble.

She'd spent the whole of her fortune on Balfurin, and brought it back to life. That first year she'd remained here alone must have been an incredibly difficult one.

She sat back and folded her hands together and regarded him steadily. "Why would you ask a question like that? Don't you remember our wedding night?"

"Perhaps I'm seeking a different perspective to the memory," he said, shrugging. "Perhaps I'm hoping there was something I did correctly. Proficiently. If nothing else, that I caused you no pain."

"I thought pain was part of the process," she said.

"So, I was a brute in that arena as well." Damn George.

She didn't respond. Why had he asked that question?

"Does everyone know how much you loathe your husband?" he asked.

She crossed her arms, cupping her elbows with the opposite hands, looked away and then looked back. "I think so, yes."

There, the answer he'd sought. How odd that he felt almost happy about the answer and was curiously disappointed at the same time. As if his true identity was warring with his role, as if Dixon had triumphed where George had failed. Charlotte's affection and respect was something George had not been able to obtain with either his vaunted charm or his title.

He closed the door to the library, and slowly turned, giving her time to protest their intimacy. But she didn't say a word.

In the silence, she stood and moved to the wall that held the massive fireplace. One of Balfurin's assets— enough wood-burning fireplaces in every room to keep the inhabitants warm, and a forest of trees to fuel them.

He entered the room to stand beside the desk. One hand reached out and touched the quill she'd just been using. The wooden staff was still warm from her touch.

Instead of calling for a servant, she lit a match and touched it to the kindling.

He wanted to apologize to her for his rudeness and insensitivity. He had no right, despite his curiosity, to pry into her life and to demand that she reveal anything to him.

"I find myself wanting to know everything there is about you," he said, abruptly giving her the truth.

She glanced over at him, evidently surprised. "Why? Why now? When you've never cared to learn anything before?"

"As I said before, I was an insensitive bastard. Perhaps there were other things on my mind."

"Whose skirt you could upturn next? I doubt you had any more serious concerns than that. You never struck me as a serious person."

She held the poker in one hand and jabbed at the wood. A shower of sparks burst upward, sailing into the chimney like a thousand tiny fireflies.

"While I was too serious, perhaps," she said, staring into the fire.

"Why did you marry? Was I that charming?"

She glanced at him over her shoulder. "You were very charming to my sisters, and to my mother, I recall. You were very polite to me. But you must remember, we had met only two or three times before we married. Hardly time enough to be charmed."

"Then why? Did you want to be Countess of Marne?"

She bent her head, her attention on the fire. "My father wanted a title and was willing to pay a fortune for it. You did not come cheap, George."

He was beginning to hate that name.

"But no," she continued, "I didn't care about the title. I could tell you that I married you only to be a dutiful daughter. I hadn't much choice. Women don't, usually. Or I could tell you that my mother insisted that her daughters marry in order of their birth and as the oldest, I was the first. My sisters were pleased to have me out of the way, I think. But the truth is that I was anxious to start my own household. I wanted a husband, a family. I wanted to be consulted by Cook as to what to have for dinner. I wanted to have a child

I could love and teach. I wanted a husband who would come to revere me."

He didn't know what to say to her. She stared into the fire, her back to him. He wanted to ask her to turn, to smile, to make this moment easier.

"I have no defense over what happened five years ago, Charlotte. All I can do is present myself to you as I am now."

"Everything I have is at Balfurin," she said. "I have nothing else other than this. Nothing," she added, turning to look at him.

"I won't take it from you."

"I'll not allow you to," she said.

"What do you need? I've already offered money and you haven't been in a hurry to accept. What else can I do for you?"

"I don't want anything from you, George. Not even an apology. Your leaving me was the best thing that could have happened. It forced me to see the world as it was, not as I wished it to be. Balfurin is my household. The students of my school are my children."

"And your husband?"

"You're very personable. And very charming when you wish to be." She looked up at the mantel and then began arranging the figurines there, pushing one back with a finger and pulling one forward. "But I'm not at all certain you are dependable."

Now was the time to confess to her. But he remained silent.

"You're very handsome. The years haven't changed that. In fact, you might even be more handsome than you were five years ago."

He told himself it was idiotic to feel a spurt of pleasure at such a compliment. Nevertheless, he wanted to thank her and then preen like a peacock.

"What other choice had I? To remain at home the brunt of jokes and sidelong whispers? There goes Charlotte, her husband left her after a week. Courageous man, that he lasted a full week."

"Surely they wouldn't have said that."

"I have five sisters, and all of them were in a hurry to marry. I would have been a mistake, the object lesson my parents could use to keep them in line. If you do not behave, you'll become just like Charlotte."

"What would you have done if I'd been here?" he asked, genuinely curious. "When you came to Scotland?"

"Shot you."

His bark of laughter surprised them both. "Shot me?" he asked when he got his breath back. "Are you serious?"

"Deadly. I'm a very, very good shot," she said. "My father insisted on teaching me."

"Did he think you were a boy?"

She looked startled. "I think he wished I was. Why?"

"I know a man in Penang who has a dozen daughters. He's alternately proud and despairing. When they were little, he treated them as if they were sons, teaching them all manner of things they would never be able to do. When they became older, he insisted that they become the epitome of all things womanly. No wonder they're confused."

"Is that what you think I was, confused?"

She didn't look at him, merely stored the poker in

its holder and turned and walked across the room to sit at the desk again.

"There isn't a moral to this tale," he said. "I've nothing further to say about fathers and daughters, since I am neither a daughter nor am I likely to be a father."

"No," she said calmly, "you aren't."

Instead of sitting by her desk, he took one of the chairs in front of the fire.

"I have always liked this room," he said. "It reminds me of my childhood."

She didn't question him and he didn't contribute further, realizing that he'd almost made a misstep. He'd almost told her about his uncle, the man who was George's father.

He studied the flickering orange and red flames, thinking that she was not unlike fire itself: brilliant, enticing, but too dangerous to touch.

Evidently restless, she stood again, and walked to the fireplace, standing and extending her hands to the fire as if to warm them. It wasn't that cold in the room. Was she nervous? Did he make her uncomfortable?

Or was she simply as aware of him as he was of her?

There was nothing visible from her neck to her shoes, no hint of skin, as if she had dressed this morning with the aim of protecting herself from his eyes. But the shape of her body was evident beneath the blue wool dress. Her waist was small, the curve to her hips making him want to touch her there. Her legs were long and no doubt shapely. Even her back, from her waist to her shoulders, was a beautiful creation.

He respected her, not only for her intelligence, but for her ambition. Or perhaps not ambition as much as determination. She'd not relied on someone to rescue her, but had decided to rescue herself.

He wasn't surprised to admire her, or even to like her, but he'd never expected to hear himself say the next words: "Can't we begin again, Charlotte? Five years wiser? You, a bit more cynical, and me a little more kind?"

She turned and faced him, and he was infinitely grateful for the look on her face, a combination of surprise and fear. Her expression brought him back to reality, made him conscious of what he'd said. Had he lost his mind? Evidently.

He stood, wanting to flee, and then realizing it was something George would have done. Yet his cousin would never have allowed himself to be caught in a net of his own words. George was too glib for that.

"Forgive me," he said in the silence.

She wrapped her arms around her waist and continued to stare at him. He wanted to reassure her that he hadn't lost his mind, that he was not indulging in any of the spirits or substances the Far East could easily provide a man. He had simply spoken his thoughts, forbidden though they were.

Loneliness had crept up on him, and regret. Added to that volatile mix was need, desire, and hunger. Not for any woman, but for a woman with caution in her eyes, and the barest tremble of her fingers.

He wanted to kiss her, to hold her, to forget himself in the sweet warmth of her embrace. Instead, they stood looking at each other silently. He bowed slightly to her, knowing that the wisest course was to simply leave the room.

That's when he noticed the pattern on the brick.

Charlotte was standing in front of the hearth, and beside her was one of the facing bricks bearing the pattern he'd seen on the first earl's coffin. The pattern was replicated on the other side of the hearth. From here, it looked simply like it was a decoration, a bit of ornament for the plain brick. How many generations had glanced at it, not even noting its presence?

He was torn between curiosity and caution. Now, however, was not the time to do his exploring. Instead, he would wait for a time when Charlotte wasn't in the room.

"I'll leave you," he said, the words sounding almost awkward. Perhaps he needed to borrow a little of Matthew's magic. Exit the room in a puff of smoke, perhaps.

At the door he hesitated. "I'm sorry I hurt you, Charlotte. Forgive me."

He didn't expect an answer. Nor did he receive one. He closed the door behind him in silence.

The minute he was out of the room, smiling that irritating half smile of his, Charlotte forced herself back to her desk and her correspondence.

I'm sorry I hurt you, Charlotte.

She couldn't push his words from her mind. Staring sightlessly at the letter from Lady Eleanor, she wondered what he'd expected from her. A breezy retort, "Oh, it was nothing. Do not concern yourself." Or,

"Don't spend another second in regret, George. I understand completely."

She didn't understand, not any of it. Not the fact that he'd left her, and not the fact that he'd returned, even more charming than before, but with a rough edge that he'd never had. As if he were slightly dangerous, more unpredictable, as if his charm was only surface deep. He'd become a man who alarmed her, frightened her just a little, and one who made her heart beat too loud and too hard.

The least he could do was feel a little remorse. Spend a few sleepless nights in contemplation of his sins against her.

Lady Eleanor's suggestion might be worthwhile after all.

There was something utterly wicked about that idea, especially as Charlotte was uncertain what she felt for George at the moment.

Why didn't she simply come out and ask him why he'd left?

He might say something horribly hurtful that she'd never be able to recover from, something like: I couldn't bear to remain married to you, Charlotte. Not even with your money. Or even worse: I was in love with another woman.

How could she bear that? It was bad enough thinking those thoughts in the silence and loneliness of her chamber night after night during the first months. Gradually, she'd ceased thinking of George at all, or when she did it was with a righteous indignation and anger.

Over the past five years, she'd gradually come to accept that George was not of good character, that he was not even a good example for the children they might have had.

Now he'd returned, the villain in her personal drama, looking even more handsome than he ever had before, with a somberness to his nature that he'd never possessed. He had character, and insight, and an introspection that was fascinating to explore. He was a different person, a person she didn't know, a man who attracted her entirely too much.

There were too many aspects to this new George that intrigued her. Not the least was his way of looking at her as if he'd singed the clothes from her body with his eyes and she stood naked and unadorned before him.

A burst of heat traveled up her spine. She sighed, folded her arms on the top of the desk, and lay her head on them.

She should look away whenever George attempted to speak to her. She should not think of the color of his eyes, so blue and arresting. Sometimes, they looked as if they were the most delicate of summer flowers. At other times, they reminded her of the dark clouds before a storm. She could sit and look at him for hours.

She was behaving as silly as her students.

Occasionally, a girl would return to school with a dreamy smile and absent eyes, staring off into space as if unable to concentrate on anything other than the memory of the young man she'd recently met. Charlotte had found that the best treatment for such a wandering mind was a good dose of castor oil and a tremendous amount of memorization. Very well, what was good enough for the student was good enough for the headmistress. She should attempt to memorize something. But what? Certainly not a love poem. Certainly nothing with a dramatic flavor. Perhaps Shakespeare, but he was forever going on and on about unrequited love. She could do without that.

What on earth was she to do?

Write The Edification Society? *Dear Ladies, I'd very much like instruction in seduction, if you please. You see, I've begun to lust after my husband, perfidious bastard that he is. I want him to ache with unrequited passion. I want him to hunger for me. Me, his wife. Me, his abandoned wife.*

Perhaps she could chain him to Balfurin with passion, if nothing else.

Had she lost her senses? What about Spencer?

That thought brought her up short. She stared at the closed door, envisioning him standing in front of her. Spencer was the most polite man she'd ever met. The kindest.

But he wasn't her husband.

If only Spencer had been home a few days ago, or had called on her since. He would have counseled her, his advice no doubt wise and compassionate. But since when did she need advice from any man? She'd made her own decisions in the last five years.

She sat up, determined to banish both men from her mind. Instead, she focused on Lady Eleanor's letter, reading it with a growing sense of horror.

My dear Charlotte,

I have addressed the rest of our membership, and they agree. Although Balfurin is some dis-

tance from our homes, it might prove to be an
excellent meeting location for our organization.

They couldn't possibly meet at Balfurin. What on
earth had possessed Lady Eleanor? No, she couldn't
allow it. What if one of her students found out? Worse,
what if one of the parents discovered it?

How did she keep Lady Eleanor and her Edification
Society from Balfurin?

She grabbed another sheet of paper and began to
write to Lady Eleanor:

As thoughtful as your invitation is, I do not feel
that it would be appropriate for me to become a
member of your group at this time. Nor do I feel
that Balfurin, as a school for impressionable
young girls, would be an appropriate meeting
place.

Dear God, let that keep them from Balfurin.

Chapter 13

Dixon waited until almost midnight, the hour when spirits were restless, according to Matthew. Balfurin late at night was the perfect setting to believe in ghosts. There were no candles or lamps kept lit during the night. No footmen were stationed in appropriate places to be of assistance.

The darkness felt like a living thing, a companion to his journey.

He wondered if the spirits of the deceased lingered in houses. Did the memory of tragedies and joys remain behind in the very brick of his ancestral home? He could almost hear the whispers of lovers, his uncle's angry bellow, the muffled laughter of children. Then, too, there were his own memories. He could almost witness his child self running through these corridors only to be shouted at to mind his manners. "Dixon! Have you forgotten where you are?"

The walls were paneled in wood, heavily carved at the ceiling and middle. They seemed to absorb sound, or perhaps that was just the new green and gold runner. As a boy, he'd slid along this hall in his stockinged feet, he and George trying to reach all the way to the stairwell. That's how he'd fallen down the stairs one day and broken his arm, a feat that had resulted in banishment to his room for a week. His uncle had fumed and his aunt had lectured. Strange, how he could barely remember her. She was short and blond, with an absent smile and a habit of smoothing her little finger over her left eyebrow.

He made his way to the library in the darkness, grateful for the windows at the end of the corridor. They let in just enough of the moonlight that he didn't stumble into any of the tables.

The handle turned easily and he let himself in, closing the library door silently behind him. He lit the lamp on the corner of the desk and went right to the fireplace. There was nothing but cold embers here now, waiting for the morning maid.

He bent and tapped at the bottom most brick bearing the earl's crest. Nothing happened. He reached into his dressing gown pocket and retrieved the hammer he'd taken from the stable for just such a purpose and hit the brick. Again, nothing. Not defeated, he began working on the brick on the opposite side of the hearth. This one moved a little when he tapped it with the hammer.

He sat on the floor, and taking an awl he'd also borrowed, wedged it between the brick and mortar. To his surprise, the brick moved easily, sliding forward into his hand.

Dixon reached inside, sticking his arm all the way into the cavity. The space was as deep as the hearth. And empty.

No, not quite empty. He withdrew something between his fingers and looked at it in the glow from the lamp. A piece of paper. A corner of a page. From a document of some sort. But what?

He reached inside once more, only to come up empty. Had George already found the treasure? It looked as if he had. And left Balfurin with no further thought of his wife or his heritage.

If George were here, he'd thrash him until he begged for mercy.

Dixon replaced the brick, cleaned up the broken mortar pieces, then stood, dropping the awl and the hammer into his pocket.

He would revisit Nan in the morning. Hopefully, she'd tell him what had really happened the last time George had come home. Loyalty toward the earl was one thing, but she needed to understand that George should be found. If for Charlotte's piece of mind if nothing else.

And for his own as well.

"It is indeed like you said, Miss Maisie. I can see all the stars that I might have seen at home."

Matthew turned to his companion. In the darkness she was nothing more than a shadow, but he could smell her scent, something that reminded him of the fields and hills around them.

"Are you certain," he asked, "that the journey here did not hurt your foot?"

"Oh no," Maisie said brightly. "I rarely have any

pain anymore. Not since her ladyship got me these special shoes. Before that, I ached a bit, but not too much. Thank you for asking, Matthew. No one else does."

"I think it is to make the situation easier for you," he offered. "Or, perhaps, they are simply uncomfortable. They do not know what to say, so they prefer not to say anything at all."

"I'd much rather they said something, even if it's cruel. It's better than feeling invisible."

"While I would much rather they remained silent."

She glanced at him. "Why would anyone ridicule you, Matthew?"

"My country is a mixture of cultures," he said. "Malay, Chinese, and Indian. My father was of one culture and my mother another. I have tainted blood." He hesitated for a moment and then continued. "There are those who see me as an abomination."

She didn't say anything for a moment.

Finally, he glanced over at her to find her smiling at him.

"Oh, Matthew, there are always those who will judge every single one of us. That's their sin, not ours. I think you are quite the most handsome man I have ever seen. I could look at your face for hours and never grow tired of the sight. You're hardly an abomination."

He didn't answer her. What could he say? She would not understand the culture of his country any more than he completely understood Scotland. On one hand, it seemed a barbarous place, but the people were genuinely kind, possessed of an innocence that had the power to charm him.

"Thank you for wanting to share the night with me," he said.

An hour ago, Maisie had knocked on his door and bid him come with her, their destination a small hill overlooking Balfurin. The rest of the castle was asleep, and few lights shone. The only illumination was the moon and the stars twinkling above them.

Maisie glanced over at him. "It's nearly morning Matthew."

He nodded. "It was kind of you to take pity on my wakefulness."

She glanced at him again, smiling this time. "I didn't take pity on you, Matthew. I was unable to sleep as well, and when I heard you walking in your room, it just seemed right that we should be awake together. Tomorrow, however, I will wager that both of us will be sleepy enough. It doesn't seem quite fair."

"Buddha teaches us that life is neither fair nor unfair."

"I don't think that's quite right. And who is this Buddha fellow, a friend of yours?"

"A great teacher," he said, hiding his smile. She could not be blamed for her ignorance because she lived in a remote part of a remote country and knew little of the world. "He was the enlightened one. He spent a great bit of time thinking on life and how man fits in it."

"Does he come from your country?"

"I think he might be considered a citizen of the world."

"Well that's easy enough, isn't it?" Maisie said. "Being a citizen of the world means you never have to obligate yourself to one place." She put her hands flat on the grass behind her, leaned back and studied the stars. "I, for one, would much rather be a citizen of some place. I like belonging. I like knowing that I'm going to see the same thing tomorrow that I saw today."

He didn't speak, didn't tell her that he'd rarely had the comfort of sameness. His adopted family had never lived in the same place more than a few months at a time, being intent on spreading the word of God.

"There is a great deal to be said for routine," Matthew said.

"It isn't to be feared, Matthew. Doing the same thing day after day doesn't make you a boring person. It's only boring if you have the same thoughts. If you never learn." She turned to him. "There's a man who came to our village not too long ago. He speaks German and he's promised to teach me. I like to learn something new every day, if I can. That's why I'm so glad that her ladyship said I may take a book from the library whenever I wish. It might take me some time to read it, but read it I shall. When I'm done, I'll get another."

He'd never met anyone quite like Maisie, so demanding of life. When he told her so, she only laughed. "It's my life, isn't it? No one else is going to live it for me. And I'd be a pretty silly person if I waited until I reached the end of it to regret all of the things I haven't done."

She sat back, staring at the sky again, all the while glancing at him from time to time. Several moments passed in perfect harmony until Maisie spoke again. "Evidently, we're not the only ones awake at this hour." She pointed to the castle below them.

A faint flickering light danced in a window. For a horrified moment, he thought it might be a fire, but then the light moved, leaving the window dark.

"They say Balfurin is haunted," Maisie said, wrapping her arms around her up-drawn knees.

He glanced at her, surprised that she'd made such a pronouncement in a calm tone of voice.

"You do not sound afraid."

She laughed merrily. "Of ghosts? Not in Scotland. Every building has its share of ghosts. We're a dour nation, Matthew. We've a great deal of tragedy in our past. I'd be surprised if Balfurin weren't haunted. Still, I don't like the idea of them wandering through the place at night." She gave him the sidelong glance. "That's why you'll have to see me to my room. To protect me."

"It would be my great honor," he said seriously, although he wondered if it weren't the other way around. He might well need protection from Maisie.

"Do you never laugh, Matthew?"

He considered the matter. "You are saying that I am too serious."

"Not serious, exactly. I think, like Scotland, that you must've had a great deal of sadness in your past."

He didn't discuss his past with anyone, not even Dixon. "And you, Maisie? Have you not had a great deal of sadness as well?"

"Oh, you mean because of my foot?" She smiled. "I've had my share of teasing, that's true. And pain in my side from time to time, because of the way I had to walk before my new shoes. But I can't remember ever being other than I am, so I don't suppose it matters. My lameness simply is, Matthew, like the dew on the grass or even Balfurin itself."

"What gives you pleasure, Miss Maisie?"

"I like chicken soup," she said, surprising him. He expected another answer, perhaps. Something to do with beautiful days or pleasant scents.

"Chicken soup? This, too, I like. With noodles?"

"No," Macy said. "With carrots and large chunks of chicken. And crusty rolls. With butter, of course."

"Of course," Matthew said, smiling.

"And clean sheets that smell of the sun. And kittens, with their eyes just opened and their little bellies fat and full and rounded. Sometimes, I hold one who is purring for the very first time and it's like God has given me a gift. What about you, Matthew? What makes you happy?"

"Being here with you now," he said honestly. "Feeling safe."

"Have you not often felt safe?"

He wished she'd not asked that question. She didn't truly want to hear the story of his life. Or perhaps he didn't wish to tell it.

"I would like to see these kittens of yours."

"The barn cat is due to have another litter soon," she said. "I hope you'll still be here at Balfurin."

"My master is in no hurry to leave."

"Why do you call him that? He does not own you."

He didn't tell her the truth. She was European and would not understand that from the moment Dixon had saved his life, the other man had owned Matthew's soul. It was up to him whether or not Matthew felt joy or pain or lived out his life with honor.

His life was not his, and once he would have railed at that. But in the last several years, he had begun to accept, to understand that his destiny was not necessarily his to command. By acquiescing to his fate, he became stronger. The stronger he became, the more he was prepared for anything destiny delivered to him.

"It is a title of respect," he said giving her the explanation most Europeans accepted. He saw her nod, grateful that the topic was done.

On this quiet hillside in Scotland, he began to feel the first rumblings of discontent. If he had been obligated to no one but himself, he would have begun to think thoughts that were forbidden him. He would've held Maisie close to him and perhaps kissed her. Because his life was not his, he focused on the stars above him rather than the temptation beside him.

Matthew stood and held out both hands for her. Without hesitation, Maisie placed her fingers within his and allowed him to help her stand. For a moment they stood too close, and he inhaled the scent of her. She smelled of the soft grass upon which they'd sat, and a curious profusion of flowers.

"In my country, I would shock your relatives by being all alone with you in the darkness."

"In my country, too," Maisie said. "Have you many relatives?"

"I have no one," Matthew said. "I do not often tell people that. But then, they do not often ask."

"Then shall we make a pledge? We'll only be honest. We shall ask each other questions that no one else dare ask, and answer them with our true heart."

He wasn't entirely certain that was wise. She was too innocent a creature, too sweet for him to touch. He felt his heart creak open and the sudden anger he felt startled him.

After extinguishing the lamp, Dixon let himself out the door, closing it quietly behind him. The corridor seemed even darker than before, the stairs enshrouded in black. The portraits hung in military precision along the stairwell wall seemed to be smiling at him, either in amusement or commiseration.

He was almost to the top of the stairs when he heard a heavy dragging sound. If Matthew had been with him, he'd have said it was the restless spirit of one of his ancestors carrying his own sins. Dixon wasn't inclined to believe in ghosts, those either burdened by earthly evil or pure and virtuous.

Something, however, was making that sound.

Stepping to the side of the corridor, he fingered the handle of the hammer in his pocket and waited.

"Damn him!"

He knew that voice.

"I'll show him! Does he think I'm going to simply sit here and allow him to dally with the maids? Where is he?"

Something heavy falling down the servant's stair was followed by a muffled comment. He made his way down the corridor, the hammer forgotten, his entire attention on the woman coming toward him.

Charlotte stepped out into the corridor. For a moment, she looked like a ghost, attired in her pale nightgown and wrapper.

A faint, almost decorous, scream escaped her at his

appearance. One hand went to the base of her throat—the other still held the weapon at her side.

"Is that a broadsword you're dragging behind you?"

"It is." She pulled the sword up beside her, allowing the tip to skitter along the rug. If it was as sharp as the other weapons at Balfurin, the carpet would be sliced to ribbons. Charlotte, however, didn't look the least concerned.

"I will not have it, George," she said loud enough to wake any ghosts—or humans—at Balfurin. "I'll not tolerate you bedding the maids. No husband of mine will shame me in this fashion, even if we do not share a bed. I will not have it! Once was quite enough, thank you."

"Surely you didn't knock on all the servants' doors to find me?" he asked.

"I didn't think it necessary. You're rather vocal in your enjoyment so I just stood and listened."

He was torn between humor and compassion.

"I assure you I wasn't bedding any of the maids, Charlotte," he said.

"Then what are you doing roaming the corridors of Balfurin at this hour of night?"

"I couldn't sleep."

"Your guilty conscience, no doubt."

"No doubt." She was closer to the mark than she knew. "Was it your intent to run me through with the broadsword?"

"Or to cut off a certain portion of your anatomy," she said, pulling the sword closer.

"You are a very bloodthirsty woman. Guns and broadswords."

"Being a spurned wife brings out all sorts of emotions."

Granted, she held the sword but he wasn't afraid of her ability to wield it since she could barely lift it.

He stepped closer and before she could pull away, leaned forward and kissed her.

A thoroughly wrong thing to do, of course.

Her lips were incredibly soft, almost pillowy. He deepened the kiss, extending his free hand around her right shoulder. He heard the sword drop, felt her hand curve around his neck. He moved even closer, lured by her response and a small, almost helpless sound she made as she opened her lips.

He had never been so aware of a woman's fragility as he was at this moment. She was nearly vibrating with fear. He wanted to enfold her in his arms, murmur something soft and comforting that would ease her terror. But to do so, he would have to end the kiss, and he wouldn't do that.

"This isn't wise," she whispered finally when the kiss was done and she was breathing hard. But, then, so was he.

"No. It isn't wise." Nothing about his presence at Balfurin was wise, let alone standing in the darkened castle with his cousin's wife in his arms.

She stood on tiptoe and linked her arms around his neck. He wanted to warn her that she was in more danger than she understood. He'd already lost his honor. By pretending to be George, he'd ignored his own sense of decency. Now he was asking himself questions he shouldn't ask: how much worse would it be to take her to his bed?

The proposition was too tempting.

He rested his forehead against hers, breathing hard and making no effort to hide her effect on him.

"Charlotte." He murmured her name. Unspoken were the words he should have said: *Forget these moments ever existed. Pretend I didn't kiss you.*

He was sorry for what George had done to her. More than sorry. He despised his cousin. He wanted to make it up to her, let her see how desirable she was, how fascinating a mind she had, and how beautiful a body. But that wasn't why he'd kissed her.

From the night he'd first seen her, she'd fascinated him. He'd wanted her when he'd stood in the Great Hall and watched as she welcomed guests to Balfurin. He wanted her when she crossed the ballroom, anger blossoming on her face. He wanted her at breakfast, when she'd saddled him with two hundred watchful girls, and when he'd rescued her in the rain.

There hadn't been a moment when he'd been free of his desire.

She stepped back, pressing her fingers against her lips and staring at him wide eyed. As if she'd never been kissed before, or so thoroughly.

He wanted to kiss her again and show her how it could be. A deep, invasive kiss that stunned the senses and numbed the mind. If she remained here, he would. And more.

She was the only one who could stop him.

"Why did you come home?" she asked. "Why did you come back?"

Not the question he'd expected, and he didn't know how to answer it.

She looked away, tucking her hands around her

waist and then in front of her. She traced the pattern of the buttons up her wrapper and down again while one hand trailed to the end of the sash that belted it closed.

"To make amends," he said, and in a way it was true.

Her fear hadn't eased, but she didn't retreat. Instead, she stood there in front of him, brave and dauntless, as courageous as she must have been five years ago.

He wanted to kiss her again, in reparation, in a sheer and selfish need to touch her. Instead, he bent and picked up the broadsword.

"Shall I return this to where it belongs?"

"I keep it in my chamber," she said.

He looked at her quizzically.

"For a year I lived here with just the servants."

"And you were their protector?" he asked.

"Someone had to be."

He hefted the sword easily, deciding it wouldn't be wise of him to comment further. She'd undergone privations and sacrifices for what she had now. A great deal more than George had ever endured. Dixon wished his cousin well, but he also wished him far away. There was one thing worse than Charlotte being without a husband—being burdened with George.

She turned and began walking down the corridor. It wasn't wise of him to watch her walk because she did so in a thoroughly feminine way, a motion that made him focus on her hips. There were only two layers of fabric hiding her body, the nightgown and the wrapper, both of a sheer material that didn't protect her from either the draft or his gaze.

The oh-so-proper headmistress of the Caledonia School for the Advancement of Females was roaming through the halls of Balfurin barefoot. He couldn't help but smile at that revelation.

He followed her, carrying the broadsword. They were at her chamber too quickly. She glanced at his door and then back at him.

"Thank you," she said, and reached out to grab the sword with both hands. Her fingers brushed against his, and for a moment he thought she might speak. But she said nothing, just retrieved the sword from his grip and held it so that the point pierced the carpet.

He wanted to tell her that such a venerable instrument of war should not be treated in such a fashion, but instead he took one more step back, away from her, and bowed slightly. Her gaze focused on his dressing gown, at the open V at his neck. Did she know he was naked beneath the garment?

God, don't let the last of my honor falter. Let me forget that she is as lonely as I, as wounded, perhaps. She was a woman of delicacy, firm in her resolve but tentative in her emotions. He could hurt her too easily, bruise when he only meant to touch.

He'd come home to find himself and instead had discovered her, a complication of immense proportions, a temptation, a trial, a test that he was on the verge of failing.

Dear God but he wanted her. In his arms, in his bed, beneath him, his mouth smothering her screams of pleasure.

Run, Charlotte. Run as quickly as you can, because I'm too close to forgetting I have any honor at all.

She only faced him, innocent that she was, unaware of her danger.

Chapter 14

There was an expression in his eyes that she'd never before seen, something heated and alarming. She should have run from that look, but instead, she wanted him to touch her, wanted him to stroke his fingers along her arm, cup her shoulders in his hands. She wanted to feel his thumb against the base of her throat, the pads of his fingers as they stole up to her chin, and his palms on her face, holding her still for another kiss.

She wanted to weep, the heaviness filling her, reminding her of those rare moments when she felt overwhelmed by grief and loss and uncertain why. She felt a pulse beat deep inside her, as if her core were coming alive, as if the ice wall inside her was melting.

Slowly, carefully, she took one step toward him, the broadsword still at her side.

"Come to my bed," he said, startling her. "Come

with me." He turned and faced his door, and then opened it and stepped inside. Only then did he turn and look at her again.

A good five feet separated them. She could flee to her chamber now and he wouldn't follow. How strange that she somehow knew she could leave her door open and yet he wouldn't bother her.

This capitulation must be all hers.

"Come," he said, stretching out his hand to her.

If she did, if she allowed him to lure her into the Laird's Chamber, nothing would ever be the same again. She would no longer be simply the headmistress of a soon to be profitable school. She would be a wife in more than name. She would have a husband, someone whose duty it was to protect her, defend her, care for her.

Someone whose bed she was compelled to share.

Should she go? Or stay? Either way, this night would change her. Regardless of her decision, she would never again look at him in the same way. She would forever recall the tenderness of his kiss, and the possibility of it.

To make amends, that's why he'd returned, why he'd come back to her. By turning now and walking away, she could pay him back in kind for those five years. Doing so would forever alter their tentative friendship and destroy whatever insisted on blossoming between them.

How much did she hate him? How badly did she want him punished?

And by punishing him, did she not also punish herself?

After a moment's hesitation, she dropped the

sword, reached out and placed her hand atop his. Immediately, his warm fingers curled around her hand. This was the George she remembered, impatient with his need and wants. She allowed him to pull her into the chamber, closing the door behind them. She stood silent as he lit too many candles as well as the oil lamp on the dresser. The room was soon as bright as day.

This was new. Before, he'd wanted the act done in darkness. And she'd been grateful for it, since he wouldn't be able to witness her reluctance. In the dark she could pretend to be willing, be nothing more than a vessel for him to fill.

"You look terrified," he said now. She shook her head, but from the smile on his face, she doubted if he believed her.

He placed both hands on the sash of her wrapper. She placed her own on top of them, thinking that he meant to undress her here in the brightness, in the yellow tint of the beeswax candles.

"Must you?" she asked.

"No," he said softly. "I won't do anything you don't wish. Tonight, let's pretend that we don't know each other very well. We're new lovers, coming together for the first time. We'll learn each other slowly and deliberately."

"We don't know each other very well," she said, forced to honesty. "There was only that one time."

He looked startled just before he pulled her into his arms.

She lay her head against his shoulder, closing her eyes tight. When she was old and frail, she would remember this moment when she touched her lips to his neck, feeling the rapid beat of his heart beneath his skin. His scent was something exotic and foreign, yet essentially his.

When had he changed? After leaving her? Or had the man she married been this fascinating personage all along and she'd been too young or too naive to see it?

"Charlotte."

Even his voice was magic, a dark ribbon like the sight of the River Tam beneath a night sky.

Never before had she felt this way. Not once in all her thirty-two years had she felt so desperate for the touch of another human being. Daring herself, she reached out and smoothed her hand against his chest. He flinched, a reaction that startled her.

"Charlotte," he said, and there was a note of warning now in his voice.

"Forgive me," she said, dropping her hands and stepping back. "I was being forward."

"Not so," he said. "Dangerous, perhaps. Enticing, of a certainty. Not forward."

"Dangerous? I've never been called dangerous."

"I'm grateful for the blindness of my fellow countrymen, then. Otherwise, I'd be compelled to defend your honor."

She was unaccountably pleased by his words, but even more so for the look in his eyes. They smoldered, and she wondered what he was thinking that could heat his gaze in such a way.

Suddenly, and without warning, he bent down and kissed her again. A kiss that captured her breath, weakened her knees and caused that odd pulsing in her lower regions.

Her hands trailed up his chest to link at the back of

his neck. She stood on tiptoe to be closer to him, startled when he cupped his hands around her buttocks and lifted her up, pressing her so close that she could feel the length of his arousal. Only a few layers of fabric separated them from each other. He raised her up and then lowered her slowly down his hardness, encouraging her to feel all of him.

He lowered her until her feet finally touched the floor and then further shocked her by removing her arms from around his neck and placing her hand against him.

Her fingers were at the base of the shaft, her palm along its length, and still she didn't measure the whole of him. Good Lord, her memory had played her false. Or had she ever touched him before? She couldn't remember doing so. George had come into her bedroom, entered her bed, and mounted her, leaving as quickly as it was done. That one night was the sum total of her experience as a wife.

"Have you grown?" she whispered, not at all sure she should be asking such a question. "Does it keep growing?" In that case, she would never accommodate him in a year or so.

It was a very disconcerting feeling to be kissed through laughter. She couldn't help but smile at the sensation, all the while she had the feeling that he was ridiculing her ignorance.

But then he pulled away and looked down at her, and in the bright light of the room she could see the expression on his face. There was tenderness there, something she'd never before seen in his gaze. As if George truly felt something for her.

"No and yes," he answered. "It's the same size it

has always been, but being close to you makes it seem larger."

"I haven't the slightest knowledge of the subject," she admitted.

"I once read a book," he said, leaning down and touching his forehead to hers, "that was written eight hundred years ago. It was called a pillow book, the diary of a maiden, I believe, who was initiated into love."

"Really?" She pulled back and looked at him with interest. "Would it be possible to acquire a copy?" She looked away. "Of course, there is the problem of keeping one here at the school. I can only imagine the hue and cry that would come from one of my students accidentally acquiring it. Every parent in Scotland would excoriate me."

"I do not have your recall, Charlotte," he said, smiling, "but I can remember enough to be of assistance."

Heat rose from her big toes, up her ankles and legs to encompass her torso, shoulders, arms, neck, and then the very top of her head. The sensation was so bewildering that she could only stand there blinking at him.

Did he expect her to answer? Blessedly, he didn't seem to demand a response. Lucidity was beyond her. Instead, he bent and kissed her again, and this kiss was without any levity at all. Heat was traveling through her body. She was dizzy, and he was the only solid thing in the entire universe.

She clung to him with both hands, her fingers clutching at his shoulders as the sensations deepened. His lips were hard and then soft, and then open, demanding the same of her. His tongue was intrusive and coaxing and tender and exciting, and every sensation all at once. She felt as if she couldn't get her breath and then felt as if she were breathing too quickly. Her heart slowed and then raced and then felt as if it liquefied as the heat in her body intensified. Her toes curled as she made a small sound in the back of her throat that sounded weak and desperate and wanting.

His hands were on her buttocks again but this time he lifted her up in his arms and carried her some distance to the bed. He put her gently in the middle of the mattress as if she were the most precious burden he'd ever carried.

She raised up on her elbows and watched him.

His dressing gown was black silk, heavily embroidered in gold, silver, and crimson threads. He threw it off his shoulders, and it slid to the floor revealing him in all his nakedness.

For the first time, she was grateful for the candles. From this moment onward, she'd be able to remember the sight of him. He was glorious, a Roman soldier of a man—though the muscles of his chest and stomach looked to be made of hammered iron, his breastplate was indeed flesh, his shoulders wide and strong. His thighs were thick and sprinkled with the same curly black hair as his chest. His calves were strong, his feet both long and wide, a firm foundation for the rest of the man.

His erection, however, caught and held her attention. As she watched, he fisted himself, pulling back the foreskin until the whole of him emerged, a most formidable weapon.

She could feel the heat cooling in her body. This was not going to work. This was not going to be a pleasurable interlude. She was certain of it. She remembered the sole night of her marriage bed and recalled all the pain of it. She did *not* want to repeat that experience.

If anything, he'd grown harder and longer as she watched. She looked away, deliberately focusing her attention on something else.

The four-poster hangings needed to be replaced. Bother the hangings. Could she leave? What would he do if she simply scurried to the door and left?

"Charlotte," he said softly. "Tonight, we're new lovers. You're a maiden, with all her innocence and fears."

"You make me sound like a child."

"Not a child. A beautiful woman who has never quite believed that fact. A woman who's never been properly loved."

She glanced at him.

"I'm to be your pillow book, remember? Shall we turn to the first page?"

Reluctantly, she nodded. Never let it be said that she was a coward.

He moved to the side of the bed and sat on the edge facing her.

"A maiden must know her own body first before she can enjoy its gifts."

"I know my body."

"Ah, but you know only the totality of it, I suspect. Did you realize all the delightful and varied parts?"

He moved his hand to the sash of her wrapper, slowly untying it. A small smile was playing around his lips and she wondered what he was thinking.

"I've wanted to undress you for an hour," he said, as if he'd read her mind.

"Have you?"

Her nightgown was a fine lawn, nearly transparent. It offered no shield from his eyes.

"I think we need to get you out of this," he said softly.

Before she had a chance to protest, he scooped her up from the bed and set her on the floor beside it. When he would have grabbed the hem of her night-gown she slapped at his hands.

He ignored her as if she were no more than a pesky mosquito.

All too quickly she was naked, and back in the middle of the bed. But just when she thought he would mount her, he reached over and put his hand beneath her breast, his thumb gently brushing back and forth over the nipple.

"This doesn't feel the same when you do it as when I do it, does it?" he said.

"I don't touch myself there," she said breathlessly. "When I do, it's by accident."

"A woman's breast is a wondrous thing," he said. "Capable of a great many sensations. The softest touch can awaken desire." He bent and blew against the nipple. A tiny, shivery breath, but she still felt an an-swering spark deep inside. He seemed to know it as well, because he smiled when he drew back. Once more his thumb strummed against the nipple and he watched his own actions with interest. She felt a tight-ening and looked down at herself. The nipple was now hard and pebbly and so was the other, even though he hadn't touched it yet.

When she would have questioned what he was about, he placed two fingers across her lips and shook his head. Evidently, she was to be as mute as her best students, attuned to listening and not to speaking. She nodded, to signify that she understood, and remained silent when he removed his hand.

He bent and placed his lips against her nipple, drawing it into his mouth. A spear of sensation raced through her as if his lips were directly connected to another, more intimate part of her. He was not content to suckle one breast, but divided his attentions between both.

She wanted to frame his face with her hands, feel his scratchy beard against her palms, hold him in place and force him to continue at his task. But he was too quick, and each breast was left feeling bereft.

Then he did something she'd never thought a man— a husband—would do. He gently parted her legs and stared at her directly. All the sensations in her body seemed to coalesce where his gaze was directed.

He smiled. "You're very responsive, Charlotte," he said. "It's a very great compliment to me. A touch on your breast and your body is already readying itself for me." He bent down and suckled on her breast again and, when she was concentrating on the sensations he evoked, he slid his hand between her legs, inserting a finger into her, nearly causing her to leap from the bed.

She hadn't expected it. When he made a soothing

sound, she clenched her eyes shut, trapped in her muteness as if he'd demanded a promise of silence from her. But what on earth could she say?

Stop. Don't touch me. Don't make me feel this way. How foolish.

Her mind failed her. There was not one single page floating in front of her eyes, no scrap of memory to be recalled, not one quote she could summon.

He touched her again, pulling his finger out of her, and inserting it again, at a different angle so that it seemed to press against a magical part of her, one capable of such pleasure that her eyes flew open to meet his gaze.

"Charlotte," he whispered, and it seemed to be a summons to another place, a land of the mind, and soul, and perhaps heart. His eyes seemed to say: trust me. His mouth curved into a rueful smile as if he knew how very difficult it would be for her to do so.

He smoothed his hand over her, and she wanted to come upright, to meet his fingers with every stroke. She bit back the inclination and forced herself to remain still. But it was the hardest thing she had ever done.

He kissed her, his lips wet and hot and then stroked a thumb down her intimate folds. She bit her lips rather than make a sound.

How very strange that what he was doing felt so absolutely wondrous. He'd never touched her before, never sounded as if he were out of breath before.

He kissed her again, and then her breasts, and when she placed a hand on his neck and let her fingers walk to his shoulder, he pulled back and smiled at her.

She wrapped her arms around his neck. "I'm not afraid, George. Really, I'm not."

Suddenly, he moved, and for a horrible, terrible moment she thought he was leaving her. She opened her eyes to find him sitting back on his thighs at the end of the bed. His gaze was solemn, and as she watched, he extended his hand to her.

Without questioning why she did so, she reached up and placed her hand in his. She knelt in front of him, their fingers intertwined. He lowered their joined hands, still looking at her. His gaze was direct, somber, allowing no prevarication, no wilting beneath it.

Caution rose along with the heat in her body.

"There's no reason to feel afraid of me, Charlotte. Not now, not ever."

What did she say to that?

"I want to love you, to show you how enjoyable it can be. Not bring you discomfort."

She stared at him, uncertain what he wanted from her. Permission? Invitation?

"I want you to feel as much pleasure as I do."

A flush traveled up her chest at his words.

"Do you feel pleasure, George?"

He leaned forward and placed two fingers across her lips to silence her.

"Not now, but I will," he said. "And so will you." A moment later, he kissed her and she spiraled down into the sensations with delight.

He'd bedded his share of women, but somehow Charlotte made him feel inept and untried, like a youth whose need was greater than his knowledge. Or a man out of his element, who didn't know how to touch a woman like Charlotte the way he wanted, with skill and talent, so that she trembled as he did.

He moved her so that she was on her stomach and then helped her rise to her knees.

"You're so beautiful," he murmured, stroking his hands from the delectable curves of her buttocks down her narrow waist to her shoulders. Only then did he allow himself to cup her breasts and squeeze them lightly. She sank to her forearms, her derriere pushing back at him.

"The pillow book says that this is the way a maiden finds her greatest pleasure."

She didn't speak, only made a little wiggle that was too enticing.

He didn't need any persuading. Despite the fact that he was trembling, he deliberately slowed his movements. He guided himself into her, stopping when he wanted to surge deeply inside. Instead, for every forward movement, he pulled back a little.

He took a deep, shuddering breath and gripped her hips, slowing pulling her onto his shaft and clenching his eyes shut as he felt every delectable, torturous sensation.

He wanted her to beg him to hurry, but she didn't make a sound. Her hands clenched at the sheets, gripping fistfuls of linen as she pushed back against him. He remained motionless, but she took up the rhythm, rising fully, bending forward on her knees, and then back, establishing a rhythm that urged him to lose his control.

The candles flickered, the shadows deepened and sweat broke out over his body as he concentrated on the incredible pleasure where they joined.

Her back suddenly arched like a cat and she pushed back against him as if she were a seductress, intent on pleasuring herself, and he was simply incidental to the act.

He wanted to whisper her name, to caution her that he was not a god, that he could not maintain such patience for long.

But Charlotte was in no hurry. She bent forward again, still on her knees, her forearms pressing against the mattress. He wanted to ask her how she felt, wanted to coax her to speak to him, but he knew that in this act, at least, she was shy, virginal in thought if not almost in deed.

His hands still rested on her hips, but he'd given up any illusion of control from the moment she first moved.

He moved one hand down to where they joined, and pressed a finger to her. She straightened her arms, her head hanging down between her shoulders. Slowly, he drew his fingers up until he found her plump and swollen and wet around his cock.

He stroked his fingers up and down, heard her indrawn gasp. Good. At least she was beginning to feel something of what he felt.

"Shatter for me, Charlotte," he whispered. "I want to feel when you find your release. I want to know what it's like when passion blinds you and you can't catch your breath."

Make it soon. Please.

She slowly shook her head from side to side as if it were an ardent and silent battle they fought there on the bed. Did she have any idea how desperately he wanted to find his release? Did she know what it would be like for her?

"Now," he said gently and pressed two fingers to

her, sliding them slowly up and down. "Now," he said again, and then put both hands on her hips and pulled her toward him.

He was as deep as he could get, and still it wasn't enough. He pressed forward on her back until she subsided on her forearms, her forehead grinding against the mattress as a series of shuddering sobs escaped her.

Again and again and again he pulled out and then pushed himself back gently and yet too slowly for his need and his own desire.

Hurry. Hurry. An internal voice screamed at him that he wouldn't be able to hold on to his restraint much longer. He wanted to erupt in her. He wanted to repeat this moment over and over. He pulled out of her and then slid into her wetness again and again, gritting his teeth when a sound like a moan threatened to escape. His hands trembled, and he gripped her hips tighter, at the mercy of his body and his craving—his need—for completion. He wanted to repeat the pleasure over and over, lock the door and refuse to let her escape for a week—a lifetime.

"Now," he said as he drove deeply into her. "Now." He felt her begin to quiver around him. He pushed forward, cupped her breasts in his hands and gently squeezed her nipples. He pressed his face against her back, smelling the scent of her skin, feeling her tremble. Only then did he allow himself to surrender to the pleasure.

Chapter 15

Dixon rose at dawn to find that he was the only occupant of his bed. Some time in the night, Charlotte had returned to her room. Perhaps it was better that way. If he'd awakened beside her, he would have loved her again, further complicating matters.

He'd already broken his resolve and dented his honor well enough. The ramifications would have to be addressed, including the fact that he wanted to repeat the act over and over again.

He dressed and left the Laird's Chamber, striding across the hall. He raised his fist to knock, but caught himself. What could he say?

I am not George. There, a small repair to his honor. *I am Dixon, his cousin, and you fascinate me too much.*

But before he spoke, perhaps he would lean forward and kiss her. Would there be a sparkle in her eyes?

Would her face be flushed, her lips slightly swollen?

Would she kiss him back? Better, would she invite him into her chamber?

For a moment, a fleeting inch of time, he relived the night, before he thrust the memory away. He wasn't at all certain she would answer the door.

Did she regret last night?

He had never considered himself a coward, but at this moment he found his courage being tested.

"She's still asleep, your lordship."

He looked up to find Maisie walking down the hall. Her limp was pronounced this morning, as if she'd been walking too much.

"I went in to see her just five minutes ago, sir, and she was burrowed under all the blankets all comfy like. I don't think she'll rouse till noon."

A reprieve, then.

"Would you like me to give her a message, your lordship?"

He shook his head. "No, I'll not disturb her, Maisie."

Dixon turned and walked down the corridor, intent on the tower room. Since he couldn't see Charlotte, he could at least visit with Nan. He knocked on the door and waited. Several moments later, he knocked again and finally heard a sound on the other side.

"Nan? Are you feeling well enough for a visitor?"

"I am old, child, not sick," came the querulous reply.

He entered the room and closed the door behind him. She was sitting beside the window, the morning sun touching the sill. In the light she looked even more drawn and more shrunken than she had a few days earlier. Time was running out for both of them, but hers was the final race.

"Are you well, Nan?"

She looked amused at the question. "I am well enough."

He reached out and adjusted her shawl. She batted his hand out of the way and he was shocked at how cold her fingers were.

"Your hands feel like ice."

"It's not the winters that make me cold, child, but my age."

There was only a small fire in the grate, and he stirred it with a poker before returning to her side.

"There are warmer rooms at Balfurin."

"I'll not move from here." She looked out the window as if to dismiss him.

"Then I'll send up more wood for the fire."

"The girl keeps it burning. Ask me, instead, what I'll do for the loneliness. Being without love brings a greater discomfort than any the flesh might feel. Longing for death is not much solace."

He pulled up a chair and sat beside her. He didn't know what to say to her. Would words have any effect at all?

After a few moments of silence, he finally spoke. "I went to the crypt," he said. "I didn't find anything there."

She only smiled.

"But the pattern on the earl's coffin was the same as the bricks in the library."

"You always were a canny lad," she said. "I've often thought you the smarter one of the two of you. It took George longer to find it."

"There was a secret compartment in the fireplace, but it was empty. Was the treasure there? Did George find it?" He withdrew the corner of the page he'd found, and placed it on her lap.

She smiled, and looked far out into the distance. For the longest time she didn't speak, but neither did he, determined to match her in patience.

"More than once George stripped Balfurin of everything he could fit into a wagon and drove off, leaving us to starve. We were too stubborn to die. Too old and too stubborn."

She managed a frail shrug. "Perhaps he was more desperate than he'd been before. He married an English. I never would have given him the first clue if I'd known." She clasped her hands in her lap, looked down on them as if the presence of her fingers suddenly surprised her. "He wanted her money. There were women in Scotland he could have wed." She glanced up at Dixon. "She doesn't come to visit me."

"From what I hear," Dixon said, "you wouldn't receive her."

"What have I to say to an Englishwoman? Her people killed those I loved many years ago. I'm not too old that I can't remember that." She gave him a shrewd look. "Are you worried that I might tell her who you are, child?" She smiled. "Let her figure it out."

"Did George find the treasure?" he asked, trying to get her back to the subject.

"He liked Edinburgh. Not as much as London, I hear. But well enough. He had too much wanderlust to remain here, Laird of Balfurin. A pity that you were not your uncle's son."

"Did he find it, Nan?" he asked again, wondering if her mind was wandering. Did she even know if George had found the treasure?

"He found the scroll. The scroll with the whole of the poem on it."

She smiled and began to speak:

> *"Three times he'll score his mark*
> *Three times a mark of grace*
> *A father, son, and holy ghost*
> *To show the sacred place.*
>
> *Beyond a river swift*
> *The current true and fast*
> *The one who seeks shall find*
> *The gold and jeweled cask.*
>
> *A treasure there to find*
> *A trunk of jewels and gold*
> *Placed there for sons to come*
> *To protect and to hold."*

She laughed, the sound so brittle he expected the air to crack.

Had age destroyed her wits?

She laughed again, and he stood to leave. She held out one frail hand, her fingers trembling. "Your grandfather bid me say the first two parts to anyone. I've cheated a bit to give you the last. But he has five years on you, Dixon."

"So he did find it?"

"If he did, he'd not stay here, child. He was the one with dust on his shoes, always wanting to be some other place. He'd spend the treasure in London or Edinburgh. Have you looked there?"

"No."

"You'll not find him at Balfurin." She closed her sunken eyes, then opened them a moment later. "Go and find him, child, and bring him back to Balfurin." She looked out the window again, staring at something he couldn't see. The past? "Bring him back to where he belongs."

Charlotte awoke and stared at the ceiling and for a moment, just a moment before recognition came to her, she experienced the most blissful feeling of peace and tranquility. The term was over for the winter. The girls had left for home to experience the social rounds of Edinburgh and London. There was money in the coffers, and it looked as if the enrollment for the next year would be even greater than this term. There was nothing she needed to do that was pressing or urgent and she felt absolutely wonderful, except for a few odd twinges here and there.

George.

Her eyes widened. George. She rolled over cautiously, expecting to see him sleeping there beside her. No, she had left his room the night before, seeking her own chamber. Otherwise, she might have turned to him.

Rolling over on her back, she blew out a breath, and frowned at the ceiling. She closed her eyes again, fisted her hands at her sides, and concentrated on something, anything, but last night.

She had been full of reckless abandon last night. Thoroughly hedonistic. Almost shockingly so.

Making a cocoon of her sheets and coverlet, she peered out of it like a frightened hedgehog.

How would she ever face him?

He was her husband. He had the right to be here in her bed. From the moment he'd returned to Balfurin he could have demanded that she submit to him, but instead he'd charmed her. He could have pushed his way into her chamber, but he'd kissed her so long and so ardently that she'd gone willingly into the Laird's Chamber.

She closed her eyes. Never mind George. Where had she gone to? Where had the cautious Charlotte, the anxious Charlotte, the determined woman disappeared? From the moment he'd returned, nothing had been quite the same.

The Edification Society was wrong: George didn't need any training at all. Heat traveled up her chest and bloomed on her cheeks.

No, she was not going to think about him. A lovely Rembrandt painting she'd once viewed came to mind, and she allowed herself to experience that memory, beginning to smile as she looked at the vision behind her closed eyes. All she had to do was train her mind on some pleasant, innocuous memory, and she could banish any embarrassing thought.

A few minutes later, Charlotte slipped from the bed and crossed the floor, turning the key in the lock. She looked down at herself, only then conscious that she was naked. She grabbed her wrapper and put it on before going to the window and opening the shutters. The view overlooked rolling hills, and in the daylight she caught a glimpse of the River Tam as it meandered closer to the old castle. She stood in the window, oblivious to the chill, staring up at the morning sky. The day would be a bright one, the blue sky clear and cloudless, but it might as well rain for all she'd enjoy it.

What in the name of all that was holy had she done?

Had she lost all her wits?

Her senses were reeling. Both excitement and fear started in the pit of her stomach and spread throughout her body. She'd never before felt like this, not even in the days after her marriage.

Five years had truly made a difference, but in him or in her?

She'd wanted to touch him, a need she'd never before experienced. Not even with Spencer. She'd wanted to take her hands and rub his strong, muscled arms. She'd linked her hands at the back of his neck and demanded that he kiss her.

Had he thought her brazen? She closed the shutters and leaned her forehead against them. How was she to face him? Was his ardor truly directed toward her? Or simply because there were no other women he wanted to bed at Balfurin? Either the maids were matronly, or they were too young to attract his attention.

The excitement she'd earlier felt dissipated suddenly to become a cold and clammy feeling. The greater question wasn't why he'd wanted to bed her, but why he'd returned at all. Or even more troubling: when would he leave?

"You look disturbed, master."

Dixon glanced at Matthew. He'd been so deep in thought that he hadn't noticed the other man's entrance.

He placed his traveling desk on the floor, having written the poem Nan had recited. His recall might not be as perfect as Charlotte's, but the poem was elementary, evidently designed to be easily remembered.

"No so much disturbed as determined," he said. "I'm no closer to learning where George has gone than I was a week ago." A great deal had transpired instead, however, with the result that his honor was in tatters. It hadn't been all that healthy when he'd returned to Scotland and he'd succeeded in complicating the issue.

"Perhaps you're not destined to know, master," Matthew said. "Perhaps your cousin wishes to remain missing."

"Are you still wishing to be away from here, Matthew?"

"Perhaps not with the swiftness I was before," Matthew said obliquely.

"A good thing," Dixon said, standing. "I need your help."

Matthew placed his arm across his body, and bowed low. Any other time, the gesture would have brought a smile to his face, but today, Matthew's obeisance annoyed him.

"I'm not a lord, Matthew. I'm not one of your obscure Oriental gods. I'm just a human being." Flawed and humbled by the magnificence of his stupidity. What the hell had he done, taking Charlotte to his bed?

Matthew straightened. "I know that, master."

"Then stop bowing to me."

"If you will it, master."

"And stop calling me that."

Matthew just inclined his head. "Are you displeased with me?"

"I'm displeased with myself."

"Because you took the Englishwoman to your bed."

He frowned at Matthew, finding some solace in directing his anger at someone other than himself. "How the hell do you know that?"

"I tend to you. I bring you water for washing. Your bed looks as if it was shared," he added, sending a look toward the offending piece of furniture. "I only made an assumption."

"I expect your usual tact in this matter," Dixon said.

Matthew nodded.

"She doesn't deserve to be shamed by this."

Matthew only smiled.

Dixon's conscience was vying with his libido for dominance. Unfortunately, the memory of Charlotte in his arms, soft, warm, and enticingly female, was easily overwhelming his honor.

Matthew inclined his head again. "You feel guilty."

He didn't answer. "I'm going to Edinburgh and then on to London."

"I will begin packing immediately."

"I want you to remain here."

Matthew, surprisingly, didn't look all that displeased. In fact, if Dixon didn't know better, there was a smile lurking behind Matthew's bland expression.

"You are going to find your cousin."

Dixon nodded.

"Will that make you feel less guilty, master?"

He didn't have an answer for that. Maybe it would. Or maybe it would only further complicate matters. All he knew was that he needed to leave Balfurin and quickly, before he was tempted to slip on George's skin and become his cousin.

And take his wife.

Charlotte heard a sound and stared at the hallway door.

"If it's his lordship, shall I tell him you're almost dressed?"

Charlotte shook her head, looked at Maisie in the mirror, and changed her mind.

"Yes, tell him."

When Maisie left to open the door, she called her back. "Never mind. I'll see him later, I'm certain."

Why should he know that she'd made Maisie do her hair twice now, and both times was displeased with the result? She'd changed her day dress three times, despairing of the contents of her wardrobe. Surely there was something suitable for a winter morning that wasn't in serviceable black or blue? She was in the mood for color, for bright reds and greens, for pale pink, sultry mauve, or something blue to match his eyes.

What a foolish woman she was being.

"Never mind," she said again. "Just help me finish. I've a hundred things to do today."

Maisie looked at her skeptically, but didn't say anything. The winter days were days of leisure, days they'd come to look on as a holiday. In truth, there was nothing more pressing ahead of her than reading a few volumes, and finishing the notes on the new history curriculum. And organizing the library, a project she'd anticipated for months now.

She heard the drone of conversation, the sound of male voices. George and Matthew? She stared at the door, certain that she hadn't heard correctly.

"Open the door, Maisie," she said.

The maid went to the door, and opened it slightly.

"If anyone wishes to know my whereabouts, tell them freely, Matthew. I have few secrets."

"Ah, but the one you do have makes up for the lack of others, master."

"Will you be all right here at Balfurin without me?"

"Most assuredly," Matthew said.

"Not afraid of any ghosts or goblins?"

"The danger I feel in this place, master, is to you. Not to me."

George laughed. "I can't imagine anything happening to me that hasn't already occurred, Matthew. Living in the Orient is not a sedate type of life."

"Still, it is your home, and as such, should be a safer place."

"Then you shall have to ensure it is," George said.

"How shall I accomplish that, master?"

"With magic, of course. Or tossing your sticks, or a hundred other things that would no doubt shock your Baptist foster parents."

"I am Baptist, it is true, master. But I never said that I believed solely in that credo and no others."

George laughed again, but this time she didn't hear what he said. She was too busy fastening her shoes.

She opened the door fully to find George—just as she thought—attired for a journey. "Where are you going? You're leaving, aren't you? Without a word? Again?"

She wasn't so much angry as she was disappointed. Despairing. Destroyed. No, perhaps she was angry as well. Furious. Enraged.

Her mother had often said that she shouldn't frown so much; it was very off putting. She couldn't help it now. She glanced behind her at the broadsword propped against the wall and contemplated finally using it. He thought her bloodthirsty? He hadn't seen anything. Wait until she coshed him over the head.

How dare he leave her!

"Forgive me, did I wake you?" he asked, his tone too smooth, his voice sounding light, unconcerned.

"You're leaving," she said, ignoring the fact that his gaze was on her face, and that his expression actually seemed to hold some regret.

She would not cry. How foolish. Of course she wouldn't cry. He'd left her before, he would again. She'd known that from the moment he'd appeared in the ballroom.

"I'm going to London. I have business there. And Edinburgh as well."

"Really?" She held on to the door and managed a smile. Did she sound disinterested enough? She was only his hostess, and that only grudgingly. It didn't matter that he'd loved her not once but twice in the small hours of the night. It didn't matter that she'd sobbed against his shoulder the second time, when he'd used his fingers and mouth with such abandon.

Surely some of what they'd done was outlawed, if not immoral? How odd that she hadn't cared. Well, it certainly didn't matter now, did it?

"I'll be back in a week. Perhaps two."

"Are you certain you're coming back?" There, the real question. The brute actually smiled. "Could you not transact your business by letter?"

"I'm afraid not. There are certain matters that demand my attention."

"You could send Matthew," she said, well aware that she was acting like an anxious schoolgirl afraid of separation from a parent.

"I'm afraid there are tasks only I can accomplish."

"Are you really coming back?" She stood tall, straightened her shoulders, and looked up at him fearlessly. Let him see that she wasn't afraid of his answer, that she could face anything. She had before, she could again. But he had never kissed her quite so softly, and enticed her to bed with a gentleness she hadn't expected of him. Nor had he ever before given her such pleasure.

What a doxy she was, to allow her body to hold sway over her mind.

"On my soul," he said, and reached out to take her hand. She relinquished her grip on the door with some reluctance, more than startled when he bent his head and placed a kiss on her knuckles. "You have no reason to trust me, Charlotte, but I ask it of you anyway. The reason is urgent or I would never leave you. But I promise I will return."

"If it snows, the roads will be impassable."

"I'll find a way," he said.

"The coach will become mired."

"We've already faced that dilemma as you recall."

"Then be careful," she said, finally drawing back her hand.

"You, as well. I am leaving Matthew here to be of assistance to you. He is a man of many talents."

He wasn't George, however, and fool that she was, she missed him already.

"Are you certain he isn't simply acting as a pledge of your honor? A guarantee that you'll return?"

"I have to come back. You have something very valuable of mine."

She drew back. "I have nothing of yours, George."

He smiled again. "It'll occur to you."

He bowed to her, and then turned and walked down the hall, Matthew accompanying him. For the longest time she stood there in the doorway watching him.

She had never before studied the way a man walked. Nor had she ever noted that George's demeanor seemed different from other men. He commanded the space he occupied. A woman's eyes naturally were drawn to him.

What did she have that was his?

A question that she was very much afraid was going to occupy a great deal of her time. Even more so was one she didn't dare ask—was he really coming back?

Chapter 16

A carriage was coming down the road. A carriage Charlotte didn't recognize, the first vehicle to navigate through the recent snows. Two weeks had passed since George had left. Two very long weeks during which she'd waited and watched, feeling both like a newly wedded wife, and an utter fool.

Charlotte flew down the stairs, wondering why George didn't simply open the door and come in, striding through Balfurin's foyer in that way of his, as if he owned every bit of the earth beneath his feet.

She hesitated at the bottom of the stairs, waiting for Jeffrey to answer the commanding knock. The old man was stiff and slow, giving her time to pat her hair into place, adjust the bodice of her dress, pull down her skirt, pull it up again to check her shoes, and wish, more than once, that she'd had time to change. She'd been polishing the pewter tankards, of all things, and no doubt the scent of vinegar and salt still clung to her.

Please hurry. Twice, she wanted to slip past Jeffrey and pull open the great iron-banded door herself. The elderly servant would have been insulted by her actions, if not hurt by them.

Hurry, he waits in the cold. You must let him in quickly.

She took a few steps toward the door, uncaring that she looked too eager. It was time for pretensions to be destroyed and a little honesty to stretch between them. Somehow in the last weeks, he'd entranced her, amused her, and charmed her. Somehow, he'd become someone she couldn't stop thinking about, someone who made her breath tight and her pulse beat wildly. She wanted to tell him her secrets, ask his advice, give him her own counsel, and sleep in his arms.

When had she begun to fall in love with her own husband?

Jeffrey finally moved back, welcoming him. Her mouth opened to greet him, her smile coming without volition. Her heart beat with a steady pounding rhythm and her palms grew damp. Even her toes seem to curl within her shoes.

But it wasn't George.

Spencer came forward, his hands outstretched, his smile wide and hearty.

"Charlotte!" he exclaimed, as if they'd not seen each other for months instead of the few weeks it had been. "You're looking lovely, as usual."

Her smile had dimmed upon seeing him, but she forced it firmly into place again, realizing she was being rude in her disappointment.

"Spencer," she said, clasping his outstretched hands. "How delightful to see you again as well. How was Edinburgh?"

"No other woman in Edinburgh can match your loveliness. Indeed, all of the females to whom I was introduced paled next to you."

When had he become so fulsome? And why was he reminding her that he was a bachelor in search of a wife? Why did he think she'd care? She was a wife in search of her husband.

A month ago, she probably would have blushed, no doubt even preened under his stare of approval. Today, however, she thought he was entirely too forward in his attentions. But then, he didn't know what had happened at Balfurin in his absence, did he?

She glanced past him to Jeffrey, who stood by the open door as if waiting to bid farewell to their visitor. There was no doubt of Jeffrey's loyalty. Jeffrey did not approve. But then, Jeffrey rarely approved of her anyway. With the opening of the school and the influx of English females, however, his disapproval had become even more apparent, until his face had stiffened into one large glower.

It is just as well that she'd learned to ignore him.

"If you would, Jeffrey," she said, "please signal for refreshments to be served in the green parlor."

He didn't answer her, didn't indicate by a nod of his head or a subservient bow that he had any intention of doing what she asked. She captured her sigh inwardly, and turned, leading the way to one of the public rooms that had been refurbished four years ago.

Spencer knew the room well, since she'd received

him here on numerous occasions. But he stopped at the threshold and looked around him appreciably, as if witnessing the furnishings for the first time. And, for the first time, she thought his glance was a bit too calculating, as if he were gauging the cost of the two facing sofas and the porcelain bric-a-brac arranged on the mantel. She almost wanted to quote him the price of the brass urn in the corner or the ornately carved table behind each sofa. Instead, she remained silent, motioning him to one of the adjoining chairs near the fire.

Perhaps it was because she'd waited so anxiously for George to return that the comparison between the two men was so striking. Spencer was tall, as was George. But his hair was blond whereas George's was black. Nor did he have George's striking blue eyes. Instead his were hazel, an almost indeterminate shade. How odd that she'd always thought them his best feature. His shoulders were broad, but not as wide as George's, and he was close to becoming portly since he did like his food. George was in much better shape, not to mention that his body was in perfect condition.

Absolutely perfect condition.

She felt the heat warm her face.

"My husband has returned," she said abruptly. The minute the words were out of her mouth, she couldn't help but wonder if she'd somehow planned to startle him with the information.

He looked shocked, but then he was also her solicitor, and such a reaction might well be a legal one.

Would he have to know that she and George—in Lady Eleanor's words—had conjugal relations?

"Do say something, Spencer."

He sat there staring at her with the same glass-eyed stare as a two-day-dead trout.

"How long has he been home?" he finally said, and the words sounded oddly strangled.

"Nearly a month ago now," she said calmly. "He arrived the night of the graduation ball. We missed you," she added pointedly.

"George is here?"

"The Earl of Marne," she said, reminding him ever so gently of her husband's title. He'd never been introduced to George, and consequently could not presume upon an acquaintance that did not exist. How odd, that up until this moment, she'd allowed him such liberties, perhaps even encouraged them. Indeed, she had never before considered that she might not like Spencer saying her husband's name in quite that insulting fashion.

Everything had changed the moment George had come home.

"Where has he been all this time? What has he to say for himself?"

Her initial reaction was to tell Spencer that the question was not any of his concern. But then, upon reflection, she realized that she'd made it his business, since she'd retained him on her divorce.

How on earth was she to settle that?

Over the years, Spencer had become her confidante, her friend. How was he to know that, well . . . everything had changed?

"The Orient. He has a great liking for all things foreign. I find that strange," she said, looking down at her hands. "I don't recall him being so curious about travel. But then, I didn't know him well."

"I confess to being confused, Charlotte," he said. "What explanation has he given for being gone? And for returning now? Has he heard of your success?" He glanced around the room as if to encompass the entire school. "Is he here for money? Has he spent your dowry and is now hoping for more?"

The questions were intrusive, almost rude, and once again she had the inclination to silence him. A word would have done it, but she'd didn't speak it, feeling curiously as if she were two people at the same time. The woman she'd been a month ago would have commiserated with Spencer, would have provided all manner of facts and details of George's return. But the woman she was now, the woman who was falling in love with a stranger, was confused and uncertain. She wanted to hold everything about George safe in her heart, to keep private for only herself. She didn't want to examine her feelings in the light of day, and she didn't want to discuss her husband with this man. If she had questions, they would be asked of George.

"He wants nothing of me," she said, feeling curiously empty as she said the words. The truth could be uncomfortable, slicing through her. Perhaps George didn't even want her as a wife, else why would he have left the moment he'd bedded her?

Was love a confusing emotion? Did it muddle the mind and lay claim entirely to the senses? She'd always heard that being in love was supposed to be a pleasant emotion. Was she supposed to *enjoy* fluctuating between euphoria and despair?

"He's offered to give me money for the school," she said. "I understand he's quite wealthy now."

Spencer didn't say anything, but she could tell just by looking at him that he doubted her words. Or George. A month ago, she might have agreed. But in the last month, she'd fallen under the spell of an increasingly fascinating man.

The door abruptly opened and Jeffrey entered, nearly staggering under the weight of a tray piled high with dishes and cups and an ancient tea service.

Since Jeffrey was not given to subtlety, she frowned at him to indicate that she'd received his message only too well. He'd treat Spencer like a king but not because he valued the man. Nor would he do so for her sake. Balfurin, however, had a reputation for hospitality, however poor their circumstances, and he would maintain that reputation even if it meant swallowing his pride.

"The Scots are a very difficult race," she said, deliberately overlooking the fact that Spencer was a Scot. "They're a very stubborn people. Abnormally so, I think. Given to their own opinion, even to the exclusion of common sense."

"Do you think so?" Spencer asked, reaching for one of the cups. Instead of waiting for her to pour, Jeffrey grabbed the teapot, sloshing the liquid in equal measure in the cup and saucer. Then he delivered the cup to her, as if challenging her in her hostess duties.

She frowned at him again but once more he blithely ignored her.

Perhaps now was not the correct time to continue her eternal battle with Jeffrey. She decided to ignore him, an easier task to think than to do. In the next five minutes he dropped a biscuit on her skirt and managed to sprinkle her with tea. But in the end, Spencer was served, and Jeffrey finally took himself off, no doubt to sulk in the kitchen.

"Is he the reason for your dislike of my nationality?" Spencer said when the door was finally closed—too hard—behind him.

"I don't dislike the Scots as a group," Charlotte said. "Most of the people in Scotland have been beyond polite to me. They welcomed me when I had nowhere else to go. But any country has its malcontents and its irritating individuals." She, unfortunately, had been blessed with two of them—Old Nan and Jeffrey.

"Is George here to stay?"

How curious that certain questions could actually sting, as if the words had little barbs that twisted themselves into her flesh.

"I suspect that George will do whatever George wishes," she said, answering him with the truth.

"What will you do, Charlotte? Welcome him as your husband?"

"Do I have any other choice?"

"I'm certain there must be mitigating factors. Do you want me to pursue the subject?"

What a very difficult question.

She brushed at her skirt, wondering if she'd be able to clean the stain. Thanks to Jeffrey, she may have to discard this garment entirely.

"He should be dismissed," Spencer said. "Pensioned off."

"Thanks to the old earl's will, he can live here until his death." Charlotte sighed. "And bedevil me until that day comes."

He reached out and covered one of her hands with his. "Do you want me to find a way to rid you of George, Charlotte? It might still be possible to divorce him."

How could she answer that question? She'd spent hours in contemplation of it. Last night, in the darkness of her room, illuminated only by the brief shadows of a lover's moon, she'd asked herself what she wanted. George. What did she truly wish to do? Have a real marriage. The two answers frightened her because they relied not on what she was capable of doing, not on her strengths but on the whims of a man she didn't know well.

She'd never yearned for love, never wished for it like her younger sisters. She'd never giggled over a casual glance or a bestowed flower. True, she'd sighed over sonnets, and shed a tear for the anguish and tragedy of star-crossed lovers, but she had never actually believed that it might be possible to feel the same way.

But love and desire had somehow come into her life and she didn't quite know how to act.

"I don't know," she said finally, hearing the hope in her own voice as well as the despair. Did Spencer note it as well? "I don't know what I'm going to do."

"You would be better off sending him away."

"How do I do that, Spencer? He's the Earl of Marne, Balfurin's laird. I can't simply banish him as if he were one of the footmen." She sent him a chiding look, but he only stared at her steadily as if attempting to convince her to banish George with the strength of his will.

"Then encourage him to leave, Charlotte. Do not give him a reason to stay."

His look was so intent that it wasn't difficult to interpret his meaning. Did he know? Did he guess that she and George had shared a bed?

"He's my husband, Spencer." There, a simple enough thought. A declaration.

She forced herself to match his stare with one of her own. Looking into his eyes was not particularly easy, and she couldn't tell if it was anger she saw there or only disappointment.

He stood, placing the cup and saucer on the tray between them so hard that the china clanked against the silver.

"I think you'll regret your kindness toward George," he said. "He hurt you once, he'll do so again."

"Forewarned," she said, standing, "is forearmed. I can't forget what he did, Spencer. But is it fair to think a man can't change?"

He looked as if he would like to say something else. Instead, he turned and left the room, leaving the door ajar. A moment later, Jeffrey appeared in the doorway.

"Is he gone, then?"

"Yes, Jeffrey, he's gone."

"Is it going to be like this all day? I thought what with the hooligans gone I'd have a chance to rest."

With some difficulty, Charlotte kept her comments to herself and forced a smile to her face. "I doubt we'll have any more visitors, Jeffrey. If nothing else, the snows will keep them away."

"Good," he said, and shuffled away.

Thank Providence that George hadn't returned this morning. Otherwise, instead of simply dealing with a surly servant, she'd have had a confrontation on her hands. She'd have been forced to explain to each man who the other was, a task from which she was blessedly saved.

Chapter 17

Londonwas an exceedingly lonely place, a discovery Dixon made with some degree of surprise. Perhaps it was because his mind was filled with images of Charlotte. He couldn't quite forget that look on her face when she thought he was leaving her. Again. Then, too, Matthew was not cowering in the corner of the carriage, alternately shooting him looks of aggravation or being wide-eyed at the scenes outside the window.

Armed with a list he'd compiled of George's friends—those he'd known before leaving for the Far East a decade ago—he began his search for his cousin.

"Haven't seen the chap," the Earl of Dorset said when Dixon found him in his favorite gaming hell. The man hadn't aged well in the last ten years, a discovery that made him wonder what George would look like now. Would he, too, have lines of dissipation on his face? Would his nose be florid and his eyes bloodshot? "Tell him to call on me when you find him. Forget the money he owes me."

The earl was the last person Dixon met to be as sanguine about George's debts. In order to obtain any information, Dixon ended up paying a princely sum to settle what his cousin owed.

George had taken himself off to London not long after his father died, amassing a surprising number of hangers-on. Unfortunately, none of them had seen him in the last few years. The closest Dixon came to finding his cousin was the drunken ramblings of the brother of a duke.

"Saw him not too long ago. A year? Two? Damned hard when they all roll together. Wouldn't speak to me, of course. Gone up in the world. Or I've gone down, either one." He'd finished a full glass of wine during the course of that speech, leaving Dixon to wonder if he'd actually seen George at all or if it had only been an effect of the alcohol.

At the Port of London, Dixon met with the Harbor Master, leaving his name and the promise of a reward for anyone who could provide him with a copy of a manifest listing George MacKinnon as a passenger on any vessel in the last five years. Because his cousin had occasionally spoken of Australia and America, although not in flattering terms, there was a chance George had emigrated to those countries. However, it was possible that he'd also traveled to the Continent, so Dixon was careful to include the packets and channel-crossing ships in his reward.

By the end of the first week, he'd lost hope of finding

George in London, and traveled north to Edinburgh. There, he'd met with his solicitor, and finished the business he wished to transact with his firm. Following the meeting, and on the recommendation of his solicitor, he found a prosperous inn, asking for the best room.

The Edinburgh day was a gray one, filled with sleet, and promising more ice before nightfall.

Dixon took his valise from the innkeeper and thanked him.

"The room looks fine," he said, surveying it quickly. It wasn't Balfurin, but it would have to do. At another time, he'd be impressed with the pristine bed and the massive furniture. Another time, perhaps, he'd notice the steam from the hot water and congratulate the inn keeper on his timing.

"Would you like to have a tray, sir? A selection of meats and cheeses?"

He nodded in agreement, and the innkeeper left, closing the door behind him before he began shouting orders.

Dixon threw the valise on the bed and joined it, sitting on the edge and pulling off his boots. He'd learned in the last few years that comfort was something to be sought without apologies. He'd spent winters in soaking rains and summers sweating in tropical forests. He'd survived oriental fevers, being attacked by pirates, and a snakebite or two. Each day of health was to be relished as was a warm, dry bed, and a good meal.

Pleasant as it was, though, something was missing in this room and he knew exactly what it was: the scent of roses and Charlotte.

Slowly, he stripped off his travel-stained clothes,

folding them and placing them on the chair. As he stood and washed, he noted his imperfections. The scar on his left side from a bullet wound. In Penang, one of his men had been aiming for a snake. He'd killed it, but in the process had also struck Dixon. Then there was the time he'd been climbing down a cliff and lost his footing. He'd forever carry the imprint of the rope on his stomach. A mishap as a child had left a scar on his left thigh. He and George had climbed out of their room on some adventure. Curious, he couldn't remember exactly what they'd done, but he recalled only too well the tree he'd used to climb down from their third-floor room. A branch had gouged into his leg, and because he'd gone against his uncle's wishes, he'd not mentioned the injury or even sought treatment for it even after it had become swollen and inflamed. Consequently, he now had a scar to remind himself of his youthful nature.

Too bad other scars weren't so obvious. Perhaps he would be a better man if they were visible.

What color was a dirty soul? Gray? Or was the soul such a delicate organ that it was tinted black for any kind of sin? And a troubled heart? What kind of scar did it reveal?

He dressed in a clean shirt and trousers, and then sat on the edge of the bed.

He'd grown accustomed to silence, to the tranquility of his garden at the end of day, to isolation when he chose it. Sandalwood and incense were his chosen scents, along with the smell of tropical flowers. Penang could be frenetic with activity, but it also offered him peace, unlike Edinburgh. Outside his window he could hear the rolling wheels of carriages, carts, and coaches as well as the neighing of the horses and the clopping of their hooves.

True, his history was in Scotland, but he felt invisible here. Since he'd come home only Nan had recognized him. In Penang he'd built a house so large that it occupied the top of a mountain. In Scotland, there was nothing that belonged to him, only those things he'd borrowed.

Even Charlotte.

One good thing about being in Edinburgh was that some distance separated them. At least here he couldn't invite her to his bed, couldn't say something asinine that would only serve to humiliate him in the morning. He was prevented from demonstrating to her the exact degree of his need and his fascination, and perhaps even deeper emotions.

Adultery. An ugly word for the pleasure they'd shared. But he couldn't take her to his bed again. Doing so might well prove to be disastrous. Twice, he'd wanted to confess his identity to her, so she'd know whose name she'd murmured softly in her pleasure.

What kind of shame would he bring her with the truth? She would never forgive him. At the moment he wasn't sure he'd be able to forgive himself.

Even now he could recall how she looked when he'd left her, her fingers stilled at the base of her throat, and her stricken look as she stared up at him.

She was intelligent and yet protective about that fact, witty and uncertain of it, and beautiful but unaware. She had the ability to strip even the most rudimentary thought from his mind, and when Dixon touched her, he trembled.

For that reason alone he wanted to find George. He'd have her choose. He'd ask her to look at each of them and take a step toward the man she wanted. Honor might keep her rooted to the spot, but he'd know. Somehow, he'd know when she chose him. Then, he'd do something rash and unwise, something that would earn him clucks of Matthew's tongue. He'd steal her away to Penang and love her for eternity.

Or perhaps she'd simply walk away from him, knowing the enormity of his sins.

He should say to hell with George, and leave Scotland. Matthew would be pleased. And, in a month or two, he would no doubt forget about Charlotte MacKinnon.

He shook his head at his own thoughts. He might be able to lie to someone else, but he'd never been able to lie to himself. He wouldn't be able to forget her. Ever. The thought of her, the memory of making love to her would rank among the most important memories of his life.

He stood, walked to the window that overlooked the street, and stared outside. The freezing rain seemed an apt accompaniment to his mood.

Why had he returned to Scotland?

"I want to go home, Dixon." A plaintive voice from his memory. "Papa said that you'd take me home."

"In a few months, Annabelle. It's not convenient to take the time for a voyage to Scotland now."

"You never say anything's convenient, Dixon. It's always tomorrow or the next day or next week or next month."

What had he said in response? Something calming, no doubt. Or he had simply left the room, nearly desperate to quit his wife's company.

His character was too flawed for comfort.

He removed the miniature from his valise, and set it on the bureau. Matthew had slipped the portrait of his wife into his case when he wasn't looking, thinking that it might be soothing on the long voyage to Scotland. The other man hadn't known that he didn't need a picture of Annabelle. She existed, full-bodied and never silent, in his mind.

For a few moments, he studied her face, set in an oval frame dotted with diamonds. A wedding present from his bride. She was a lovely woman, someone who deserved to find happiness in her life, despite the fact that she was occasionally annoying. Her character might have changed with the years; she might have become less strident, more patient. Now she would never have the chance.

He'd been desperate to obtain her father's influence, hungry for the beneficial terms of the new trading agreement. He'd acquired all he'd wanted, as much income as he'd desired. Everything he'd planned for, he'd obtained, along with a few other, less pleasant encumbrances: a troubled conscience, and a guilty spirit.

He'd wanted money and power and over the years, he'd acquired both. His word was respected in Penang; his name had a certain cache.

Was that why he'd come back to Scotland? To become simply Dixon again, without the notoriety, the prestige? To walk through the streets of Edinburgh without people bowing to him? Without people currying his favor?

Or had he simply come back to Scotland to hide?

George had been gone exactly seventeen days, and in all that time, Charlotte had caught up on the paperwork she needed to do. She'd paid all her bills, made a list of courses she'd like taught in the near term, wrote recommendations for the teachers who wouldn't return to Balfurin, looked over the qualifications of the applicants for the posts, and generally satisfied herself that she'd nothing left to do.

Then why was she feeling as if something was left undone?

She'd been in the library for four hours without interruption. Maisie hadn't even bothered to peer inside the room to see if she wanted anything. Of course, Maisie was being very coy lately. She would much rather see if Matthew required her assistance than her employer.

George's servant had taken to going to the top of the hill and looking down the road to Edinburgh as if he were a lost cur seeking its master. Maisie, more often than not, joined him, the two of them standing there, Matthew's embroidered robe and Maisie's gray wool cloak blowing in the cold wind. A strange pair, one that looked remarkably as if they belonged together.

She would not allow Maisie to be hurt by an odd Oriental man. Matthew Mark Luke and John. What sort of name was that? When she'd asked the question of Matthew a few days ago, he had only bowed to her, folding his arms within the voluminous sleeves of his robes.

"I had no say in my naming, your ladyship. I was but a child," he said. His face was devoid of expression, as if it had been made of clay and a celestial sculptor had smoothed any emotion from it.

"Did you never think of changing it?"

"To what purpose, your ladyship? A man is who he is."

Now she pulled on the bell rope summoning one of the footmen. When he arrived, she gave him instructions. A few minutes later, Matthew appeared in the doorway.

"You wished to see me, your ladyship?"

Curiosity had taken hold of her—or had never truly left—ever since the moment George had appeared in the ballroom door.

"I would ask the question of my husband, Matthew, but he isn't here. Does George have a concubine in Penang?"

Matthew stared at her, the expression in his eyes unreadable. "I am not a source of information on your husband, your ladyship."

She returned his look, annoyed. "Why did he choose Penang for his destination? Why the Far East? It seems a very long way to travel."

"I do not know the workings of his lordship's mind," he said.

"Would you tell me if you did know?" She studied him. "Are you truly that loyal?" she asked him. "Do you ever answer a question about George?"

"I will answer anything it is of my ability to answer, your ladyship, but I must warn you, I do not know a very great deal about George."

"Haven't you been with him some length of time?"

Matthew bowed, a habit that was growing exceedingly irritating. "Your ladyship, I have been with my master for some time."

She frowned at him. "I don't understand your way of talking, sometimes. Are you trying to be deliberately enigmatic?"

"Indeed, I am not, mistress. I am trying to answer your questions. If I do not speak in the clearest of English, it is my lack, not your understanding."

"Your English is perfect, Matthew, which you know quite well. If everyone at Balfurin spoke as perfectly as you I would be quite pleased."

Matthew allowed himself to smile, a sign that their conversation was over. She knew she wasn't going to get any more information about George from his servant. He bowed once more before leaving her.

"Isn't he the most fascinating man?" Maisie said, coming into the room just at that moment. Charlotte wasn't fooled; she knew her maid had been waiting for the end of the conversation.

"You needn't feel as if you have to protect Matthew from me," Charlotte said. "I am not going to breathe fire on him like a dragon. I can't dismiss him, and I'm not about to put him in irons, if that's what you're afraid of. Matthew is as safe with me as you are."

"Oh, I know that, your ladyship, but he doesn't. I do think he's afraid of you."

She glanced at Maisie. "What has he said about me?"

"Nothing. Absolutely nothing. But then, Matthew doesn't say a very great deal about anything. He has just now begun to tell me about his homeland."

"Does he never speak of George?"

"Sometimes," Maisie said. "I think Matthew is worried about him, but I don't know why."

"Is he ill?" Was that the reason he'd suddenly come home? Dear God, had he come home to put his affairs in order? Had he needed her forgiveness before dying? Charlotte felt so strange that she abruptly sat in one of the chairs before the fire. No, surely a man as vigorous looking, and as virile as George could not be dying.

"I don't know, your ladyship. Shouldn't you ask the earl?"

Charlotte nodded, lifting her hand in a gesture of dismissal. She'd lost her maid to George's servant, and her peace of mind to George.

Seventeen days. What had George found to do for seventeen days?

Maisie sat beside Matthew at meals, not to shield him from the other servants, but because she felt protected by him. He never made a comment about her foot. Nor did he ever say anything about her occasional ungainly stride. He never raised his voice and he always had fastidious manners as if he were a lord or something. Even if he didn't like something Cook had prepared, he always made a point of thanking her for her effort.

Sometimes, especially when they were out walking together in the evening, he would put out his hand and she would put hers on top.

"What a lord and lady we are," she said once, and he smiled.

"Does it concern you, Maisie, that you were not born to be a lady?"

She'd never considered it before. She was simply

who she was. "I can't say so," she told him. "I really don't think I'd like to be a lady. Her ladyship doesn't look very happy, for all her title is Countess."

He nodded and they didn't discuss it further.

Now she did something terribly shocking. She put her hand on his leg under the table. He glanced over at her, so abruptly that she was startled almost into moving her hand. But she kept it where it was atop the silken material of his robe.

The silk felt wondrously smooth to her palm. What must it feel like to wear such a garment?

He made a sound with his lips, as if he clicked his tongue against them. When their table mates were making the most noise, he leaned over and whispered to her. "What are you doing, Maisie?"

"I am being forward," she said, staring down at her food. In truth, she wasn't very hungry, but she had learned to always accept a meal when it was presented. There was no telling when another might come along.

"To what purpose are you being forward?"

She looked at him out of the corner of her eye.

There was a small smile playing around his mouth, and for a horrified moment she wondered if he was mocking her. But the expression in his eyes was filled with warmth.

She squeezed her hand over his knee.

"Because I very much wanted to touch you. You were too far away, and I didn't want to wait until after dinner."

He abruptly stood, startling her.

"Come." That was all he said, just that one word command. He didn't ask if she wanted to be with

him. Nor did he try to convince her. Simply that one
word as if he knew she'd obey.

She nearly tripped over her own feet in her haste to
follow him outside.

There was no moon tonight, and she was grateful
for the darkness. She wanted to call out to him to not
walk so quickly, because there was no chance she
could keep up. But he stopped at the other side of the
barn, turning to face her, such a looming dark shadow
that she halted, cautious of him as she'd never been.

She'd not had a chance to grab her cloak. Patches of
snow were still left on the ground and the wind was
cold. She cupped her arms in her hands and stared up
at him.

He was angry. She'd never seen Matthew angry.
Normally, his temperament was even, his words calm.

"Have you no wisdom? Do you not know those
things all women do?"

"I knew what I did was wrong," she confessed. "I
shouldn't have done it, but I very much wanted to."

He didn't say anything for the longest time.

"I really wanted you to kiss me, but I couldn't wait
until we went outside. It might have snowed, or we
couldn't take our walk."

"You wanted me to kiss you?" he asked.

"What's a girl to do, but be forward? What with
you being all proper all the time?"

"Maisie," he began, but now she was the angry
one.

"I've a right to touch you, Matthew. I do. You're
walking out with me, and it means something in Scotland even if it means nothing in the Orient."

"What does it mean?" he asked cautiously.

She put her hands on her hips and glared at him. "That you think I'm special. That you want to talk to me where prying ears can't overhear. That you want to spend time with me, and tell me things you don't tell anyone else. And if you don't like that, well you can just be angry all over again."

When he didn't speak, she took a few steps toward him. "I'm not afraid of you, Matthew. You can be just as angry as you like."

"There is no reason to be afraid of me. I do not hurt the weak and the defenseless."

"Don't call me weak," she said. "I may be smaller than you. But I'm not weak."

"You are filled with pride. Such a thing can be good but it can also be bad. Pride gives you a wrong view of the world, Maisie. It makes you think that you can do things that you cannot do. It makes you brave in the face of danger. Sometimes a person *is* weak, and it is better to admit such a thing."

"I'm weak near you," she said.

"You must not say such things."

"I only touched you," she said, uncomfortable with his tone. There was something in his voice that hinted of sadness.

"You touch me the way a woman does when she wants a man to respond. You want me to put my mouth on you, to take you to my bed."

"All that?" She smiled up at him.

"All that," he said somberly.

"And if I do?" She wished there was more light. She didn't want to see kindness or pity in his expression. Let his eyes reveal that warmth she'd seen at the dining table.

"That would not be wise."

"No," she agreed. "It probably isn't wise. But must we be sensible all the time, dearest Matthew?" She took another step and when she was close enough, flattened her hand against his chest.

"Kiss me, Matthew. Please."

He took one step back, but that was all. She smiled and approached him once more and this time he didn't move.

"Does a Malay man kiss differently from a Scot?"

"I do not know how a Scotsman kisses."

She reached up and placed her hands on his shoulders, gently drawing him down toward her. "I shall tell you if it's any different."

"Have you kissed a great many men?"

"Only one man has ever kissed me before, and he was my brother's friend. He married last year and I couldn't help but think of that kiss when I watched him taking his vows."

"And if it is different?"

"Then I shall probably like it more," she said. "I didn't like his kisses all that much."

He placed his hand on her cheek, the action stilling her.

"And if you don't like it?"

"How can you say that, Matthew? It's better already." She smiled and stood on tiptoe. "Because it's you."

Then, before he could prevent it, she kissed him full on the mouth.

"There," she said when she pulled back. "I've been thinking of doing that for quite a few days now."

"You have?" he asked.

"Oh yes, and see, it's not something I'll regret in the future. I'll never have to simply wish that I'd kissed Matthew, because I did."

"No woman in my country would have dared to kiss me first."

"What would the women in your country do?" she asked.

"They would wait until I kissed them."

"Pity them," Maisie said. "You might never be brave enough."

He reached over and, before she had a chance to react, framed her face with his hands and gently lowered his lips to hers. When the kiss was done a moment or so later, he pulled back. Her lids fluttered open and her eyes grew wide.

"It is not simply good enough to do a task, Maisie," he said tenderly. "One must do a task well."

She sighed in response, wrapped her arms around his neck, and whispered, "You're going to kiss me again, aren't you? Just to show me how it's done?"

Matthew smiled, and extended his arm. From his sleeve came a burst of light, a small bluish glare that had her smiling in delight. Then he leaned down and kissed her again, and she forgot all about one kind of magic and experienced another.

Chapter 18

During the school term, Charlotte insisted that all her students attend chapel every morning in addition to Sunday service. Once a month, a minister came from Inverness to preach a rousing sermon. On the other three Sundays, she and the teachers took turns reading a lesson. They sang hymns, and read from the Book of Common Prayer. Altogether, it was a very short, but very worshipful ceremony.

Since all of the teachers and students had left the school, Charlotte had thought of simply avoiding Sunday service. But this morning, she'd felt the need to be closer to God.

Ever since coming to Balfurin, she and God had engaged in a *quid pro quo* arrangement. Charlotte showed Him some measure of prayerful piety and He in turn let her have her way in a few things.

However, she'd learned to make her requests to the

Almighty in such a way that she didn't neglect any of the necessary elements. If she were praying for a new cook, for example, someone with the ability to create appetizing meals in the abundance required to feed a school of this size, she didn't neglect the fact that the woman be healthy or that she have some sense of thriftiness when it came to purchasing supplies.

God had a way of being literal, of giving her exactly what she asked for and nothing more.

What would be the proper prayer for George? As the music swelled around her, and the enthusiastic voices of the staff rose to match the sounds of the organ, Charlotte found herself composing exactly the right petition.

What did she need to incorporate into her prayer to ensure that the Almighty handled George in just the right way? She didn't want anything bad to happen to him.

Dear God. There, a good start. She had a problem addressing God as Father. It reminded her too much of Nigel Haversham. He would have been pleased to know that as a child she'd thought Nigel was God. No, Dear God was best.

Please have George . . . what? She hesitated.

George had effectively trapped her, and the knowledge only added to her annoyance. She couldn't divorce him for desertion since he'd returned, and she couldn't divorce him, period, unless they were separated. George needed to move out of Balfurin, perhaps live in Edinburgh for a period of years. Then, she could go through the cumbersome steps in the divorce proceedings. She doubted, however, that she could convince him to do so since he was so enamored of the

Orient. But if he returned to Penang, the Scottish courts would decree that he was out of their jurisdiction, and she'd be right where she'd been for the last five years.

Did the Almighty look askance on a woman who prayed for a divorce in the middle of a church service? She didn't think it was quite fair if God punished her for doing so since she was somewhat trapped by circumstance, but just in case God was not feeling charitable, she modified her prayer somewhat.

Dear God, please let George leave Balfurin with all possible speed.

Dear God, please let me be able to frame questions to Matthew in a way that he will answer. There, a more acceptable prayer, certainly. Surely God wouldn't be annoyed at her for asking that.

Now, for the important part of the prayer.

Dear God, please do not let George be attractive to me in any way. Please do not let me wish him to my bed. Please do not let me evince any curiosity whatsoever in the reason he's been gone for twenty days. Twenty, God. What on earth can he find to do that would take him twenty days?

Dear God, give me some sense. Help me not to fall in love with my own husband. She hesitated. Surely that prayer wasn't entirely wise. *Dear God, I'm so very confused. I don't know what to do or what to pray for. Please, help me. Please, show me what is best. Send me a sign, please God. A little assistance would not be amiss.*

She listened to the droning of the voices and sang a verse or two. Sometimes she thought she had a lovely voice, but that's when she sang alone in front of the fire in her tub. But what she lacked in skill she made up for in gusto. Surely God would approve of her enthusiasm.

Matthew glanced at her once and then away. How odd that he knew the service so well. She would have expected him to be Buddhist, or some other esoteric religion, but he seemed very much at home with the Presbyterian service.

Dear God, please let George return soon. We must solve this difficulty between us. I am very much afraid that he's going to abandon me, and I don't wish to be cast aside like an old pair of boots. I want to feel love in my life, and while I appreciate the relationship of mankind to you, and while I choose a close relationship to you, God, is it wrong to pray for love with a . . . man?

God was regrettably silent, and so was the congregation, the hymn finally over. Charlotte moved to the front and recited today's verse.

She couldn't imagine what had been on her mind when she'd chosen it. It was an exceedingly dull selection, having to do with the fruits of one's labors.

She looked out at the congregation, numbering no more than fifteen people, servants she'd employed from the early days at Balfurin. Each one of them looked up expectantly, as if she were a minister herself, as if she knew exactly the right words that would give them comfort and ease their days.

She'd always been a bookish child, and a shy young woman, so odd in appearance that she might have been overlooked in the marriage market except for her fortune. It was only in the last few years that she'd seemed to change, to grow into her features. Her hair had darkened in color a little, had become less blindingly red and more auburn. Her nose hadn't seemed quite so long. Her chin was not quite so pointed anymore.

But as her appearance had become more acceptable, her role had grown. She had piled more and more responsibility on herself until every moment of her day was planned. There were such time constraints on her that sometimes she knew she would not get everything done and consequently spent the waking hours worrying about those incomplete tasks, and her sleeping hours dreaming about everything she needed to do.

Why? So that she would have no free time at all in which to examine her life? Or like now, staring out at a sea of murmuring people, realize that the life she had created for herself was one that should have been lived by a woman thirty years older.

Where had her youth gone? When had her joy disappeared? Was she not to have any fun at all in life?

To her horror, she realized she'd become more straitlaced than her mother and more governing then her father. She'd become her parents. Where had the girl gone who'd defied them both? Where was the Charlotte who had decreed that she would remain at Balfurin in defiance of everything?

That young woman still lived somewhere inside her, a little afraid of what she'd become. Staid, determined, wrapped in propriety as tightly as a bandage. Priggish.

She caught herself and began to read the passage aloud again. The congregation would have to make of it what they would, extract the meaning for themselves. She was not in the mood to be profound. She didn't want to be their religious leader. Right now she didn't want to be the matriarch of Balfurin, its chatelaine. She didn't want to be the headmistress of the Caledonia School for the Advancement of Females. She only wanted to be Charlotte, a little wild, and a little wicked.

Someone who would shock people with her daring. Someone whose hunger for life would overwhelm rational thought.

Just then the chapel door flew open, and the wind blew snow along the aisle and up to the podium as if it were being batted there by a thousand angel wings.

"My dear, we are sorry to interrupt your service," Lady Eleanor said from the doorway. She began to remove her coat. "It was a long and grueling journey from Inverness. The snow did not stop in all this time."

Lady Eleanor and her entourage had arrived. Angels—or devils—here to coax her to wickedness.

She really should have made her prayers a little more explicit. God truly had a sense of humor.

"I think it's quite auspicious that the snow stopped just before our arrival, my dear," Lady Eleanor said while reaching for a pastry. She blew on it as if it were too hot to consume, but perhaps she was just ridding the offending cake of any extraneous crumbs. The napkin she held in her right hand was spotless. So were the gloves neatly folded together and resting on the left chair arm. She sat properly, her knees pressed together and, no doubt her ankles together, the skirt revealing only the tips of her highly polished shoes. She was the epitome of all things polite, graceful, and refined, which was probably why Charlotte was having such difficulty with the conversation.

"We would have been here earlier, but dear Amanda has a tendre for her brother-in-law. We had to settle that before we traveled here to assist you."

"Assist me?" Charlotte asked.

"Have you given any thought to our discussion, my dear?"

"I sent you a letter, Lady Eleanor. You should have received it more than a week ago."

The older woman waved her hand in the air. "I received it, my dear, and proceeded to pay it no attention. We've all felt a little reluctance to change, to broaden our outlook. It's what society hopes for, after all. Whatever would the men in charge do if we women put aside our reticence and talked to each other?"

Charlotte looked helplessly around the room. Each of the seven women who'd accompanied Lady Eleanor to Balfurin were sitting in the Green Parlor partaking of Cook's new batch of biscuits and cakes. Thank heavens the woman had not gotten out of the habit of cooking for a large number of people in the past month.

"Dear Eleanor was so helpful to me," a woman said. Charlotte glanced in her direction. She knew four of the women, but the others had been introduced to her in the walk from the chapel to the parlor. Now she couldn't recall the woman's name. Barbara? Beatrice? It had started with a *B*, she was certain of that, because of the woman's bonnet. There was a plethora of flowers attached to it, in such profusion that Charlotte had immediately thought of bees.

How odd that her memory failed her just at this moment.

"I think dear Eleanor has been helpful to each of us, in our time. It's a shame that such ignorance has been left to fester for so many generations."

Another stranger, one with a very narrow face and a pair of thick spectacles tied to a bilious green ribbon resting on her chest. Margaret. There, she'd remembered.

"I think it best if we began our meeting, dear," Lady Eleanor said. "Unless you wish to delay it until this evening? I'm certain we can find something or someone to help us pass the time."

"Now is fine," Charlotte said quickly, wondering if her footmen would ever know how much she'd sacrificed to protect them from The Edification Society.

One of the women stood up and went to the parlor door, a thickly banded oak door that was part of the original castle. This room had been intact when she'd first occupied Balfurin, but she'd opened up the room by having three more windows created in the thick walls, and having the fireplace and chimney expanded. The result was a space that could accommodate a group of people in relative comfort in any season.

"Does it lock?" the woman asked.

Charlotte shook her head. "No one will interrupt us."

The other woman nevertheless took up a position in front of the door as if to physically block anyone from entering.

Charlotte's palms were growing damp. Not a good sign.

Lady Eleanor reached into her commodious valise

and came up with a sheaf of papers. She gave them to a woman sitting to her left.

"Take two and pass them down, please, Hortensia," she said.

Since she was sitting on Lady Eleanor's right, Charlotte was last to get the information handed out. She took one look at the graphic drawing and clasped the paper to her chest. She was the only one whose initial reaction was horror. The other women were either sighing or smiling, and more than one was commenting upon the size of the subject in question.

She closed her eyes and pretended she was not here. She was not in the parlor at Balfurin. She was in her schoolroom, and the titters of laughter were from a group of mischievous girls in the back of the class, not eight matronly women.

"A friend of mine, a physician, provided me with this drawing, anatomical in nature, I grant you, but we must begin with science in order to understand the amatory arts."

Charlotte opened her eyes and stared at Eleanor.

She held the sheet up by the corner. "It's a drawing of a man's . . . parts."

"Why of course it is, my dear. The penis is quite attractive, but in its flaccid state it leaves a great deal to be desired. It looks like a pig's bladder that's been drained. But in glorious tumescence, why, that is something to behold!" She stared down at the drawing. "I do wish he could have drawn it erect," she said sadly.

Eleanor looked at the assembled group. "One day, we shall simply have to encourage a young man to come before us, and show us how quickly a male can go from flaccid to erect. *Hominus erectus*. What a glorious state!"

"Not today," Charlotte said weakly.

"Oh no, my dear," Eleanor said, "we're not quite at that stage yet. There are many things we have to learn first." She leaned over to Charlotte and spoke in a low enough tone so that the woman across the circle could not hear her. "We're going a little in reverse, my dear," she said, "in order to bring you up to the rest of the group's understanding. We've all passed this particular stage, but it was so enjoyable that I'm sure none of the other women are having difficulty revisiting a subject already taught."

"That's very kind of you, Lady Eleanor, but it's not truly necessary."

"Nonsense, Charlotte. Now if you will release your death grip on that particular paper, you'll notice that there's another drawing to note. Again, a physician friend of mine assisted me in this matter."

If she'd thought the first drawing was shocking, Charlotte didn't know what to say about the second. It was a drawing, evidently, of a woman's nether regions, as if she had her legs spread wide open for anyone to see.

Her feet were sweating and her palms were cold. Even if she hadn't such a splendid memory, she'd never be able to forget either illustration as long as she lived. She'd be a very old woman, she was certain, lying on her deathbed, and these pictures would be there in her mind.

She closed her eyes, again, but it didn't help. Lady Eleanor was still talking and the group of women were still conversing, saying things that Charlotte truly didn't want to hear.

"Now, who would like to discuss the quickest way to get the male penis from flaccid to erect?"

Charlotte's eyes flew open.

Eleanor looked from one woman to the other. A very small woman with a very large bosom held up her hand tentatively.

"I have heard that placing warm hands on either side of the penis is conducive to an erectile state."

"Very good, Honoria. Anyone else?"

"I speak the most vile words to my Harold," a woman by the name of Susan said. "The more vile, the better."

Charlotte had to look away. For the last three years, she'd known Susan as the very strict mother of two daughters, both students at the school.

"He likes to pretend that I'm a woman of the docks. In fact, there are many occasions when I don't let him into my bed until he pays a fine for the privilege."

She would never be able to face the woman again.

"When the night is over," Susan continued, smiling, "I don't return the funds."

"I have found that a judicious application of the tongue works the fastest." This from a woman Charlotte had never before met. "Even mentioning that I might wish to mouth him causes his John Thomas to rise rather quickly."

"No euphemisms, Darlene. We are pledged to truth in this group."

"Penis," Darlene corrected.

"I have found the same," Lady Eleanor said. She

leaned back in her chair and folded her arms and nodded sagely, as if she were agreeing on the proper bordering plant to be installed in her garden. "But there's a technique to mouthing, ladies. You must pay some attention to your drawing now." She held the illustration of the penis up and pointed to the bulbous tip. "Use the shape of your mouth, and ring it around the penis very gently. Suck just slightly, as if you're tasting an orange."

Charlotte had always wondered what hell was like. Now she knew. Hell was being in this room, at this moment, with the relative of a duke instructing a group of women on the proper mouthing of a penis.

"There's a great deal of hair there, isn't there?" This from the lady with the spectacles. "I tend to avoid the testicles, but I understand it's a source of great pleasure for the male."

"Indeed it is," Eleanor said. "But it is also a source of great pain if you do it incorrectly. You must ignore the hair there. If you do not wish to touch the testes with your mouth, a gentle cupping motion with your hand is sufficient to incite great pleasure in your partner. Also, if you will inject your longest finger just behind the testicles to a small inch of skin, that, too is a great source of pleasure."

She turned to Charlotte. "Have you found these techniques to be useful, Charlotte?"

"Me?" She looked wide-eyed at Lady Eleanor. "I don't know. I was only married for a week before George left me," she added.

Not one woman spoke, and the silence was so thick that it was almost a presence in the room.

"George is larger," she said, and then clapped a

hand over her mouth as the other women began to smile. Why on earth had she said such a thing?

"How very fortunate you are, my dear. I thought that he had a very substantial package when I saw him."

"Indeed," Susan said. "I do thank heavens that Harold is still a young man."

"An old man is not as preferable a lover as a young one," Sylvia said. "The organ turns an unbecoming shade of purple with use."

"Blue in some," Hortensia said.

Would they never stop?

"A younger man, especially one of lesser means, is a great deal more grateful than an older one," Lady Eleanor said.

A maid named Sally tapped at the door and opened it slowly. Charlotte raised her hand, a signal for the girl to enter. Blessedly, the other women fell silent. Good, at least the maid would not be scandalized, which was more than could be said for her mistress.

Perhaps she should pay attention to Lady Eleanor after all. She'd gone to George's bed and afterward he'd acted no more impressed than if the gardener had told him he'd found weeds in the flower bed. Instead, he'd gone off to London and Edinburgh for twenty days.

"Even a magnificent creature such as yourself could benefit from some knowledge, Charlotte."

"I would not call myself magnificent, Lady Eleanor."

"Which just contributes to your charm, Charlotte. You do not take on airs. But you have the most delicate ivory skin."

"My mother has the same."

"It's true your nose is rather large, my dear. But your Titian hair makes up for it. And the quite unusual shade of your eyes."

"They're just green," Charlotte said.

"Nonsense, they're very unusual. They have flecks of blue, don't they?" Lady Eleanor peered closer. "Do they change color depending upon what you wear, my dear?"

"Sometimes I've thought so."

The older woman nodded in satisfaction. "Tell me," she said leaning closer, "is he a very good lover?"

Charlotte closed her eyes again, and this time she murmured a prayer to the Almighty who must be clutching His stomach and rolling with laughter.

Please, God, let these women leave. Please let no one in Edinburgh or Inverness or the whole of Scotland know of their visit. Please let them be gone. I shall not complain about anything forever. If the French teacher wants to go on and on about how barbaric a country Scotland is, I shall not correct her. If the linguistics instructor wants to criticize the state of the library, I shall not complain. If Cook wants to use the most costly cut of meat for her stew, I will no longer cavil at the cost.

God, however, was not cooperating. Either He had tired of bargains, or was genuinely amused at the situation. All eight women remained firmly in place.

"Well, my dear?" Lady Eleanor said.

He was an absolutely glorious lover. He was so adept at the task that she missed him more than she'd ever thought possible. More than once, she'd awakened feeling hot and damp, the memory of their night together making her yearn for him. But that was not a confession she'd make to these women.

"I think it's time for me to begin arrangements for dinner."

"Nonsense, my dear. We're in the midst of a very interesting discussion."

She only looked at Lady Eleanor.

"Very well, I can sense your reticence. Your husband has returned; has there been no sexual congress in the interim?"

"No," Charlotte said, lying straight-faced. "There has not."

The woman with the spectacles looked at her pointedly, as if unable to understand English.

Finally, after sighing deeply, Charlotte answered. "I have every intention of divorcing my husband." Another lie. At the moment, she didn't know what she was going to do.

"On what grounds?"

"Desertion," Charlotte said.

"But he's come back."

"Wouldn't it be better to simply punish him another way, my dear?" Lady Eleanor asked. "Keep him in thrall with his penis."

She blinked at the older woman, wondering if there would ever come a time when Lady Eleanor ceased to shock her.

"He's an earl, my dear. He is quite good-looking, and he's the heir to this marvelous place. Whatever would you get out of divorce except for the satisfaction?"

Without waiting for Charlotte to answer, she went

on. "I should think keeping him in delicious agony would be much more satisfying."

A demon, evil, malevolent, and curious, made her ask, "How do I do that?"

Lady Eleanor reached over and pulled free the illustration of a woman's nether parts from Charlotte's grip.

"You must begin to know yourself, my dear. I suggest you take a mirror and match the parts listed here with your own. You'll find that the body has a very great need to enjoy itself. If you do not allow yourself to feel pleasure, you're cheating yourself of one of the great joys of life itself."

One by one, the women in the group nodded.

"Pleasure to the human body is as necessary as food and drink."

Charlotte took back the drawing, turned it upside down on her lap and kept her hand over it. If she agreed to everything Lady Eleanor said, would that mean the meeting would end sooner?

"Very well, I shall try."

"And that is all that we can ask," Lady Eleanor said brightly. "A willful end to ignorance. Now, how are we to assist you in seducing your husband?"

Chapter 19

Dixon was determined, upon leaving Edinburgh, to tell Charlotte who he was the minute he entered the doors of Balfurin. Halfway home, he decided that he would wait and talk with Nan first, to surmise if there was something else he could learn about George's disappearance. When he could see Balfurin in the distance, he decided that he needn't be hasty about divulging his identity.

From his conversations in both London and Edinburgh, Dixon learned that George had simply dropped off the face of the earth. No, first he'd married Charlotte, and then a week later he'd disappeared.

Had Charlotte's father aided in that disappearance? Had the man been greedy for a title but unwilling to have a wastrel and a drunkard for a son-in-law? Another tidbit of information he'd discovered. The memories of George's so-called friends were harsh and unrelenting. "He was more often in his cups than standing upright." "I found him lying in the street, singing at the top of his lungs." "There wasn't nobody like Georgie when he wanted to fling a girl's skirts up over the top of her head. More often than not, though, he was already three sheets to the wind. Lots of talk and no action."

In the three weeks he'd been gone, Dixon had found no sign of George. He'd frequented the gambling establishments his cousin had liked to visit, along with a few new ones where the manager claimed to have no knowledge of a spendthrift earl wasting his wife's dowry.

Nor was there any sign of him at Leath, where the oceangoing ships berthed every day. No captain there, no clerk in the sprawling counting houses, no one seemed to have ever heard of George.

His cousin had simply vanished one day and no one but Charlotte seemed to note his absence.

He arrived at Balfurin just as night was falling. He tapped on the ceiling and waited for the coach to stop, then dismounted and walked some distance in front of the horses just as he had more than a month ago. Nothing had changed.

Charlotte. She was there, just minutes away.

His chest hurt, as if he couldn't breathe.

He'd tried to avoid thinking of her, and all he'd succeeded in doing was fixing her face firmly in his mind. He could hear her voice, and see the sparkle in her eyes as she waited for him to serve the next volley in their conversation. He'd never known another woman like her. Women in the Orient were submissive as a rule, catering to a man's whims and wishes even before he knew what they were. Women in Scotland were more demanding.

Charlotte was neither and both, an amalgam, an enigma, a puzzle. When she loved, he suspected, she'd love deeply and forever.

Had she loved George? That was a question he'd never asked along with another for which he hadn't yet found the answer: why had George left her?

Balfurin looked the same as it had three weeks earlier, but this time the castle seemed almost welcoming, as if humor and gaiety and a host of other pleasant emotions dwelled inside its red-brick walls. There were no students in attendance now, and fewer staff, but the atmosphere would still be cozy. A hint of spice, the warmth from the fire, a tentative smile from one of the maids, even old Jeffrey's rusty grin would all welcome him.

And Charlotte.

What was he going to do about Charlotte? He'd not wanted to leave her for a moment, let alone the three weeks it had been. Had she missed him as well? Or counted herself fortunate that her long-lost husband had disappeared again?

Of the two of them, his actions were more suspect. He knew he wasn't George, knew that Charlotte was not his wife. She had no such inkling.

Was he going to be able to leave her alone? There, the question that had followed him all the way from Edinburgh. He wanted her, in a way that both fascinated and disturbed him.

At the moment, he wished he'd never seen Balfurin

again, had never wanted to mend those broken ties that had kept him far from Scotland all these years.

Matthew was right. He'd stirred up the ghosts of the past, and they weren't pleased.

He turned and walked back to the carriage, giving the signal to the coachman. He didn't have the answers for the questions he'd raised, but then he hadn't in the last few weeks, either. Perhaps the best thing he could do was to see her again, come face-to-face with his errant desire, and tell her the truth.

The task might well prove to be impossible, or more than he could manage. He didn't want to leave her. Instead, he wanted to become George, more now than at any time in his life.

Jeffrey was there to open the door for him.

"Do you never sleep, Jeffrey?" he asked, entering the castle.

"The countess is entertaining, your lordship," he said, bowing. "Shall I inform her of your arrival?"

Dixon consulted his pocket watch. "At this hour?"

"I believe so, your lordship. I've heard a great deal of laughter coming from the parlor."

"Really?"

Jeffrey bowed again, a gesture Dixon wished he wouldn't make. The old man looked incapable of rising. He waited until he was certain Jeffrey had gotten his balance, and then strode past him to the stairs.

"No, leave her. God knows she deserves a little levity. Who are her guests?"

Jeffrey sent him a look from beneath his bushy brows.

"I take it you don't approve?" Dixon asked as he began to mount the steps.

"In my day, women acted like ladies, my lord. They were accompanied by proper chaperones, escorts and the like. Lady Eleanor's entourage was only women. Silly, giggling females, the lot of them."

He was halfway up the stairs when he turned and looked down at the elderly servant.

"You've been here a very long time, Jeffrey."

"Aye, your lordship."

"You've seen a great many things in all that time."

" 'Tis true. I have."

"Is there anything you'd like to tell me?" Dixon asked.

Jeffrey eyed him as if he knew full well that he wasn't George. "About life in general, your lordship? Or is there some other reason you'd be asking me?"

"Disregard the question, Jeffrey."

"She's got a suitor," Jeffrey said.

Dixon turned and looked down at the elderly man. Jeffrey looked in the direction of the parlor. "The countess. He called on her the other day. A so-lic-i-tor," he said, elongating the word.

"Indeed," Dixon said, pushing back the sudden anger he felt.

"Spencer McElwee. He came to tell her how beautiful she was, and she, lapping it up like a cat to cream."

"What else did he tell her?" At the older man's offended look, Dixon rephrased the question. "Did you happen to accidentally overhear any more of his remarks?"

"He was all for getting her divorced," Jeffrey said. "Wanted to marry the countess himself, I think." Jeffrey's smile, thin and twisted, seemed to indicate he knew they were playing with words. "Of course, until you showed up, your lordship. Your returning stopped his plans."

Dixon didn't question the elderly servant further, merely headed up the stairs.

"Your lordship."

He stopped and looked down at Jeffrey.

"Finding the treasure might solve a lot of problems at Balfurin," Jeffrey said.

"The treasure?"

"I'm thinking that a great many people have gone looking for it, your lordship. Whether or not they found it is the question."

There was a wealth of meaning in Jeffrey's words, but Dixon was only left with more questions. He was tempted to ask the elderly retainer if he was speaking about George, but the time wasn't right. He had to talk to Charlotte first before revealing his true identity to the servant.

"Money isn't the answer for everything, Jeffrey." Dixon continued up the stairs, well aware that both of them had only hinted at the real issue: where was George, and how much longer was Dixon going to pretend to be his cousin?

Returning to Balfurin was proving to be as complicated as he'd feared and he'd yet to greet Charlotte.

Tonight was the first occasion Charlotte could ever recall that she wished she didn't have the kind of memory that held dear every single word she'd ever read. One of Queen Elizabeth's poems seemed oddly appropriate for the occasion:

I grieve and dare not show my discontent,
I love and yet am forced to seem to hate,
I do, yet dare not say I ever meant,
I seem stark mute but inwardly to prate.
I am and not, I freeze and yet am burned.
Since from myself another self I turned.

Stanza after stanza of poetry filtered into her mind, along with treatises, lectures, and other bits of writing. Perhaps her mind offered up the series of documents for her to peruse instead of thinking about George.

Why hadn't he greeted her upon his return? Why hadn't he even knocked on her door to tell her he'd come home?

She closed her eyes, placing her arm over her forehead, deliberately concentrating on anything else but her husband. Immediately, she envisioned Lady Eleanor's anatomical drawing of the male organ, except this one was fully erect.

A muffled sound of disgust escaped her. What had happened to her? Lady Eleanor's influence, no doubt, but she didn't even have that excuse, did she? She wasn't an impressionable girl. She was a grown woman.

She'd defied her parents, and lived at Balfurin essentially alone for a full year. She'd started the Caledonia School for the Advancement of Females by herself. Ample reason, therefore, to think that she was not without some measure of courage. But tonight she was beginning to realize that she wasn't as brave as she thought. In fact, she was beginning to believe that she was a coward in a great many ways. Otherwise, she would knock on George's door and demand to know why he hadn't even shown the most rudimentary politeness to her.

Why didn't she?

Charlotte sat up in bed in the dark. Was that him? She listened for his footfall in the corridor but the sound didn't come again.

She leaned against the headboard, frowning at the door.

Forget about George. Instead, she should concentrate on organizing the volumes in the library, a task she'd set aside for herself and one she truly anticipated. In all these years at Balfurin, she'd never spared the time to catalogue the books left behind by all the generations of MacKinnons. The library was the only true heritage left, since the rest of the castle had been allowed to fall into ruin.

Why hadn't he even said hello? Something. Anything. Anyone else would have demonstrated a little decency, a smidgeon of politeness.

Think about the books. There were treatises on philosophy, some very fine illustrated texts that looked to be old.

Pity she didn't have any books on how to garner the attention of one's husband. Hadn't Lady Eleanor mentioned something? Charlotte focused her attention on the night-darkened ceiling, wishing she could recall conversations as easily as she did the written word.

"My dear, it's no sin to be ignorant. Ignorance is only a sin if it's willful, if you reject knowledge. I have several books I would suggest to you, if you are of a mind to procure them. Queen Marguerite of

France wrote a series of tales, called Heptameron. They are shocking in some aspects, but a good primer, all in all."

Dear heavens, did she really need a book? She'd managed well enough on her own the other night. She'd done quite well, as a matter of fact. So well that she hadn't been able to forget it.

Or George.

She didn't need instruction as much as she needed her husband. They would teach each other.

She reached over and grabbed the matches, lighting the candle. She set it back on the table, and began to unplait her braid. Slipping from the bed, she stripped the nightgown from her body and bathed in the cold water from the ewer before slipping on another, prettier nightgown. This one was taken from the bottom drawer, where it had sat for five years. Since it was part of her trousseau she'd thought of disposing of it more than once, or giving it to one of the maids upon the occasion of her wedding. But she'd worked long hours on the intricate embroidery on the yoke, and couldn't bear to think of it being worn by another woman. In a way, it represented her marriage, unused, unnecessary. Or maybe herself: unwanted.

But not tonight.

She bent down and retrieved an item from the drawer of the chest beside the bed, and only then left the room. She knocked on his door, wishing that the sound did not echo down the corridor. But there was no one else with chambers on this floor, and none of her servants were assigned to patrol the hallways of Balfurin at night.

He didn't answer, but she wasn't going to retreat.

She knocked again, and this time she heard a noise beyond the door. She fixed a smile on her face, thinking that she should have brushed her hair. As it was, it cascaded past her shoulders in an undulating wave.

When he opened the door, he was attired in his dressing gown, but it was all too evident that he was naked beneath it. How odd that she didn't know if he liked nightshirts or not. She should know something as elemental as that.

What had she wanted to say?

He needed to shave. He looked swarthy and dangerous, almost menacing. Surely that was the only reason her heart was beating so heavily.

Come to my bed.

Horrified, she wondered if she'd said the thought aloud, but evidently not, because he stood there regarding her with no more interest than if she was one of her students. They stared at each other for a long moment. She'd lost the ability—or had she ever had it?—to know what he was thinking. His gaze was hooded, his expression unreadable.

"Was your journey home uneventful?" she asked.

"Yes,"

"You were not injured on the trip?"

"No," he said.

Was he going to give her a one-word answer to all her questions?

"You haven't taken ill, I trust?"

His mouth curved up in a smile and she was startled into silence for a moment—for just a moment, until his sheer beauty dimmed a little. It truly wasn't fair that he'd grown so attractive in the last five years.

"No, I'm fine," he said.

"Are you very certain? You really are in good health?"

"I'm in fine health. Thank you for your concern."

There, that question was answered. He hadn't returned to Balfurin to die.

"I was worried about your leg," she said.

"My leg?"

"The broken one," she said, looking down at his bare feet. "The one that prevented you from crossing the hall and giving me the courtesy of a greeting."

His smile broadened.

"Forgive me, I was rude. I was given to understand you were entertaining."

She gripped both edges of her wrapper with one hand and stared at him. "You were never so accommodating in the past."

His smile disappeared. "This isn't the past." He looked from her to the open door behind her. Was he telling her to return to her room? Very well, she would not shame herself any further.

She turned and walked across the hall.

"Charlotte."

She glanced over her shoulder at him. "What is it, George?"

His face hardened.

"What are you holding?"

She glanced down at the object in her hand. "It's a velvet whip, I believe."

Several long moments passed before he spoke again.

"Would you care to tell me why you have a velvet whip in your hand?"

She studied it with great care as if she'd not been

half horrified when Lady Eleanor had given it to her along with a few whispered instructions.

"No, I don't think so," she said, wishing she'd never knocked on his door.

"Thank you for missing me."

"Don't be absurd," she said, and closed the door before she could admit that she'd missed him every hour of every day.

Chapter 20

Charlotte bid a relieved farewell to The Edification Society, determined to keep them from Balfurin for their next semi-monthly meeting. However,
she doubted she'd be entirely successful. Lady Eleanor
was as determined a personage as Charlotte had ever
met. Nor did it help matters that she'd caught the
footman winking at the older woman.

When George was exceptionally pleasant to the
women, Charlotte wanted to kick him. They needed
no enticements to remain. In fact, she was very concerned that the snow might block the road to Inverness,
thereby keeping the group at Balfurin.

Thankfully, however, the weather cooperated, the
snow holding off until after their departure. Then
winter blanketed Balfurin, enshrouding the trees with
ice so delicate that it looked like lace and freezing the

River Tam. Balfurin's chimneys chuffed white smoke against a perpetually gray sky.

The women's departure, while a welcome event, also marked a turning point in her relationship with George. To the staff, they no doubt appeared perfectly amicable. He nodded to her when they passed in the hallway and Charlotte nodded back at him. They occasionally shared a meal in the family dining room, the sheer size of the enormous trestle table making conversation inconvenient. Any other communication between them was assisted by Maisie and Matthew, neither of whom appeared put out by being placed in the position of messenger.

But while the world might see them as polite to a fault, Charlotte knew that the situation was really quite different. She was annoyed with George and made no pretense of hiding it when the servants weren't present. He, on the other hand, was evidently under the delusion that she was invisible. He was ignoring her. No, not simply ignoring her, but making a point of ignoring her, which only annoyed her further.

Therefore, any rational person would understand why she'd had enough. She'd ordered a tray sent to her room rather than sit with George and endure another hour of his carefully averted eyes. He never even smiled at her anymore, nor did he make any pretense of civility.

One would think he endured her presence because he was forced to do so. She hadn't made him return to Balfurin.

In fact, the very last thing she wanted was to have George underfoot. She was used to being left alone in her pursuits, unencumbered by a husband. She didn't *want* to be disturbed by George's proximity or his irritating ability to make her heart beat faster and her chest feel tight.

She especially didn't want to think about that night nearly a month ago. But it was there just as it had been every moment since it had happened. She'd gone to her husband's bed, and yet she couldn't regret it. How else would she have known the pleasure from lovemaking?

But he didn't seem in a hurry to repeat the act, did he?

Charlotte stood at the window, watching as night surrounded Balfurin. They hadn't a marriage. They had a . . . Her thoughts ground to a halt. Exactly what was their relationship? An arrangement? Certainly not a union.

A hint of snow lingered in the air, and Charlotte had given orders that the fires were to be replenished through the night. One thing she'd learned about the castle: if the walls were allowed to grow cold and damp, it would take days to warm them again.

George was acting strangely. He'd begun to cultivate an odd routine of leaving Balfurin early in the morning and not returning until afternoon. Charlotte pretended not to be interested, adopting an attitude that whatever her once absent husband did was of no consequence to her. As long as George left her alone to run the school and maintain order at Balfurin, she was content.

However, her curiosity was getting the better of her, especially since he left the castle every morning attired in little more than a kilt, the ends of the plaid thrown over his shoulders. The man was blessed with muscular legs, and very attractive ones at that. She knew Cook prepared him lunch; whatever else he carried in his pack was a mystery. Nor did he share the information with her. When she asked Matthew why George seemed so intent upon walking the length and breadth of Balfurin land, the servant only bowed and refused to comment.

She heard him say something across the hall, and then he laughed. Who was he talking to, Matthew or one of the maids, forever lurking around him waiting to do him a service? Perhaps she should think about rotating some of the staff, especially since they were acting so decidedly lovesick.

She was not going to think about George again.

Charlotte had given orders to have a bath readied in her chamber, and when the knock came, she called out and then watched as a procession of footmen emptied a series of steaming buckets into the large copper tub. When she dismissed the last of them, Maisie entered the room with her arms around a large canvas satchel.

"Matthew threw his sticks last night," she said, emptying the contents of her bag on the seat of a chair. "He says the elements are there for good fortune. He says that his lordship will find the treasure, and you should seek good fortune in a flower bath."

Charlotte looked at her maid, uncertain which part of that statement to question first.

"He's looking for the treasure?" she finally asked. "The treasure of Balfurin?"

"You know about it, your ladyship?"

Charlotte nodded. "There is no treasure," she said. "It's an old tale told by old people."

"Oh, his lordship believes in it all right. It's a cask of gold, saved by the first earls for when there was need in the family."

"I thought he was wealthy."

"Oh, indeed he is, your ladyship. At least, that's what Matthew says." Maisie shrugged, evidently the issue of George's wealth being of no interest to her. "But maybe it's like being hungry, your ladyship. You can't imagine ever being full, so you keep eating."

"I've never heard greed explained so beautifully, Maisie," she said. "What's a flower bath?"

"A *mandi bunga*," Maisie said.

"I beg your pardon?"

"It's not just a bath," Maisie said. "It's a tradition, a part of Matthew's culture. A woman hoping to attract good luck or a husband takes a *mandi bunga*. Or she takes one if she wishes to expel bad luck."

"What about expelling husbands?"

Maisie only sent her a quelling look. An altogether odd experience, being chastised by her maid. But because she no doubt deserved it, Charlotte remained silent.

She walked toward the chair and looked down at the array of ingredients. "I don't suppose it could hurt," Charlotte said. "What's all this?"

Maisie lifted the items one by one. "These are all dried flowers. Seven different types of them. The rest are coconut leaves, betel nut, something else that smells like unwashed feet, I'm afraid. Wax, chalk, and one other thing." She moved to Charlotte's dressing table and poured out a little of her expensive face powder into her palm. "Face powder," Maisie said.

"Are you sure we're not doing magic?" Charlotte

asked. "Nothing is going to explode into flames, is it?" she asked, looking doubtfully at the chair heaped with the ingredients for the bath.

"I don't think so," Maisie said. She reached over and grabbed the dried flowers, dumping them into the steaming water. "I'm supposed to weave four strands of coconut leaves into a shape."

"What kind of shape?"

"I don't know," Maisie admitted. "I think a bowl."

"Perhaps there's a skill to it," Charlotte said when Maisie had finished. The coconut leaves didn't resemble a bowl at all, merely a very small mat. "What are you supposed to do now?"

"I think you're supposed to get into the bath," Maisie said, "while I act as the *bomoh*." At Charlotte's inquisitive look, she explained. "A *bomoh* is like a minister."

Charlotte took off her wrapper and slipped into the steaming water, thinking that the dried flowers didn't add much to the experience. They weren't fragrant, but they were scratchy and she pushed them out of her way and set them bobbing toward her feet.

Maisie picked up some thread and molded the wax around it until it appeared like a long, skinny candle. Then she took one of the betel nuts and gave it to Charlotte. "I believe you're supposed to rub it back and forth between your palms."

"Are you quite certain?"

"I am," she said, but her voice lacked any degree of conviction. She gave Charlotte a quick look before going to the door and pulling it open.

After a whispered conversation, she shut it again.

"Is Matthew on the other side?"

"He was," Maisie said. "But now it's his lordship. He says he should be the one to instruct you on the *mandi bunga*."

Charlotte sank back into the water and stared up at the ceiling. Should she ask for divine providence to interfere in this ceremony, or should she take advantage of the situation as Lady Eleanor had advised on her departure?

A husband needs to be snared like any other animal, my dear. Sometimes the creature will not see what's before its nose until you make him pay attention. A woman as attractive as you should have no difficulty in doing that.

This very strange situation of being neither married nor unattached could last until death claimed George. Since George was a very strong, very healthy man, who didn't appear to be sickening in any way, that could be years. Decades, actually. The only real solution, the only viable answer for her situation was to convince George to remain at Balfurin, to become a true husband.

She sat up, dislodging one of the dried flowers—a chrysanthemum. It floated away on a small wave.

"Ask him to come inside," Charlotte said.

Maisie quickly turned and glanced at her. "Are you very sure, your ladyship?"

"I am," she said resolutely, lying with a smile on her face. She sat up, draping her arm over her breasts as she surreptitiously pulled her wrapper closer to the tub. Just for good measure, she drew up her knees. There, she was almost presentable. However, if she was going to seduce her husband, she was going to have to be a little more courageous.

George entered the room and immediately seemed to dwarf it by his presence. How did he do that? As he strode through the room, she recalled only too well what he looked like naked. How he'd touched her with his fingertips.

The muscles of her stomach clenched.

"I don't remember all the instructions," Maisie explained to him. "I'm not a very good *bomoh*."

"It takes a little practice," George said, smiling at her.

"Would you help?" Charlotte said. She glanced over at him. Was her look sultry? Was her voice seductive?

He didn't seem the least affected.

Maisie slipped from the room as George took the rest of the ingredients, eight pieces of something dark green and dried, four leaves, and a few betel leaves rubbed with a little chalk. These he put into a wooden bowl he'd unearthed from the bottom of the satchel.

He walked to the bath and dipped the bowl into the water. "I'm surprised you agreed to such a ceremony."

"I would be a fool to ignore the chance for good luck," she said. Her voice sounded low. Did he notice?

Her breasts felt tight, and she pressed her arm against her chest to minimize the sensation. Had his eyes always been that brilliant a blue? At least he was looking at her directly now, not ignoring her as he'd done these last few days. Was that what she needed to do? Sit naked before him and dare him to look away? Her cheeks flushed, and her lips felt dry.

"I'm supposed to anoint you now," he said. "It's customary to have the maiden wearing a sarong."

"I'm not a maiden," Charlotte said, drawing her knees closer to her chest.

"Then we'll dispense with the sarong." He sprinkled the water over her shoulders, all the while softly speaking words in a language Charlotte didn't understand.

"What are you saying?"

"I'm imploring the spirits to grant you good fortune if you are worthy."

"And if I'm not worthy?" she asked.

"Then you'll have to petition them again."

Charlotte looked up at him, and wondered what he was thinking. He was back to ignoring her again, his gaze carefully focused on the other side of the room.

She removed her arm from across her breasts, and gripped either side of the copper tub. It was easier to look at the fire than at him. Had he even noticed that her breasts were exposed, that her nipples were bobbing in the water like little corks?

"How long does it take?" she asked. "Before I know if my luck has changed?"

That I'm able to seduce my husband into remaining at Balfurin? Is that a terrible thing to want? And is it acceptable to almost pray to God while indulging in a heathen ritual?

"Not long if the spirits of Balfurin grant it," he said.

"Not Oriental spirits?"

"You'll find they're much the same."

"I've often thought Balfurin haunted," she said, and then wondered why on earth she'd mentioned that.

He halted in sprinkling the water over her head. "Have you?"

She nodded.

"If there are such things, I would imagine Balfurin is as good a place as any for spirits to reside."

"I half expected you to counsel me not to be foolish," she admitted.

"I've seen a great deal that I can't explain. I've learned not to dismiss anything out of hand."

Except your wife. But she didn't say that. Instead, she smiled sweetly and asked, "Even ghosts?"

"I've sometimes had the feeling that I wasn't alone in an empty room. Who's to say it wasn't a ghost?"

She nodded again. "I've felt the same," she conceded. "Once, in the library, I felt as if someone were standing right beside me. I even asked if someone was there. I think I would have screamed if anything had answered."

"Perhaps our inability to communicate to the departed is not in our hearing but their speaking. Perhaps they can only turn over objects and make the wind whisper."

"Or make it cold," Charlotte said, sliding down in the water a little.

How very odd that they were talking to each other with more accord than they'd done in days. How very strange that the conversation was so proper, one they might have had in the drawing room, and not with dried flowers floating into her breasts and her nipples all coral and hard.

George had ceased sprinkling her. Now he dipped the bowl in the water and allowed the ingredients to sink to the bottom of her bath.

"Or perhaps what we feel is only the voice of our conscience," he said.

"Do you have a troubled conscience?" she asked, forcing herself to sit up a little. There, her breasts were no longer covered by the water. He couldn't help but see now.

He looked at her somberly, his gaze direct and unflinching. "I do."

She hadn't the slightest idea what to say to his confession.

Suddenly, he knelt at the side of the tub, entirely too close. But it was what she wanted, wasn't it? He trailed his fingers in the water, not looking at her. With great courage, she reached out and touched his hand, fascinated at the path of a droplet between two knuckles. She followed it with the tip of a finger, feeling as if that small, insignificant touch was almost intimate.

Her breath felt tight.

She wanted his hands on her.

"Is there anything you want? Besides good fortune, I mean."

To seduce my husband. No, she wasn't about to tell him that.

He only smiled as if he knew what she was thinking.

A few tendrils of hair, made humid by the heat, escaped to trail down her cheeks. He used one finger to push them away, a gentle touch. She'd gotten her wish, then. He'd touched her, but not in the way she wanted. She reached up with one hand, and touched his inner wrist, feeling how fast his pulse beat.

He was looking at her, but his gaze was carefully directed to her face.

She splashed water on her breasts, and he looked down.

"Perhaps it isn't wise to act as your *bomoh*," he said, his voice lower than its usual tone. He used one finger to direct the path of a desiccated rose.

"Why would you say that?"

"You might wish me gone, and what would be the point of that? I would be the instigator of my own despair."

"Now you're jesting," she said. "You don't appear to be in the throes of despair. I doubt my wish will inconvenience you even a little."

"Ah, so you do wish me gone."

"No," she said softly. "I wish you in my bed."

The moment stilled. Time seemed to stop, hesitating on a breath. A droplet fell from his hand and landed on the surface of her bath, and it seemed to Charlotte that she could hear it.

"Charlotte."

He made her name sound longer than two syllables, drawing it out on a sigh.

"I want you touching me," she confessed, feeling as if she'd opened up her chest with such words and exposed her beating heart. Would he know how difficult it was for her to be so defenseless? So helpless?

She closed her eyes, and leaned her head back against the curve of the tub.

Do not be afraid of your urges, my dear. Lady Eleanor again. *Act upon your body's craving. It's only nature. It's time that women demanded their share of pleasure in the world.*

"I've never forgotten that night, you see, and I

wondered when it would happen again." Her cheeks warmed, flushed with the memory.

She opened her eyes to find him looking at her. Not just her face, but her breasts and the rest of her body, magnified by the water, offered up to him without a trace of hesitation.

He was her husband. He owed her five years of pleasure. Five years of kisses. Five years of gasping wonder.

"Why don't you come to my bed?"

"Because it wouldn't be right," he said.

"It wouldn't be right?" she asked, confused.

"My conscience, Charlotte, has been winning over my libido, but for how long? Especially if I remain in your chamber."

He stood, looking down at her. She looked away, staring at one of the flowers, something vaguely orange with tightly furled petals. She couldn't identify it in its current state. Perhaps it was something indigenous to the Orient.

"There's nothing wrong with a man and wife loving each other, George."

Before she could further attempt to convince him, or give in to those silly tears that threatened, a noise from outside her room startled them both.

"What the hell?" George went to the door, looking out into the hall. "Stay here, Charlotte," he said, as he took a lamp from its hanger on the wall.

She did hate being commanded, especially by a man who'd just repudiated her.

"I'm coming with you," she said, but he'd already left the room. She stood and dressed in her wrapper, pulling at the garment when it became instantly damp. She really should have taken the time to dry.

By the time she caught up with George, he was down the hall, picking up the large candelabra that had fallen to the floor.

"How did that happen?" she asked.

"A careless maid. A cat."

"I don't allow the barn cats inside," she said.

"It's been my observation that cats go and come as they will," he said.

That was true enough.

He began mounting the stairs to the third floor.

She hung back, and he glanced down at her. Until that moment, she didn't think he'd actually seen what she was wearing, or in this case what she wasn't wearing. His expression stilled, and his eyes darkened. The lamp in her hand seemed to make the fabric invisible.

"Perhaps it would be better if you went back to your room," he said softly.

"I'm not a coward," she said, but she was speaking of confronting an intruder. Not him.

"No, but you are nearly naked."

"There's no one but the two of us. You've seen me naked before."

"Not in the middle of Balfurin," he said. "As I recall, it was in my bed."

"It doesn't matter, does it? You've already said you've no intention of repeating the experience."

"Do you think it's because I don't want to? Surely you're not that foolish." A noise from above them made him look up. "Someone's up there."

He took a few steps upward, but she didn't budge.

"I'd rather you went back to your room, but if you won't do that, then come with me."

"I'm not in any great hurry to go to the third floor," she confessed. "I try to avoid it when I can."

He looked at her. "Why?"

"I often hear noises from there. And at this time of year, it isn't fully occupied. Most of the servants have gone back to Inverness until the new term."

"I'm afraid the only spirits at Balfurin are alive. Someone knocked down that candelabra, and I intend to find out who."

She reluctantly went to his side, climbing the winding steps right behind him, following so close that she could feel the heat from his body. When they reached the landing, he turned toward her.

"I'll not let any ghosts harm you," he said, the humor in his voice easily detectable. She didn't care if he ridiculed her. There were nothing but shadows on this floor, and there wasn't a carpet to absorb their footsteps, only long wooden floorboards that creaked and groaned with every step.

He took the lamp from her and, one by one opening doors shone it inside each room. Before he approached another room, however, she stopped him.

"That's where Maisie sleeps," she said.

Abruptly, the door opened. Charlotte didn't know who was more startled, the two of them or Matthew. He stood in the doorway, attired in a crimson robe, but since he was barefoot, she suspected he was also naked.

"What is it, Matthew?" Maisie called out.

Matthew stepped into the hall, closed the door

behind him, and with calm, deliberate, movements closed his robe.

"Have you heard or seen anything amiss tonight?" George asked as if they'd not just disturbed his servant in the act of cohabiting with her maid.

Maisie had evidently lost no time in going to Matthew. How odd to be envious of her maid.

She wondered if the occasion called for some words of censure, and then decided that she'd let the opportunity pass. Besides, Maisie hadn't sounded distressed, only well loved.

Charlotte sent a look of irritation toward George.

"I've been doing my meditations, master. I've heard nothing that would disturb me."

There were a dozen things Charlotte could say—or should say—but for some strange reason she'd lost the ability to form a coherent sentence.

"Do you need me, master?"

"I'd be grateful for the loan of one of your jackets," George said.

Matthew disappeared for a moment, returning with a lit candle and a beautiful burgundy robe that he handed to George.

He helped her on with the garment, rolling up the sleeves so her hands were visible. Until that moment, she hadn't realized how very cold she was. She remained silent as George buttoned her from neck to ankle, and then tied the sash tight around her waist. It was one thing to aim to seduce one's husband, and quite another to appear almost naked in front of his servant.

"There is another floor," George said looking from one end of the corridor to the other.

"It's only used for storage. No one ever goes up there. I haven't gone up there in months." She only went reluctantly, when she needed to inventory the furniture or give orders to one of the footmen to bring down a table or an extra chair for the dining room seating. To her consternation, however, George was bent on exploring the area.

There was nothing to do but follow the two men up the narrow steps. She didn't suffer from a dislike of small spaces, but she could see how someone might when traversing the stairs. It was like entering a cave. The steps were shallow, designed for one person at a time. The shadows from the candle cast eerie shapes along the wall. Without much imagination, she could envision a wolf with snarling teeth.

At the top of the steps she moved closer to George, wishing he'd not chosen to come up here. This was the tallest part of Balfurin, higher than even the tower rooms. Had there been any windows up here, she'd be able to see the expanse of Balfurin land.

Suddenly, out of nowhere, a shape moved toward them. George swore and swung the lamp. It shattered against the figure, fiery oil spilling on the floor. The fire might have spread had Matthew not thrust the candle he held into Charlotte's hand, before slipping past her and beating at the flames with his robe.

Charlotte turned away, shocked. But it wasn't the sight of Matthew's nakedness that she'd forever recall, but the image of his back, scarred with deep, long gouges. As if he'd been whipped, and often.

The writhing shadows played across the wall. The sound of blows made her wince, a prayer coming quickly to her lips. *Please don't let George be hurt.*

The sound of the struggle gradually subsided, and slowly one shadow disengaged from the other. She turned to find that Matthew had disappeared, and only George stood there, his arms around another figure.

"George?"

She held the candle aloft.

He turned his head to look at her. "I'm all right," he said. "I'm not so certain about our intruder."

George pushed the man down the dark stairs in front of him. At the bottom of the stairs, she turned toward George and only then recognized the intruder.

"Spencer?" She stared at him, shocked.

"Your admirer?" George asked.

"Hardly that," she said. "A friend."

"Your solicitor."

"Yes," she said, frowning at him.

Matthew emerged from his room, once more properly dressed. He took back the candle from Charlotte, and she willingly relinquished it, stepping into the shadows. Even though she was decently covered in Matthew's robe, she felt almost naked, especially since Spencer was staring at her.

"What are you doing here?"

"It would have been all right, Charlotte, if he'd never returned," he said, sending a look of derision toward George. "She was going to be my wife. And all my money problems would have disappeared."

Charlotte stared at him, annoyed. Didn't the idea of poor timing occur to the man? Now was not an opportune moment for him to mention their previous relationship.

She brushed at the front of Matthew's robe, carefully

avoiding both George and Spencer's eyes. "Perhaps once we did mean something to each other, Spencer. But my husband has returned, and that has changed everything."

"Are you saying you feel something for him, Charlotte?" Spencer asked.

George folded his arms and looked from one to the other as if he were inordinately amused. If she had shoes on instead of her flimsy slippers, she might have kicked him in the shins.

"I think you should answer questions instead of asking them, Spencer. What are you doing here in the middle of the night? For that matter, how did you get in?"

He remained silent.

"Perhaps he'll talk to the authorities in Inverness," George said. "Are you up for a trip to the magistrate, Matthew?" George asked.

"You're going tonight?" Charlotte asked.

"Have you other plans?" George asked. The humor was still there in his eyes, but something else flickered there. Was it simply the candle's flame or her own wishful thinking?

"Not at all," she said, and turned and left them. She descended the stairs, walked down the corridor, and entered her room, closing the door softly behind her.

An altogether ladylike journey, giving no hint of the desperate disappointment she felt.

Chapter 21

The day was chilled enough that it felt like snow again. Perhaps the weather would halt George's exploration for today. He'd have to remain inside, and engage in conversation like a normal person. Unless, of course, he was like a winter hare and capable of walking atop the snow.

Charlotte blew out a breath and stared out the window. The servants were being very quiet, and the only sound in the room was the spitting and hissing of the fire. Someone—Maisie?—had thought to toss some dried flowers among the wood and the result was a delightful floral scent.

The Green Parlor was a pleasant place in winter, warmed by an eastern sun so that even the mornings were comfortable. Today, however, her thoughts were disturbing, marring her sense of peace and even troubling her determination.

"I found what Spencer was looking for," George said, entering the room. He crossed the room and handed her a drawstring bag.

"You're back," she said, turning to face him. Did she seem as eager as she sounded? When had she lost the ability to control her emotions?

"It's not all that long a journey."

She nodded.

"Spencer was silent throughout," he said. "So Matthew and I went exploring when we returned." He dropped a canvas bag on the table between them. "There had to be a reason he was on the fourth floor."

If there was, she couldn't think of it. The fourth floor was the only place where the castle and the recently constructed dormitory met. A covered walkway connected the two buildings, in case of fire or weather so bad the students couldn't use the courtyard.

She had a thought, and looked at him in horror. "He wasn't used to getting into the dormitories, was he? He didn't go there while the girls were sleeping?"

"On the contrary." He bent forward, opened the bag, and sent the contents tumbling onto the table top. She stared at the assortment before her.

"It's Juliana's brooch," she said, fingering the marcasite and pearl ornament. "And Penelope's ring." One by one, she listed the items, all reported lost or stolen in the last month of the term.

"I thought the girls were careless," she confessed. "At the most, I thought perhaps there was a student with sticky fingers, but not to this degree."

"Oh, I think she had sticky fingers all right, but I think she was Spencer's accomplice."

"Among my students?"

"Someone who actually stole the items, and hid them there for Spencer to recover. Since he was in Edinburgh for a month, he couldn't get to them until now. I've no doubt the snow held him up as well."

"Someone silly enough to be flattered by his attention," she said, thinking of more than one girl who would have been pleased to have attracted the attention of the blond-haired solicitor.

"I think it goes beyond flattery, Charlotte," he said. "The girl who did this stole from her fellow students for him. Or perhaps for herself. Either way, they conspired to rob your students."

Charlotte looked up at him. "How will I explain this?"

"You don't have to," he said easily. "Simply return each item to the girl with a note that it's been found."

She nodded. "That would be the wisest course." She replaced each of the items back into the bag.

She should have known that Spencer wasn't interested in friendship. Or even in marrying her, despite what he'd said. He'd be concerned with what she'd owned and in what he could steal.

She glanced at George, but he'd left her to stand by the fire. "Did your journey go well?"

"Well enough. The magistrate was impressed enough with my title and Matthew's appearance to need no further witnesses."

"You sound annoyed."

"I've no reason to be. I'm the Earl of Marne."

"And I'm the Countess of Marne." Now why had she said that?

"Yes, you are, aren't you?" He turned and studied

her. "A comment guaranteed to put me in my place."

"You *are* annoyed. At me? I'm not responsible for Spencer's feelings for me."

"Aren't you? I've always been amazed at women who say that. You entice, and flirt, and charm a man, and then act entirely surprised when he's captivated."

"I did not entice and flirt with Spencer."

"Perhaps I wasn't talking about Spencer."

Silence, while she gave that comment some thought.

"It looks like snow. Not a day for walking," she said, changing the subject. She didn't know why he was irritated with her, and it was best, perhaps, to avoid the topic of Spencer. Or of men and women.

Perhaps she should just come out and address the issue directly.

Come to my bed, George. Let's pleasure each other. We have some feelings between us, I think, some common way of thinking. We make each other smile, and there are no pauses in our conversation. You fill in my hollows, and I soften your edges.

What would he say? What if he said no? Could she bear it? Quite possibly not.

"No," he agreed. "Not a day for walking."

"Will you stay inside, then? Or will you go exploring? There isn't a treasure, George. It's a tale, nothing more."

At his look of surprise, she continued; "From the moment I arrived at Balfurin I was accused of coming to steal the treasure. I grew heartily tired of hearing about it."

He smiled. "It's something I have to find," he said.

"An enigmatic statement. You were never before given to mystery."

"A man can change. Will you allow me that?"

"You've plenty of money, do you not?"

He glanced at her and then back at the fire.

"Then why this desperate search?" she asked.

"It keeps me honorable."

She sat back in the chair, still clutching the cloth bag.

"It's a tattered thing, my honor. I would prefer to hold it close and keep it safe, allow it to mend, perhaps. Do not ask me to give up my search, Charlotte. It reminds me of who I am and what I must find."

"What must you find, George?" she asked softly, not understanding his words.

"Myself. Answers. Dignity. Forgiveness."

"What have you done that you wish forgiveness with such earnestness?"

"Adopted greed as my way of life, perhaps. Coveted another man's possessions. Damned him to hell for everything he had and threw away."

"Why do you do that?"

"Do what?" he asked.

"Hint at something but never say it outright."

"I don't know what you're talking about," he said. But something flickered over his face, some emotion she couldn't quite read. She was adept at discovering the secrets of nearly grown girls, but she doubted she was up to the task of deciphering George MacKinnon.

He smiled again, his features becoming less hard, his face more approachable. Geniality favored him. She had the feeling that she didn't know him at all, only what he allowed her to see.

Who was George MacKinnon? Not the first time

she'd asked that question, but she was no closer to an answer than she'd been from the day he arrived.

Except, of course, that she'd fallen in love with the parts she had seen.

She stood and forced a smile on her face. "If you're going exploring, then I'm coming with you," she said. When he didn't speak, didn't turn, she repeated herself.

He finally nodded, and faced her. "Then come, damn it."

As she stared, he left the room. She hurried to catch up with him, wondering why she bothered.

The last thing he wanted was Charlotte accompanying him. She didn't understand, and he wasn't about to illuminate her, that her presence was both a blessing and a curse. More curse than blessing lately, because his conscience was losing no time reminding him exactly who she was.

He wanted to touch her, so damnably much that he clenched his hands into fists every time he was around her in case his mutinous fingers reached out to stroke an auburn lock of hair or measure the curve of her smile. He wanted to watch her walk slowly toward him, allow him to nestle his cock right in that spot nature had carved for it. He wanted to cup her breasts and suckle her nipples, and swallow her surprised little cry when she found her release. He wanted to fill her with his seed, hold her when she sobbed aloud in the aftermath, and cradle her when she grew round and plump with his child.

Despite the sin and dishonor, he would not have

traded these weeks for any other memory. To meet her, to know her, to lie with her, to love her—he would recall these memories until the day he died, however soon or far-flung that event.

But he couldn't trust himself with her.

The night of the bath he'd come too damn close to pulling her out of the tub and throwing her on the bed and keeping her there until her lips were swollen with his kisses and her body bore the imprint of his.

He knew what she didn't. He wasn't George, Earl of Marne. He was just plain Mister MacKinnon, a wealthy importer, a land owner, and proprietor of many businesses located in various places in the world. But he wasn't Charlotte MacKinnon's husband, and it wasn't right to be her lover.

Damn George.

Dixon, on the other hand, was a man who'd carved a future for himself from the dregs of his envy. A man filled with flaws, not the least of which was greed. He'd proven that, hadn't he? And he was no better now, wanting Charlotte so much that he was half tempted to tell her the truth and beg her to escape Balfurin with him. He'd keep her safe and in luxurious comfort for the rest of her days. She'd need for nothing, especially love.

He bent and retrieved a branch from the ground, stripped it free of leaves, before digging it into the snow at his feet, all for something to do to appear occupied until she caught up with him. It would never do to be honest with Charlotte. He had difficulty even looking at her lately, risking a glance into those expressive green eyes of hers. There was something about her look, as guileless as a summer day, that pulled at him. As if she were part angel, and could implore his better self to honesty.

What would she do if he told her that being with her on this day was both a complete joy and a source of great pain? She didn't know anything of his conscience, of the fact that he had not been able to sleep well lately, that he'd spent most of the night pacing back and forth, trapped in his web of lies as completely as a dying spider.

He stood on the crest of the hill, the twig held like a staff at his side. Abraham, welcoming the tribe. Or a shepherd waiting for a recalcitrant lamb. Charlotte, attired in her burgundy cloak, stood at the base of the hill looking up at him, a somewhat perplexed smile on her face.

"You're not wearing your kilt."

He smiled. "Even a Scotsman knows there's a time for a kilt and a time for trews. Are you disappointed?"

She didn't respond, and he didn't force the issue.

The day was a splendid one, the clouds overhead being pushed away by a fierce wind. If anything, it had grown colder, but the sky was a brilliant blue, as if Mother Nature had sprinkled it with lapis lazuli at dawn.

She grabbed her skirts in both hands and lifted them slightly so that she might climb the hill with greater grace. He could watch her walk all day, the undulation of her limbs beneath her skirts reminding him of the vision of her unclothed. She had a beautiful body, and he suspected, was only recently becoming aware of that fact.

Who would help her realize who she truly was? George? He doubted it. George had never realized her worth. If he had, his cousin would never have left her. Instead, he would have kissed her feet every day and blessed his good fortune.

He reached down for her hand, and pulled her to the crest of the hill.

"I'm surprised you waited for me," she said. "You haven't been very welcoming of late."

He didn't answer her but stared out at the vista in front of him. To his far left was the old castle half hidden by another hill. The river arched around and passed some distance away. To his right was Balfurin. The builders of the castle had taken the precaution of placing the new structure on an elevation above the level of the River Tam.

"Are you truly looking for the treasure?"

"I am," he said.

"Why?"

She'd asked that question before and he couldn't answer her then, either. Because he had no other clues to George's whereabouts. Because he didn't know if his cousin had ever located the treasure. Because none of his efforts in Edinburgh or London had born fruit, and he had no other ideas. Because it was there, because he wanted to accomplish something before he left Balfurin, because it kept him occupied and away from her.

None of those were reasons he could articulate.

"Do you believe it's real?" she asked.

He shrugged. He believed that George thought it was real, enough to abandon his marriage and his new bride. But how did he tell her that?

"It makes sense that it would be," he said. "When

my ancestors abandoned the old castle, the MacKinnon family was a great deal more prosperous than now. Perhaps there was a treasure chest that they thought should be relocated as well."

"And in the move, it was lost?" she asked doubtfully.

"Either that, or it was saved so securely that it couldn't be found again." He glanced at her to find her smiling at him. "Did Nan ever repeat the poem to you?"

She shook her head. "Nan limited the times she absolutely had to communicate with me to the barest of necessities. If Balfurin was on fire, I think she would have only grudgingly informed me."

From his pocket he pulled out the sheet of paper on which he'd written the poem and recited it to her.

"So, you've been looking for these clues?" she said when he'd finished.

"I've spent the last week investigating the caves along the river. My cousin and I played there as boys."

"But you didn't see anything like the three marks." She recited the stanza perfectly.

> "Three times he'll score his mark
> Three times a mark of grace
> A father, son, and holy ghost
> To show the sacred place."

"It would have to be marked in a way that would make it obvious to someone looking for it."

"But ignored by anyone else," she added.

He nodded, unsurprised by her quick understanding.

"Perhaps it isn't a mark at all," she said, walking beside him.

He glanced at her. "What do you mean?"

"Perhaps it's something natural that your ancestors just took advantage of, like three stones together, or three hills. That sort of thing."

"I hadn't considered that. This area is riddled with caves, however, and it just seemed more reasonable to investigate them."

"We've passed two or three of them already," she said, surprising him.

"I didn't realize you knew the topography so well."

"When I first came to Balfurin, there was little occupation but daily walks. I found myself exploring every inch of these hills."

"Did you find anything of interest?"

"No," she said. "Nothing but loneliness."

"You miss your students, don't you?"

She looked surprised at the question. "My students? Normally, by this time of year, I am so heartily tired of the noise and confusion that I don't miss them at all. But when the spring comes, I'll be eager for a new year to start."

"If you weren't occupied with the school, what would you do?"

He found he very much wanted to know. In fact, he wanted to know everything there was to know about her. What she thought, what she felt, what stirred her to tears, or admiration. What made her laugh? Did she sing when she was happy? Could she even carry a tune? What made her sad?

"If I could do anything in the world?" She considered the question for a moment. "I'd be loved," she said simply. "I have never had enough of that."

He didn't know what to say to her directness, to the anguish of her honesty. For a few moments an awkward silence stretched between them. Finally, he spoke again. "Love is not like betel nuts, Charlotte. It's not a commodity."

She smiled. "I know my parents loved me, at least I hope they did. My father never said the words to me, not once. And neither did my mother. But they were good to me and to my sisters. Still, I would've hoped for a little greater fondness from them, some more affection."

The question wasn't a wise one, but he asked it nevertheless. "Do you not have enough love in your life now?"

She looked directly at him. "I thought there was a chance of it," she said. "Now, I'm not so certain."

There was an odd confusion in her eyes, an emotion he couldn't decipher but that pained him to see. He began to walk, striding down the hill and through the glen, wondering if she'd keep up. She did, and without a word of protest for his pace.

Charlotte didn't speak again, but followed him like a disciple. If she were angry, she didn't mention it, and if she were hurt, she didn't punish him for it. She remained a ghost at his side, close enough that he was always intently conscious of her presence.

Against his better judgment, he offered her his free hand. Neither of them wore gloves, and the touch of their palms was surprisingly intimate. She linked her fingers with his, and he wanted to pull back and away. The act of either a coward or a wise man. He did neither, only squeezed her hand lightly and smiled at her.

She smiled back, the gesture making her face appear luminous. He wanted to caution her that such a look was dangerous near him. He was so captured by her soul and her mind that it was just one step closer to be enthralled by a smile.

There was no future for them.

He really shouldn't have gotten closer to her. She smelled of roses, or some other garden flower. He wanted to ask if she'd preserved the petals herself or had purchased the scent in London. Did she sprinkle it on her underclothing, or only dab it behind her ears and at her breast? Questions he had no business asking.

Questions that were better asked by a husband.

"Will you leave Balfurin once you find the treasure?" she asked.

He stopped and faced her. "I expected the question earlier," he said. "I congratulate you on your restraint."

"If you knew I was going to ask, have you formulated an answer?"

"Part of one," he said. This moment was coming for weeks, from the exact second he'd seen her marching across the ballroom, fire in her eyes. He needed to tell her the truth, but it came hesitantly to his lips. His conscience warred with his honor, but amazingly his honor won.

"Charlotte," he began, reaching out and touching the edge of her jaw with his bare hand. She didn't use her beauty like a number of women did, as a weapon in her arsenal. She was simply who she was, Charlotte MacKinnon, capable, determined, talented, and intelligent. "I'm not the man you think I am," he said. The words stuck in his throat.

"I know. I've sensed from the first that you've changed, George, and I thank God for it."

They were on the crest of a small hill with a flat, almost concave, top. She walked a few feet away, her back to him. He hoped she didn't turn. It would be so much easier to tell her the truth with her back to him.

"Can we not have a true marriage between us?" She examined the horizon, as if the words were written on the sky above the mountains in the distance. "I'm tired of loneliness. I would have laughter in my life and contentment. I want to waken in the morning knowing I was loved, and spend the day smiling. I think you and I could have that, if we tried."

Her words ate at the boundaries of its restraint, tempted him to lie when he should speak the truth. Once again he cursed George, wanting to punish his cousin for every tear she'd shed in the last five years. But the pain Charlotte would feel at his departure would be his burden alone. George had no part of that.

The time had come for honesty, and it was nearly killing him.

She turned and faced him. "I've waited in my bed this last week, thinking you would come to me. But you haven't."

He glanced at her, wondering why he was surprised at her frontal assault. Being direct was so much a part of Charlotte.

"I am not very practiced at seduction, but I am more

than willing to attempt it." She began to unbutton her cloak. He was struck dumb as one button after another fell open. She was not wearing her serviceable blue dress. Nor was she attired in any of her more fashionable gowns.

"You're naked," he said, somewhat stupidly.

"No," she corrected, "I have my cloak on."

"Your cloak," he repeated.

He was Dixon Robert MacKinnon, of the Balfurin MacKinnons, a long line of Scots stretching back at least six centuries. They had been reivers once upon a time, and barbarians.

They were men to be reckoned with.

Then why did he feel like such an innocent at the moment? As if he'd never seen a naked woman? Because he'd certainly never seen one standing on the edge of a moor, in the middle of a Scottish winter, with the remnants of snow dotting the hills, and a brisk wind whistling up his greatcoat. Because he'd never seen one smiling exactly like that at him, and crooking her finger at him.

"Why?" It seemed a reasonable request, and the only word he could utter at the moment. His hands gripped her shoulders still cloaked in a heavy wool, and he dared not think that only inches away was her unclothed body. He concentrated on the green of her eyes, instead, and the very mischievous smile playing around her lips. Except that beneath his hands, she trembled.

"Why?" he asked again. She moved her hands to place them on his chest, unbuttoning the buttons of his greatcoat, sliding her palms to rest against his vest. How strange that he could feel the imprint of her fingers against his skin.

"You wouldn't come to my bed. And if you will not come to me, then I simply must coax you."

"Must you?"

"I must," she said, nodding.

"Why?"

"I liked our lovemaking," she said softly. "Didn't you?"

"Above all things."

"Then why didn't you want to repeat it?"

"I did. But it wouldn't be wise. You don't know how many nights I wanted to come to you, how many times I stopped myself. Once was dishonor enough, but it would have to last me for the rest of my life."

She pressed both hands against his chest as if trying to push him away. "You're leaving, aren't you? And you don't want me burdened with a child. At least this time be honest enough to tell me before you go. Or write me a note. Don't make me wait like I did before, wondering which one of the maids you took with you."

"I would never leave with one of the maids," he said, smiling down at her.

She startled him by dropping to her knees before him and reaching for him.

"Charlotte."

"Don't leave me, George. Because if you leave me and Balfurin one more time, you can never come home again."

She never let her gaze drift from his face. Her eyes were intent, her mouth smiling. If he'd truly been

George, he would have been the most idiotic man alive to think of abandoning her.

But he wasn't George and there was no future for them. And any moment his cousin could come home. What would he find? An adulterous wife and a man who coveted her.

He would no doubt be damned in the future for his actions of the past. In the afterlife, if there was one, and he was summoned to stand before Satan himself, he would answer for his sins. To Satan's question: what do you have to say to save your immortal soul, he would have only one answer. I loved. Not wisely, but well.

She parted his greatcoat, undoing his trousers with a speed that shocked him. Or perhaps she was not as quick as he had imagined and he was just too slow to comprehend. He was being well and truly seduced, and his libido reared up in great delight and marked this day as something he would forever recall.

She withdrew him from his trousers with fingers that were not adept at the task, but she made up in enthusiasm what she lacked in skill. And damn him, he was more than willing to assist her, but she slapped his hands away and then put her mouth on him. In this task, she was not skilled, either, but he allowed himself to be used for practice.

One last time. He'd touch her one last time before leaving.

Wisps of her hair had come loose. He reached down and spread his fingers through it, dislodging the last of her hairpins and scattering them on the ground.

"Charlotte," he softly said, and it was both an entreaty and praise.

She was intent on her task, her hands on either thigh, the nails of each hand digging into his buttocks as if to punish him if he moved. As if he would. He was transfixed, amazed, and utterly delighted.

He was growing harder with each touch of her tongue along his length. When she mouthed him, pulling her lips completely around him and flicking her tongue back and forth over the tip, he almost exploded there and then.

"Is your quest to unman me, then, Charlotte?" He fingered her cheek. "I'd much rather spend myself in you."

She pulled back and looked up at him, gently cupping his testicles with one hand as she smoothed her other hand down his shaft. All the world like he was a recalcitrant puppy that she soothed with a gentle petting.

His skin was flushed and he was hot and needy and not in the mood to be toyed or trifled with. She stood, her mouth reddened, her nipples tight. She grabbed his hand and put it between her legs. "Feel how wet I am for you."

He was neither a god nor a saint.

He stripped off his greatcoat and tossed it to one side. He divested himself of his garments, throwing them out of the way. Later, he would worry about grass stains and other telltale signs that he'd indulged in a tryst. For the moment, his most important task was wiping that smile from Charlotte's face and changing the sharpness of her gaze to something more satisfied.

Once more. One more time of loving her and then he would leave Balfurin.

Finally, he was naked and he pinned her to the ground with a kiss. He nuzzled her neck, following an invisible path down to one impudent breast half shielded by the burgundy cloak.

"What are you saying?" Charlotte murmured between kisses.

"It's a prayer," he confessed. "That I might last long enough to give you satisfaction."

Her laughter was warm, inciting his own smile.

The world abruptly changed, the ground buckling beneath them. He only had time to roll her on top of him and wrap his legs and arms around her before they were falling. When he hit the ground it was with such force that the breath was knocked out of him. For a moment, he thought he'd lost consciousness. An eternity later, he heard Charlotte calling his name.

"Are you hurt?"

He opened his eyes and smiled at her. "I think my arm is broken," he said, feeling a spear of pain travel from his forearm to his shoulder. "No, not my arm, my shoulder." If he was right, his shoulder was dislocated.

"And you?" he asked.

"I'm fine. You broke my fall."

He sat up with her help and looked around them. They were in what appeared to be the ruins of a cave. The hill on which they'd rested only minutes earlier had been the ceiling, now collapsed and lying in chunks on the cave floor.

"It wasn't a hill at all, was it?" Charlotte said. "We were walking on top of a cave."

He nodded.

"The weight of all the snow must have weakened it."

"And we did the rest," she said.

"Thank God it's a sunny day," he said, "or we wouldn't be able to see a thing."

Charlotte knelt beside him, brushing off bits of rock and dirt and grass from his shoulders.

"You realize that your clothes are up there, and you're down here."

"At least one of us is dressed," he said. "Well, half dressed," he amended, grateful that she was still wearing her cloak. "Still, we're not exactly attired for exploring a cave," he said.

He stood and extended his good hand to help her. It was not a moment to feel amusement, but he couldn't restrain his smile.

The cave was hollowed out of the side of a hill. The portion where they stood was nothing but earth, but farther in, it was rock, and the tool marks on the stone indicated that while the cave might have been created by nature, man had amended it.

The top of the ceiling was shaped like an inverted bowl, the part where they had fallen at the very top. But the sides, curving down to the ground didn't look any more stable.

"There must be a way out," he said, looking into the darkness. He had no torch with him, nothing to light and no way to light it. His lantern was in the pack and the pack was above them. All he had was the staff that he'd fashioned earlier from a sturdy twig. He picked it up, wondering if he looked as foolish as he felt, exploring like the first man, naked and without even a loincloth.

What was that biblical quotation? The wages of sin are death? He had no intention of dying in this place.

He didn't believe in a vengeful Almighty. If God was of that temperament, Dixon would not have survived a dozen or so disasters in the last year alone.

There were two corridors stretching off into the darkness. Even the bright afternoon sun could not illuminate the pockets of shadows. He glanced at Charlotte. "Stay here," he said. "I'll be right back."

"I detest being commanded, George."

"Please. I may become lost and the sound of your voice will lure me back." In actuality, he didn't want to take a chance with her safety.

"Very well," she said, giving him a look that left no doubt in his mind what she thought of his plan.

As he walked away, he had the distinct notion that she was watching him. An odd feeling but not an uncomfortable one, to know that a woman was watching him walk, no doubt studying every inch of his body.

He left the light with great reluctance, descending deeper into the cave, following a corridor hewn out of the rock itself. It narrowed and then abruptly ended in a stone wall. There would be no escape here.

He turned and followed the second corridor, expecting to find the entrance to the cave. Instead, there was only a mound of dirt and boulders and a smell of something vaguely unpleasant.

"George!"

"I'll be there in a moment," he called.

"Now, please," Charlotte said, her voice quavering.

He turned and retraced his path, returning to where she stood, the dust stirred by the cave-in settling in a nimbus of sunlight around her.

"What is it?" He came to her side, realizing she was trembling violently.

"Look." She was staring in the opposite direction, where the other corridor led away into the rock.

"What is it, Charlotte?"

"There. Look." She raised her arm and pointed.

He didn't see what she was looking at right away. But as the dust began to settle even more, he realized that it wasn't an outcropping of rock he was seeing. He took a few steps toward the shape, his mind reeling with the knowledge even as he approached the skeleton. The skeleton of a man, his dark hair thinning and long, half covering the head.

At the skeleton's side was a cask of coins and small nugget-sized pieces of gold. Beside his hand was a large onyx ring, the stone carved with the first earl's crest, a ring Dixon had seen often enough on his uncle's hand.

George.

A surge of grief nearly sent him to his knees.

"Who is it?"

Shouldn't she know? Shouldn't something have alerted her? He looked up at the cloudless blue sky as if to see the laughing face of God.

Dixon turned and faced her, naked and defenseless. "It's George."

He watched as her eyes changed, watched as confusion filled her face, and her features smoothed in protection.

She stared at her husband, and then looked back at him.

"I don't understand." Her mind's last attempt to refute the obvious. Her inability to believe was temporary and as swift as his own recognition had been.

"If that's George, then who are you?" Her voice

was so faint that he could barely hear her, but he didn't need her words.

"Who are you?" This time, she nearly shouted the question.

"My name is Dixon Robert MacKinnon. I'm George's cousin. Some say I'm ruthless; few would say I'm kind. I'm the chairman of the MacKinnon Trading Company, and I'm the largest landowner in Penang. I have over forty ships in my fleet. I'm wealthy beyond my boyhood expectations and yet at this moment, I'm greedy and envious and damned."

She pulled her cloak tighter around her in a gesture more revealing than if she screamed.

"Why?" she asked, staring at him with wide eyes and a stricken expression on her face.

He knew what she was feeling, the clarity of his empathy startling. She couldn't speak because the words wouldn't come, but her mind was filled with questions, protests, and arguments. She was in turn angry and hurt. But all she'd asked was a simple, one-word question. An impossible question: why?.

She didn't speak, didn't move. She might have been a statue hewn from unforgiving rock.

"You thought I was George. I allowed myself to continue the pretense."

"A word was all you needed. A simple explanation."

"Nothing about this entire situation has been simple from its inception, Charlotte."

"Why didn't you tell me?"

"Perhaps I was curious," he said. "Perhaps I wanted to find out what happened to George. You were a stranger; I didn't know you."

"Didn't trust me."

He nodded.

"Is that why you came to Balfurin? To find George?"

Silence stretched between them.

"No." The whole truth had to come out, didn't it? Every scar, every hidden secret. "I didn't know George was missing until I arrived."

All he really wanted to do was protect her, to keep her from being lonely. He wanted to be there in the middle of the night when she woke and couldn't sleep. He wanted to pull her into his embrace and love her, hold her until dawn stretched across the horizon.

He wanted to laugh with her, and marvel at the complexity of her mind. He wanted to reassure her, complement her, and simply be in the same room so that she could look up and find him there.

Instead, he'd hurt her, and he was going to hurt her more.

"I came to Balfurin to hide, I think. I came to find my roots, to understand myself. Matthew thinks it's part of my grief."

If anything, she grew more still.

"I was married. To a beautiful woman whom I no doubt used as George did you. I had more money, but her father was a high-ranking member of the English East India Company. I wanted his influence more than I wanted her."

She took a step back as if poisoned by proximity. Very well, she might as well have it all, every chunk and morsel of it.

"Annabelle was an excessively tiresome woman," he said, realizing exactly how he sounded. Cruel and uncompromising. But better Charlotte see him as he had been. Perhaps as he still was.

"She complained about the weather, about my absences, about Malay. She refused to learn the language, or adapt. She wanted to go home to England."

Charlotte remained silent.

"She also complained about her health. Endlessly. She broke a nail and it was a tragedy. She acquired a bruise and the world must stop. I learned to ignore her to my shame and endless guilt. I had a choice to summon the physician for her stomach pain or attend a meeting. I chose the meeting."

"She died," Charlotte said.

He nodded. "She died."

He turned to face George's skeleton. "Matthew thinks I'm grieving. I'm not. I didn't love her. I'm ashamed. Ashamed that greed made me marry her, ashamed that greed kept me from insisting upon proper treatment for her. Who is more guilty of the two of us for that sin, I wonder? George or me?"

She didn't speak.

George had been trapped here in the darkness. Dixon's mind shied away from the thought of that death, and he turned to face Charlotte again.

She'd not changed her stance, nor had her gaze veered from him. He'd never felt so exposed in his life, or as vulnerable in his nakedness as he did at that moment.

"I didn't want to tell you who I was. Perhaps, in some way, I thought that I could simply go on as I was, pretending to be George, becoming the husband you deserved."

She shook her head and he held up one hand to halt her words.

"I didn't want to feel what I did for you. I didn't want to envy George. I didn't want to resent him. But I did, and the longer I knew you, the more I knew I wouldn't be able to simply walk away from you. But the one thing I did, and it was the most difficult task I've ever set for myself, was staying away from your bed."

She looked away, her gaze fastened on the far wall. Very well, let her avoid the sight of him, but let her have the truth at least.

"I've wanted you from the moment I first saw you, Charlotte. If that's a sin, then I'm a sinner."

She took a deep breath before speaking. "I have to get out of here," she said. "I will scream if I don't, and I'm not given to screaming." She finally looked at him.

"You can stand on my shoulders. You should be able to pull yourself to safety."

She nodded.

He bent down in front of her, a gesture that spoke to him of allegory. He was a supplicant, she the grantor of his wishes. But she wasn't in a generous mood, and only mounted his back, her knees on his shoulders. When he stood, slowly, balancing her as if she were the most precious of burdens, she wavered a little, clutching at his hands. He could feel her tremble and wondered if it was because of her precarious post or the discovery they'd made, only minutes old.

Slowly, she gained her balance, stepping onto his shoulders. The resulting pain felt like torture. He moved his hands to her legs as she steadied herself.

He moved a little closer to the edge. She stood on tiptoe on his shoulders and he bore the agony without a sound. He was not a martyr by inclination or choice, but he probably deserved whatever pain she inflicted on him.

His hands still rested on her calves, feeling her tremble. He wanted to say something to comfort her, to strengthen her, but the gulf that stretched between them was too wide and too deep to cross with words.

"There's a rock here," she said. "I think I can reach it."

He remained motionless as she reached up, and then she was gone, the pressure on his shoulders abruptly lighter. He stepped back and looked up, shielding his eyes from the sun.

She knelt on the edge and threw his clothes down to him.

"Will you send help for me?"

She looked past him to where George sat against the wall.

"I'll send help," she said. "My husband must be properly buried. Although I'd prefer to let you rot."

There was nothing but silence as she left him. He donned his clothes before returning to George.

What had his cousin's last hours been like? Had they been filled with regret? Anger? One of a myriad of questions to which he would never know the answer.

"Ever since your father drummed it into me that I would never ascend to the title, I've been doing my damnedest to be better than you in every way. I learned to shoot better, to be a better horseman. I made a fortune, George, not by winning it or finding it, but earning it. And I discovered something that I wish to God you'd learned. Greed isn't enough. Not nearly enough."

He plucked a gold coin from the cask and watched as it gleamed in the sunlight. "All in all, George, everything I fought to acquire doesn't mean very much right now."

He tossed the coin back into the chest. "I feel as though I've fallen into hell. You've heard me confess all my sins, cousin. Is it practice, do you think, for my ultimate interview with Satan?"

How odd that George seemed to smile at him.

Chapter 22

No more than an hour later, rescue arrived in the form of a ladder and a rope. Two young footmen, possessing more brawn than curiosity, assisted Dixon out of the cave, then in raising and carrying George home.

When they arrived at Balfurin, Charlotte stepped out of the shadows and motioned the footmen into the parlor. A bier had been set aside for George's remains, and they carefully placed him there.

Only then did she turn and address Dixon, looking at the floor as she did so.

"You're the Earl of Marne now," she said.

He nodded.

"Despite that, I hope you'll respect my request."

"Charlotte," he began, but she held her hand up as if to stop his speech with her fingers.

"Please leave," she said softly. "Our solicitors can

work out the arrangements of my surrendering Balfurin to you, but in the meantime, I just want you gone."

"Forgive me."

She didn't respond, didn't say another word, just stood in front of him with her head bowed. It was the sight of her tears that silenced him.

Dixon turned without another word, heading for his room where Matthew relocated his shoulder and helped him improvise a sling for his arm. Although he was still in pain, he refused Matthew's potion, intent on a final errand.

At the door, he turned and addressed the other man. "You'll be pleased to know we're leaving Balfurin."

Matthew was as silent as Charlotte had been.

Dixon left the Laird's Chamber, intent on the tower room. When he knocked, the door was opened by a young maid.

"I'm sorry, your lordship," she said, "but Nan is not feeling well today."

"Nevertheless, I have to speak with her." Nan was ancient; it was very possible that she would not last to see another dawn. Before she died, he wanted the truth. "I'm afraid it can't wait," he said, and gently pushed the door open.

The girl stepped back, reluctantly allowing him entrance.

He'd thought Nan diminutive before, but in her wide and deep bed, she looked little larger than a child. Her white hair was wispy upon the pillow, her face so lined that it resembled wrinkled cloth. She turned her head when he entered her chamber, but she didn't smile in greeting. Instead, her gaze locked on his and she nodded slightly.

"You've found him."

"Yes. But then, I think you knew I would."

"I hoped for it. I wanted him to find peace before I did," she said, her voice so low and raspy that he had difficulty hearing her. He pulled up the chair to sit at her bedside.

"Tell me what happened," he said.

She smiled. "So autocratic, young sir. Very well. He came home, just like you thought, to find the treasure. I think he was ashamed that his wife had more money than he. It is the way of the world sometimes, when a man has more pride than sense.

"I gave him the first verse, like I was supposed to. When he found the rest of the poem he asked me if I knew where the treasure was buried. I told him no more than I told you, but he was hungrier for it, I think, and every day he went out with his shovel, determined to find it."

"But one day he didn't come back," Dixon said.

She nodded weakly. "One day he didn't come back. And we waited. The next day passed, and the next, and then a full week. We knew he never would come back." She raised her shaking hand and pointed at the floor. "The third board," she said.

He stood and walked to where she pointed, pushing back the rug. One of the boards wasn't nailed down completely, and he lifted it easily. Inside the hole was a leather valise and inside the valise were a few clothes. At the bottom were George's brush and shaving gear, all inscribed with the Marne crest.

"Why did you hide his things?"

"I didn't hide them," she said faintly. "I kept them safe. Especially from the English. Some of the money he brought we used to feed ourselves for a time. The rest is in there."

Now was not the time to try to reason her out of her lifelong hatred of the English. She was dying, and making her peace, such as it was, with what had happened.

"Jeffrey knows, doesn't he?"

She nodded. "Aye," she said faintly, her voice fading.

Dixon didn't answer, just came to sit beside her again. He knew she wasn't going to live long. Despite her actions, he didn't want her to be alone, especially not after witnessing how George had died.

"You're named for him, you know. My Robbie."

"I know," he said softly. "My grandfather was a great man."

"Not great," she corrected. "Sometimes foolish, sometimes wise. He knew how to live, however, and that's a gift most people don't have. Do you, Dixon?"

He thought of the vision of Charlotte, naked beneath her cloak, her smile tremulous yet daring. "I thought I did," he said, knowing that there would forever be a hole in his life where she should be.

"Don't be a fool, boy." Her eyes closed.

He smiled, and reached out to hold her hand.

Less than an hour later, she opened her eyes. "Robbie," she said, and smiled. In that instant, he knew that she no longer saw him, but another man, the companion of her youth, and the love of her life.

He sat by her bedside for an hour, maybe more, drawing a curious kind of peace there. When it was time, he left the tower room, seeking out the elderly retainer who'd been her friend all these years.

Jeffrey didn't say anything to the news, only bowed his head for a moment. "She was old when I came here, your lordship, and I'm no youth. It's to be expected." He shook his head. "But it won't be the same without her."

As he left, Dixon turned and studied the elderly retainer. "You weren't confused that night, were you?"

Jeffrey looked at him from under his bushy white eyebrows. "What night would that be, my lord?"

"When I first arrived at Balfurin. You called me the Earl of Marne."

"I'm not so feeble that I didn't recognize you, your lordship."

"You already knew what had happened to George."

Jeffrey inclined his head. "I only suspected."

"Is that why you wanted me to look for the treasure?"

For a moment, he didn't think Jeffrey would answer him. When the old man finally spoke, his voice was low and raspy, as if he were holding back emotion. "We weren't all that sure he'd come back to Balfurin if he found the treasure. He'd never shown any loyalty to the place before. I reasoned that if you couldn't find the treasure, then he was alive somewhere. If you found him, then I had my answer."

"Didn't you look for him?" Dixon asked.

"I was too old to go traipsing over the countryside."

"George might have survived if you'd found him in time," Dixon said.

There was a pause, and then Jeffrey looked up at him, his eyes rheumy and sunken. "You can't make me feel more guilty than I already do, your lordship.

Why do you think no one came out and told you the story from the first? Nan and me were aching for our actions. Shamed. We've got to go to our Maker knowing we're partly responsible. You saying it's so doesn't make it more of a burden."

They exchanged a long look.

"It would have been better if you'd told me," Dixon finally said.

Jeffrey nodded. "But it's a sight easier to look backward than it is to face the future, your lordship."

Dixon could only agree. He retreated to the Laird's Chamber and began packing. In an odd way, it was fitting that his departure from Balfurin be so precipitous and without fanfare. He'd come home without warning and he was leaving in the same manner.

Charlotte arranged for George's body to be placed in the Green Parlor prior to the service that would inter him in the chapel. She sent word to the minister in Inverness, and had notices delivered to those who should be informed, and proceeded to become the widow of the Earl of Marne. Only a few days later, when thanking the guests for attending George's funeral, did Charlotte realize that it was possible that a few of them believed the man who'd attended the ball had also been the one they buried.

She didn't correct them.

When it was over, and the guests had left Balfurin, Charlotte gave instructions that the floor was not to be reset after George's interment. Instead, she wanted Nan to be buried beside George's grandfather, a decision that probably confused most of the staff and no doubt would anger a few of the MacKinnon ancestors had they been present to voice their disapproval.

They would simply have to haunt her.

Future generations would no doubt look on the three names inscribed on the plaques on the floor and try to reason out the triangle, George's grandfather, his wife, and his mistress. Let them wonder. Or perhaps they would stand on the stones as she did now, and reflect on a life that had spanned ninety-two years.

"They say she lived in the tower room because she could see the chapel from there," Maisie said from beside her.

Charlotte glanced at Maisie and then away. The maid had been quiet and reserved ever since Matthew had left, as if the spark of life in her was dimmed by his absence.

"She loved him even after he died," Maisie said. "Thirty years it was."

Charlotte didn't respond. What could she say? That the sadness and the loss seemed insurmountable to her, that Nan's life should have been spent in joy and not in grief.

She had to make decisions, and yet she felt incapable of doing so. Balfurin belonged to Dixon now, and she had to leave. Either that or possibly lease the castle from him since it had effectively been converted to a school. Would he accept those arrangements?

My name is Dixon Robert MacKinnon. I'm George's cousin. Some say I'm ruthless; few would say I'm kind.

She cursed her memory.

Why hadn't she known?

He'd told her he was George, and she'd believed it. What kind of stupid, foolish woman did that make her?

Poor Charlotte MacKinnon—unable to tell her own husband from a stranger. She might well be the brunt of a child's taunt. Charlotte MacKinnon, husband gone missin'. Her skill at rhyme exhausted, she shook her head as if to clear it.

There, that was the crux of the matter, wasn't it? Her shame. Her embarrassment. How could she face people? They would all be asking themselves the very same question she now asked. Didn't she know?

No, she hadn't.

Instead, she'd been fascinated from the very first by the man who'd claimed to be her husband. A man who had left Balfurin on the very same day George had been found.

She'd told him to leave, and he had. She'd refused to allow him to speak, and he'd remained silent. She wanted to be alone, and everyone had carefully respected her wishes.

Didn't anyone understand that she didn't *know* what she wanted?

"I've a letter, your ladyship," Maisie said.

Charlotte faced her maid. For a moment, brief and fleeting, and filled with unbearable hope, she thought it might be from *him* and stretched out her hand. But the handwriting was female and familiar.

"What is it, your ladyship?" Maisie asked. "Are you unwell?"

"No," she said numbly, opening the envelope and staring down at the words.

"Is it bad news?"

She glanced over at Maisie. "Strange, I almost expected it. No, it's not bad news." She stared down at the letter. "It's from my mother, Maisie," she said. "My parents have invited me to England for a visit." She held up the letter, read, " 'It's time our rift was mended. We so desperately wish to see you, Charlotte.' " She looked at Maisie again. "They're willing to send their best carriage for me." Had they learned of George's death? Somehow, was she now deemed acceptable? Or had enough time simply elapsed that her parents were willing to overlook the fact that she'd defied them?

How very odd that it didn't seem to matter right at the moment.

"Isn't that what you wanted, your ladyship?"

"I don't know," Charlotte said, honestly. "I've waited for them to write me for years. I don't need them now."

Maisie smiled, but it seemed an effort for her to do so. "We don't need many people in our lives, your ladyship. But it's another thing to want them, isn't it?"

"You're talking about Matthew, aren't you?"

"I am. I expect it will not be always easy, him being Chinese and me being Scot."

"But you want him in your life?"

Maisie's smile broadened. "No, your ladyship, him I need. And you, your ladyship? Do you not need someone?"

Charlotte ignored the question, but Maisie wasn't deterred.

"Sometimes men need a bit of coaxing. Or they

don't understand the signs we send out. Like the ones you gave his lordship."

"I wasn't aware I was sending out any signs."

Maisie sent her a remonstrative look. Charlotte decided that perhaps silence was the best recourse. But her maid would not allow her to remain mute, it seemed.

"You cannot mean to say those longing looks were accidental?"

"I never once sent him a longing look," Charlotte protested.

"Indeed, your ladyship, you did, and often. And sometimes, you would simply sigh, and stare into his eyes like a lovesick girl. It's a good thing that the new term hasn't yet started. You'd not be a good example to all those tenderhearted girls."

"I've never heard anything more unfair in my life, Maisie."

"Perhaps you didn't know you were doing it, your ladyship. It's quite possible. I, myself, knew that I was gazing on Matthew like a silly child. But I think women are supposed to be admiring of men. It makes them feel manly and handsome. But then, they're supposed to act the same around women. How are we to know that they think we're beautiful otherwise?"

She glanced at Maisie.

"Dixon never looked at me in such a way."

"Perhaps not when you were looking, your ladyship. But he did."

"Really?"

Maisie nodded.

"How did you become so wise in the ways of men and women?"

"Well, it wasn't from listening at the door to The Edification Society," Maisie said. She glanced at Charlotte, whose face was warming with embarrassment. "What a bunch of silliness that was. My Mam used to say that love was the best teacher of all, that you find out what to do with all the arms and legs and things when you love the one you lie with."

"Your mother seems like a very wise woman."

"She should be. She had twelve of us, and enough grandchildren to occupy a village. I wonder how she'd feel about a little Oriental one?"

"Are you with child, Maisie?" Charlotte asked.

Maisie didn't look the least offended by the question. "I'm not, but I would be happy to be." She looked down at the stones at her feet. "I don't want to live the whole of my life like Nan, your ladyship, always wanting something that God can't give you."

She turned and left Charlotte alone with the dead.

Always wanting something that God can't give you. Maisie's words seemed almost prophetic. Was she to be like Nan for the rest of her life? Waiting for the end of it to be joined to the one man who made her heart smile?

How could she walk the halls of Balfurin, either quiet and sedate or raucous and noisy as they would soon become, without thinking of him? Was she to live the rest of her life in longing?

He'd taken advantage of her. She closed her eyes and forced away the thought that she had attempted to seduce him not once but twice. After that one night, he'd acted with honor, but she hadn't.

What would Lady Eleanor say? She might advise her to take one of the footmen as her lover. She didn't want a lover. She was quite done with men, with love, forever. She had lived quite well for five years without any thought of companionship or intimacy. She could live another five, ten, fifteen years without love.

No, she couldn't.

Since Dixon had come to Balfurin, every morning had been a new adventure. She couldn't wait to end her sleep, to dress, and leave her room. Her heart had stuttered on witnessing him on the stairs, and she'd begun to look for him at the window. The day was not complete until she'd seen him. Sometimes he'd wave, and she'd felt as if the world was a perfect place once again.

She'd never before considered that love might have so many nuances—from laughter to friendship to admiration to joy. Sometimes she experienced a warm hollow feeling in her stomach or an ache in her chest, as if her heart wept. Sometimes, she was ecstatic, and sometimes sad.

No one had told her that desire might be possible as well, that she might want to be touched by another human being, crave it so much that she would dream of him. No one had ever explained that her body would be a traitorous entity, that she would feel as if she were not in control but that he commanded her heartbeat and the escalation of her breath. She could still feel his hands on her breasts, could close her eyes and feel his thumbs on her nipples, softly strumming as if to coax them to harden. Every pore seemed to open, as if yearning to savor every exquisite sensation.

She wanted to take him to her bed, again and again and again. She wanted to use him up, familiarize herself with the feeling of passion until she was replete.

She wanted young women to come to her for advice and older women to look at her with a knowing eye.

She couldn't help but remember what he looked like in the cave. He was the most beautiful creature she'd ever seen, with the sun hitting his shoulders, with his muscled stomach and his broad chest and slim hips. He'd touched her with his hands, and covered her body with his, and made her think ineffable, impossible things, recall snippets of poetry about beauty and love.

He'd lied to her. He'd admitted to flaws and faults that distressed her. He was no god, but a man with blemishes on his soul.

I didn't want to feel what I did for you . . . But I did, and the longer I knew you, the more I knew I wouldn't be able to simply walk away from you.

But he had. He'd left her, and she was in love with him.

Dear God, how was she to bear it?

Not by waiting. Not by sitting beside a window and watching as life passed by in an endless panorama. Not by wishing. Not by weeping at night.

Charlotte said her final farewells, not only to Nan and George, but also to the woman she'd been as well.

Chapter 23

❧

"Balfurin is warmer," Matthew said, making a clucking sound with his tongue. "As large as the castle is, it has a feeling of coziness."

"That's because there's a fireplace in almost every room," Dixon said.

"It's a very strange country, your Scotland," Matthew said. "It's very cold, but its people are warm. They seem very accepting."

"Unless you're English," Dixon said.

"That is one disadvantage that I do not have." Matthew smiled.

"Are you glad you came to Scotland with me, then?"

"There are compensations for remaining here," Matthew said. "I doubt I shall ever grow accustomed to the cold, but a smile can sometimes make up for the chill."

"Would that smile belong to a certain young lady by the name of Maisie?"

"I find her very personable. A very direct and honest young woman." He stared out the window as if he saw Maisie's face in the reflection.

Dixon didn't bother to hide his smile. He'd never before seen Matthew enamored of a woman. No, it was more than that. "Are you in love, Matthew?"

Matthew sighed, as if he'd both expected the question and dreaded it. "Who knows what love is?"

He did, but Dixon kept that thought to himself. Love tore him up inside like shards of glass, but had the capability of healing as quickly. One smile from Charlotte would do it. The sound of her laughter would keep him buoyed for hours.

"Are you going to simply leave it at that, Matthew?"

"I have nothing to give her, master. Even my life is not my own."

"I give it to you."

Matthew turned to look at him, surprised.

"I've done it before, you know, at least thirty times, and each time you've refused to accept it. I'm damn tired of feeling responsible for you. You owe me nothing, except for your happiness, and I'll not stand in the way of that. One of us should be happy, don't you think?"

"I'm of mixed blood, master. Your lordship."

Dixon threw down his quill, uncaring that ink spotted the papers he'd been given. "Malay was settled by people of all races. If Maisie is so petty as to consider your bloodlines, then she isn't worthy of you at all."

"She does not care, your lordship."

"Dixon."

Matthew studied him for a long moment.

"A servant would call me your lordship," Dixon said. "But a friend would address me by name. Either Dixon or MacKinnon. I think, after all this time, that we're friends, don't you?"

He returned to signing the documents his solicitor had given him.

"Is there nothing I can do to assist you?"

"No," Dixon said. "Most of these have to do with ascending to the title. I had no idea that there was so much I was responsible for. No wonder George found it necessary to wed an heiress."

He looked down at the stack of papers still to be signed. He was the Earl of Marne, the Laird of Balfurin. Why wasn't he more pleased? He had proof of his responsibilities in the papers before him, in the fact that people addressed him as *your lordship*. Not a pretend title as when he'd masqueraded as George, but rightfully his.

Why didn't it mean more?

All his life, he'd wanted to be master of Balfurin. He'd wanted to be laird. He'd wanted to be the Earl of Marne. He'd been desperate to be the next in a proud line of men, *the* MacKinnon.

Now, he was more than ready to turn his back on everything, to escape Scotland.

He couldn't evict Charlotte from Balfurin, and he couldn't see himself living there in the shadow of her memory. What would he do with an empty school for girls? For that matter, what would he do with an empty life?

"Your fortune will be put to good use, then. Balfurin needs upkeep."

Dixon nodded. He'd already settled a fair amount on Charlotte, in addition to making her his heir in case anything happened to him.

"Are you going to do something about Maisie?"

"I do not like leaving you alone," Matthew said.

"I've been without your companionship most of my life, Matthew. As long as I was assured of your well being, I'd be happy enough with the arrangement."

"You will be lonely."

Dixon smiled.

"So I shall be, but perhaps it's what I deserve." He stared at the end of the quill for a moment. "I never loved her, you know. Annabelle. I don't want you thinking that I'm grieving for her. She deserved a better husband. She deserved a better fate."

"I never believed you were grieving for her," Matthew said. "But for the death of your honor."

Dixon studied the other man for a long moment. "You never cease to amaze me, Matthew."

"It was not difficult to see that you were shamed by your actions. You are a man of principle and you did not act according to your own conscience."

"Nor have I in Scotland."

Matthew shook his head. "I think you did what you must in order to solve the mystery of your cousin's disappearance."

"At the risk of insulting you, Matthew, you're too kind. Perhaps you could impart that opinion to a certain countess of my acquaintance. It might change her mind about me. She's brushed my explanations aside as if I'm a raving lunatic. Although I don't suppose I blame her."

He glanced at Matthew again. "You'll stay here,

then? Even with the Scottish winters? They can be brutal."

Matthew smiled. "As you say. But I think I will be warm enough."

Charlotte had earlier directed that her coach be readied for a trip to Inverness. She'd learned from a groom that Dixon's coachman, in his eagerness to arrive in Inverness, was vocal in his dislike of Balfurin. Beyond that, Charlotte didn't have a clue as to Dixon's plans. But if she had to visit every single inn in the entire city, she was more than willing.

She descended the broad steps of Balfurin, pulling on her gloves. At the bottom of the stairs she glanced back at the castle.

She had come to Balfurin seeking answers. For years the castle had sheltered her, protecting her from loneliness and even despair. Here, she'd found purpose and a feeling of worth. She'd changed her life single-handedly, and Balfurin had seemed to approve, almost as if it were a sentient being.

Now, however, a cloud loomed over the structure as if Balfurin chided her for her anger, for her stiff-necked pride.

Maisie ran down the steps after her.

Charlotte stared at the younger woman. "What are you doing here?"

"I have come to accompany you, your ladyship."

"It is not necessary, truly. I'm a widow, the headmistress of a school. I need no chaperone."

One of Maisie's eyebrows rose. "May I ask where you're going?"

"To Inverness."

The second eyebrow joined the first. "Why?"

Was she to have no privacy? "Is it necessary that you know?"

"No," Maisie said calmly. "But I know where his lordship and Matthew are staying."

"How do you know that?"

"Matthew told me."

She and Maisie studied each other. In the girl's eyes was the same resolve that had stared back at Charlotte from the mirror this morning.

"He was going to come back for you," Charlotte said.

"He was." Maisie nodded, and it was a curiously proud nod, as if the girl had blossomed into a confident woman overnight.

"I suppose that would save time," Charlotte admitted.

She still hadn't entered the carriage, and Maisie looked steadily at her.

"If you don't allow me to come with you," Maisie finally said, "I'll simply have to steal a horse from Balfurin and journey there alone. Unlike you, your ladyship, I am neither a widow nor a headmistress. But I am determined."

"But you just said he'll be back."

"But I don't know when. I miss him, your ladyship."

The girl folded her hands and continued to regard Charlotte impassively.

Charlotte sighed. "Then who am I to refuse you? I wouldn't dare."

Half the way to Inverness, Charlotte decided that what she was doing was foolish. A dozen times she decided to return to Balfurin but every time she did so, she glanced over at Maisie, marveling how brave and composed the maid appeared.

Charlotte's stomach lurched with every turn of the wheel. If it hadn't been for Maisie, she might have knocked on the roof and had the coachman slow even further, giving her time to compose herself. But the closer they came to Inverness, the more impatient Maisie appeared.

Inverness was crowded, the city noisier than she remembered. When the carriage finally halted in front of a red-brick inn, Maisie exited first, Charlotte following at a more sedate pace. The inn looked to be a charming place, a prosperous establishment. Maisie lost no time in admiration, but strode past her and entered the taproom, asking to speak to the owner. When had she become so demanding? Had love changed her? Or was it simply that she felt no fear?

They received directions, and this time Charlotte led the way up the stairs. The door was opened at her knock not by Matthew, but by Dixon himself.

"Please, your lordship," Maisie said, stepping in front of Charlotte, "I'd like to talk to Matthew."

He nodded, and pointed to the room across the hall. Only then did he look back at Charlotte.

Good Lord, he was handsome. She wanted to ask about his shoulder, but his expression halted her solicitousness. He was unsmiling, looking more stern and severe than she'd ever seen him.

He didn't look as if he was happy to see her at all. Instead, he turned and walked across the room, halting beside the window, leaving her to follow or to remain where she was.

Slowly, she entered the room, closing the door softly behind her.

She clutched her gloves in her hands and wished she'd put her bonnet on instead of leaving it on the seat inside the carriage. It would have acted as a barrier, a helmet.

More because of a wish to do something than to appear proper, she began to pull on her gloves, jerking them at the wrist. Her hands were damp, and the gloves weren't cooperating, and the task did nothing to ease the passing of the silent minutes.

He still didn't speak. What had she expected, for him to act overjoyed at her appearance? Yes. She had imagined that he would enfold her in an embrace, and then kiss her, and together they would plan their future.

This tall, handsome man with the watchful eyes was not what she'd expected.

She forced her shoulders back, and her head erect, facing him.

"I will not be deserted by another MacKinnon," she said, her voice carrying over the distance between them. It was not what she'd planned to say, but she didn't excuse away the words. Instead, she calmly folded her gloved hands around her reticule and regarded him the way she would a rebellious sixteen-year-old.

Dixon, however, was not looking the least bit cowed. Instead, he regarded her coolly and steadily.

"I was the one who asked you to leave. Make sure you remember that when you go back to Penang. You haven't left me. I want that understood."

Oh dear. Why had she said that?

"Is that really why you came, Charlotte?"

At this moment, it was difficult to remember exactly why she'd come to Inverness. To see him one last time? To marvel at how handsome he was? To see the light surrounding him like a nimbus, to recall how tall he was, how broad his shoulders?

To force him to admit that he'd been a cad? To make him explain, in minute detail, why he'd done what he had? Or why he thought he could escape any ramifications for his actions?

One of the tenets she taught her students was that there were consequences to behavior. Wisdom brought reward; impulsiveness often resulted in ruin.

A foolish woman was the most pitiable creature of them all.

Perhaps it was understandable that initially she might have confused the two men. She'd only been married a week to George, and he'd been missing for five years. Yet honesty now compelled her to admit that seeing Dixon, she could no more compare him to George than she could liken a lion to a chicken.

She looked down at her reticule, and then slowly turned, waiting, waiting. For what? For him to say something to keep her there? What could he possibly say?

A host of remarks, all of which she'd accept. Instead, silence stretched between them, broken by another pronouncement, one she heard herself say with something like horror. "I don't want you in my life, Dixon MacKinnon. I don't want you in Scotland."

"Indeed?"

"When you go back to that paradise of yours, please remember that I was the one who sent you away. You didn't leave me."

At least she'd refused to be abandoned again.

She opened the door, walked out into the hall, and closed the door behind her so hard that she was certain the sound could be heard down in the taproom. The noise, however, was not sufficient to separate her maid from Matthew. The two of them stood in the doorway of the opposite room, engaging in a form of welcome that could only be called enthusiastic.

Charlotte cleared her throat, and Maisie finally looked in her direction, but she didn't remove her arms from around Matthew's neck.

At least someone had a bit of happiness.

"You'll be staying, then?" she asked Maisie.

The girl only nodded, joy adding beauty to her face.

Charlotte took a sum of money from her reticule and pressed it into Maisie's hand.

"You'll marry her, Matthew?" Charlotte asked, looking at him.

"If she'll have me, your ladyship."

Maisie's expression was answer enough.

What was pride, when happiness was at stake?

She should knock on Dixon's door and say what she'd really come to say: *I'll cling to you like a burr, a barnacle, a thistle. I'll badger you with my presence until you accede to my every wish. I'll tempt you or torture you. However I do it, I'll not let you leave me.*

She turned, intent on doing just that. Her knock, however, wasn't answered. She knocked once more, but he didn't open the door. Evidently, Dixon had had enough of conversation. Or of her.

"Your ladyship," Matthew began, but she waved her hand at him, knowing that she wouldn't be able to speak without crying. She'd lost her pride after all, it seemed.

She made it down the stairs and out to her carriage, desperate to leave Inverness. She straightened her shoulders and before the footman could assist her, opened the carriage door. One foot was on the step when she glanced inside.

Dixon sat against the cushions, occupying the whole corner of the interior.

He smiled at her, a bright, disarming expression that rooted her to the spot.

"Are you coming inside, Charlotte?"

As if to remind her that she'd been brokenhearted a moment earlier, one tear escaped her eye and rolled down her cheek. She angrily brushed it away.

How odd that she'd lost the ability to speak.

"If you delay any further," he said, "it'll be dark by the time we arrive at Balfurin."

A thousand comments came to mind, but the only one that left her lips was silly and unimportant. "How did you get here?"

He pointed upward. She glanced back at the steeply canted roof of the inn.

"You climbed up on the roof? With your shoulder?"

"Actually," he said, "I climbed *down* the roof. Did I ever tell you how we cleared some of the tropical forests in Penang?"

She shook her head.

"A story for another time. Suffice it to say I'm very

good at climbing trees. And roofs, shoulder or no."

"Why?" Another silly question, but she was trying to understand. The streets were congested, the pedestrians passing them looked alternately curious or annoyed that she blocked their way with the open door. All she could think of was that he looked too handsome, and she wanted to throw herself into his arms.

His smile faded a little, and he leaned forward, extending a hand to her. She put her hand in his, entered the vehicle, and sat opposite him.

"I had to stop you," he said. "A grand gesture, if you will. Something to get your attention. Regrettably, I don't have Matthew's talent in magic."

At her silence, his face changed, his half smile fading. "I don't believe what you said, you know."

He didn't give her time to respond, which was just as well. She was feeling very bemused at the moment.

"I had no intention of leaving for Penang, Charlotte."

"You didn't?"

"I was observing the requisite mourning period. Or attempting to do so."

She'd had five years to mourn George, but it sounded wrong to say such a thing aloud, so she remained silent.

He'd never released her hand, and now he bent his head to study it.

"How long were you going to stay away?" she finally asked.

"Another week. More than that would have been too long, I think. Too unbearable."

He looked up. "At the end of the week I was going

to make camp around Balfurin. I was fully prepared
to engage in a siege."

"Another grand gesture?" she asked.

"Something to convince you of my feelings."

She didn't answer him. She couldn't. Could her
heart swell to encompass the whole of her body?

"Consider yourself kidnapped, if you will." He gently released her hand and leaned back against the cushions. "I've given Franklin orders to return to Balfurin,
and I've no intention of releasing you until you agree."

"To what?"

"To marrying me, of course. I love you. Will you
marry me, Charlotte? I warn you, I intend to be a very
demanding husband. Not an absent one at all, I'm
afraid. I'm remaining in Scotland, right beside you.
There are several additional conditions to this union,
so weigh your answer carefully."

"What conditions?" she asked, wishing that the
dress she wore had pockets. She would thrust her
hands into them and clench her fists so he wouldn't
know how terrifying it was to ask that question.

"I demand that you love me," he said, "that is not
negotiable. It would be nice if you could forgive what
happened in the past. But we can work on that. However, I want your laughter, and your intellect. I want
your opinions, and your energy. I want your knowledge, your hope, your optimism, and your strength.
And I want your loyalty, as you have never given it to
anyone or anything before. I want you to believe in me
the way you believe in yourself. I want you to recall
every conversation we've ever had the way you do a
page in a book."

He reached out and touched her cheek, tracing a line to her chin with his forefinger. "And I want you to come to my bed with joy and eagerness. Do you agree?"

Before she could speak, before she could say anything in defense or protection of herself and her sudden vulnerabilities, before she could agree with the utmost enthusiasm, he leaned over and scooped her up, depositing her on his lap. Then he kissed her, softly, sweetly, tenderly.

"What do I have that's yours?" she asked a moment later when the kiss was done and she was feeling more than slightly dazed.

At his quizzical look, she reminded him. "Before you left for London, you said that you'd come back because I had something of yours."

"You've had my heart from the very first. I love you, Charlotte MacKinnon. A pity that I'm not a better man. God knows you deserve one, but you'll have to settle for me."

"I will?" She smoothed her fingers over his face, allowing her thumbs to rest just below his lips. How utterly handsome he was, and he was hers.

He nodded. "With all my flaws and faults. I'm sorry for those, but I'll work on them with your help."

She sighed, wishing she didn't feel so close to tears. "Saints are overrated, Dixon. I'm as far from angelic as I can be."

He reached out and touched her face, gently pushing back a tendril of hair from her forehead. "What would those flaws be? I've seen none, Charlotte."

"I'm guilty of pride, more than my share, especially since you think me so perfect. I'm stubborn and opinionated, fiercely loyal and dogmatic at times. I'm determined, but I think that is an asset rather than a flaw, don't you?"

He put two fingers against her lips. "Do not read me a litany, Charlotte. Allow me to discover all these failings myself."

She took a deep breath, only now realizing that she'd been barely breathing for the last few minutes.

His face seemed to loosen, his expression not quite so severe. There was a hint of a smile at one corner of his mouth. "Shall I engage in a siege, or will you allow me into Balfurin?"

Her heart was beating so fast that she felt light-headed. "Balfurin is yours, Dixon."

"And you? Are you mine?"

She tried to smile but gave up the effort. "From the very first," she said, using his words.

"You agree to my conditions?" he asked, brushing his lips against hers in the lightest of kisses.

"I do," she said. "I'll share everything I know or think or remember, and I'll give you my loyalty, my laughter, and my forgiveness. But most of all, I'll give you my love." She sighed and stretched her arms around his neck, feeling strangely like weeping, not in sadness this time, but in joy, pure joy.

Epilogue

Charlotte Haversham MacKinnon turned at the sound of footsteps.

Dixon's head emerged from the opening, just before he pulled himself up to the floor of the tower roof. His grin was infectious, and she couldn't help but smile in return. How odd that she'd seen him only an hour ago and missed him already.

She strode forward and extended a hand to him. When he took it, she bent forward, kissed his knuckles, and then executed a flawless curtsey.

"My lord," she said, dipping her head.

"My lady," he said, and drew something from behind his back.

She opened the velvet box while glancing at him from time to time. "You needn't give me presents every day, Dixon," she said.

"I don't," he said. "Only when I see something that reminds me of you."

"Everything seems to remind you of me," she teased.

"Can I help it if you're my world?"

The box forgotten, she kissed him softly.

"Open it," he said.

She did so, finding a length of gold rings ending in a set of keys that looked to be gold. She blinked back tears. Once, she'd told him of her first thoughts upon seeing Balfurin, and he'd evidently not forgotten.

"It's beautiful," she said, her smile a little watery as she looked up at him.

He helped her fasten it around her waist and then stepped back.

She didn't have a chance to kiss him again. Matthew's shout could be heard from the base of the tower.

"MacKinnon!"

Matthew had taken to calling Dixon by his surname, as if he were a proper Scot and Dixon his laird. She, herself, was still referred to more formally, despite her request to the contrary. She'd begun to accept that Matthew would always be a little reserved with her.

He emerged from the stairwell, but despite his exertion, his face was deathly white, his eyes huge in his face. He looked rather like an owl that had its nest in the tallest tree in the adjoining forest.

"MacKinnon?"

"Is there a problem, Matthew?" she asked. "We don't have guests, surely?"

She looked in the direction of the road to Inverness.

Dear heavens, was The Edification Society here again? Last month she'd received a letter from Lady Eleanor asking her if a year of marriage had proven to be instructive. She'd only written back that, unfortunately, she was too busy to entertain the group. There were some things meant to be kept private, and her life with Dixon headed the list.

As Maisie had once said, love was the best teacher of all.

"Have any of the students been left behind?" They were at the end of another term, another autumn, for which she was grateful. Two hundred fifty lovesick girls were too much to endure, especially since they were all sighing and threatening to swoon over *her* husband.

"No guests and no students, your ladyship. I have news." He glanced at Dixon and then at Charlotte. "I am a father, MacKinnon, your ladyship. My Maisie has given birth," he said, looking alternately terrified and proud about the news.

Maisie had begun her labor this morning, but Charlotte hadn't expected the baby to be born so soon.

"Why didn't you say so, Matthew?" Charlotte said. Picking up her skirts with one hand and holding Dixon's hand with the other, she headed toward the tower steps. "Is it a boy or a girl?"

"A girl, your ladyship, and we would like to name her Charlotte in honor of you."

Charlotte stopped and turned, facing Matthew. She'd come to understand the man in the year of her marriage. Her respect for him had grown as well as her affection. "That is the most wonderful gift you could give me, Matthew."

"Then you do not mind, your ladyship?"

"Charlotte," she corrected. "If Dixon can be the MacKinnon, I can be Charlotte."

She smiled at her husband, and then reached up to kiss Matthew on the cheek. At his look of surprise she only smiled.

This autumn day in Scotland was perfect; the past months had been joyous ones. The years stretched out in front of her like a banquet to sample and savor. She smiled at Dixon again, and he responded by pulling her into his embrace and kissing her.

A moment later they separated, and she glanced at Matthew descending the staircase. He was impatient to join his wife and his new daughter.

"Let's go see Maisie, shall we?" she asked Dixon, and together they left the tower roof.

Author's Note

The poem quoted in this book by Queen Elizabeth I (1533–1603) is entitled "*On Monsieur's Departure.*"

Captain Francis Light, known as the founder of Penang, landed in Penang in 1786, renaming it Prince of Wales Island. Light had convinced the Sultan of Kedah to cede Pulau Pinang (island of the betel nut) to the British in exchange for military protection. In order to get his sepoy forces to clear the site, Light is supposed to have loaded gold coins into his cannons and fired them into the jungle. Light's attempts to introduce agriculture to the island were largely unsuccessful, but Penang soon became a major trading port for tea, spices, china, and cloth. The city of Penang is today a blend of Eastern and Western cultures and a bustling metropolitan city.

Women in Scotland had freedoms not available to

females in other parts of the British Empire. Scottish women had the power to petition for separation and to divorce their husbands. An excellent text on the subject is *Alienated Affections: The Scottish Experience of Divorce and Separation 1684–1830* by Leah Leneman.

Balfurin is fictional and is based on an amalgam of wonderful Scottish castles.

Next month, don't miss these exciting new love stories only from Avon Books

Surrender to a Scoundrel by Julianne MacLean

An Avon Romantic Treasure

Evelyn Wheaton swore she would never forgive Martin, Lord Langdon, for breaking her friend's heart. But Martin has never met a woman he couldn't charm and he won't give up until he's won Evelyn—for a lifetime.

Love in the Fast Lane by Jenna McKnight

An Avon Contemporary Romance

Scott Templeton thought he had seen everything during his racing career. But that was before the ghost of the legendary Speed Cooper appeared in his car. Now Scott's being haunted, Speed's family is up in arms, and Scott has to navigate the most dangerous track of all—love.

Wild and Wicked in Scotland by Melody Thomas

An Avon Romance

After being stood up at her own betrothal ball, Cassandra Sheridan escapes to Scotland. When she encounters a handsome and dangerous stranger on the road, she's intrigued—and horrified when she realizes he's Devlyn St. Clair, her missing fiancé! Now Devlyn must convince Cassie to forgive him before he loses her once and for all.

Desire Never Dies by Jenna Petersen

An Avon Romance

Lady Anastasia Whittig may be a spy, but she greatly prefers research to the more dangerous field work. But when one of her friends is nearly killed, Anastasia teams up with fellow spy Lucas Tyler to track the villain down. Little do they know that this mission will test the limits of their courage—and their passion.